Spindrift
A SEAL COVE ROMANCE

ANNA BURKE

Bywater
BOOKS

Ann Arbor
2020

Bywater Books

Print ISBN: 978-1-61294-177-6

Bywater Books First Edition: August 2020

Printed in the United States of America on acid-free paper.

Cover designer: Ann McMan, TreeHouse Studio

Bywater Books
PO Box 3671
Ann Arbor MI 48106-3671
www.bywaterbooks.com

For veterinarians everywhere.

And for my wife, who saves lives every day.

Spindrift

A SEAL COVE ROMANCE

Chapter One

Emilia Russo stared at the sailboat. *What the hell have I gotten myself into?* This whole idea was insane. Then again, so was she, although her therapist had encouraged her to use kinder language to describe herself. *Fine. This is just another symptom of my spiral of doom.* She rested her hand on her greyhound's shoulder to steady herself.

"It's just a boat, Nell," she said. The black dog leaned into her leg in unmistakable animal solidarity. *It's just a boat,* she told herself again. She'd sailed it a hundred times with her father. The old wooden rail was smooth with oil from their hands, and the fiberglass hull with its fading paint even bore her name: *Emilia Rosa.*

That was the catch, though, wasn't it? She'd sailed it with her father. Now he was gone, the worst of the trifecta of disasters that had marked the past year. Her eyes stung. She would do this for him.

The new engine on the back of the small sailboat reassured her. It had been years since she'd sailed, and with the engine she would worry less about getting lost at sea. First, however, she had to get herself and her dog out to where the boat bobbed peacefully on its mooring in the calm evening water. Rowboats lined the dock. She scanned them, looking for the old blue one she'd grown up with. It wasn't there. Frowning, she pulled the bowlines of a few of the nearby boats to see if hers had gotten lost in the mix. Her heart plunged when she finally found it.

"Nell," she said, staring at the decrepit dinghy riding low in the water, a milk jug bail floating in the small pond at the bottom, "I've got a bad feeling about this."

The dog watched with interest as Emilia pulled the rowboat closer. It definitely had a slow leak somewhere, and she lay on her stomach on the sun-warmed wood of the wharf as she bailed out the worst of the water. Only then did she dare step into the boat to finish the job. When she was satisfied she wouldn't sink immediately, she grabbed her bag and tucked it into the driest corner. Then she turned to Nell.

"Your turn."

Nell's expression didn't require translation. *Oh hell no*, her narrow face said, and she backed up against the end of her leash.

"It's okay, baby. Come."

Sixty-five pounds of stubbornness splayed her paws on the deck.

"Nell." Frustration leaked into her voice, and she took a deep breath. Animals needed their humans to be calm and confident. Unfortunately, Emilia felt neither of those things at the moment.

Footsteps vibrated down the dock, and she groaned. An audience would really ice the cake. "If you come right now I will buy you a cheeseburger."

Nell remained unimpressed. The footsteps came closer. Emilia closed her eyes, took a deep breath, and braced herself for unwanted human interaction.

"Need a hand?" The voice, low and calm, came from the woman standing a few yards away with her hand on the collar of a sable German shepherd. Emilia assessed the dog's body language and gauged his reaction to Nell, who rarely showed an interest in members of her own species. Then she raised her eyes to the woman. "He won't bother your dog," the intruder said, as if reading Emilia's mind.

Fuck. Emilia's cheeks flushed with embarrassment. Life just wasn't fair. She recognized the woman standing before her, even though it had to have been at least fifteen years since she'd last seen her. Morgan Donovan.

She was taller now than she'd been as a teenager, but those slate-blue eyes remained unchanged. Her wardrobe hadn't altered much, either. Carhartt work pants, slung low over lean hips. Practical boots. A simple brown sweater that Emilia's fingers itched to smooth over shoulders broadened from a lifetime of rugged athleticism. The impulse quickened her irritation, and she jerked her eyes back up, noticing the most significant change: Morgan's hair was no longer bundled into a sloppy ponytail. She'd cropped it short, and the dark curls brought out the contrast with her fair skin.

"Classic Black Irish coloring, just like her mom," her father had said once when he saw Emilia staring at the Donovan's' girl in the harbor. Emilia had pined after Morgan the last two summers she'd spent in Seal Cove, before her mother had sued for full custody and her father lost visitation rights. She recalled with humiliation that Morgan hadn't so much as said hello in all that time.

It hadn't occurred to her she might run into Morgan now, and even if it had, she wouldn't have thought much of it. Unrequited love was one of those universal adolescent experiences that prepared children for the inevitable heartbreaks to come. She'd gotten over Morgan years ago. Still, seeing her when she was barely managing to keep her shit together smacked of cosmic sadism.

She met Morgan's open gaze with a glare. "I'm fine, thank you."

"Sure." Morgan's eyes swept over the milk jug and Nell's stubborn ears. "You look like you have things under control."

"I do. Nell, come." Perhaps it was the unmistakable command in her voice, or perhaps Nell had taken pity on her, for the dog leapt lightly into the boat and settled between Emilia's knees like she had done so a hundred times before. "See? We're peachy."

Peachy? What are you, five? She flipped the oarlocks into place and fumbled the oars into them. Then, realizing Morgan had shown no signs of moving on, she popped one oar back out and used it to push off. She got six feet before the bowline snapped taut.

"Shit on a stick," she said under her breath.

Morgan knelt with a grin and tugged on the line, which gave her enough slack to unclip it from the dock and toss the rope into the dinghy.

"Thanks." Emilia's face felt hotter than asphalt in July.

"No problem." Morgan's smile deepened, and then faltered as her eyes slid to the name painted on the stern of the boat.

Emilia put her back into the oars and pulled hard against the water's resistance before Morgan could begin offering condolences for her loss, or whatever other bullshit phrase she chose to employ. Her efforts were clumsy at first, but her body remembered the steady rhythm of the motion as Morgan shrank in her peripheral vision. Nell helped block her from view by craning her neck around to kiss Emilia's face at an improbable angle. When she reached the *Emilia Rosa* and dared to look up again, Morgan had vanished.

"Thank god," she said to her dog as she unsnapped the canvas boat cover enough to make room for Nell. "All aboard."

Nell stiffened as Emilia hauled her in by her harness, but quickly proceeded to sniff around the musty, salt-smelling cave she'd found herself in. Emilia finished pulling the cover off the boom and stowed it in the small cabin. The furled sail felt cool and familiar under her fingers. She didn't undo the rope that kept it tied down, nor did she attempt to hoist the boom. Instead, she pulled a flat boat cushion out from the cabin and sat, fishing in her bag for the bottle of wine she'd brought with her.

"Cheers, Dad." She took a swallow. The wine soothed her throat. Nell lay down beside her, inspection complete, and rested her long snout on Emilia's knee.

Chapter Two

Morgan stared at her hand. It remained on the ignition, where it had lingered for ten minutes while she watched Ray Russo's daughter struggle with the dilapidated dinghy a few moorings over. She quelled the desire to offer further assistance. The look in those brown eyes had been clear: *I don't want your help*. That didn't mean Morgan hadn't noticed how desperately she clearly needed it. The grief in the other woman's face had hit Morgan like a mule kick to the gut. *She doesn't need you to save her.* The way the woman's knuckles had whitened on the oars flashed across her mind. What was she afraid of? And her mouth, before it had twisted with determination, with her lips parted and vulnerable—*stop*. She didn't normally have this level of empathy for complete strangers, no matter how attractive. Then again, the woman wasn't exactly a stranger, was she?

"I should've said something." Her dog pricked his ears at her voice, but when she didn't add anything else, he lay back down on the deck. A lump rose in her throat as she sat in the captain's chair and let her hand fall to her lap. She still couldn't believe Ray was gone. Over the sunlit water, his daughter curled up on the bow of his boat. Morgan saw the glint of light on glass and a deep red glow: wine. The sight made the lump larger. Drinking alone on her boat was what had first brought Ray into Morgan's life, back when she didn't know the first thing about operating her twenty-one-foot Bayliner. She had been afraid to take it out and just as afraid of admitting to herself that she had no idea what she was doing. Ray had set her straight.

Well, not about the drinking. She'd helped him home several times over the past few years. Seeing his daughter with a bottle to her lips roused a bittersweet pang. She hoped the girl knew when to stop. Ray never had. The thought settled the decision. She'd stay in the harbor instead of nipping up the tidal river for a little fishing. Being on the water, even if she didn't move, was better than the chaos of the house she shared with her friends. She leaned back in the chair and watched the clouds turn pink, then orange, as the sun descended further into the western sky. The late May light softened the grays and blacks of the rocky shoreline with its shuttered summer homes and brooding pines.

Emilia. That was her name, same as Ray's boat. Ray had mentioned she'd come to stay with him in the summer when she was younger, but Morgan had no memory of anyone who looked remotely like Emilia Russo ever setting foot in Seal Cove. She let her gaze drift back down to the sailboat, remembering the coldness in those brown eyes and the flush of embarrassment across Emilia's olive skin. Hot and cold. She wiped her palms on her pants, aware that the sudden prick of sweat heralded danger.

The majority of the moorings were empty this early in the season. Few of the summer people had arrived, and only the locals and the lobstermen and women had their boats in the water. Morgan preferred it this way. Quiet. Tranquil. It gave her a break from the hectic schedule of the clinic, which had lost its other full-time large animal veterinarian in April, and it also gave her a break from her housemates. It wouldn't be the same this year without Ray, though. Settling deeper in her chair, she propped her feet on the dash and closed her eyes.

Morgan jerked awake some time later as her phone vibrated on her hip. A message from her friend Stevie glowed on the screen: *You're late.*

She ignored it. Sunset brought cold air in from the ocean, and she inhaled the lingering winter chill.

A splash caught her attention. She shoved her phone back in

6

her pocket as a string of obscenities carried over the water. Her dog woke at once and bounded to the rail with his tail upright and alert. Morgan stared around the harbor for the source of the disturbance. The fading sunlight cast long shadows, and the water surrounding the neighboring boats looked nearly black.

Emilia no longer sprawled over the bow of the sailboat. This, paired with the frantic barking of the woman's dog, clued Morgan in.

"Shit." She fired up the engine and sprang to unhook her boat from its mooring. The Maine water was still dangerously cold this time of year, especially for someone drinking. She gunned the engine as much as she dared in close quarters, not wanting to slap Emilia with wake, and circled around to bring her boat alongside the *Emilia Rosa*. She tossed a bumper out of habit and looped a hasty line around a cleat to keep the boats from drifting, then leaned over the bow to extend a hand to the woman clinging to the sailboat's hull.

"Here."

"I'm fine," Emilia said through chattering teeth. The anger in her voice made Morgan flinch.

"Like hell you are. Give me your hand."

"No."

"Seriously?" Morgan leaned over farther and grabbed Emilia by the wrists. She pried her grip away from the sailboat and hauled Emilia over the rail, thankful for the rigorous requirements of her job. The greyhound stopped barking at once.

Emilia looked too startled at the sudden change in her circumstances to speak right away, and instead stood in a steadily growing puddle on the deck of Morgan's boat. The thick wool sweater she wore—one of Ray's, Morgan realized—sagged on her slender frame, and her brown hair dripped into her face. Morgan rummaged through the storage cabinet in the bow and pulled out a beach towel. Surfing penguins emblazoned the worn cotton, but if Emilia found it insensitive she kept it to herself.

"Your dog okay with other dogs?" she asked Emilia. She didn't love the idea of an unknown dog on her boat, but neither did she

7

like the thought of leaving an animal behind. If it was anything like Emilia, it might decide to go for a swim, and greyhounds were notoriously cold intolerant. Two hypothermia victims weren't on her docket for the evening.

Emilia nodded.

"What's her name?"

"Nell."

"Nell, come," Morgan said in the soft but firm voice she reserved for skittish animals. The greyhound leapt onto the boat in a scrabble of claws and flung herself at her owner. Her own dog, Kraken, grumbled at this invasion of his space, but obeyed Morgan's sharp command to stay put.

"There's a shower at the boathouse. It'll warm you up."

"I don't have a change of clothes," said Emilia through chattering teeth.

"Makes sense. I assume you weren't planning on going for a swim?"

Emilia grimaced in reply.

"I can lend you something to wear."

"You don't need to do that."

Morgan stifled the derisive snort before it could escape. Emilia's clipped politeness, which bordered on bitchy, obviously covered up the woman's embarrassment. Morgan wanted to call her on her bullshit like she would have done with Stevie. That, however, didn't seem like it would go over well. She untied her boat from the *Emilia Rosa* and took them into the dock a short distance away. Emilia stared at her soaked feet the entire ride, huddled in the seat next to Morgan and shivering in the wind. Even soaking wet and draped in tropical penguins she was gorgeous, an observation Morgan couldn't help making despite her better judgment.

"Okay." She killed the engine and tied up. "Let's get you warmed up."

"I'm fine," Emilia said again.

"Look. Emilia, right? You're not fine. The water is fucking cold, and no offense, but you look like you drank a bottle of wine."

8

"Half a bottle."

"Close enough. Do I need to explain vasodilation to you?"

Indignation flashed across Emilia's face. *Good*, thought Morgan. Indignation was proof she wasn't totally wasted—and that she had a decent vocabulary. Morgan held out her hand, and despite the resentment evident in Emilia's eyes, this time she allowed Morgan to help her off the boat and up the ramp to the boathouse. Morgan told herself she didn't notice the strength in Emilia's hands or the way her cold fingers locked around her own. Noticing things like that would only get her in trouble.

Idiot, Emilia berated herself as hot water from the grimy shower chased the cold out from underneath her skin. *You're a fucking drunken idiot.* This was lower than she'd been in a long time, and the irony of the situation gnawed at her. How many times had her mother ranted about her father's irresponsible drinking? How many times had she herself asked him to be more careful? And yet, here she was, drunk and freezing in a boathouse shower.

Nell whined and poked her head underneath the gap in the shower stall door. She bent over and stroked her dog's head with a wet hand, wishing she was anywhere but here.

At least Morgan was a woman. Emilia didn't think she would have been able to stop herself from throttling one of the salt-of-the-earth types she'd seen eyeing her around the harbor, or worse, one of the hipster men who gathered around the bars and talked about building their own boats with money from their trust funds, though they never put it that baldly. She would have preferred, however, to be rescued by a less attractive woman, or at least someone who wasn't Morgan Donovan.

Or to not have required rescue at all.

You're lucky there was someone here, an irritating and logical part of her brain informed her. She shut the thought down, but not before an icy wave of nausea washed over her. If she'd drowned, her mother would have thought she'd done it intentionally, and Emilia never wanted to see that kind of fear in her mother's eyes again.

9

The wine made her head spin in the cramped space of the shower. Morgan probably thought she was an alcoholic. *Just like my dad.* She closed her eyes and let hot water beat against her lids. Yes, she had downed half a bottle of wine while sitting in the boat her father had named after her, but sitting in the boat sober had been out of the question. It had too much of her dad in it. *Next time I'll wear a life jacket,* she promised herself. *And I'll leave the wine behind.* That wouldn't prevent the dinghy from sinking or a bank of fog from whisking her blindly out to sea, but it was a start.

On the other hand, at least she'd gotten her first swim of the season out of the way. She used to compete with her dad to see who could brave the cold water first, both of them shrieking and shouting as the frigid water of the Atlantic closed over their belly buttons. Hot tears joined the water flowing over her body.

A dry towel appeared over the door a second after she shut off the shower. The reminder of Morgan's existence helped distill the fresh bout of grief, and she fanned the spark of irritation because she preferred it to the alternatives. Morgan didn't know anything about her. Sure, she was grateful for the rescue, but the smugness in the other woman's bearing galled her. She clearly found Emilia incompetent, and while nothing that had happened tonight, admittedly, suggested otherwise, the assumption hit too close to home.

"Thank you." She whipped the towel over the side of the door and around her body. *Now please leave.*

"No problem. I've got some clothes, too. They'll probably be too big, but they're dry."

"I don't—" she began, but a green flannel shirt and a scuffed pair of work pants followed Morgan's words. She contemplated putting her wet clothes back on. The idea felt childish as well as cold, and so she shrugged into the soft, worn shirt and tried to ignore the shiver of gratitude from her traitorous body. The fabric smelled like pine and salt and something else—sandalwood? She shook her head to free her hair from the collar. The pants, unlike the oversized men's shirt, fit snugly. Almost too snugly. She cursed Morgan's slimmer hips as she shimmied into the dungarees.

Nell thrust her snout into her hand when she emerged, barefoot and still shivering, into the darkness of the boathouse.

"Still alive," she told the dog as she shoved her feet into her sodden sneakers. Morgan was nowhere in sight. "Think we can sneak away?"

Her dog licked the lingering salt from her skin and did not offer comment, but hearing her own words out loud sobered Emilia more than the cold water. Her humiliation was no excuse for downright hostility. She owed Morgan a thank you for the clothes, and more importantly, slipping away would make her look even more ridiculous than she already did. She squared her shoulders and walked out of the boathouse.

The tiny Seal Cove marina boasted lockers, a bathroom and shower, complimentary parking, and a few picnic tables in various stages of decay. Morgan sat at one of the tables idly scratching her dog's ears. The easy confidence in the way she lounged on the bench made Emilia want to grind her teeth. She would kill for an ounce of that self-assurance. Instead, her feet slipped in her wet sneakers, and her soaked clothing dripped from her hands.

"Better?" asked Morgan.

"Yes. Thank you for . . . well, you know."

"No problem. Do you need a ride?"

Shit. Her keys, wallet, and phone were still in the boat, and her skiff bobbed on the mooring out of reach and probably taking on water. She could wait around until Morgan left and then borrow another skiff, retrieve her possessions, and pretend that none of this had ever happened, or she could ask Morgan for more help. *Not happening.*

"I'm fine."

"You keep mentioning that."

"I mean, I don't need a ride. I walked here. You don't need me taking up any more of your time."

"Actually, you're doing me a favor. I'm avoiding my least favorite social event of the year."

"High school reunion?" Emilia guessed, wondering how she could get out of this increasingly mortifying situation.

11

"I think you have to go to an event for it to get ranked, and I've managed to avoid those reunions. I'm Morgan, by the way. You might not remember me, but you're Ray's daughter, Emilia, aren't you?"

"I remember you," she said to forestall the kick that came with the words *Ray's daughter*. The German shepherd tilted his head as he appraised them. Knowing the next words out of Morgan's mouth would be condolences, she seized on the opportunity. "What's your dog's name?"

"Kraken."

"Kraken?"

"My housemate named him. She wanted to be able to use the phrase 'release the kraken' at least once a day."

Emilia couldn't help the smile that tugged at her lips. The idea was ridiculous, and therefore made her feel slightly less so. "Well, I appreciate that you didn't let him pull me into a watery grave."
Not that I needed the help.

"I keep his tentacles trimmed."

Emilia opened her mouth to crack a joke about the veterinary politics surrounding declawing and if they applied to de-tentacling, but stopped herself. She wasn't Dr. Russo, here. She wasn't sure if she ever wanted to be Dr. Russo again.

"I'll get the clothes back to you. And wash them."

"Don't worry about it. Just drop them in my skiff. Last name Donovan is painted on it."

"Okay."

"Look, Emilia . . ."

"It's fine."

"No, I mean—" Morgan paused and took a deep breath. "Your dad was a friend of mine."

"Oh." At home in Boston, no one had known her father. She'd accepted that coming here things would be different, but this was the first time she'd had to face the reality of the life Ray Russo had led when she wasn't with him. Of course he and Morgan were friends; they kept their boats at the same marina. Had he talked about his daughter? She didn't remember seeing Morgan at the funeral, but then again she hadn't paid much attention to the other mourners. Her own grief and its ensuing complications had consumed her.

The problem with condolences, she'd learned, was people expected the bereaved to say something in return. For a while she'd said "thank you," but as the weeks passed and things didn't get easier, "thank you" grew harder to say. She observed how other people responded in situations like this, watching movies and listening to podcasts, but how could she say "yes, he was a good man" when his drinking had deprived her of a father? How could she say "I am sorry for your loss, too," when she had no idea what he had meant to these people?

Isn't that why you came here? asked the voice in the back of her head that enjoyed playing devil's advocate far more than conscience. *No.* She'd come here to settle his estate and get away from the dumpster fire of her own life, not to immerse herself in his. She didn't want to know about his legacy.

Too much time had passed since Morgan had spoken and she had said "oh," that terminal word, killer of conversations the world over. A chorus of peepers filled the silence of the chilly late May evening. She wrapped her hands around Nell's collar and clung to it, feeling the warmth from her dog's body against the backs of her fingers.

"Well, it was nice to meet you," said Morgan, in a voice too full of understanding for Emilia to tolerate. "I'll see you around?"

"Yeah. Sure."

"And you might want to think about taking a boating safety course."

Heat exploded in her chest. A boating safety course? Really? Who did this woman think she was? She glared at Morgan, who visibly flinched. She savored the small victory.

"I'll consider it," she said in a clipped voice. "Nell, come."

Morgan pulled into the long, winding gravel drive of 16 Bay Road, wincing as the truck nearly disappeared into a pothole.

She'd have to see if Bill would grade it for a discount on his herd's spring exam again. The grass needed to be cut, too—something else she didn't have time for. The patchy spring growth shot up in some places and remained stunted in others, a testimony to the cruelty of the past winter. There were four of them in the house, Lillian and Angie in addition to Morgan and Stevie—someone else could do it. Lillian liked plants. Grass was a plant.

Her shoulders tightened as she saw the number of cars parked in the small gravel lot in front of the barn-turned-doggy-day care and boarding facility for Angie's start of the summer season staff party. She didn't actively dislike Angie's employees, but after a day like today, all she wanted to do was curl up on the couch or crash into her bed. Mingling with a group of teenagers and college-aged kids who still believed in their dreams didn't enter that picture.

She parked in her customary spot in front of the sprawling farmhouse. White paint peeled off the northwest side of the house, but they'd gotten the gardens under control last fall, and carefully pruned shrubs and lilac bushes covered up the worst of the rotted siding.

"Let's get this over with," she said to Kraken. He leapt out after her and performed a quick inspection of the darkening yard before bounding onto the porch. He waited with obvious impatience for her to kick off her boots. Kraken didn't mind Angie's employees. They all showed him the admiration he felt he deserved.

Inside, voices clamored to be heard above the bursts of laughter. The sound of claws skittering on the hardwood floors alerted her to the arrival of the house's other resident canines. Stevie's brindle pit bull wagged his tail enthusiastically with his face split in a goofy grin. Lillian's two dogs followed: an obscenely fluffy seventy-pound mutt and a tiny Italian greyhound. Both were one leg short of a complete set.

"'Sup, gang," Morgan greeted the dogs. Kraken raised his muzzle and sniffed. Morgan's nose caught the same scent: pizza. In order to snag a slice, though, she had to pay her dues.

"Ange?" Morgan said as she entered the farmhouse kitchen. Exposed beams and cluttered granite countertops were eclipsed by Angie herself as she pulled Morgan into a hug.

"I feel like I haven't seen you in ages," Angie said. Her messy bun of wavy brown hair tickled Morgan's nose.

"That's because you haven't."

"Pizza? Beer?"

"Yes pizza, no beer. I'm still on call."

"Ouch. Pizza it is, then." Angie waved her hand toward an open box and a stack of paper plates. She'd put on more clothes than she usually wore around the house, thanks to the presence of her employees, but she'd paired her work polo with yoga pants and a pair of thick wool socks Morgan recognized as her own.

"Nice socks."

"You're welcome for doing your laundry."

Morgan couldn't argue with that. She'd been too busy the last month to do more than brush her teeth. The clinic desperately needed to hire another large animal vet, or at least someone comfortable working in a mixed practice.

"You're late." Stevie flung an arm around her shoulders and shoved a beer in her hand.

"I'm not drinking."

"Course you're not. Don't worry. I drank half of it for you."

Morgan eyed the can of beer. She wanted nothing more than to relax. Maybe half a beer wouldn't kill her. It wasn't like she'd, say, downed half a bottle of wine and fallen out of her boat. A vivid image of Emilia's brown eyes filled her vision.

"Fine," she said, taking a sip. "And I'm not late. I was delayed."

"Delayed?"

"Someone fell off their boat. I pulled them in."

"Brrr."

Morgan considered telling her more, knowing Stevie would get a kick out of teasing Morgan about rescuing a damsel in distress, but she remembered the grief and humiliation in Emilia's face and kept her mouth shut. She also recalled how Emilia had looked wearing Morgan's spare clothes. *Down that road lies peril.*

15

Her mind quoted one of the books or shows her friends were so fond of.

"They okay?"

"She'll be fine." Morgan hid the smile that rose to her lips behind her beer as she repeated Emilia's favorite words.

"Anyone we know?"

"No. Nice dog, though. How's the party?"

"It's devolved into Cards Against Humanity." Angie jabbed her thumb toward the living room, where her employees lounged on the mismatched couches and armchairs that filled the space. "I forgot how vulgar Alexa is."

"Is she the one with the dildo earrings?" asked Stevie.

"Yes."

"And you hired her why?"

"Because it is hard to find people who enjoy getting barked at all day for minimum wage. Plus, those earrings double as earplugs."

"Among other things."

"You're gross." Angie swatted at Stevie, who had ducked behind Morgan, who fielded the blow.

"Pizza me, Ange," Morgan said.

Angie grabbed three slices at random and piled them on a plate. Morgan devoured the first slice of pepperoni in four bites. Coming up for air, she asked, "Where's Lil?"

"Still at the clinic. Emergency came in right before close."

"I love that you still know more about the clinic than we do," said Stevie. Morgan had to agree. Angie had been a vet tech before inheriting this house and enough money to open the clinic's affiliated boarding and day care facility. Despite this, she always seemed to have a line on what was going on back at the office.

"One of my many skills." Angie crammed an entire slice of pizza into her mouth to illustrate yet another skill, smiling around a rogue olive.

"Why is that so gross and yet so sexual?" Stevie asked Morgan.

"Only in your mind." Morgan tousled Stevie's hair, which she had taken out of her ponytail. The blond strands still bore the crease from their long day.

Angie examined Morgan more critically. "Fuck this party. You look exhausted, Morgan. Lillian will be here soon to play vet. You need to get some sleep."

"You sure?" Since Angie's business was technically a part of the clinic, she advertised on-site veterinarians. This meant one of those veterinarians had to show up for staff events occasionally.

"Of course. Stevie will defend me from my minions."

Stevie gave Morgan an exaggerated look of horror.

"Thanks, Ange," said Morgan.

Alone in her room, she eyed her bed, weighing the pros and cons of a shower. She smelled like horse and cow manure. Those smells hadn't bothered her for years, but she'd feel better if she at least rinsed off.

The bathroom she shared with Lillian had been cleaned recently. She made a mental note to thank Lillian as she shucked off her clothes and stepped into the claw-foot bathtub, which had been effectively, if inelegantly, retrofitted with a shower head and a hideous, dinosaur-themed shower curtain Stevie had bought as a gag gift. Hot water sluiced down her shoulders. She let it soak her hair and run down her face, washing away the grime of the day. Emilia's profile with its tight jaw and taut smile drifted across the backs of her eyelids again. Wary. Guarded. Morgan wondered what the hell she'd been thinking when she fell into the water. Emilia obviously didn't know her way around a boat well, although maybe she had at one point. Drinking on top of inexperience was downright stupid. On the other hand, Morgan had seen the spasm of grief that seized Emilia's entire body when she'd mentioned Ray. Emilia had lost her father. That was reason enough.

The ancient water heater needed replacing, and she knew from experience that the sudden drop in temperature indicated that approximately forty-five seconds remained before it went from warm to frigid. *Wouldn't that be fitting, all things considered?* Her mind conjured up the way the wet clothes had clung to Emilia's body when Morgan pulled her from the freezing ocean, and how she'd gasped as the wind had hit her.

Damnit. It had been too long since Morgan had let someone else touch her, and this was the result. Her mind had reverted to desperate measures, even while her heart and her schedule insisted there was neither time nor space for anyone else right now, and hadn't been since the collapse of her last relationship six months ago. Besides, what was the point of going on a date that could be interrupted at any moment by a call from the clinic? That likelihood was exactly why Kate had called off their engagement in the first place.

She shut off the water. Thinking about Kate still made her jaw ache, and she forced herself to unclench her teeth. Kate had moved on, leaving Morgan here, living in a house with three other people instead of the apartment she had shared with her fiancée. She stepped blindly out of the tub and elicited a yelp from the dog lying on the bath mat.

"Sorry, bud."

Back in her room, she set her pager and her phone on her nightstand, then shoved her head through the worn hem of her favorite Cornell T-shirt (the one that featured a donkey's head on the front and its rear on the back, courtesy of the livestock club at school). Barely conscious, she measured out Kraken's dinner, ruffled the hair around his ears, and slipped into an exhausted sleep.

Emilia unlocked the door to her father's house with shaking fingers. After Morgan had left, she'd borrowed her skiff and rowed back out to her boat to retrieve her bag and tow her leaky dinghy to the dock. Nell looked up at her reproachfully and made a beeline for her dinner bowl as soon as Emilia hefted the old wooden door open. Entering her father's house still felt strange. Set back on an acre of land that abutted a small corner of the estuary, the log cabin-style home smelled like old tobacco and musty leather furniture. Taxidermy animals adorned the living room walls, and one corner of the sunroom was dedicated to his fly fishing supplies. She'd have to decide what to do with it all at some point, but not while she wore a stranger's clothes.

Not a stranger. Morgan Donovan.

"Eat, you monster," she said as she fed Nell in the dim kitchen. Painting the dark wood white would be the first thing she did, she decided. Her father had liked the constant twilight of his home, but she did not enjoy living in a cave. Her therapist would no doubt agree. *White curtains would help, too.*

She changed into an old sweatshirt and sweatpants, dumped her wet clothes and Morgan's into the washing machine, and curled up in the recliner that overlooked the window to the yard. It was more of a meadow than a yard, really, overgrown with tall grass and old, dry stalks painted silver by the moonlight.

"Well, Dad," she said to the room, "I fell off the boat."

He would have laughed at that. Prior to the divorce he'd laughed a lot. Even after, during the years when she had spent the summers with him, he had been full of laughter. She hadn't spent much time with him during the intervening decade and a half. Vet school and work made it hard to get away, but she imagined his laugh would have remained the same—so long as he hadn't been drinking. *Not that I can judge right now.*

A deer crossed the meadow, followed by a fawn. Nell finished her dinner and settled herself on the vacant couch to watch the deer with interest. The peepers chirped in the gathering night, joined by the calls of animals Emilia didn't recognize. It was louder here in its own way than in the city, though she didn't miss the omnipresent serenade of distant sirens.

Her phone buzzed. She scanned the notifications. A missed call from her mother, and a text from her stepsister, Anna Maria. Both could wait, as could the emails mustering their forces in her inbox. At least one would be from a shelter director, reminding her that she had a job waiting whenever she was ready to return.

19

Whenever. Not if. So far only her therapist had acknowledged the possibility that she might not be ready to return to any of it: Boston, her job, even the veterinary field. Remembering what her therapist, Shanti, had taught her about thought blocking, she redirected her mind away from her breakdown and the responsibilities she'd put on hold, and back to the present.

Tomorrow she would stop by the hardware store and pick up some paint palettes. While she was there, maybe she'd see about grabbing a fiberglass repair kit to fix the leak in her skiff. One day at a time, as Ray Russo was fond of saying—not that he'd ever managed to stick with AA. No major decisions. She could do this.

Chapter Three

The hardware store in town boasted a slim selection of paint chips. Emilia eyed the palette, wondering if she should venture farther inland in search of a larger chain home improvement store. The thought exhausted her.

Maybe it's good to have fewer options. She selected a handful of white, cream, and ivory chips and tried to visualize them on the rough pine walls. Should she leave the walls and just paint the trim? And what about the ceiling? *No.* Light walls. She'd play with leaving a few exposed beams, but the house needed a face-lift, and she couldn't bear to think about her father sitting alone in the dark, smoking his pipe and drinking until his heart gave out. *Fresh paint, fresh start.*

"Need any help?"

The store clerk looked to be about sixteen. Hardly old enough to be an expert in anything, despite the "Ask Me" pin above his nametag.

"Fiberglass repair?" she said.

"Aisle six," replied Ask Me Doug. He led the way, his work shirt rumpled and his hair that peculiar brand of disarray known only to teenage boys. "Boat?"

"Yes. Just a skiff."

"Ever repaired one before?"

"I helped my dad once."

"It's super easy." He grinned, apparently enthusiastic about the subject, as he launched into an explanation about the proper curing conditions for fiberglass that made her eyes glaze. Emilia amended her earlier assessment. Perhaps Doug *was* an expert in repairing leaky rowboats.

"Thanks," she said when he finished.

"No problem. There's lots of YouTube videos if you need more help."

She would *definitely* need more help.

Laden with paint chips and a fiberglass kit, she left the store and stepped into the spring sunshine. Nell waited in the car with her long neck stretched out the window, tracking the progress of a squirrel in a neighboring tree.

"Oh no you don't." Nell had two gears: potato and full speed. Emilia would never catch her if she took off after the fluffy-tailed creature. She grabbed her dog's leash forcefully as she dumped her supplies in the trunk. Nell gazed after the squirrel with longing, but did not attempt to give chase.

The idea of going home made her teeth ache with claustrophobia. To postpone it, she took Nell for a walk to see how much of the town had changed since she'd last been here.

The harbor town was small and slightly run-down in a quaint, coastal way that pleased the eye and attracted tourists in the summer months. Flower boxes offset fading paint and missing shingles, and the few boutiques open for business this early in the season carried the usual tourist fare. Emilia passed several seaside restaurants, the main wharf, a small lobster dock, and the town's only hotel, which was little more than a large bed and breakfast.

The smell of freshly brewed coffee caught her attention, and she saw a small shop she didn't remember from her youth: Storm's-a-Brewin' Coffeehouse and Brewery.

Another microbrewery. *Just what the world needs*, she thought, but the "Pets Welcome" sign took the edge off her cynicism. Keeping Nell at heel, she pushed through the glass door and into the warmth of the coffee shop.

"Good morning," said a short woman with thick black curls, bright red lipstick, and an infectious smile from behind the counter.

Emilia blinked at her, then looked around. A wooden bar wrapped around one corner of the café, and a chalkboard advertised local beers on tap while another boasted various gourmet coffee beans. Exposed brick walls complemented the potted succulents and air plants that hung from the beams. She didn't need to look to know that the case of artisanal products by the checkout was outside her budget. Tables occupied the floor space, although most of them were empty, and a small raised platform suggested the shop held live performances. The effect was too hip for Seal Cove, but the coffee smelled delicious.

"Good morning," she said. "Just a cup of your dark roast."

"For here or to go?"

Emilia considered her options. She could kill some time and think about painting, or she could get to work on the boat or the house. "For here."

"And for your pup? Puppaccino?"

I'm a vet, so no, she almost said, her mind filled with images of obese dogs downing whipped cream. She settled for a "no thank you."

"Dog biscuit?" The woman's smile spread faster than the parvovirus in a puppy mill. Emilia felt her lips twitch in response.

"Sure. What do you say, Nell?"

The greyhound sat and swiveled her ears forward, her impossibly long snout waiting expectantly for praise.

"Well, aren't you a perfect angel," said the barista. Her nametag identified her as "Stormy." *Great,* Emilia thought darkly, recalling the name of the café. *I just love puns.*

"She certainly thinks she is."

"Did you adopt her from the tracks? I heard they closed a bunch last year."

"I did. Not last year, but a few years ago."

"You speedy snoot of a doggo," Stormy said as she handed Nell the biscuit. *Snoot of a doggo?* Nell, however, didn't mind the gibberish and took the biscuit delicately. "Any treats for you?"

Emilia eyed the pastries. "Maybe a scone."

"Definitely a scone. Blueberry is the best. Maine berries. Last year's, of course, but they freeze well."

Emilia paid and settled into a corner with her coffee and her scone. Both exceeded her expectations. The scone boasted the perfect combination of moist and crumbly, and the coffee tasted like coffee smelled, unlike the disappointing stale breakfast blend she'd found in her father's cupboard. She rested her fingertips on Nell's back. Food hadn't tasted good for weeks. Months, if she was being honest. She closed her eyes to savor the sensation of her taste buds responding appropriately to stimuli and took another bite of the scone, then a sip of coffee. *Perfect.*

The little bell above the door broke her blissful reverie. Nell perked up, her tail wagging, and Emilia's tenuous good mood burst.

"Stormy?" Morgan Donovan called as she pushed through the door, followed by a petite blond in matching Carhartts and polo. Emilia tried to shrink behind her mug and wished she had grabbed a copy of the local paper as a shield.

"Stormy, your boyfriend's here," said Morgan's companion. *Boyfriend?*

"Hey, babes," Stormy said. "Glad to see you're still alive."

Morgan leaned on the counter. Emilia studied her shoulders, acutely aware of the muscles visible beneath Morgan's shirt.

"Barely," said Morgan.

"I can fix that. Drinks on me today."

"You don't need to do that," said Morgan.

"I know." Stormy smiled and blew the woman beside Morgan a kiss. "Morning, sunshine."

"Sunshine" put a hand on Morgan's shoulder and peered around her to examine the pastries. The casual touch made Emilia shrink further behind her cup.

"How's business?" Morgan asked.

"Starting to pick up. Morning rush is over, as you can see." Stormy gestured at the café.

Don't look, don't look, don't look, Emilia prayed. Morgan turned. Emilia stared into the depths of her mug, hoping Morgan would get the hint. Being reminded of her most recent humiliation held zero appeal.

Nell betrayed her. She felt Morgan's gaze hone in on the dog, and she ordered Nell to stay out of the corner of her mouth. Nell shot her an all-too-human look, then wagged her tail at Morgan. Aware that feigning further indifference would border on rude, Emilia looked up.

Slate-blue eyes met hers from across the room.

"Hey there," Morgan said, an easy smile on her lips. Emilia's stomach dropped just as surely as it had at age thirteen.

"Hi."

"How's the boat?"

"I picked up some fiberglass repair."

"Sunshine" glanced back and forth between Morgan and Emilia, her forehead furrowed. Stormy rested her elbows on the bar, revealing her generous cleavage, and gave Emilia a considering look that turned the scone to a lump of cement in her stomach.

"Emilia Russo," Morgan said to her friends.

Damn you, Emilia thought as Stormy straightened in recognition.

"You're Ray's daughter?" asked the woman Emilia guessed to be the café's proprietor.

"Yep."

"I'm sorry about your dad. He was a nice guy. Always tipped. He played for us a few times in the off-season." Stormy nodded toward the stage.

The thought of her father playing guitar in this hipster hideout brought a surge of unexpected emotions. Jealousy, first, that he'd played for other people. Grief, of course. Pride, too, and gratitude that here, at least, he'd be remembered for something other than a failed marriage and a drinking problem.

"Ray?" asked Sunshine.

"Russo Construction," said Stormy. "Real nice baritone. You remember him."

Emilia found the small lump in Nell's shoulder that had been there for as long as she'd had her and traced it with the pads of

25

her fingers. Morgan stared at her, and she felt, rather than saw, the compassionate sympathy in her gaze.

"He has that beautiful house up on Pleasant Street. Are you putting it on the market?"

"Ease up, Stormy." Morgan accepted the to-go cup Stormy handed her.

"Yeah. Ignore her. I'm Stevie, by the way." Stevie approached Emilia with a slight swagger that set off her gaydar.

"Emilia." She took the offered hand, noting the calluses. Stevie's blue-green eyes—much lighter than Morgan's—shifted to Nell. "And this is Nell."

"Why hello there, gorgeous," Stevie said in a surprisingly throaty voice. Nell responded without her usual reserve and stepped forward to present herself for adoration. "How long are you in town for?"

"I'm not sure. A month, at least, Maybe two."

"Nice. Well, we'll probably see you around. Small town. And I *will* be seeing you," she purred at Nell.

Emilia smiled despite herself.

"You got my coffee?" Stevie asked Morgan.

Morgan slid another to-go cup down the bar and met Emilia's eyes again. A shiver ran down her back. Morgan's boyish appeal had matured into soft-butch perfection, and she remained unfairly attractive. Embarrassment gnawed at the scone in Emilia's stomach, producing unpleasant byproducts.

"See you later," Stevie said as she headed for the door. Morgan followed after with a wave to the room, but she paused at the door with a crooked grin.

"Stay dry," she said to Emilia.

Emilia clenched her jaw at the reminder about her unexpected swim. The doorbell jingled in Morgan's wake.

"*That's* who you pulled out of the ocean?" Stevie said as soon as the door shut behind Morgan.

"So?"

"So, she's fucking gorgeous. Did you at least get her number?"

"Jesus, Stevie. That's inappropriate."

"How? You rescued her, didn't you?"

"Pretty sure she didn't want to be rescued."

"See if she's on Tinder."

"No."

"Give me your phone."

"Absolutely not," said Morgan.

"Fine. I'll use my account." Stevie pulled her phone out of her pocket and perused it for a few minutes in concentrated silence. "And nothing. She's not on Hinge, either."

"Maybe she's seeing someone."

"Or she doesn't use dating apps because people who look like her don't need technology. Either way, she's definitely queer," said Stevie.

"You just want her to be gay because she's hot." Morgan turned off the main road and onto a side street, swerving to avoid yet another pothole.

"Ah hah. You *do* think she's hot."

"I'm not blind."

Stevie fiddled with the radio and settled on an '80s station that made Morgan's head throb. At least they only had three appointments scheduled for the day, plus she had gotten a full night's sleep. No calls. With luck, they might even be done at a reasonable time. She knew better than to say the words aloud. The veterinary gods loved to fuck with their followers.

"Has Dr. Watson found anyone to hire yet?" Stevie asked as they pulled into the driveway of a small farm.

"Not that she's told me. Apparently, no one wants to move to bumfuck Maine."

"We're not in Bumfuck. You're thinking of our hometown."

"Which is two towns over."

"Whatever. Anyway, Emilia. When did her dad die?"

"February. Heart attack."

"That sucks. Maybe she needs a friend." Stevie propped her chin on her fist and stared up at Morgan with dramatically widened eyes. "If only you'd gotten her number."

"Why don't you ask her for it?" Morgan parked the truck by a pile of old tires.

"Because she's not my type," said Stevie. "And she's totally yours."

"Shut up."

In a different time and in a different place, she admitted to herself, she might have made a pass at Emilia. Dark-eyed brunettes, especially tall, dark-eyed brunettes, had a history of getting under her skin. A different Morgan would have asked her out for coffee or a beer without thinking twice.

Kate had shattered any chance of that.

Abby Killmore greeted Morgan with a firm handshake at the barn door, her coveralls smeared with all the shades of green and brown found in barns. "Good to see you, Dr. Donovan."

"How's the flock?"

"Most of them lambed without a problem. I've got one ewe with mastitis, but something's up with Percy."

Morgan stifled a groan. Percy, Abby's livestock guardian llama, had a foul temper.

"I didn't know you had a horse, Abby," said Stevie. Morgan followed Stevie's gaze and frowned. A stout chestnut walked across the pasture toward them. Belgian, Morgan guessed, or a draft cross. The horse's flaxen mane blew in the late spring breeze. She recognized the odd snap to the horse's left hind immediately: stringhalt.

"I don't," said Abby, her brow creasing. "That's Olive."

"Are you boarding?"

"Something like that. She's my cousin's daughter's, but she's got stringhalt. Kid wanted a new horse, and my cousin's an idiot and got her one."

"And now you have Olive?" said Stevie.

"Yep."

"Want us to take a look at her?"

Abby's hesitation was more pronounced this time. Morgan kept her expression neutral. She understood what Abby wasn't saying. The cousin wouldn't pay for another vet visit, and Abby wasn't interested in coughing up more money, either.

"Who was your cousin's vet?"

"Dr. Baker, over in Scarborough."

Morgan made a mental note to give Dr. Baker a call the minute she left the property. "Any history of injury to that leg?"

"Not that I know of, but that doesn't mean much."

"Let's take a look at Percy, then."

Percy, after an examination that resulted in several wads of spit landing on Morgan's torso and one nearly hitting her face, had a suspicious swelling on his breast. She took a few cultures from the abscess, then checked over the flock. Some bacterial causes of abscesses were contagious. When she turned up an ewe with similar symptoms, she turned to Abby.

"It could be pigeon fever. I won't know for sure until I get the cultures back, but it can affect horses, too. I'll need to check Olive."

"I'll grab her," said Abby, relenting. Olive didn't need much coaxing. The mare had been hanging out by the gate with bright, curious eyes. She nuzzled Abby as Abby slipped a halter over her head and led her into the barn. Her left hind leg snapped up and then down to the cement floor of the barn with a hard clunk that made Morgan wince in sympathy.

Stevie headed up the horse while Morgan performed her examination. Olive, despite the stringhalt and an overly round stomach, was in remarkably good health as far as Morgan could tell without running blood work.

"What did your cousin do with her?"

"Kid wanted to barrel race."

"With a Belgian?"

"She's supposed to be a quarter horse cross."

Morgan looked at Olive. Any quarter horse blood had been obscured by her Belgian heritage, save for her shorter stature. She wouldn't be racing any barrels with a weak hind end.

"You could probably still do something with her. Stevie, try her at a trot."

Stevie led her out of the barn into the yard and clucked a reluctant Olive into a trot. The stringhalt affected the trot, too, and without a round pen or a ring Morgan doubted they could convince the mare to canter.

"I don't ride," said Abby.

"I can keep an ear out if you're looking for a home for her," said Morgan. Stevie returned to them with the horse trailing her, ears perked forward.

"Thank you. She's a sweet horse." Abby watched Olive with a resigned expression. "She deserves better than this. And she needs a job. Follows me around like a dog."

Morgan stroked the mare's shoulder and studied her vet tech. Stevie had an odd, almost dreamy, expression on her face as she tickled the horse's lips. Morgan knew that look. It was how Stevie had ended up with her pit bull, but there were vast differences between bringing home an unwanted stray dog and bringing home a horse.

Emilia held one paint chip after another up to the wall. None of them spoke to her, but all looked like they'd be an improvement over the tobacco stains. Her options consisted of eggshell versus gloss versus whatever other type of paint she somehow needed to select, and she had no idea what each term meant. *I could Google it.* She thought of Doug and his YouTube advice and pulled out her phone, but before she could start her search, it rang.

Shit.

"Hi, Mom," she said in a forcibly bright voice.

"Hi, sweetie. How are you doing? I haven't heard from you since you got to the cabin."

"I texted you."

"You know how I feel about texting. So? How is it? Did they clean it for you?"

Cleaned. What her mother really meant was *has the company we hired removed all signs and smells that might suggest a man had died in this house alone in a chair with his beer and his pipe?*

"It's fine."

"What about those horrible hunting trophies?"

She glanced at the deer head mounted on the wall in front of her, then flopped into an armchair. "They're still here."

"Maybe you can sell them on eBay."

"Mom."

"I'm just saying you don't have to surround yourself with dead things. You know I worry about you."

"I'm *fine*."

"Are you taking your meds?"

"*Mom*. I'm thirty years old."

"And only a month out of treatment."

"Do you want me to hang up on you?"

Silence filled the line. Emilia tugged on the frayed edges of the hole in the knee of her jeans. Yes, she was only a month out of Morse Hill's residential program, but they'd deemed her fit to return to society and normal human activities. She was fine. Maybe if she repeated that often enough people would believe her.

"Well, at least you have Nell with you."

"She's doing the thing where she lies on top of her own head on the couch."

"Silly dog. Oh, Anna Maria told me to tell you to stop ignoring her texts."

She pulled a thread all the way out and let it fall to the scuffed hardwood floor. Ignoring her stepsister wasn't intentional. She just didn't know what to say. Anna Maria hadn't known her dad, so Emilia's grief was foreign to her, opening up a rift that had been barely noticeable while they were growing up.

"I'll talk to her."

"Good. She wants to visit you."

"You mean she wants to get away from her children."

"You're deflecting."

"You're not my therapist." She didn't mean to snap, but she wished her mother could understand how much effort it took for her to do even as little as she was managing. There wasn't any effort left over for patience.

"Emmy."

"Sorry. It's the paint. There are too many choices."

"You're painting? You've only been there a few days."

"You never liked how dark Dad's house was."

"And he liked it because it hid the dirt."

"Did you know Dad did open mic at the new coffee shop in town?"

More silence. "No. I did not know that."

"It was weird. The coffee shop people knew who he was."

"I forget how small that town is. Any familiar faces?"

"Nope," Emilia said, thinking of Morgan.

"Don't be afraid to make friends."

Emilia pinched herself to keep a rein on her frustration and decided to feed her mother a few scraps to get her off her back. "Actually, I have met a few people."

"Good. Promise me you won't hole yourself up in that dark house?"

"I promise."

She hung up after a few more minutes of small talk and stared at Nell, wondering how her mother always managed to make her feel twelve again. She couldn't even blame her too much, which just made it worse.

Emilia had always been the most responsible of her siblings, as well as the oldest. Her breakdown had taken everyone by surprise. Now, her mother coped with her fears by babying Emilia, which she supposed was an improvement from sitting outside her door in case she tried to hurt herself, as her mom had done in the days immediately following her discharge.

She took a deep breath and let it out slowly. The past year had dealt her one too many blows. Between her father's sudden death and the crushing reality of shelter medicine, she'd cracked.

Don't think about it, she told herself, but it was too late.

Multiple professors had warned her about shelter medicine during veterinary school. The psychological toll it took on vets, known as compassion fatigue, was even more profound than in the rest of the field, and a lot of the work involved euthanizing animals deemed unadoptable or whose medical needs exceeded the reach of the shelter's limited budget. The work mattered. Emilia understood the necessity behind it. Government-funded shelters did their best to help as many animals as they could, and since part of their contract usually meant taking in any animals that came their way, space was an important commodity. So were funds. Shelters served the greater good. So Emilia did what she could and offered a peaceful death to those the shelters couldn't afford to help. Without more funding and more shelters, there was no other choice.

She'd gone into shelter medicine because she wanted to make a difference. Half of the week she worked at a low-cost spay and neuter clinic, and the rest of the time she traveled from shelter to shelter as needed, examining new arrivals and checking up on the health of the other residents. Perhaps she could have lasted another year or two, but she'd gotten the call about her father right after injecting Euthansol into a one-year-old dog with a bad fracture. Something had snapped.

Hannah had left soon after, unable to handle Emilia's depression, and it had taken two months of intensive therapy before she felt human again. Not happy, but human. She no longer burst into tears at the grocery store. She remembered to wash her hair and cook herself meals. Most importantly, her brain had stopped suggesting all the ways she could kill herself, pointing out telephone poles while driving or calculating the dosage of the drugs she'd need to administer to herself the same painless death she gave her patients. Thinking about how close she'd come terrified her now. This was a good sign.

"This one." She chose a paint chip at random: Alabaster Dream, satin latex. *Who names this stuff?* Holding it up to the dark wall, she pictured the living room in her mind's eye. White walls, exposed beams, and perhaps a touch of nautical blue somewhere. Rustic cabin meets seaside resort. HGTV always played in patient waiting rooms, and while the budgets of the homeowners on the renovation shows made her want to laugh hysterically, she found the demolitions and the subsequent renovations soothing. An obvious metaphor for recovery: tear something down, throw enough money at it, and you'll create something better. She made a mental note to tell her therapist she was on to her office's subliminal messaging the next time they spoke.

"But do I need to sand you?" she asked the walls. "Or will primer be enough?"

The animal heads on the wall stared back at her, and she could have sworn the taxidermy coyote by the fireplace smirked. Her mother was right: she needed to do something about her stuffed housemates. The attic would suffice for now.

Said attic, when she forced her way up its fold-out stairs, revealed a jumble of boxes, old bedframes, broken furniture, and decaying life jackets. She wiped a cobweb out of her eyes and frowned. Her Toyota Corolla didn't have nearly enough space to haul the debris to the dump. She needed someone with a truck.

Morgan's face popped into her mind.

She clarified her assessment: someone with a truck who *hadn't* seen her fall into the Atlantic Ocean. *I'll rent one*, she decided, and shoving aside the attractive alternative of taking her tea on the porch in the sunshine, she set to work.

Morgan pulled into the clinic at half past six.

"I'm starving." Stevie dug around the glove box for a snack, and several syringes tumbled to the floor.

"Lil's here." Morgan nodded at the Subaru Crosstrek in the parking lot.

"But does she have snacks?"

"She has dog biscuits, and those really meaty chewy treats that smell like bacon."

"Don't tempt me." Stevie jumped out of the truck and grabbed the kit to restock supplies while Morgan double-checked that none of the paperwork had fallen out of her battered clipboard. Content that all cases were accounted for, she headed for the back door, intentionally avoiding the lobby and the pet owners sitting in the chairs. At least ambulatory vets knew their schedule was going to get fucked, she reflected as she passed the sign that showed their office hours: 8:00-5:00. A beautiful lie.

Danielle Watson poked her head out of her office when Morgan entered the building. Short, gray-haired, and with the cold confidence common among livestock veterinarians, she looked out of place in her lurid sweater.

"What the hell are you wearing, Watson?" Morgan asked as she eyed the kittens frolicking on the lime green cotton.

"A client gave it to me, and it's cold back here."

Stevie, reappearing at the sound of Danielle's voice, made the sign of the cross and backed away slowly, asking, "What's wrong with cookies? Or a fruit basket?"

"There's an Edible Arrangement in the kitchen. Morgan, I need to talk to you."

Stevie slapped Morgan cheerfully on the back and made a beeline for the kitchen.

"What's up?" Morgan asked as she settled into the spare chair in Danielle's office. Danielle owned and managed the clinic, but she also saw appointments as needed. Today, she looked like a woman who had been puked on and/or shat on by too many fractious animals.

"Still no luck finding another ambulatory vet. Or even someone interested in a mixed practice with ambulatory on-call duties." She took off her glasses and rubbed her eyes. "I know you need a break, Morgan."

"I'm hanging in there."

"We could start referring clients to the Davis Clinic."

"I don't want to lose clients just because Sellers left us in the lurch." Dr. Sellers's abrupt resignation still rankled. She'd trusted him. Bailing without warning was unprofessional at best, and she wasn't feeling generous: it was a shit thing to do.

"And I don't want you burning out. I'm cutting you back to weekends and Wednesdays for emergency services. That gives you three nights off."

"I'm fine." The words reminded her of Emilia, and she deflated in her chair. She wasn't fine. She was exhausted and needed a break, even if it meant some of their clients switched to Davis Animal Clinic.

"It's nonnegotiable. Tired doctors make mistakes."

"I know. I just don't understand why no one's biting. Have you had any phone interviews?"

"A few, but the wrong personalities. We need someone willing to stay here for more than a year, and the job market for spouses is nonexistent unless they're willing to commute to Portland."

None of this was news. That was why Maine was called Vacationland. People came to visit, not to stay.

"Keep me posted."

"I will."

"And hold still." Morgan snapped a picture of Danielle in her cat sweater and sent it to Danielle's wife.

"Get out of my office, Donovan."

Morgan found Stevie by a wilting bouquet of fruit and ornamental kale.

"I saved you a strawberry," said Stevie.

"Thanks. Find anything else?"

"Brownies. Counter."

Morgan peeled back a sheet of tinfoil to reveal a tray of homemade goodness. Perks of the job. At least on the road she and Stevie were not exposed to sugar and carbs all day long like the small animal staff. No wonder Lillian ran every day. She shoved a brownie into her mouth and accepted the last strawberry.

"Just kill me," Lillian Lee said from behind them. She sank onto one of the stools at the table and rested her chin on her hand to stare mournfully at Morgan. A few strands of her black hair escaped her ponytail, and dog hair covered her clothes.

"What's up?" Morgan asked Lillian.

"This dog's pressures. They aren't responding to anything, and the owners don't want to go to optho, but they also don't want to remove the eye."

"Fruit?" Morgan gestured at a sagging cantaloupe.

"No thanks. Unless it's soaked in vodka?"

"Sorry. But Danielle is making me take a few nights off, so I'll buy you a drink later."

"By buy me a drink I hope you mean bring me a beer while I turn to mush on the couch."

"Deal."

"Dr. Lee?" an assistant called from a treatment room.

"And here we go again." Lillian slid off the stool, straightened her white coat, and strode out of the room.

"Think any of the leftovers in the fridge are still good?"

"No, I'll buy us burgers on the way home," said Morgan.

"Doctor bucks." Stevie popped the cantaloupe into her mouth. "Burgers and beer for everyone queer."

"You're giving me a headache. Make sure we have enough vet wrap for tomorrow. And duct tape and diapers. There's a hoof abscess on the schedule."

"Sure thing, boss."

Stevie sauntered out, leaving Morgan to wonder, as she often did, whether her technician mainlined Red Bull whenever her back was turned. Sighing, she retreated to her office and the paperwork awaiting her. There would be no stopping by the dock tonight. Paperwork, beer, and bed. Idly, she wondered if Emilia had been back to her boat, or if her dip in the Atlantic had scared her away. The latter thought brought disappointment. Whatever Morgan had told Stevie, Emilia Russo offered a welcome distraction.

Chapter Four

Renting a sander had seemed like a straightforward venture. All she needed were the sander, belts, extension cord, safety goggles, and a face mask. Nell would spend this time on the porch. Just because Emilia wasn't sure if she wanted to practice medicine anymore didn't mean she was going to forget about the risks exposure to dust and chemicals posed to dogs.

The reality proved a little more challenging. The hardware store in town didn't rent out tools—at least, not the ones she needed—so she had to track down the nearest ACE Hardware. Then she spent a good thirty minutes of her life listening to a white man several years her junior explain in terms better suited for a five-year-old how the tool worked, all while staring at her chest.

The acquisition barriers, however, paled in comparison to the real challenge: the walls themselves. Smoke darkened the wood by her father's favorite chair. Elsewhere, oil from the fur of long-dead dogs revealed their preferred nooks and routes. She couldn't just sand them away. These walls were proof her father had lived, proof that for all his faults, he'd sat here in this room, listening to his bluesy music while the sun set over his meadow. Who was she to sand and paint this house, erasing all traces of that man? Who was she to judge his life?

She put down the sander and touched the worn leather of his chair beneath the drop cloth. Perhaps this had been a terrible idea. Perhaps she should have taken her mother's advice and left the house in the care of an industrious real estate agent practiced in dealing with the possessions of others, someone who didn't balk at hauling the refuse of spent lives away in dumpsters and luring new tenants into the haunted remains.

No. She squared her shoulders and faced the empty room, turning in a slow circle to take in the knots and whorls of the pine boards and the faded wood of the windowsills. Her father's last gift to her was this house. She needed this time and this house and something to do with her hands besides administering death. She would do right by all of them: the house, her father, and herself.

Still, she didn't need to do everything today.

"Let's go out on the water, Nell."

No one was at the wharf. She dug a life jacket out of the small locker that now belonged to her until the lease ran out and grimaced at the grimy film covering the fluorescent orange. Better a dirty life jacket than another water rescue, she reminded herself as she shrugged into it and adjusted the straps. Morgan could take her safety course and shove it up her ass.

Water had accumulated in the bottom of the skiff again. She pulled it close to the dock and bailed it out, glad no one was around to laugh at her clumsy motions. *I should have brought the kit to fix this piece of shit.* Since she hadn't, she coaxed Nell into the boat, rewarding her with a treat from the pocket of her jeans, and began to row.

The motion felt more natural this time. Her shoulders and arms burned pleasantly as the oars sliced through the calm water of the harbor. A flat, overcast sky arced overhead, and the slow ripples barely disturbed the glassy sheen of its reflection. Nell didn't share her serenity. The dog sat hunched in the bow with her ears pressed flat against her skull.

"Almost there." A few more strokes brought her parallel to the sailboat. She pulled the oars into the skiff and grabbed the edge of the sailboat to steady them. "Up, Nell."

Nell turned her narrow head to stare at Emilia in disdain, then scrambled into the boat. Emilia secured the bowline to the mooring and followed, managing not to fall into the ocean. She took this as a good omen.

Setting the boat to rights didn't take long. Despite the slow, steady breeze, she had no intention of actually sailing. Not until she followed hardware store Doug's advice and watched a few hours of YouTube tutorials to refresh her memory. The sailboat's small engine, however, would take them around the harbor until then. Grinning at her dog, who had curled up on the pile of seat cushions Emilia had assembled for just that purpose, she fired up the engine with a few tugs of the draw and a muttered prayer. It sputtered twice and then turned over with a little cloud of blue-gray smoke that cleared quickly. She climbed into the bow to release them from the mooring—her second successful dry feat of the day—and took a seat with her hand on the tiller.

"Ahoy, matey," she said to Nell. The dog ignored her. "Or not."

She guided the boat around the nearby moorings, noting Morgan's small speedboat, the *All Paws on Deck*, as she passed. Morgan Donovan could fuck off. She wondered at the intensity of the thought. Morgan hadn't done anything besides rescue her and make a stupid—and deserved—comment. Well, that and ignore her over a decade ago when they were kids, but Emilia couldn't hold her accountable for teenage angst. Still, something about seeing Morgan again had set off her defense mechanisms, and all the logic in the world couldn't quell them. Morgan had known her dad. She couldn't tell if that made her jealous of Morgan or her father or both—as if her jealousy could change any of this. Her father was gone. Morgan was just a girl she'd had a crush on once, and that was where those feelings belonged: in the past, not here in her grief.

The harbor opened up into a large sheltered bay perfect for sailing had she been inclined. Instead, she kept to the coastline, watching for harbor seals and porpoises and enjoying the way the wind tangled her hair. She had no bad or complicated memories of being on the water with her father. He'd been happy here.

She stayed out long enough to start worrying about gas for the engine. May sunshine pierced the clouds toward evening, turning the horizon a tranquil rose-gold. Reluctantly, she navigated once more toward mooring eighteen.

"Nice ride."

Emilia's hand jerked on the tiller, and she corrected it hastily, knocking into a red and purple lobster pot in the process. Morgan lounged on the bow of her boat. Her pants were cuffed above her ankles, and her tousled curls blew in the slight breeze. A fishing pole rested in her hands.

"At least I take mine out."

"*Touché.*" Morgan gave her a friendly smile as Emilia passed.

"Asshole," Emilia said to Nell under her breath. The calm that her sail had earned her floundered and drowned as she killed the engine. She could feel Morgan's eyes on her as she leaned over the bow of the sailboat to secure it to the mooring.

Sorry, bud. Not playing damsel in distress today.

Putting the boat to bed took only a few minutes. She glanced over at Morgan to make sure she stayed put in her own boat, then heaved Nell into the skiff and set off toward the dock. Unfortunately, rowing meant she had to face Morgan the entire way, and something about the other woman's posture made her suspect Morgan was enjoying the situation.

Don't let her get under your skin, she told herself. *Clearly, you're going to run into each other. She knew your dad. She docks her boat here. She hauled your drunk ass out of the water.* Her jaw clenched. She hadn't come here to be humiliated. *On the other hand*, a more rational part of her brain argued, *What if you'd hit your head when you fell in the water? She could have saved your life.* But she hadn't hit her head, and now Morgan probably thought Emilia, like her father, was an alcoholic, which shouldn't have mattered but did. Morgan's casual wave as she neared the dock made her grind her teeth. Soon she'd need to start wearing a mouth guard.

I'm allowed to blame her and still understand that it's my fault and I'm being ridiculous, she decided. Everyone else on the planet managed to hold conflicting beliefs at the same time. Why not her?

41

Nell leapt out of the skiff in a hurry. Emilia, however, frowned at the boat. More water. She weighed her options: haul it out and examine the damage, risking Morgan's unwanted advice, or wait for another day. *I'm being an idiot.* She gathered her tangled hair into a messy braid. Morgan didn't matter. Her boat did. Shedding her life jacket, she gripped the prow of the skiff and hauled it onto the dock.

Nell cocked her head at this new turn of events and approached the boat hesitantly.

"You don't have to get in this time."

The dog contented herself with watching as Emilia removed the oars and flipped the skiff. It weighed more than she expected, and she panted as she surveyed her craft. A hairline crack ran one-third of the length of the hull. She traced it with her finger, aware that a second rowboat was, predictably, approaching the dock, and vowing not to look up.

Nell greeted the sable German shepherd warily. Snouts and tails swapped places, until both dogs appeared to decide on a policy of live and let live, and the shepherd nosed Emilia's pocket. She blinked into his warm, brown eyes.

"Oh hello there," she said as her heart melted. "Aren't you handsome."

He smiled a dog smile and waited expectantly. Emilia's hand went to her pocket automatically, but she paused, looking from brown eyes to slate-blue. "May I give him a treat?" she asked Morgan.

"It'll make his day."

She slipped the dog a cookie, saving a second for a jealous Nell, and ruffled both sets of ears. Most of the shepherds she'd known were reserved with strangers, but then again this was their second meeting and she had cookies. The odds were in her favor.

"What's his name again?" she asked, though she remembered well enough.

"Kraken."

"Right. Your roommate's choice."

"Only tentacle he has is his tongue, though." The tongue in question lolled.

"And you've met Nell twice now." She glanced at her dog, who leaned against Morgan's leg and was enjoying a chin scratch.

"We're old pals."

Damn it, she thought as Morgan found Nell's itchy spot and the dog's lips curled in ecstasy. Some of her defenses crumbled, along with her resentment. She couldn't hold hard feelings against someone who appreciated her dog, and Nell's seal of approval was hard to ignore. She shoved her hands into the sorry excuse for pockets in her jeans, envious of Morgan's work pants and their capacious, practical ones.

"I wanted to apologize," Morgan said.

"For what?"

"I get the feeling we got off on the wrong foot."

Emilia tucked a rogue strand of hair behind her ear. She didn't say anything, and Morgan smiled ruefully.

"For the record, you're not the first to fall off your boat here. I've done it. You just got unlucky enough to have a witness."

Emilia grimaced. "I don't know about unlucky. You did pull me out, and I'm not sure I could have managed that on my own."

"Be honest, though. You hate me a little for that, don't you?"

"Maybe," she allowed as her skin prickled with embarrassment and an unexpected surge of relief tugged the corners of her mouth up in a smile. It felt surprisingly good to be called out by this woman. Morgan, by all rights, should have written her off as a bitch and walked away. She hadn't.

"Can I make it up to you with a drink?"

Emilia's budding smile faltered. Being called out? Sure. Being asked out? That she wasn't ready for, even as friends. Not with Morgan.

"I'm not coming on to you, if that's what you're worried about." Morgan's voice kept its easy timbre, but Emilia's face flamed.

"Oh god. No. I'm so sorry. I didn't think—I mean—I'm gay, so I'm not offended, but . . . Jesus." She sat on the skiff and buried

43

her face in her hands. Next to her she heard Morgan take a seat on the dock. This was even more embarrassing than falling in the water.

"Shit. That was a dick thing to say. Look, I know I don't know you, and I can't imagine what you're going through right now, but your dad was a good friend to me. I miss him."

Emilia pressed the heels of her palms into her eyes to prevent them from doing anything stupid, like crying, and spoke to her knees. "He was a complicated person."

"He also took terrible care of this boat." Morgan rapped the hull. Emilia emerged from the shelter of her hands. Morgan's expression held compassion, but no pity. "Have you ever done this kind of repair?"

"I've watched some videos."

"Then you probably know more than I do," said Morgan.

Fuck it. "Actually, I have no idea what I'm doing. About this. Or, honestly, about anything."

"Hey." Morgan spoke to her the way Emilia remembered her speaking to Nell. The gentle voice felt like a soothing hand on her back. "Tell you what. I'll watch some tutorials to get on your level, and if you want, I can help you get this lady seaworthy. You're obviously totally capable of doing it yourself, but like I said, I miss your dad. You can think of it as a favor to him."

"Okay." The word hurt coming out.

"Good." Morgan stood and offered Emilia a hand. "And now, you look like you really could use a drink. I'm not on call, and Stormy's is on both of our ways home. Plus she allows dogs, so if you want to grab a drink . . ." She trailed off.

Emilia accepted Morgan's hand. Her palm was warm and rough. "Sure."

"All right. Did you drive or walk?"

"Walk," said Emilia, and this time it wasn't a lie.

"Mind if we keep walking? Parking the truck is a bitch in town, even during the off-season," said Morgan.

"I don't mind. What should I do about this?" She nudged her boat.

44

"We'll carry it up to the boathouse. It's pretty obvious it needs repair, and no one will steal it. This way it will also be dry when we work on it."

We. Well, at least she hadn't lied to her mother. She'd made a friend.

Her eyes slid to the flexed muscles in Morgan's arms and shoulders as they carried the skiff. *Friends*.

Morgan walked beside Emilia down the weathered sidewalk, their dogs pausing to sniff at things she could only guess at. Emilia kept pace easily with her, unlike poor Stevie, and Morgan idly wondered if she was a runner. She had a runner's long muscles, although her jeans hugged hips that made Morgan swallow. Her dark hair hung in a messy braid that managed to look artful, and she had Ray's olive skin. The wool sweater she wore also looked as if it had belonged to her father. She'd rolled the over-long sleeves up to her wrists in a way that stirred a dangerously protective instinct in Morgan.

Stevie, she thought darkly. Her friend's insistent prodding had gotten to her, and now she was spinning fairy tales for herself. Emilia Russo's father had died, and Morgan had no desire to complicate Emilia's life further. The woman clearly had a lot going on. More to the point, so did Morgan. She could be friendly, though, and try not to dwell on Emilia's sputtered, "I'm gay" for too long, or the curl of hair trailing down the open collar of her sweater. Morgan cleared her throat.

"So," she asked. "Where are you coming from?"

"The dock."

"In general," said Morgan, noting the slight curve of Emilia's lips. Had she cracked a joke?

"Boston."

"Ah. That makes you a summer person. I'll try not to hold it against you."

"Appreciated. Did you grow up here?"

"Born and bred. I spent some time in New York—upstate, not

45

the city—for school, but this is home." She waved her hand at a row of buildings that took "weathered" past the borders of quaint and into derelict.

"Is that a bad thing?"

"Depends on your perspective."

"Which is?"

"I love it here. Granted, the winters are long and the roads are shit, but it's worth it."

"My dad thought so, too. He and my mom split when I was eight. He came back here. I spent the summers with him until I was a teenager."

"Emilia of the *Emilia Rosa.*"

"Yes. I have a boat named after me."

The wry note in Emilia's voice made Morgan laugh.

Storm's-A-Brewin' came into view around the corner with its dark blue awnings hanging over the cheerfully lit windows.

"Before we go in, I have to ask—was she named Stormy or is it a nickname?" Emilia asked.

"Her mother named her Victoria, which she hates, by the way. Apparently, she had terrible temper tantrums as a kid. Her brother started calling her *Vic-stormia*, and *Stormy* stuck."

"I suppose Stormy is better than Vicky."

"If you ever feel like living on the edge, call her that." Morgan opened the door, and as Emilia stepped through it, she caught some faint hint of scent. Floral. Sweet. Emilia's perfume, or maybe just a fancy brand of shampoo—whatever it was, it inspired the unhelpful urge to lean in and breathe deeply.

"Boifriend!" Stormy waved from behind the bar. A red bandana held her tempestuous black curls in place. Morgan caught Emilia's raised eyebrow at Stormy's exuberant greeting.

"*Boi* with an *i*. It's a long story," Morgan said as she approached the bar.

"Not really," said Stormy. Only two other customers were in the shop, which didn't bode well for business. It also gave Stormy an excuse to insert herself into their conversation. "Morgan's my stand-in partner. Whenever some creep hits on me, I tell him

46

about my big, strong, truck-driving boyfriend." She snapped the bar towel at Morgan's biceps.

"Ouch." She rubbed the spot where the towel had hit.

"One time, I had a customer who just wouldn't let it go, and Morgan happened to be here . . ."

"Got it. She likes playing the hero, doesn't she?" Emilia took a seat at one of the bar stools and shot Morgan a sardonic look that quickened her pulse.

"I see you know all there is to know about the Don. Do the doggos need any water? Morgan's finicky about community water bowls. Kraken gets his own cup."

"Lucky boy," said Emilia.

"Lucky owner. I know he drinks out of the toilet at home," said Stormy.

"He does not." Morgan put her hand on Kraken's head, only half feigning her wounded tone. No dog of hers would ever drink out of some bacteria-filled cesspool.

"Mhmm. What can I get you ladies?"

"I'll take a stout," said Morgan.

"And I'll try your porter."

"Excellent choices, though I would have pegged you as an IPA drinker," Stormy said to Emilia. "How are you liking Seal Cove?"

"I feel like I dove right into the middle of it."

Another joke? Morgan couldn't tell.

"Not something I'd recommend. I don't touch that water until July, and that's with padding." She patted her curvy figure.

"And a wet suit," said Morgan.

"Why haven't I seen you in ages? Buying coffee doesn't count," Stormy asked as she set Morgan's foaming stout down in front of her.

"I've been on call and it's spring. Everything wants to be born or die, usually at the same time. Danielle made me take three nights off a week, though, so maybe you'll see more of me."

"I'll believe it when I see it, but thank you for darkening my door."

"I don't darken doorways."

"Oh, but you do. You're all dark and brooding."

"And I don't brood."

"She broods," Stormy said to Emilia.

"Brooding is better than pouting," said Emilia.

"True. Although Stevie is a cutie when she pouts. Tell her I miss her, too. Does she know you're here? I'm surprised to see you two separated."

"Stevie?" Morgan felt an unwanted heat rise in her cheeks. "I left her at the house. Emilia and I ran into each other at the dock."

"I won't tell her you're cheating on her," said Stormy.

Emilia's eyebrows contracted in confusion, and Morgan contemplated tossing her drink in Stormy's direction. The last thing she needed was Emilia thinking she and Stevie were an item.

"Cheating on her with beer," she tried to clarify.

Emilia's eyebrows continued their trajectory inward.

"I'm not dating Stevie." Why was she saying these things? She looked to Stormy for aid, only to find her friend smirking at her in amusement.

"Well, now that you've thoroughly established how you feel about Stevie, I'll get back to work," said Stormy as a group of high-schoolers came into the shop.

"Let's grab a table." Morgan fled Stormy's knowing smile. Damn her friends. They meant well, but they were also mortifying. She chose a corner away from the boisterous youths in pursuit of a caffeinated jolt. Kraken heaved a sigh and collapsed by her chair. Nell, Morgan noticed, sat close to Emilia and watched her surroundings with some of her owner's wariness.

"I don't remember you on a boat growing up," said Emilia.

"My folks didn't have a boat. They live on a farm a few miles outside of South Bristol."

"Is it a working farm?"

"Not really. They have twenty acres, and my mother keeps a flock of Dorset sheep. Sometimes we use it as overflow for the clinic."

"The clinic?"

48

"Seal Cove Veterinary Clinic."

"You're a vet." Emilia didn't phrase it as a question. Morgan tried to interpret the expression in her dark eyes. Most people reacted with enthusiasm to her career, followed by a variation of one of the following statements: A) I wanted to be a vet when I was younger! B) Cool! So my dog does this weird thing . . . C) You must love playing with puppies and kittens all day.

Emilia did none of the above. She simply sat there, looking at Morgan with a strange, almost wistful smile.

"What do you do?" Morgan asked to break the awkward silence.

"Right now I'm just trying to figure out what to do with my dad's house."

Morgan didn't miss the evasion, but she didn't push it. Had Ray mentioned what his daughter did? He must have. It swam at the edge of her memory, but try as she might, she couldn't reel it in. "I've never been inside the house, but I've seen the outside. Looks like a nice place. Rustic. I know he built it himself. Will you sell it?"

"I think so. Or I could rent it out, I guess."

Morgan tried to imagine what she would do if she inherited the Donovan farm sooner than anticipated. The answer came easily. Keep it, move in, and continue paying off her student loans. Her situation and Emilia's, however, were drastically different. Morgan had a life here. Emilia just had memories, and Morgan didn't think she'd be able to rent out her parents' house if their places were reversed.

"I'm on the road most of the time, but we've got all kinds of tools lying around if you need to borrow anything. Here." She pulled her wallet out of her pocket and removed a business card, scribbling her cell on the back. "Seriously. Shoot me a text if you need anything."

Emilia accepted the card, and the unreadable expression changed to something more familiar. Wariness again, but this time mixed with gratitude.

"I feel like I'm starting to owe you."

"Don't worry about it. Like I said, Ray is a friend. Least I can do is help his daughter, right?" She couldn't bring herself to use the past tense to describe him.

Emilia traced lines through the condensation on her glass. The motion had a hypnotic effect on Morgan. Maybe moving away from the bar had been a bad idea. Their conversation had flowed freely there, while now it stuttered and tripped over unseen obstacles. *And you just gave her your number*, she reminded herself. *Might want to clarify your intentions.*

"Look." She took a draught of her stout before continuing, mostly for something to do with her hands. "Cards on the table, pun definitely intended."

Emilia cracked a small smile.

"I don't normally go out of my way like this, but you seem like a good person in a tough place, and since we keep running into each other, I think we should be friends. Friends help friends. Unless, of course, you'd rather keep glaring at me from your sailboat?"

Emilia's cheeks flushed. "You saw that?"

"I worried you'd burn a hole in my hull."

"What makes you think I didn't?"

Morgan raised her hands in defeat.

"Okay," said Emilia.

"Okay, what?"

"Okay, yes, maybe friendship isn't such a bad idea. I just have one condition."

"Which is?"

"You can't tell anyone I fell off my boat."

Morgan winced.

"You already did, didn't you?"

"Technically I didn't say it was you."

Emilia leaned back in her chair. She had nice shoulders. Feminine, but strong. Morgan stopped the thought from progressing past casual observation into more dangerous territory, like what it might be like to grip those shoulders while—*shit.*

"Then tell me something embarrassing about yourself," said Emilia.

"I've only had half a beer."

"I'll buy you another," said Emilia.

"So that you can blackmail me?"

"Friends keep secrets."

"Fine. Let me think." *My ex broke off our engagement. I'm probably going to die alone, crushed to death by a cow. The last time I had sex was six months ago. I can't even touch myself without thinking of Kate.* "I eat cheese in the middle of the night."

"How is that embarrassing?"

"You don't understand. I eat a lot of cheese. No cheese is safe. Cheddar, brie, mozzarella, cheese labeled, 'Stevie's, don't eat.' Cheese dip. Cheese sticks. If it's cheese, I'll eat it."

"How much cheese are we talking about?"

"So much. I could eat it by the block."

"I still don't think that's on the same level as falling off a boat."

"What if I told you I was lactose intolerant?"

"Are you?"

"No."

"Not good enough. Sorry." Emilia crossed her arms across her chest, a motion Morgan refused to let her eyes dwell on. The old blue wool sweater might have been too big for Emilia, but it didn't conceal nearly enough.

"Okay. How about this. First time I drove a tractor."

Emilia smirked.

"Is something funny?"

"That's just . . . very gay."

"This is Maine. You'd be surprised how many people can drive tractors. Anyway, I didn't realize you had to engage the clutch to use the brake. I was working for a friend of my dad on her farm, and all I wanted to do was put a new round bale on the hay spike and feed it out to the herd. But I couldn't stop. I didn't even make it out of the parking lot. My boss had just bought some new fence posts, and I drove right into the pile. Most got busted, and the tractor only stopped because I drove into a hill. The worst part was that I had a huge crush on my boss's daughter, who was obviously watching the whole thing."

"Did you get fired?"

"No, but I wasn't allowed to drive the tractor again for a long time."

Emilia tapped her fingers on the table. "That's pretty bad. I accept your proposal. Friends?" She raised her glass.

"Friends," said Morgan, clinking her drink to Emilia's.

"I have one more question."

"Shoot."

"Do you eat cheese from a can?"

"I do have some standards."

"But do you?" Emilia mimed squirting cheese from a nozzle.

"Totally." She leaned in. "I've even tried the cheese they sell at pet stores for dogs. It's not half bad."

"I've actually tried that too," said Emilia.

"I knew I liked you."

"If questionable judgment in cheese is your criteria, then we'll get along fine. What about beer?"

"I know more about craft beer than I want to." Morgan nodded at the bar and at Stormy, who was foaming milk for a lobsterman Morgan hadn't figured as a latte kind of guy. Just went to show that stereotypes didn't always hold up under scrutiny.

"Believe me, I can sympathize," said Emilia. "Boston is the home of the Craft Beer Bro. I've had the incredibly complicated and holy process of drinking fermented plant matter explained to me more times than I care to count."

Morgan relaxed as they stayed on safe ground. Dogs. Drinks. Food. Music. Nothing too personal, besides the story she'd told her about the tractor. As they talked, she studied her companion. Emilia had a way of glancing down before she smiled that revealed the absurd length of her eyelashes. She wore no makeup, though Morgan had no way of knowing if this was normal for her or not, and her full lips were slightly chapped from a day on the water. Faint dark circles suggested she didn't sleep well. Morgan's mind categorized these details with the same level of attention it gave the rest of Emilia: too much. She wanted to run her thumb along Emilia's lower lip to soothe the dry skin. Chapstick would be more effective, she told herself, and jerked her eyes away. They fell on the clock on the wall.

"Oh, shit. I've got to get home and feed this guy." She patted a perturbed Kraken, who eyed her with reproach. He was too well behaved to whine, but she knew he was hungry.

"I'll settle the tab," said Emilia. She rose before Morgan could protest, forcing her to leap to her feet and chase after her. They arrived at the till—and an amused Stormy—at the same time.

"You don't need to pay for my drink," Morgan said.

"Why not?" The challenge in Emilia's voice as she leaned back against the counter did unfair things to Morgan's heart rate. That blend of hauteur and femme confidence had always been her weakness.

"You could always split the bill," Stormy suggested with a grin that Morgan longed to wipe off her face.

"No, I'll pay." Emilia tapped her phone to the card reader before Morgan could pull out her card.

"Technology. Amazing, isn't it? Boifriend, say 'thank you, Emilia,'" Stormy instructed.

Morgan shoved a ten into the tip jar. Her face felt hot and her throat was dry despite the beer. She glared at Stormy before turning to Emilia. "Next one's on me."

"Sure." Emilia patted her dog's head. "Ready, Nell?"

Stormy raised her eyebrows as Morgan moved to follow Emilia to the door. Morgan shook her head at the question in her eyes.

Chapter Five

Of course Morgan was a vet. Emilia stared at the business card, her mouth full of the coppery taste of disappointment. Morgan Donovan, DVM. Why couldn't she have befriended a lobster-woman or an investment banker or an artist—or a person in any profession, really, besides veterinary medicine? She'd left Boston to get away from her old life. Enmeshing herself in that world again was a terrible idea. She wasn't ready and, besides, eventually she'd have to tell Morgan she was also a vet, which would mean explaining her breakdown and her doubts. She had her hands full already. She didn't need more complications.

She also couldn't deny to herself any longer that she liked Morgan. Her hands curled around the smooth stainless-steel curve of her father's urn. The dark bedroom surrounded her with the familiar sounds of the house. Tree branches on the roof. Joints and joists creaking. A few smaller scuttlings that could be mice. She smiled as she recalled Morgan's confession. Morgan Donovan, thief of cheese at midnight. Morgan, whose easy smile made the ache of Emilia's grief a little less sharp. Maybe her mother had a point. She did need a friend, and Morgan didn't need to know everything about her recent past. It gave her a fresh start.

And she knew my dad. The urn's smooth surface comforted her. "What do you think? Is she good people?" she asked his ashes.

Her father didn't answer.

Restless and still a little buzzed from her evening, she pushed back the covers and got out of bed. Nell groaned in protest. Outside, moonlight illuminated the meadow. She wrapped a thick blanket around her shoulders and padded out to the porch to curl up in her father's Adirondack chair. Dew coated the grass. It was too early in the season for fireflies, but tree frogs peeped and the boldest spring insects chirped in chorus. Something that might have been a coyote yipped.

This was nothing like her Boston apartment. No car sounds. No sirens. No neighbor's television blaring the Patriots game through an open window, and no wafting cigarette smoke. Just clean, cool air.

No wonder he'd loved it here.

One day at a time. It was good advice, but she'd have to make decisions about her future eventually. Summer was the best time to put a house on the market anywhere, and especially in Maine. If she waited too long, she'd have to deal with the house over the winter. Empty houses didn't fare well. Pipes froze and burst. Renting would make sense, but as she'd nearly told Morgan, she couldn't stand the thought of a stranger in her father's house. Selling provided closure. A clean break.

A herd of deer picked their way across the meadow. She watched them, grateful for the break in the repetitive cycle of her thoughts. *One day at a time.*

Morgan considered Joanna Mason and her father, Jack, from the side of the sheep pen. Two ewes milled about inside. Both were still pregnant, thanks to a later-than-usual breeding, and one had a lamb's head peeking out from her vulva. The tongue hadn't turned purple yet, which meant it had not been stuck long. That was a good sign.

"Okay, Jo."

The kid looked up at her with wide eyes. These sheep were part of her 4-H flock, and the fourteen-year-old scuffed the toe of her muck boot against the cement floor of the small barn.

"You're going to let her do it?" Jack asked.

"Only if she wants to learn."

"I do." The girl's brown ponytail bobbed.

"This way, you can try helping on your own first, next time. That can make a big difference for the lamb. Saves your dad some money, too." She winked at Jack.

"What do I do?"

"First, get the sheep."

Joanna caught her ewe and tipped her gently into the straw. Her competency impressed Morgan. The kid had good handling instincts. Morgan knelt beside the sheep and motioned for Joanna to do the same, and she was further impressed by the leg the girl placed carefully over the ewe's neck to prevent her from getting up during the birth. She handed her a pair of disposable birthing sleeves and put a pair of normal latex gloves on herself.

"Now, hold out your hands." She poured a liberal amount of lubricant onto Joanna's gloves. "What do you think is going on in there?"

"I think the legs are stuck."

"You're probably right."

Lambs were supposed to enter the birth canal nose and front toes first. The keywords were "supposed to," as several things could go wrong during the process. One front leg—or both—could remain behind, which jammed the shoulder blade against the ewe's cervix. Lambs could enter the canal backward, tail first or back feet first, or with their heads turned to the side. Multiple lambs could present a confusing array of body parts, requiring the shepherd to trace each one back to the unborn owner. This case, however, looked simple enough, and would be a good learning experience for Joanna.

"See if you can gently feel around the head and get your hand in there."

"I won't hurt her?"

"Be gentle, but she's already uncomfortable. This will help her."

Joanna's tongue pressed between her lips in concentration—rather like the poor lamb's—as she worked her small hand into

56

the ewe. The sheep groaned and pushed as a contraction wracked her, and Morgan felt sympathy for Joanna, whose hand had just received a painful squeeze.

"Whoa," said the girl.

"They're strong, right? Okay. Do you feel anything?"

"I . . . I can't tell."

"That's fine. You're looking for any bony parts that could be a shoulder."

Joanna's forehead wrinkled as she put all her concentration into her fingers. Morgan remembered the first time she'd assisted in a birth. She'd been much younger than Joanna, and she'd had the benefit of watching her mother do it countless times, but it still felt alien to be inside another living thing.

"I think I found something?"

"Remember to breathe," she told her.

Joanna took a breath. "I didn't realize I was holding my breath."

"That's normal. What do you feel?"

"I think . . . I think it's a tiny hoof!"

Morgan visualized the possible orientation of the lamb's body. Both shoulders stuck, but one leg almost in the right position if Joanna could already feel the hoof.

"Good. Pull it through slowly."

"I won't break it?"

"I promise you won't break it."

Joanna did as Morgan had instructed, and a yellow hoof, followed by a slick leg, emerged. The ewe strained, and the lamb slid out into the straw with a rush of fluids.

"Really nice job. Okay, let her up."

They moved out of the sheep's way. *Baa*ing, the new mother struggled to her feet and set about cleaning the lamb.

"That was so cool!"

"Right? If it's a really big lamb, you might have to find both legs, but we got lucky. Do you think she has another one?"

Joanna bumped the ewe's abdomen and nodded. "Definitely. Do I reach in?"

"Let's give her a chance first, but you did a really good job. She's lucky to have you as her shepherd."

Thirty minutes, two healthy lambs, and one very excited teenage girl later, Morgan emerged from the barn and went back to the truck where Stevie waited.

"Good news or baaaad?"

"No sheep puns."

"Fine. You've got a recheck on that evil paint mare next, and the clinic called in a melting ulcer we'll need to fit in this afternoon. How did it go?"

"Showed Jo how to lamb."

"She do okay?"

"Kid's a natural." Her cell phone buzzed before she could add more. She glanced down, expecting a text from the clinic, and saw an unknown number instead.

Sorry to bother you. It's Emilia. Any chance you have a shop vac lying around that I could borrow?

"What's up?" Stevie asked.

"Emilia wants to borrow a shop vac."

"I'm sorry, what?"

"Emilia wants—"

"I heard you. Why does she have your number?"

"We grabbed a drink the other night."

Stevie stared at her. "Uh huh."

"Jesus, Stevie. She's nice. We're friends."

"Okay, Morgan." Stevie imitated Morgan's tone. "Why does your *friend* need a shop vac, and what makes her think you're willing to loan her ours? Wasn't her dad in construction? He should have one."

"I don't know the details. She's doing some renovation on her dad's house. Maybe his is broken."

"She's hot and she can use power tools?"

"The two are not mutually exclusive."

Stevie opened the passenger sunshade mirror and flashed herself a smile. "Believe me, I know."

"Guess we can stop by the house and grab it. She's on the way to the Murphy place anyway."

"Oh, speaking of Angie—"

"Were we?"

"Angie, the house—same thing. Anyway, her birthday is next weekend. We should do something now that we're not on call twenty-four seven."

"Like a party?"

"God no. Then we'd have to invite her employees. A small thing. You, me, Lil, Stormy, the Watsons. Get the grill out if it's nice. I could make a cake!"

"What kind of cake?"

"She likes red velvet."

"Red velvet? What about chocolate?" said Morgan.

"What about it's Angie's birthday, so we make the cake she likes?"

"Fair point. I'll do some steaks and those big-ass mushrooms Lil likes." She'd been itching to get the grill out since the beginning of May.

"You should invite Emilia."

Morgan twisted Stevie's words back at her. "It's Angie's birthday. Angie hasn't met her."

"So? She's new in town. Maybe she wants to make friends. I'll stop kidding you about her. I'm serious, though. Ange won't mind, and you were friends with her dad. That reminds me. Didn't he say his daughter was a vet that one time?"

"What?"

"You don't remember? While we were fishing? That one time I came with you? He asked you about your loans because he was worried about her."

Stevie's words jarred her memory. Ray *had* mentioned something about his daughter's medical school loans, but then why had Emilia reacted the way she had when she found out about Morgan's profession? Had she lost her license? Morgan found that unlikely, but she supposed it was possible. Regardless of the

59

reason, if it was a sore spot, thrusting Emilia into the midst of a group of vets and vet techs didn't seem like a good idea.

"We'll see. We don't want to scare her away."

"We're charming. Who doesn't love talking about abscesses over dinner?"

"Exactly."

"But she's one of us."

"Because all vets are the same?" said Morgan.

"When it comes to abscesses, yes. Speaking of abscesses, I do not want to get kicked again by this next one."

The sound of tires on gravel rescued Emilia from the cloud of dust filling the living room. Nell barked from her refuge on the porch. She set down the sander and pushed her way outside, jerking her facemask down for a welcome breath of fresh air and shedding her safety goggles.

Morgan's truck idled in her driveway, then shut off. Emilia unclipped Nell's lead, and together they went to greet the women stepping out of the truck. The contrast between Morgan and Stevie amused her now that she had let her resentment toward Morgan go. Morgan had a good six inches on Stevie, maybe more, and her strikingly dark hair accented Stevie's honey blond ponytail.

"Hey," she said, suddenly aware of her ragged T-shirt and old jeans. Morgan and Stevie were dressed for the field, but their clothes, at least, didn't hang off their shoulders because the neckline had disintegrated with too many washes. She tugged it up.

"What's the emergency?" Morgan asked.

"Rabid dust bunnies?" said Stevie.

Sawdust covered even her eyelashes, and she tried unsuccessfully to brush it away without introducing it to her cornea. "Something like that. Something chewed through the cord of my dad's shop vac, and the things I've seen . . ." She trailed off, trying not to dwell on the ancient civilizations she'd discovered beneath the couches, chairs, and cupboards.

"You didn't get bit by anything, did you?" Morgan asked her with a frown. "Bats, squirrels, raccoons?"

"So far I've only seen a few mice."

Morgan's face relaxed. "Good. We found a family of raccoons in my parents' barn last summer. Eviction was . . . eventful."

"This is a nice place." Stevie looked around the yard, her blue-green eyes scanning the overgrown shrubs along the east side of the house, then the long front porch. Emilia looked, too, trying to see the house from an outsider's eyes. The log home stared back at her with her father's gentle smile.

"Could be yours," she said, swallowing past the lump in her throat. "I hope I didn't interrupt your work."

"You're on the way to our next appointment."

Morgan's reassuring smile slipped. Emilia saw her eyes flick down to her shoulder, which her shirt had revealed yet again. *Friends*, she reminded herself firmly as her body suggested more appealing alternatives.

"I'll grab the vac." Stevie paused to greet Nell before opening the truck's door. "Mind if I release the Kraken?"

"I told you," Morgan said to Emilia. Was there a hint of a blush on Morgan's cheeks, or was that her imagination?

"Release away."

The sable German shepherd leapt out of the truck and circled Nell, his tail wagging with enthusiasm. Their previous aloofness dissolved as they began to romp around the yard.

"Where do you want it?" Stevie asked as she hefted the shop vac out of the vehicle.

"I can grab it." Emilia took it from Stevie hastily, needing an excuse to look away from Morgan. When she returned from depositing it on the porch, she found Morgan and Stevie exchanging heated whispers.

"Is everything okay?"

"Peachy. What are you doing this weekend?"

Morgan shot Stevie a glare.

"Probably still cleaning."

"Do you want an alternative?" Stevie asked.

"That depends on the alternative," said Emilia.

"We're throwing a small birthday party for our friend Angie this Saturday. Beer, steaks—or mushrooms if you're vegetarian or vegan—and a few people from the clinic. Morgan doesn't think you want to hang out with a bunch of vet med people, but that's only because she's boring as fuck. The rest of us are cool."

A party. Emilia wished Nell would leave off romping with Kraken and sit beside her for moral support. How could she explain to the women in front of her that the offer both warmed and terrified her? She wasn't ready to be surrounded by her own world. *I came here to get away,* she thought, but Stevie's smile and Morgan's reddened cheeks were hardly threatening.

"I would love to," she said before she could change her mind.

"Awesome. Morgan will text you the address."

"What can I bring?"

"Nothing," Morgan said before Stevie could speak. "Ange isn't a huge birthday person. It's not really a party. Just bring yourself and Nell, if she doesn't mind a house full of dogs."

"And a demon cat," Stevie added.

"Oh?"

"James. You'll see what I mean." Stevie pulled up her sleeve to reveal several long, thin white scars.

"I'll take that as a warning."

"Do you like steak?" asked Morgan. "I can put something else on the grill for you."

She had a vivid image of Morgan "womanning" a grill in a tight black tank top. "Steak sounds great."

"Speaking of steak," Stevie began.

"Don't," said Morgan.

"It would be a mis-steak not to try one of Morgan's."

She couldn't help laughing at the terrible joke.

"And on that note, we've got to hit the road. See you around." Morgan flashed her a smile and steered a snickering Stevie to the truck. "Kraken, come."

62

Emilia watched the truck pull out and bit her lip to keep from smiling as she saw Morgan punch Stevie in the shoulder. It would be nice to have a friend like Stevie. She'd never been good at friendships. The turnover rate at work was too high, and she'd allowed herself to rely on Hannah's friends for the past few years. Some of them still kept in touch, but things were different now, and she had never experienced anything like the familiarity between Morgan and Stevie.

"You don't count," she said to Nell, who had collapsed at her feet to pant.

A party. She hadn't been to a party in . . . how long? She wracked her brain. Something thrown by one of Hannah's people probably, with loud music and the occasional line of cocaine. Too many people had always overwhelmed her, and now more so than ever. Could she trust Morgan and Stevie that this was a low-key affair? Could she trust herself around Morgan? Her shoulder still tingled where it had felt Morgan's gaze.

Definitely not.

Chapter Six

Sanding took longer than anticipated and was also infinitely more physically demanding. The soreness in Emilia's arms from the work, combined with the effort of moving furniture and cleaning did, however, have an upside: she was too exhausted to think about unanswered emails or her long list of recent failures, leaving her alone with her grief. She felt it fiercely, in bursts that took her breath away and left her sobbing on the floor, and she felt it in the quiet moments between Nell's sleeping breaths. At night she sat on the porch with her father's ashes and her dog and listened to the early summer rain falling on the tin roof.

June brought the first June bug. Nell started up from her bed on the porch and watched the fat beetle with interest as it flung itself at the light.

"No bugs," she told her dog, her mind on internal parasites, but Nell ignored her and stalked toward the insect on stiff legs. The bug vanished in a crunch.

Her phone rang as she reprimanded her unrepentant companion. "Hey."

"Sister from another mister."

"Are you ever going to get tired of that?" Emilia asked as she leaned back in her chair and let her stepsister's voice wash over her.

"Probably not. How are you doing?"

"I'm fine."

"Don't bullshit me. I have toddlers, remember?"

"How are the twins?"

"Driving me nuts. April's chewing on everything. She's worse than the dog, and Ruby only chews on her sister. Little cannibal."

"And Mark?"

"I will kill the next person who congratulates him for being a good dad just because he switched to working part-time to be home with the kids more."

"Don't do that. You'd go to jail, and I'd end up with the girls," said Emilia.

"I'll give them to you for free now if you want."

"Nell isn't ready for babysitting."

"Anyway," said Anna Maria, "Mom says you're painting or something? It's really irritating that you don't post anything. It makes it hard to stalk you. Although maybe it's for the best."

"Haven't gotten that far yet."

"You know I'd be there in a heartbeat if you need me, right?"

"I know."

"So how are you doing? Really. No bullshit."

She let out a deep breath. "I'm okay. It's hard."

"You don't need to do it alone."

"I do, though."

"You sure?"

"Yeah. And it's peaceful up here."

"Well, that's something. Oh, Christ." A child's wail nearly shattered Emilia's eardrum as Anna Maria paused to coo over her offspring.

"Do you need to go?"

"In a second."

Something about her tone alerted Emilia to trouble. "What?"

"Look, I don't want to tell you this, but I don't want you hearing about it from anyone else, either."

Emilia waited.

"Hannah's seeing someone else."

The words stole her breath. She'd been expecting them, but that didn't make them any easier to hear. "Anyone I know?"

"That friend of hers I never liked."

"Skylar."

"Yeah."

She faked a shaky laugh. "Well, that figures."

"You were too good for her anyway, Emmy."

"If you say so."

"I do say so."

"Is that April or Ruby screaming?"

"How would I know?"

"You're their mother?"

"I'm their hostage. I didn't know it was possible to love something that drives you this crazy. Don't bite your sister!"

"Go save your children from each other."

"I think I have to. Call me if you need me, and try not to think about Hannah."

"I won't," Emilia lied. Quiet settled over her again, made more pronounced by the absence of her nieces' screams.

She'd managed to come to terms with her breakup with Hannah. Her depressive spiral and subsequent hospitalization, on top of her father's death, had been too much for her ex. Hannah didn't tolerate extended emotional duress well, and Emilia had been too lost to care when Hannah broke things off. The hurt came later, but by then it was just one more hurt, like a broken limb when her organs were all on fire.

Knowing that Hannah had found solace with Skylar was different. Skylar, with her perfect teeth and Hollywood complexion, who always stood a little too close to Hannah when Emilia left her side. Hannah had sworn she had no feelings for the other woman. Maybe she hadn't. Maybe Skylar had been there for Hannah when Emilia fell apart, or maybe—and she couldn't help focusing on this last possibility—Skylar had been there all along. She pressed her fingers against her temples and told herself she didn't care. She didn't want Hannah anymore. Let Skylar deal with her uncompromising opinions and her anal retentiveness.

Her phone buzzed again. She moved to shove it far away from her, not wanting any more bad news, and then saw the name on the screen: Morgan. The text notification cast its harsh glow over her arm.

MD: *16 Bay Road. White farmhouse. 6 PM Sunday. You really don't need to bring anything.*

Her heart ached a little less at the words.

ER: *Not even your shop vac?*

The bouncing dots that indicated Morgan was typing further suppressed her dark mood.

MD: *Keep it for now. Might be more rabid dust bunnies.*

Should she respond?

She hesitated, then typed: *Do dust lagomorphs transmit rabies?*

She deleted the text. Lagomorphs was a vet word, and she wasn't ready to tell Morgan about that part of her life. Not that she'd be able to avoid it much longer without lying. "What do you do for a living" was one of those questions that tended to come up between strangers, and this party would be full of them.

ER: *These are more like dust bears.*

MD: *Do you need a chainsaw?*

ER: *How about something with a longer handle?*

MD: *Weed whacker?*

ER: *That works. Metal blade, though. Not string.*

MD: *Want it Saturday or do you need it sooner?*

Her heart thudded in her chest. Morgan was joking, but she couldn't help wondering what might happen if she asked Morgan to come over now. Would she? Or would she think Emilia was crazy? Or, and she tried to push the thought away, did she only want Morgan to come over because of what Anna Maria had just told her about Hannah and Skylar?

ER: *I made a barricade out of old fly fishing rods. Think I can hold out.*

MD: *Let me know if you need reinforcements.*

ER: *Will do.*

She set the phone down on the armrest and watched the colors bleed into the trees as night fell. Perhaps she should contact her therapist. *And if she tells you to steer clear of Morgan Donovan?* Or, worse, Shanti might ask her how she felt about the situation, and she didn't have any answers. Her attraction was obvious; everything else lay beneath murky waters. If only Morgan wasn't a vet. If only she hadn't known Emilia's father, or docked her boat at the same wharf, or been the first girl Emilia had crushed on. If they'd met at a bar—not that Emilia went to many bars—she might have kept the rest of her life separate. One-night stands were not something she did either, though. She needed friends, not complications, and she was an adult. She could control herself, no matter how much her body wanted Morgan.

I'll bring cookies, she decided. Everyone liked cookies.

Her phone buzzed for the third time. She grabbed for it, but her heart fell when she saw the ID. Anna Maria again.

AM: *Miss you. Children are tyrants.*

ER: *Miss you too. <3 u and the girls.*

Anna Maria sent a picture of Emilia's nieces tucked into their beds. Ruby had her thumb in her mouth, and April had snuggled up to the stuffed lion Emilia had given her. Her disappointment that it hadn't been Morgan melted into a wash of affection for her nieces.

"Did you get the beer?" Lillian called as soon as Morgan and Stevie walked through the door that Saturday. Morgan had arranged to switch her evening on-call shift to Monday so that she and Stevie would not be called away in the middle of the party.

"Shit."

"I texted you to remind you."

"No," said Morgan. "I mean we're covered in shit. Beer is in the truck."

Lillian poked her head into the mudroom and wrinkled her nose. Her dogs, on the other hand, sniffed appreciatively at the scent of manure.

"I see you've been playing with cows again."

"I should have gone into small animal medicine," said Morgan. She pulled off her shirt and jeans and shoved them into the washer they kept in the mudroom for this purpose.

"Cute undies," Lillian said as she vanished.

Morgan's briefs sported paw prints and dog bones. "Thanks," she shouted after Lillian.

"Don't you want to see mine?" Stevie added.

"Definitely not," Lillian said from the kitchen.

"Rude."

Morgan raised an eyebrow as Stevie wriggled out of her pants. "Dinosaurs?"

"Roar."

"Where do you even buy those for adults?"

"I have my sources." Stevie bounded into the house, and Morgan heard Lillian laugh. She shook her head at the assembled dogs, all of whom looked disappointed they had not been allowed to roll in the caked muck.

A hot shower rinsed her last appointment off her skin. Emilia would arrive in an hour, assuming she still wanted to come, and the prospect was doing not entirely unpleasant things to her stomach. She wanted to get to know her. *Know* her, or know *her*? asked an inner voice. Too many years of talking to Stevie had done permanent damage to her psyche.

The evening also had the potential to turn into a disaster. She did not need her friends playing matchmaker, however well-intentioned. She would date when she was ready. The fact that Emilia was exactly her type made their insinuations all the more aggravating, and she prayed Stevie would behave. Angie and Lillian, she knew, would at least wait until Emilia left before pouncing.

The hot water gave out with its customary lack of warning. Two showers plus the laundry were more than it enjoyed handling at one time. Stevie yelped from the bathroom at the other end of the house.

Morgan dressed in her favorite pair of jeans and a soft button-down that would keep off the chill of the coming evening, but was still cool enough to withstand the heat of the kitchen. The fact that, as Lillian often pointed out, this particular shirt matched her eyes did not enter her consideration. Or so she told herself.

"Where's Ange?" she asked Lillian and Stevie when she returned downstairs to help set up.

"Dealing with the kennel," said Stevie. "And pretending she's pissed we're throwing her a party."

"Did you check the propane tanks on the grill?" Lillian asked as she surveyed the kitchen.

"Yeah," said Morgan. "And there's a spare just in case. House looks good."

Lillian wiped her hand across her forehead. "Thanks. You got it from here? I'm going to go get cleaned up."

"We can handle it," Stevie assured her. "Sorry about the hot water." Stevie had blow-dried her hair, and it fell in soft waves around her shoulders. The effect still surprised Morgan, even after years of witnessing this transformation. Tomboi Stevie still reigned as far as her mannerisms were concerned, but the skin-tight jeans and loose white tank top left little to the imagination, and the barest suggestion of mascara graced her lashes.

"Hot date?" asked Morgan.

"Shut up." Stevie flung a pretzel at her from one of the snack bowls Lillian had arranged. "Out of clothes. I need to do laundry."

"Uh huh."

"Speaking of hot dates—"

"If you say 'speaking of' one more time I am going to slice out your tongue with a dirty scalpel."

"Brutal. Okay, fine. What time did you tell our new friend to come over?"

"Same time as everyone else."

"So we'll find out if she's the kind of person who arrives fashionably late, on time, or early. Clever."

"It doesn't matter when she gets here."

"As long as she comes?" Stevie smirked at her own joke. "Let's get the beer in the fridge, and then Lil wants us to get a fire going in the yard."

The farm property consisted of seven acres. The barn and the house stood on one, and an old apple orchard took up another. The rest had reverted to meadow and woods. A fence high enough to keep the dogs in closed off a manageable expanse around the back of the house, and a brick patio with a fire pit abutted the back door. Living with her friends and coworkers had its rough spots, but she loved their little piece of heaven.

Angie waited for them in the kitchen with an open beer.

"Hey, birthday girl." Morgan hugged Angie, who made a face.

"Tell the birthday girl to go shower," said Lillian, emerging into the kitchen with a glare for Morgan and Stevie. "Not that there is any hot water left."

"I'm clean." Angie gestured at her clothes. Dog hair coated every inch of them.

"Go. I want a nice photo of you."

"You," said Angie as she beat a retreat, "are worse than my mother."

"That's because your mother has to love you. I don't," said Lillian.

"Beer?" Morgan handed one to Lillian without waiting for a response.

"Thank you." Lillian straddled a bar stool and clasped her hands around the bottle. Her damp hair clung to her neck. "What a shit week."

"Work?" said Stevie.

"Yeah. And Brian."

"What did Boring Brian do?" Stevie pulled a stack of paper plates down from a cupboard as she spoke.

"He's not coming for the summer anymore. School stuff."

"Who takes classes during the summer?"

"No, he's ABD, but—"

"All But Dead?" Stevie never missed an opportunity to remind Lillian she found her boyfriend dull.

71

"All but dissertation, dumbass. Apparently he needs to do more fieldwork for said dissertation, so there go the plans we've been talking about *all year.*"

Morgan bit back a snarky comment. She didn't mind Brian. He was nice, and even though she didn't fully understand the obscure branch of geology that took up so much of his time, she did understand the single-mindedness that graduate work required. She did not, however, like seeing Lillian upset.

"Can't he do the research here?" she asked.

"Apparently not. He's going back to Brazil."

Morgan heard the repressed pain in her voice. "I'm sorry, Lil."

"It's fine. The house is full anyway."

"This is why I keep telling you to find a man muffin here," said Stevie.

"A man muffin?"

"Yeah. Big and muscly on top, maybe sprinkled with sugar, and the bottom is fun to unwrap."

"Thank you for that image," said Lillian.

"Is he at least coming to stay for a few days?" asked Morgan.

"Maybe."

The defeat in Lillian's slumped shoulders reminded Morgan of Kate. Guilt and heartache soured her mouth. "Are you guys okay?"

"No? Yes? I don't know. Career first, right?"

That had been their motto in vet school when it came to relationships. Morgan hoped it would work out better for Lillian than it had for her.

"At least you have Circe. She'll be with you forever."

"Thanks, Stevie. Everlasting love with my tortoise."

Stevie scooted onto the counter. "Maybe this house is cursed. Morgan's single, I'm single, you might as well be single, and Angie is at least getting laid, but she doesn't date."

"The ghost of spinsters past." Lillian perked up and looked at Morgan. "Wait, isn't your new friend coming over?"

"She said she was."

"The one you rescued?"

72

"Yeah, maybe don't mention that, though."

"Why not?"

"She's not into damsels in distress," said Stevie.

"Morgan? Not into damsels?"

"No, I mean Emilia didn't appreciate the rescue." Stevie gave Morgan a sidelong glance. "Which is a first for you, isn't it?"

"Shut up. I save lives every day."

"You also stick your hands up assholes. Oh my god. Asses' assholes. Get it?"

"That's a new low for you," said Angie. Her wet hair was wrapped in a towel and piled on her head, and another towel did its admirable best to cover the rest of her body.

"Nice outfit," said Stevie.

"My clothes are in the dryer."

"You do realize people will be here any minute?" said Lillian.

Angie smiled sweetly. "Yes. I thought I would wear my birthday suit . . ." She let her towel slip a few inches. Stevie's cheeks pinked, and Lillian and Morgan met each other's eyes.

"Angie," said Morgan, "as much as we all appreciate the female form, I can't let you near the fire pit naked, and I definitely saw mosquitoes. So, unless you want your ass bitten, clothes might be a good idea."

"She might be into the ass biting," Lillian said under her breath.

Angie and the armful of dry clothing vanished.

"Beers for queers?" called a voice from the front hall.

"Stormy!" Stevie pushed herself off the counter as Stormy arrived bearing a growler of Angie's favorite beer and a kiss on the cheek for the three of them.

Stormy filled them in on the latest drama from the bar, which consisted mostly of overheard conversations about lobster fishing rivalries. Not much happened in their sleepy harbor town. She broke off to squeal over Angie a few minutes later.

Like Lillian's, Angie's hair was still wet, and she'd looped it into a loose, heavy braid that tumbled over one shoulder. She wore a simple three-quarter sleeve dress that hugged her curves, made of

73

a material that looked so soft Morgan felt an immediate desire to stroke it. She refrained. Acknowledging clothing was dangerous: it often sparked long conversations about fashion and thrifting, topics Angie, Stormy, and Lillian could debate at length.

Danielle Watson and her wife showed up loaded down with a cheese dip that smelled heavenly, followed by a cluster of veterinary technicians and assistants. Morgan checked her watch: 6:05. Still no sign of Emilia, but there was plenty of time. She exchanged a few jokes with her friends and then went to prepare the steaks.

Emilia pulled into the driveway of 16 Bay Road and slid into a spot on the grass next to a Jeep with a zombie stick figure family, complete with an absurd number of pets, stuck to the back window. The white farmhouse gleamed in the evening light. She could see people through the porch window, and wood smoke flavored the air. She wished her heart would relocate from her throat to her chest, where it belonged.

She killed the engine and got out of the car. Dogs barked somewhere nearby, an echoing, contained sound that she remembered from working in shelters. So many unwanted animals. So many wasted lives. *You're done,* she told herself. *You don't have to do that anymore. You don't have to care.* Her therapist had termed part of her condition compassion fatigue. It was common among health care professionals, and an unavoidable result of the sheer volume of cases seen in a day. The formula was simple: too many pleading eyes, plus limited resources, equaled a psychological distancing that ultimately made it impossible to connect with anything at all. This, in turn, often led to crippling depression and other coping mechanisms, like drugs and alcohol. She'd known what she was getting into when she'd decided to go into shelter medicine. Like so many others, she'd thought she could handle it. She'd believed in the necessity of her work.

Now here she was, afraid to enter a house full of her peers, shattered by the sound of a bark. Her hand fumbled for the car door. *Leave*, her mind urged. She could text Morgan with an excuse. Flat tire. Sudden illness.

Laughter floated toward her as a door opened and shut somewhere in the house. If she left, she'd be running. Running was different from taking space and time to heal, and she knew herself well enough to understand that once she started running again, she'd have a hard time stopping. *I can always leave early if it gets to be too much.* She checked her mascara in the car's mirror, smoothed the front of her shirt, and forced her legs to march across the drive, up the steps to the porch, and to the green front door.

A slender woman answered with a laugh still on her lips. Thick black hair fell to her shoulders, and her loose shirt and tight dark jeans softened her muscular build.

"Hi. Um, Morgan invited me," Emilia said, feeling lost as the warmth from the house spilled over her. The woman offered her an equally warm smile.

"Emilia, right? Lillian." Lillian stuck out her hand and shook Emilia's firmly, ushering her inside. Emilia caught a hint of perfume, something floral and rich that reminded her of a summer garden. "Hope you don't mind dogs. We've locked them outside for now, but they'll track you down the minute they realize there's a new person in the house who might not be immune to their charms."

"I do like dogs." She followed Lillian into the hallway and noted a jumble of shoes, jackets, hanging dog leashes, and what looked like a tangled collection of sheep halters. She raised the tray of cookies. "Where should I put these?"

"Cookies? Here, I'll take them so you don't get mobbed. Come on in. Morgan's out back with the grill."

Lillian led her down the front hall—decorated with photos, not of the human inhabitants, but of a collection of dogs, cats, horses, and even a tortoise—and into a crowded farmhouse kitchen. Exposed beams spanned the ceiling, and granite countertops were partially visible amid the group of people gathered around the island. A few glanced up as she entered. Stevie extricated herself

75

from the small crowd and sauntered over with a grin. Emilia did her best to hide her surprise at how well Stevie cleaned up.

"Glad to see you're still with us. Last time I saw you, you looked like you'd been in a war zone," said Stevie.

Emilia looked down at her black jeans, double-checking that no lingering traces of sawdust had made their way onto her clean clothes. "It was a close call, but I was promised a steak. Had to hold out for that."

"I had faith in you. Ange," Stevie called over her shoulder. A pretty brunette in a black dress that looked enviably comfortable, as well as stunning, perked up at her name and joined them.

"Happy birthday," Emilia said. "And thanks for having me. I hope I didn't crash your party."

"My party?" Angie bumped Stevie with her hip. "More like Stevie's party. It's really nice to meet you."

"This is a beautiful house." She wished she didn't sound so stilted. The ease with which these people interacted was foreign to her.

"Let me introduce you; then I'll give you a tour."

"I'd love that. Should I let Morgan know I'm here?" Emilia scanned the room, remembered that Stevie had said Morgan was grilling, and tried to catch a glimpse of the grill through the glass door on the far side of the kitchen.

Angie waved away the suggestion and took Emilia's arm, towing her gently into the light of the kitchen overhead lamps.

"Emilia!" Stormy looked up from her conversation with an older couple and waved.

"Everyone, this is Emilia," Angie said to the group.

"Hi." Emilia wished she had brought Nell after all for emotional support.

"Danielle Watson," said one of the older women. Her short hair and firm grip reminded Emilia of every large animal veterinarian over the age of fifty she had ever met. Something about her confident stance, weathered face, and no-bullshit aura just radiated "I've wrestled cows bigger than you into submission."

"My wife, Patricia," Danielle continued.

"Call me Patty." Patty gave Emilia a motherly smile that balanced her partner's stoicism.

The entire queer population of Seal Cove must be in this room right now, Emilia thought as she shook more hands.

"Can I get you something to drink? We have beer and wine, and liquor somewhere, and soda and tea," said Lillian.

"Beer sounds wonderful."

"Take your pick. The rest is out back," said Stevie as she opened the fridge. "But if you go out there, Morgan will steal you."

Emilia's cheeks warmed at the words, but she laughed it off and chose a beer at random.

"Ready for a tour?" asked Angie.

The first floor of the sprawling house opened from the kitchen into a large living room. The two rooms shared a partial wall, which was occupied by a large stone fireplace.

"Wow."

"Right?" said Angie. "We don't leave these two rooms in the winter if we can help it. Morgan gets free firewood from one of her clients."

Comfortable couches and armchairs filled the rest of the living room. Piles of veterinary magazines and journals littered the coffee table, and while someone had clearly vacuumed and dusted recently, a fine layer of dog hair had already reclaimed lost territory. Bookcases lined the walls. More veterinary texts filled the shelves, along with an eclectic assortment of novels. Lillian caught her scanning the titles.

"The detective novels are mine," she said.

"Along with the period romances, not that she'll admit to it," said Stevie.

"And these are Stevie and Angie's," Lillian said in a tone that suggested she did not share their appreciation for speculative fiction. Tattered science fiction and fantasy paperbacks abutted the detective series.

"This is neutral territory." Angie pointed to a collection of Harry Potter and Tamora Pierce books.

Past the living room and down another hallway lined with

animal photographs they came to a smaller room that would have been suitable for an office had it not been occupied by a large TV screen, beanbags, and a plush carpet. Several gaming consoles kept the TV company.

"Angie and Stevie's lair," said Lillian.

"Are you into gaming?" Hope shone from Stevie's face.

"Sorry. Last thing I played was a Nintendo, before they were retro."

"They have one," said Lillian. "Consider yourself warned."

"And down here is Lil's lair." Stevie led them through a door with steamy glass panes.

Emilia froze on the step, feeling like her eyes might fall out of her head. "This is incredible." Greenery exploded at her feet, and it took her a moment to find the glass walls of the greenhouse through the jungle. Tropical plants shared space with citrus trees and vegetables, and the sound of trickling water came from a fountain in the center, which poured into a pond. She walked down the brick path toward it, entranced.

Something rustled through a collection of potted ferns.

"Don't worry. It's just a velociraptor," said Stevie, then added an *Ow,* as someone slapped her.

Lillian appeared at Emilia's elbow and crouched down as a tortoise shoved its way past the nearest pot. "This is Circe."

Lillian stroked the shell affectionately, and the tortoise bumped against her hand in a surprisingly dog-like gesture. "Someone dumped her at the clinic, and now she guards my greenhouse."

"And eats strawberries. It's adorable," said Angie.

"Any idea how old she is?" Emilia asked. The tortoise's carapace was at least a foot in diameter, maybe more.

"Not really. She's mature, and my guess is that someone's relative died and they didn't know what to do with her."

"And didn't care enough to learn," said Angie.

"Honestly, I'm glad. So many people think they want exotic pets without understanding the care and responsibility that goes into them."

"Lillian is an exotics vet," Stevie said.

Lillian stroked Circe once more, then stood. "Exotics and small animals. Morgan and I went to vet school together at Cornell. Do you garden?"

"I just had house plants back in Boston. My dad did, though. He's got a big plot at the house I might do something with."

"Well, if you need any seedlings, let me know. I always have extra." Lillian pointed toward a table with trays of young plants.

"That would be incredible, actually."

"Pick some out before you leave tonight, or come by another time."

"They're talking about plants," Angie said to Stevie. "What do we do?"

Lillian gave them the middle finger with a graceful motion that belied the crude gesture, then looked past them out the window. "Oh good. She's got the grill going."

Emilia followed Lillian's gaze out through the glass walls. The greenhouse bordered the backyard, forming an L between the house and the fence, and she saw Morgan shut the lid of a large grill and wave. She raised her own hand in recognition and felt her heart leap for its new home in her throat again.

"She's seen you," Stevie said with a pout. "Now we have to give you back."

Morgan met Emilia's eyes with a grin that lit up the room when Emilia reentered the kitchen. "You made it."

"After burning some cookies. Dad's oven is a little off." Emilia eyed the plate. Quite a few of the cookies were already missing.

"That's why I stick to cooking over open flame. They give you the tour?"

"The downstairs," said Lillian.

"Not much to see upstairs anyway," said Stevie. "Just beds and Lil's hamster wheel."

"It's called a treadmill."

"You're a runner, too?" Emilia asked her.

"Oh no," said Angie.

"It's happening," said Stevie.

79

In unison, they broke out in an off-key rendition of "Can You Feel the Love Tonight" from *The Lion King*.

"Let me know if you need a jogging partner," Lillian said as she clapped her hands over her friends' mouths. "Since I clearly don't live with any."

"I could use some motivation," said Emilia.

Lillian released her grip on Stevie and Angie. "Sorry, Morgan. I'm stealing your new friend."

"Not if I weigh her down with red meat first."

"But then I'd have to jog it off," Emilia said.

"But would you?" said Angie.

"I keep hearing about all these dogs, but I don't see any," Emilia said to shift the subject away from her body.

"They're out back, supervising the grill. Want to meet them?" asked Morgan.

Emilia nodded, and Morgan walked to the back door. The others remained inside.

"Brace yourself."

Kraken skidded to a halt on the patio flagstones first, his tail wagging. A brindle pit bull bulldozed into him seconds later and presented his butt for her to scratch, only to be upstaged by the hopping arrival of a three-legged monster of a mutt with a black muzzle, brown body, and absurdly fluffy white tail. She did her best to greet the three of them at once with two hands.

An insistent scratching at her pant leg caused her to glance down. Another tripod dog stared up at her out of an Italian greyhound's slightly neurotic eyes. She presented her hand to the tiny black button nose.

"You can pick her up if you want," said Morgan.

Emilia scooped the slender dog onto her lap. "Introduce me?"

"That little demon is Hermione, and before you ask, she does have a Hogwarts sweater. She and the other tripod are Lil's."

"Two tripods?"

"We're trying to find her a third so she has a complete set, but yes. Muffin was a rescue, and Hermione had a bad fracture. Owners couldn't pay for it."

"Did someone step on you?" Emilia asked the dog.

"Marvin—that's the pittie—is Stevie's. I believe she named him after a robot from some book. In case you didn't notice, we're all exceptionally cool."

"Well, they're cool," said Emilia. "But you don't seem to have any visible nerdoms, so I'm going to have to reserve judgment."

"Let me know what you decide."

Morgan left Emilia in her sea of dogs and walked over to the grill, giving Emilia a chance to glimpse her ass in jeans. The cool evening air warmed several degrees. Emilia ripped her eyes away and examined the rest of her surroundings.

The back patio had an eclectic collection of lawn furniture gathered around a brick fire pit. She moved to stand beside it, which the little dog seemed to appreciate, as she stopped shivering.

"I have a big one of you," she told the dog as she watched Morgan. The blue of her shirt emphasized the dark blue-gray of her irises, which seemed even darker in the gathering dusk.

I'd fall into that *ocean.*

"All right." Morgan gave the grill a tap with her tongs and nodded her approval of the temperature.

"Need a hand?" Emilia asked.

"I got it, but you can tell me how you like your steak."

Served by you. She really had to turn off her internal commentary.

"Medium rare is fine, or however it turns out. I'm not picky when it comes to food cooked by someone who isn't me."

"Not a fan of cooking?"

Emilia hesitated before answering. She had liked cooking, once. Hannah hadn't cooked at all, and her schedule had been even crazier than Emilia's, so Emilia'd done most of the work involved in feeding them. Cooking for herself, however, felt like a chore. It also reminded her of her father.

"I used to." She couldn't lie to those eyes.

Morgan had to have noticed the past tense, but she didn't push it. Emilia put that as one more mark in her favor. At this rate, the boating safety comment would soon be buried.

"Your cookies were good."

"You must like them crunchy."

"I do, actually. I have to grab the steaks. Do you need another beer?"

"What about this precious angel?" Emilia tucked Hermione against her chest.

"Clearly she's made herself at home. Keep her." Morgan's eyes trailed slowly down Emilia's chest, then jerked away as if she'd just realized where she was looking. Emilia glanced down to discover that Hermione had tucked her nose into her shirt, nestling into—and revealing—her cleavage.

"Yes, she has," she said, suddenly happier than she could remember being in months. Maybe it was the beer, or the way the little dog sighed in contentment, or maybe it was the intoxicating thrill of power that Morgan's poorly disguised attraction inspired, but she didn't care. "And I do need another drink."

Chapter Seven

Morgan hoped her friends would attribute the flush in her cheeks to the heat of the grill, and not because she'd done anything so idiotic as getting caught staring at Emilia's chest. *Stop acting like a teenage boy. You know better.* That didn't erase what she'd seen.

"Aww," chorused the largely female audience when Emilia and Hermione entered the kitchen. Stevie smirked as she met Morgan's eye, no doubt correctly gauging Morgan's reaction. Emilia had managed to tug the loose, silvery material of her shirt back up, but it was still provocative.

"Someone give that dog a steak," Stevie said when she leaned past Morgan to grab another drink from the fridge.

"I will kill you."

"Mhmm."

"Hey." Lillian raised her voice over the buzz of conversation. "I made Morgan build a fire, so let's move this outside."

"Plus all the fridge beer is gone," said Stevie.

That wasn't entirely true. Morgan grabbed the last one and tossed it to Emilia, who caught it one-handed.

"Opener?"

"Toss it back." Morgan looped her belt buckle around the top and popped it off.

"Show off." Stormy patted her on the back. "I could use you at the bar if you're going to pull stunts like that."

"She'd make good money in tips," said Emilia. Her face was smooth and unruffled—unlike her eyes. They met Morgan's for only a second, but the look in them hit her dead center. She handed Emilia the beer wordlessly as Stormy laughed.

Steaks. She grabbed the first platter and returned to the grill.

Morgan took the few moments of solitude to ground herself. *This shouldn't be this hard.* She barely knew Emilia. Yes, she was attractive. Her eyes followed the curve of Emilia's waist as she took a seat by Lillian and the Watsons. Scratch attractive. Emilia was *hot.* Breathtakingly, inescapably, hot. She'd worn just enough makeup tonight to highlight her long lashes and the red of her lips, as if Morgan hadn't already noticed those qualities. As if she hadn't thought about how Emilia's long hair would feel running through her fingers, or how the smooth skin—

"Shit." She jumped as she burned her hand on the grill. Pain seared, and the first layer of epidermis turned a perfect medium-rare.

"Morgan?" Lillian was at her side in an instant, grabbing Morgan's hand to inspect the damage. "Inside. Now."

She towed Morgan behind her and shut the door, then turned the cold water on in the sink. At least the calluses on her palms had spared her from serious damage. She tried unsuccessfully to wriggle out of Lillian's grip.

"It's just a burn."

"Your hands are your livelihood, moron. Shut up and do as I say."

The cold water soothed the worst of the sting. She had placed her palm on the grate, and red lines rose across it where her skin had come in direct contact with the scorching metal.

"What were you thinking?"

"I wasn't, clearly."

"I've got some burn cream upstairs. You're normally the one I can trust not to hurt yourself, you know."

"Sorry, Mrs. Lee."

"Do not call me that, or you will wish a burn was your biggest problem. I am not either of my mothers."

Morgan raised her unburnt hand in surrender.

"I like Emilia, by the way," Lillian continued. If she'd made the logical leap between Morgan's uncharacteristic distractedness and Emilia's presence, she was merciful enough not to point it out.

"It's been nice having a friend at the dock."

"You don't need a new friend."

Morgan focused on the feel of cold water on her burnt skin. "But she does."

"Not if the way she looks at you means anything."

"Lil, please. She's got a lot going on right now, and I don't think she's going to stick around for long. I can't do that."

Lillian slumped. "I know you can't. I'll tell Stevie to lay off you. It's just nice seeing you happier."

"Trust me," Morgan said, grimacing as she examined her hand. "I know. That's why I know I can't do it."

Happiness lied. It hid things, painting the world with a brightness that concealed the cracks in the foundation. In *her* foundation.

"Not even a fling? Maybe something with an expiration date would be good for you."

"Didn't you try that with Monique?"

Lillian winced. "I forgot about that."

"And you haven't dated women since."

"That's a little different. I'm bi. You're the biggest homo I know."

"Just don't push me on this one, okay?" She hated the vulnerability in her voice. Hated the naked need beneath the words.

"Jesus. If you're like this after only knowing her a week or so . . ." Lillian shook her head. "I do like her, though."

"Which is why we'll all be friends until she goes back to Boston."

"And if she doesn't?"

Morgan clamped her mind shut against Lillian's suggestion. "She will."

"Secret conference in here?" Stevie asked.

"No," said Morgan and Lillian together.

"Okay . . . but we want to know what to do about the steaks you abandoned."

"I'll be right out."

"Your hand okay?"

"It's fine."

"Speaking of fine . . ."

"No," Lillian said firmly.

Stevie looked back and forth between Lillian and Morgan. "Are we not rooting for this anymore? Because she's real hot."

"I'm going back to the grill." She pushed past Stevie and left Lillian to explain however she saw fit.

"Are you broken?" Stormy asked from her seat by the fire when Morgan returned to the site of her injury.

"Nope." She held out her wounded hand as proof, not looking up. If she looked up, she'd see Emilia, and she needed another minute after her chat with Lillian before she was ready for that. Instead, she listened to the conversation.

"So," said Danielle. "What do you do, Emilia?"

Morgan tensed. This was the moment she'd been dreading.

"Right now, I'm taking some time to focus on my dad's estate."

"I'm sorry to hear that he passed. I lost my parents a few years ago. It's never easy, and I can only imagine it is harder when it's unexpected."

"Thank you."

"What do you do professionally?"

Damn Danielle and her need for facts.

"Actually," Emilia said with a laugh that Morgan could tell was forced, "I'm a vet."

Morgan wasn't the only one who'd heard. Lillian, who had returned with a tube of something Morgan suspected was burn cream, exchanged glances with their other friends. Stormy looked straight at Morgan with her eyebrows raised.

"Really?" Danielle leaned forward, and Morgan silently begged her not to offer Emilia a job on the spot.

"I was in shelter medicine."

Now it was Lillian's eyes that bored into Morgan's. She ignored them. Emilia had managed to keep a smile on her lips, but Morgan noted how white her knuckles were around her drink.

"Ah," said Danielle, her voice softening. "That's hard work."

Emilia nodded but did not say anything else.

"Well, try to enjoy Maine while you're here, if you can. Did I hear you saying you sail?"

"Badly, but yes." Morgan saw some of the tension leak out of Emilia's shoulders as Danielle steered the conversation elsewhere.

Shelter medicine. Morgan plunged a meat thermometer into a steak as the pieces assembled. Shelter medicine was like one of the carnivorous plants Lillian kept in the greenhouse: it tended to attract the sort of people who didn't survive long, some quite literally. The suicide rate in veterinary medicine was higher than almost any other profession. Shelter medicine was even worse. Underfunded government clinics and struggling private rescues did their best to accommodate thousands of unwanted animals, which meant problems like severe skin allergies or even an ear infection could end in euthanasia. Shelter medicine required more than professional detachment. It required incredible mental discipline, and few people could euthanize healthy animals day after day without breaking. No wonder Emilia didn't want to talk about it.

She served up the first steaks, along with the mushrooms she'd cooked carefully to one side of the grill, then moved on to the next batch and the vegetable kebabs Lillian had prepared as a side.

"Those look delicious," Emilia said from behind her. Morgan caught the undefinable scent of her perfume.

"You didn't get some this round?" She turned in time to catch Emilia tucking a lock of hair behind her ear.

"I gave mine to Stevie."

Morgan glared at Stevie, who didn't notice. She'd chosen a particularly fine slice for Emilia. "I'll make sure some gets to you this time."

"I'm fine."

"You're always fine," Morgan said, keeping her voice light. "I see you lost your hitchhiker."

"She left me to go beg."

"Her, 'I only have one front paw, look at how sad I am' routine is pretty effective. Nell didn't want to come?"

"She sometimes gets overwhelmed in crowds, and then I stress over her, and . . ." Emilia trailed off and made a looping gesture with her hand.

"Where'd you get her?"

"Greyhound rescue I worked with. She had a really bad case of anaplasma, and the rescue couldn't afford to treat it. I couldn't bring myself to put her down." She looked away. "I've put down hundreds of animals. But not Nell."

"Some dogs are just like that. They reach up inside you—" she brandished the tongs she was using to rotate the kebabs—"and steal your heart."

"They really do." Emilia's voice was soft and sad, and Morgan barely refrained from wrapping her arms around her.

"A client gave me Kraken. Her bitch had a huge litter. I was at the farm, and the little fucker clamped onto my boot with his teeth and wouldn't let go. Followed me all over the place."

"Does he still bite shoes?"

"Steals them. Sometimes he buries them in Lil's garden, which is actually convenient, because it means we get them back."

"Nell's into dirty underwear."

Morgan shook her head. "Classy girl. Dogs, man. What do you think cat people talk about?"

"Mr. Twinkly knocked my drink off the counter again!" Emilia said in a high, nasal voice.

Morgan burst into laughter.

"What?" Emilia said in the same voice.

"I did not expect that."

"You live with Stevie. Shouldn't you expect anything?"

"Yeah, but Stevie's a freak. You're . . ." She trailed off.

"You don't think I'm a freak?" Emilia asked in her normal voice. Well, not quite normal. It was the same voice she'd used to tease Morgan about how she'd get tips working at the bar. Her pulse leapt.

"I'm still compiling evidence."

"Thank you for inviting me, by the way. I like your friends a lot."

"Don't be too nice to them, or they'll end up being your friends, too." She shoved her hands in her back pockets to avoid a second burn.

"I'd like that."

"Really?"

"Really."

"Listen." Morgan looked around to make sure nobody was about to demand more food. "Whatever's going on with you and the field, you don't have to talk about it. I mean, you can if you want to, but don't feel that you owe any of us an explanation."

Emilia's fingers touched Morgan's arm. The grill hid the gesture from the rest of the party, and Morgan reflected that she might as well have touched the hot metal again as Emilia's fingertips burned against her skin.

Emilia didn't say anything. She gazed at Morgan, her eyes the golden brown of amber honey in the firelight, and Morgan read the silent *thank you* in their depths.

The third beer was a mistake. Emilia realized it halfway through when the buzz hit her hard. She needed to stop if she wanted to drive home tonight, and she needed to drive home tonight because Nell was there. She dragged her concentration back to the conversation around her. Stormy and two people she assumed worked at the clinic were deep in discussion about a TV series she didn't watch. Danielle and her wife chatted with each other across the fire, and Angie, Stevie, and Lillian were looking at Emilia expectantly. She gnawed her lip. What had they just said?

"I'm sorry. I was just thinking about Nell. What did I miss?"

"Do you like food?" asked Stevie.

"Like, any food?"

"Maybe we should spare her," said Angie. "She's innocent."

Stevie let out a solemn sigh. "No. The truth will set her free."

"I live with total losers," Lillian said. "Ignore them. Sometimes I cook for these hellions."

"The things that woman can do to an eggplant should be illegal," Stevie agreed.

"Like, eggplant parmesan?"

"You poor thing," said Angie. "There is so much more you can do with an eggplant. You need to come over."

"Yes, you should. I don't know when we're doing it next, but I'll let you know. Angie makes amazing pierogies, too," said Lillian.

"Polish grandmother," said Angie.

"Well, I'm very Italian, in case you couldn't tell. We do olives."

"I'm a mutt," said Stevie. "No foodie heritage. But Morgan's family is so Irish they shit leprechauns and potatoes."

"Ouch." Morgan, who had finally finished feeding the guests, stood over them with a plate of food. "Got room for one more?"

Lillian glanced at Emilia, who currently shared a wooden bench with Stevie's dog. "If you move a dog, yeah."

"Marvin, off," said Stevie.

Marvin didn't move. Lillian's larger dog, however, loped over from the Watsons' side of the fire to pant at her feet.

"Does that happen a lot?" asked Emilia.

"Nearly every time."

"Marvin," Morgan said in an excited voice. "Is that a squirrel?" The bench rocked as Marvin sprang to life. Morgan dove for the vacant seat.

"Cruel, but effective," said Emilia.

"He's never caught a squirrel in his life." Morgan sat, leaving only a few inches of space between them, and cut into her steak. The perfectly done meat parted like butter beneath her knife. Emilia tried not to watch. Lusting after a person was one thing; lusting after their steak was another.

Morgan noticed her staring.

Emilia didn't bother to hide her indiscretion. "I'm sorry. That was the best steak I've ever eaten."

"Do you want mine?"

"Yes, but I refuse to take it. Now eat faster so I don't start drooling."

Morgan speared a bite of steak and waved it in the air. "You sure?"

"No." Emilia reached out and took the fork. Her fingers brushed Morgan's. *I really should have stopped at two drinks*, she thought as she bit into the steak with Morgan's hand still on the fork. It occurred to her, too late, what this must look like to everyone around her. Especially Morgan.

Shit, shit, shit.

Nobody spoke. She thought she saw Lillian and Stevie exchange a look, but that could have just been paranoia.

Morgan cleared her throat. "So, Ange, how does it feel to be thirty?"

"This is your big three-o?" Emilia hoped she didn't sound as eager to move past the previous seconds as she felt.

"I officially no longer have to give a shit about what other people think." Angie raised her beer.

"You should be proud," said Lillian. "You own your own house, and you run your own business. That's more than the rest of us can say."

Angie noticed the frown on Emilia's face and laughed. "Morgan didn't tell you?"

"Tell me what?"

"Angie has one of those the-truth-is-stranger-than-fiction stories. Are you familiar with Flannel Works?" asked Morgan.

"The world's softest and most durable work shirt?" Emilia quoted the New England drawl of the popular advertisement. Her father had a drawer full of them, and she herself had at least two.

"Apparently Angie's great-aunt bought up a bunch of their stock when it first started. She knew the founder or something."

"Which basically proves my theory that she was a secret lesbian," said Angie. "She died two years ago, and since she didn't have any kids, she left it to my mom, me, and my brother. No one had any idea she was loaded. She lived in a cabin up past Gardiner with a bunch of cats—I kid you not—and hardly spoke to the rest of the family."

"Living the dream," said Stevie.

"I bought this house because I've always liked it, and because it had a barn for the doggy day care—"

"And now you have nothing else to live for."

"Shut up, Stevie."

"Wait. Your secret lesbian great-aunt, who got rich from the *flannel shirt industry*, left you enough money to buy a house that you have gone on to populate with more queers?" Emilia asked. Amusement overrode her earlier embarrassment.

"Yep."

"That's . . ."

"There are no words," said Stevie.

"Happy fucking birthday works." Stormy wrapped her arms around Angie's head and planted a kiss on top of it. "You ready for cake?"

"Always. Do you need help?"

"With your own cake? Absolutely not. Stevie and I will get it. Stevie, come," said Stormy.

"I am not a dog." Stevie rose anyway, the white of her shirt vibrant in the twilight. Only a soft glow purpled the horizon.

Emilia leaned back on the bench and tucked her legs up underneath her. Morgan finished her meal, unmolested by any further attempts on her food, and then laid her arm on the wicker back of the bench. It didn't touch Emilia, but she was acutely aware of it anyway.

Angie turned her eyes onto Emilia. "Someone said you have a sailboat?"

"It was my dad's."

"Will you take us out sometime?"

Emilia thought Angie looked smaller, somehow, without Stevie beside her, as if she'd shrunk in on herself.

"I haven't sailed in years and it's a pretty small boat, but sure."

"You should take someone with you the first few times you

go out." Morgan's voice was serious, and Emilia tensed, remembering the boating safety comment. Even if she knew Morgan well enough by now to guess she hadn't meant the comment as an insult, the idea of being in the boat with anyone other than her father stiffened her spine.

"I'll . . . I'll think about it."

"Take Morgan. She knows the water," Angie suggested.

"I don't know much about sailboats," said Morgan.

"But you know the currents."

"Emilia might have other friends," Lillian said to Angie. "Or family in the area."

Stormy began singing "happy birthday" at that moment, sparing Emilia the need to think up an excuse. She stood with the rest of the group to enter the house.

A hand on her elbow stopped her.

"Hey." Morgan searched her eyes. "I know I'm being an ass about this, but I'm serious. The currents are dangerous. The river's full of ledges, and the harbor isn't much better."

"I'm aware."

"Are you?"

"Yes, actually." Anger heated her cheeks. "And while I appreciate your concern, I am quite capable of taking care of myself." So many people had questioned her decisions of late—herself included—and she couldn't handle Morgan adding to the list. She needed to believe she knew what she was doing.

"I get that. But you said yourself that you haven't been out in that boat in, how many years?"

"If I want a lecture, I'll take that boating safety course."

"My engine died on me once. I hadn't told anyone where I was going, and I'd left my radio in my locker. It was one of the scariest moments of my life. If a lobsterman hadn't seen me drifting I could have been seriously fucked."

"I have sails and an engine. If one dies, I'll use the other."

Morgan raked a hand through her short hair. "Just tell someone when you go out, okay? I don't need your dad haunting me."

Emilia sucked in a breath of cool night air and dug her nails into her palms, although whether to keep from striking Morgan or from showing just how much the words had knocked the wind from her, she didn't know.

"Emilia." Morgan started to reach for her, then dropped her hand. "Fuck. I'm so sorry."

She shouldn't have come. She missed the steady presence of her dog and the quiet of her father's porch. "I think I should go."

"Emilia, please."

Stop saying my name. "What, Morgan?"

"I . . ." Morgan glanced around the empty yard, then back to Emilia. "I'm protective of the people I care about. I overstepped. It's your boat, and I'm sure you know what you're doing. Will you stay for cake at least?"

"Will you try and tell me how I should eat it?" Hearing Morgan group her among the people she cared about wasn't enough to overshadow the warning that word, *protective*, raised.

"I won't even judge you for taking a piece with extra frosting." Despite Morgan's words, her tone remained solemn.

"I don't need protection."

Morgan held her hands up in a gesture of surrender.

"But I will let someone know when I take it out under sail for the first time. Which, by the way, I was already planning on doing." Anger crept back into her voice. She'd had women use protectiveness as an excuse before.

"I'm sorry," Morgan said again. "Will you stay?"

Emilia considered her. She'd only known her two weeks. During that time, Morgan had come to her aid, both in the water and when she had needed a tool, invited her into her home, and been kind and respectful if occasionally, as she put it, protective. Her attraction to Morgan aside, she'd felt more herself around Morgan and her friends than she had in months. Was she willing to throw that away because Morgan had expressed worry, especially since Morgan's first impression of her had been seeing her pitch, drunk, into the frigid ocean? She hadn't exactly radiated "competent sailor." Maybe Emilia had overreacted, just like Hannah always said she did.

"I'll stay."

"Still friends?" Morgan asked.

"Still friends."

Emilia didn't remember moving closer to Morgan, but as the tension ebbed from her body, she realized she could see the freckles spanning Morgan's cheeks and nose even in the darkness, and she smelled the notes of wood smoke, clean laundry, and sandalwood that clung to Morgan's clothes and skin.

"We'd better get in there if we want cake," Morgan said without making any move to act on her suggestion.

Months of numbness burned away like morning fog. It would be easy, so easy, to let her body purge some of her cloying grief beneath this woman. The catch in Morgan's breath told her all she needed to know about what Morgan wanted. If she let herself go, if she let herself act on the impulse to lean in and kiss Morgan, if she let Morgan touch her, would it dull the blade of her accumulated losses?

Could anything?

"Morgan," Stevie shouted from the back door.

"Right." Morgan shot Emilia a rueful smile and turned to walk into the warm glow of the kitchen.

Emilia allowed herself one muffled, sobbing exhale, then followed.

Stevie scowled at Morgan as she joined her at the counter. Morgan shrugged an apology. The cake topper dripped hot wax onto the chocolate buttercream frosting Stevie had spent the previous evening perfecting into small rosettes.

"Sorry."

Stevie handed her a slice of cake. "Whatever. You can't sing anyway."

Morgan met Emilia's eyes from the other side of the island counter. Desire lanced through her, sharp and sudden. *Fuck*. It had been a long time since anyone had been able to get her this distracted with a look alone.

Friends. That's what she'd told Emilia, and that's what she'd told Lillian. Tempting as it was to consider the prospect—dangled so infuriatingly by Lillian when she needed it least—of a fling, she knew herself too well to entertain the idea for long. She'd proved as much already this evening. Pushing Emilia about her safety had been way out of line.

Her eyes returned to Emilia of their own accord as Emilia laughed at something Stormy said. It wasn't just the curve of waist and hip and the way her hair moved as she spoke that held Morgan's eyes. There was a deep wariness there, and something else; she'd seen it in her patients. Some animals were well-behaved because they wanted to please. Others knew the shape, smells, and tastes of their limits. Morgan wanted to hold Emilia in her arms as she broke free of hers.

"You're drooling," Stevie said in a low voice. "And since it's not over my masterpiece of confection, I'm offended *and* disgusted."

Morgan ate her cake.

"Picture time," said Lillian a little while later, interrupting Morgan in a conversation with Danielle about the clinic. "Ange, get in the middle. Tall people in the back."

Morgan saw Emilia hesitate. "I can take the photo," she offered, and Morgan guessed she didn't want to intrude.

"Nope. Get in the back. I'll use the timer." Lillian propped her phone on the bar and surveyed the jumble of people around Angie. "Morgan, move closer to Danielle. Emilia, stand by Morgan. Stevie, do not make that face again, and Stormy—you look flawless. You're making the rest of us look bad."

"Paging Dr. Lee, you're needed in pediatrics," Danielle whispered into Morgan's ear.

"Hush or she'll put you in time out."

"Are you sure I should be here?" Emilia asked from Morgan's other side. "I just met Angie. I don't want to ruin her photo."

"Don't worry about it. If she wants, she can always crop out your face, right? Photoshop—"

"Act like you like each other, people," said Lillian.

Danielle slung her arm around Morgan's shoulder. She

debated the wisdom of doing the same thing to Emilia, but before she could come to a decision, Emilia leaned her hip against Morgan's and turned sideways to face the camera. The pose was completely normal and even made sense, given the angle of the camera, but it rendered a comradely shoulder grip awkward. She put her arm around Emilia's waist instead. Emilia shifted her weight and leaned in closer.

She felt too good. Morgan bared her teeth in a smile for the camera as she grew instantly and acutely aware of the warmth of Emilia's skin and the inundating scent of her perfume. This close, she picked up hints of violet and blackberry.

"Smile," said Lillian as she stepped back to join the group. Her phone flashed several times, and she strode back over to it. "Nobody move. Stormy, your eyes are closed in all of these."

"What? No way."

"Way. Okay, let's do this again."

"There's that doctor personality. I was beginning to think she was too chill," Emilia said in her ear.

Morgan's fingers tightened on Emilia's hip as her whisper traced its shivering way down her spine. She saw Emilia's lips curve in a self-satisfied smile out of the corner of her eye, and she suppressed a groan of frustration.

"Didn't they teach you that in vet school?" she said.

Emilia didn't answer, but she placed her left hand on the small of Morgan's back, and the slow drag of her thumb across the fabric of Morgan's shirt felt intentional. She needed a cold shower. Now.

"Much better," said Lillian.

Morgan didn't know if she was furious or relieved at Lillian's dismissal. Danielle dropped her arm as the group began to disperse, and she braved a look in Emilia's direction.

"If Angie crops out my head, who will she put there instead?" Emilia asked.

"Her cat, probably."

"Might be an improvement."

Morgan tried for a laugh and managed a strangled croak.

Every nerve in her body hummed and her muscles tightened, poised to act on a variety of appealing impulses, none of which were appropriate for a crowded kitchen.

"Where is the cat, anyway?" Emilia continued.

"Hiding." Her ability to form complete sentences was fading fast. Words would be next.

"Guess I got lucky this time."

"Mhmm." *And there go all language skills.*

Emilia's fingers brushed her back again. "Where could I grab a glass of water?"

"I'll get you one." *There. Four words in a row.* Morgan pulled away, but she let her hand trail down Emilia's waist as she did so, and Emilia's pupils widened.

Fuck.

She fled to the sink and filled two glasses from the tap. Cold water soothed her dry throat, but she wished she could pour it over her head.

"Excuse me for a sec," she said to Emilia as she handed her the second glass. "I need to go check on the fire."

The night air offered a lackluster alternative to an icy bucket of water, but it helped. She settled into an empty chair and greeted the dogs, who had reclaimed the yard in the absence of humans.

"Hey, buddy," she said to Kraken. He flopped at her feet with a sigh.

The door opened and shut at her back, and she heard the suction break on the seal of the cooler as the footsteps paused.

"Beer?" asked Stevie.

Morgan held out her hand and accepted the drink, grateful Danielle had given her the night off.

"Cake turned out better than I expected," Stevie said, still standing. Morgan looked up at her.

"You did a great job. Did Ange like it?"

"She said she did."

"Why do you say it like that?"

"Like what?" Stevie downed half her beer in one gulp.

"Like you don't believe it. It was fucking delicious."

"So good she's saving a piece for Lana." Stevie finished her drink and plopped into an empty chair, twirling the bottle in her hands.

"I thought she broke up with her."

"Apparently not."

"Is she coming over?"

"Later." Stevie scowled, and they sat in silence for a moment.

"I could put some horse tranq in her slice. Might lose my license, but it would be worth it to see her hit the ground."

"I fucking hate her."

"I know, bud." Morgan didn't want to think about Lana. More specifically, she didn't want to think about the marks she'd see on Angie's body the next morning.

"Why are you hiding out here, anyway?" asked Stevie.

"I was checking the fire."

"It's almost dead."

"I'm letting it die."

"Rather heartless of you. It had so much to live for."

"What time is it, anyway?" she asked.

"A little after nine."

"We should get back in then. Danielle will be heading out any minute."

"And the exodus begins." Stevie extended a hand to Morgan and hauled her up.

Back in the house, the Watsons were indeed saying their good-byes. She overheard Danielle tell Emilia how nice it had been to meet her and warmed at the sight of Emilia's smile. Stormy hung close to Emilia, keeping her company in Morgan's absence. Barring her inability to control her own emotions, tonight had gone well. Perhaps too well, her subconscious added. She ignored it. What she'd said to Lillian was true. Emilia needed friends. Morgan owed Ray that much, and that was what she was going to keep telling herself, regardless of what other less altruistic motivations might be at play.

A knock on the door distracted her. Exchanging a look with

Stevie, she left the gathering, hoping to forestall the worst of any barking a second knock would rouse from the backyard pack.

"Hey," she said to the slouching figure on the doorstep. She couldn't help giving Lana a disapproving once-over. Pin-straight hair beneath a snapback cap. Low-slung jeans. Trendy graphic tee with a reference Morgan didn't get and didn't care to get. None of the parts damned the whole, but Lana's cocky devil-may-care posture made Morgan itch to knock her down a peg. Or maybe it was the coldness in her pale eyes. They were almost the same color as Stevie's, but where Stevie's sparkled with energy, Lana's glittered like glass.

"Ange around?" Lana asked when Morgan didn't move to let her in.

"She's inside."

"Cool."

She had at least three inches on Lana. With the added height of the doorstep, she loomed over her, and the effect forced Lana to tilt her face up to meet Morgan's eyes. Morgan didn't bother hiding her appreciation for the disparity.

"You gonna let me in or what?" Lana's smirk looked forced.

"Sure." She stepped aside. Lana had to squeeze by first Morgan, then the Watsons. Morgan wished the couple goodnight and returned to the kitchen, where Lana already had a possessive arm curled around Angie's waist. Stevie wore a sickened expression.

"I should head out soon, too," said Emilia from where she leaned against the kitchen counter. Morgan couldn't help imagining what it would be like to pin her against the granite. So much for cooling off outside.

"Thanks for coming."

"Thanks for inviting me."

"This crowd can be a lot to digest."

"I really like them. And dinner was amazing. Any time you're on the grill, feel free to call me."

"I wish I had more free time," said Morgan. "That's one hell of an incentive."

"Next time I promise I won't steal any of yours."

"Yeah, well." She cleared her throat as the memory of Emilia's lips closing over her fork rocketed her internal temperature.

"Do I want to know who that is?" Emilia nodded toward Lana.

"No."

"So, not a friend?"

"She's Angie's . . . thing."

"I take it you don't like her?"

Morgan turned and leaned against the counter next to Emilia. The change in perspective brought her closer to Emilia, even if it also brought Lana, who looked bored and moody as she exchanged glares with Stevie, into view.

"We don't."

"But you hide it so well."

"Shut up."

"I know the type. Anyway, I really should get back to Nell."

"You good to drive?"

"Would you send me to driver's ed if you thought I wasn't?"

Morgan rubbed the back of her neck and grimaced at the reminder of her earlier misstep. "No, but I would offer to drive you."

"You've had more to drink than I have."

"True." Morgan grinned and bent her head to whisper in Emilia's ear. "Then again, you haven't seen my drunk ass fall into the harbor."

"You did not just go there."

"Too soon?"

"Just be grateful you're in a roomful of witnesses, Morgan Donovan."

Hearing her full name from Emilia was almost more than she could handle. "I could walk you to your car."

"Are you sure that's safe?"

"Definitely not." Morgan meant the words, even if not in the way she suspected Emilia had intended hers to be taken. Or maybe that was exactly what Emilia had intended, for her mock outrage slipped and her brown eyes flickered to Morgan's lips. *Oh fuck.*

"Let me say good bye to your friends first." Emilia pushed off the counter slowly, her movements deliberate, and bade the remaining members of the party goodnight. Lana's eyes lingered on her longer than Morgan liked.

"I'll text you," Lillian said as Emilia waved good-bye.

"Looks like they're your friends, too," said Morgan.

"I'm reserving judgment until after I run with her. Is she in as good of shape as she looks?"

"Probably better."

Emilia had parked by Stormy's jeep. Morgan wished she'd parked farther away even as she recognized the inherent problems in that thought.

"Offer to drive still stands."

"And how would you get home?" asked Emilia.

"I'd figure it out. Uber. There has to be one around here somewhere."

"Seriously, I'll be okay. I'm sober now. I never finished my third beer, and driving in Maine is nowhere near as dangerous as driving in Boston."

"But Boston has fewer moose. And potholes."

"True. Those are really, really bad."

"Right?" Morgan patted the hood of Emilia's car. "Some of them could swallow this thing. Or were you talking about the potholes?"

"Very funny." Emilia bumped Morgan with her shoulder. "Potholes. Good thing I have a friend with a truck."

It took Morgan a second to realize Emilia meant her. *Friend.* The word woke her out of the buzz she'd allowed to cloud her judgment. She took a step back as she spoke. "Anytime you need it, holler. Say hi to Nell for me."

"I will. See you around, Morgan." Emilia slid into her car and shot Morgan a smile that erased any remaining hope Morgan had harbored of getting much sleep.

Chapter Eight

Anna Maria's text interrupted her afternoon sanding session two days later.

AM: *Call me.*

She put the phone on speaker as she stripped the mask off her face and settled onto the porch.

"You okay?" she asked when Anna Maria picked up.

"I am. You are not."

"I don't follow."

"You got tagged in some photos. Are those your new friends?"

"You know I haven't been on social media. Why, am I drooling or something?"

Anna Maria snorted into the phone. "Basically."

"What?"

"Check your Instagram."

"No." Instagram was full of reminders of the life she'd stepped out of, and she had no desire to go anywhere near the magenta icon on her phone.

"Just do it."

Emilia clicked the icon. Avoiding looking at any posts from friends and former colleagues—though there was a very cute greyhound she double-tapped—she scrolled to her most recent tagged posts. Leave it to Anna Maria to stalk her regularly. Lillian, it appeared, had found her, too, and she'd posted a few photos from Angie's party. Morgan and Emilia stood in the back row in the first, and Morgan's grin made her stomach flip. She inhaled sharply at the second photo. The fact that Angie's eyes were closed and Stevie was making the face Lillian had told her not to pull made her suspect Lillian had posted it as a joke, but the real joke had been on her. Morgan's face was turned slightly toward her—she remembered whispering something—and the look in her eyes could only be described as smoldering. Then there was her own face: lips twisted in a half smile, eyes glancing up at Morgan through her lashes, every visible inch of her radiating *fuck me*.

"I'm assuming you forgot to mention your new friend was totally fuckable because you didn't want to offend my delicate sensibilities."

"She's not—"

"Totally fuckable? Yeah, okay."

"Anna."

"Emilia."

"We're just friends."

"Honey, if any of my friends looked at me that way my husband would kill them."

"Mark? He's harmless."

"Even Mark. Want to tell me what's going on, Em?"

"Nothing is going on."

"Do you want something to be going on? Because she does."

"It's not like that." Emilia stared at the porch roof. "Don't you have kids to boss around now instead of me?"

"I'm living vicariously through you. Trying to get laid with toddlers in the house is impossible."

"You must be so disappointed in me."

"You have no idea. But in all seriousness, are you okay?"

She pinched the bridge of her nose at the gravity in her sister's voice.

"Yeah. And yes, Morgan's hot. But I've got too much going on."

"You don't think maybe a distraction would be a good thing?" Anna Maria asked.

104

"She's a vet."

"So? You don't have to talk about work. You don't need to talk at all."

Emilia wondered if it was possible to *hear* eyebrows waggle suggestively.

"She knew Dad."

"Even better. You don't have to pretend to be fine, which, by the way, you're terrible at."

"Why are you pushing this?"

Silence answered her, then, "You deserve some happiness, Emmy. Life's been a shit to you."

"And what if this just messes me up worse?"

"Then leave and come home."

"I don't do flings."

"Try it. It might help you get over Hannah, and honestly I don't like you being up there all by yourself."

"You sound like Mom."

"Mom told you to have a fling?"

"No. The being alone part."

"We're allowed to worry about you."

"I keep telling you I'm fine."

"Jesus Christ! You were suicidally depressed three months ago. You're not all right." Anna Maria's outburst over the speaker sent Nell slinking to the far end of the porch. Emilia felt just as stunned.

"I'm sorry," Anna Maria said. "Twins. No sleep. I didn't mean to yell at you. I just don't like you being so far away."

"I know. I miss you, too."

"I'm glad you're making friends."

"Thank you."

"Even if Morgan is hot enough to make me consider switching teams."

"Gross."

"Sexuality is fluid. Shouldn't you know that?"

"Unlike you, I don't like thinking about my sister's fluidity."

"Or fluids," said Anna Maria.

"Hanging up now."

"Just try to have fun!"

"Bye."

"Sex is—"

She didn't wait to hear what else Anna Maria had to say about sex. Flings were easy to suggest when you were happily married, she thought, trying not to feel a surge of jealousy. In real life, flings ended in messy feelings. Or at least, Emilia's always had.

Even if she did want Morgan—and her body had been painfully clear on that account—she hardly knew her. If, once she got to know her better, she decided a fling was a safe idea, then maybe she'd consider it. She couldn't afford another blow to her mental health so soon. Self-destructive behavior didn't suit her. It also tended to get other people hurt. For now, she'd focus on the house.

Her phone buzzed again later that afternoon: Lillian.

LL: *Down for a run?*

ER: *I can be there in 10.*

"Want to go for a run, Nell?" she asked her dog as she threw on her workout clothes. Nell's ears perked up, and she nosed Emilia's sneakers enthusiastically.

Morgan's truck was not in the driveway when Emilia pulled in. She swallowed her disappointment and parked, letting Nell out on a leash. Lillian came to the door a minute later without either of her tripods.

"Hey," Lillian said, dressed in a short-sleeved sweatshirt, running pants, and neon sneakers. "You chose a dog with the right number of legs."

"She peters out after a few miles, though. How far do you usually go?"

"Depends on how much time I have. Anywhere between three and six, and longer if I'm training for a race."

Emilia noted the runner's gleam in Lillian's eyes. "I usually call it quits at five," she admitted.

106

"Let's do three and see how we feel?"

Emilia nodded and hoped she wouldn't slow Lillian down.

She stopped worrying after the first mile. They ran well together, and to Emilia's relief Lillian kept the conversation to a minimum, allowing Emilia to take in her surroundings. Lillian led them along a paved road at first and then onto a dirt one. Wildflowers bloomed alongside the gravelly edge. Beyond, the trees opened onto marshland. Tall reeds and salt grasses blew in the late afternoon wind. They startled a heron as the road curved deeper into the marsh. Its wings spread as it took flight. Sunlight sparkled on the water shining through the grass.

"I bet this road floods," she said to Lillian over the crunch of their shoes, because to comment on its beauty seemed somehow inadequate.

"All the time."

She felt, rather than saw, the gradual incline as her calves burned. Grass fell away to one side as granite appeared beneath the mud flats. After another half mile, she could see the river and the distant harbor, along with summer houses peering out of the pines. Nell's tongue lolled and sweat poured down Emilia's face. Lillian ran on. Sunlight shone off her bronzed skin, which was as slick as Emilia's from exertion.

Another mile brought them down again. Emilia recognized the stretch of paved road from her hunt for a hardware store, and the houses and farms they passed rose out of emerald green yards. Hard to imagine winter, she thought, catching the scent of lilacs on the wind.

Lillian slowed to a walk just as Emilia sensed her own stamina flagging for good.

"Whew," Lillian said with an exhilarated laugh. "Good, right?"

"So good." She ruffled Nell's ears. "How far is that loop?"

"Just over four miles."

"It sounded like you're the only runner in the house."

"Yeah. Angie and Stevie will use the treadmill in the winter sometimes."

"Not Morgan?"

"Morgan likes to do things. Deadlift sheep, or whatever."

Emilia laughed at the image.

"It really isn't fair, though," Lillian continued. "I bust my butt and she does one push-up and gets ripped."

"I still can't believe you all live and work together."

"We don't really. Stevie and Morgan are hardly ever home. I see Angie a lot, but she's got the kennel, and I can hide in the greenhouse when I need a break."

"And Stevie and Morgan don't fight?"

"Oh, they do. But they've known each other since elementary school, and they can work together even when they're angry."

"I couldn't do that."

"Me neither. Sometimes I'm even glad my boyfriend is four hours away."

The farmhouse came into view a quarter mile up the road. Emilia didn't see the truck now, either.

"How long have you worked at Seal Cove?"

"Two years. I went to school with Morgan—I think I told you that already—and she got a job here right after graduation. I specialized in exotics, and Morgan convinced me to come here once I passed my boards."

"Did you know each other before Cornell?"

"No. I'm from Bath, and she's from a little farther up the coast. Both of us swore we'd never come back to Maine." She shook her head. "You can see how well that turned out."

"Your greenhouse must be nice in the winter."

"It is. Come on in for a second and I'll grab you a glass of water, and then we can get you some plants."

"You sure?" Emilia glanced at Nell.

"I'll put the dogs out back. She can meet them there, or not at all if you prefer."

Emilia, who had a bottle of water waiting in her car, hesitated, then nodded. Nothing but dust waited for her at home.

Lillian put the dogs out and then beckoned Emilia in.

"Hey, stranger," Angie said, waving from the couch where she sprawled with a book propped on her chest.

"Missed you on our run," said Lillian as Emilia waved.

"Liar. Oh hi, gorgeous." Angie's voice rose into a coo as Nell approached.

Nell greeted this new human with a cautious sniff. The reason for her caution rumbled to life as a black shape Emilia had taken for a throw pillow hissed.

"Shut up, James," said Angie.

Nell beat a fast retreat to Emilia's side. "I've heard about your cat."

"The rumors are all true." Angie prodded him with a socked foot. "He's the worst of all time."

"Here you go." Lillian handed her a glass of water. Angie, for her part, put down her book, rose, stretched like a cat herself, and sauntered into the kitchen.

"You staying for dinner?" she asked.

"Oh. Um, I should probably get home and shower."

"We have showers."

"Stop peer-pressuring her. You're always welcome, not that there's anything to eat," said Lillian.

"Maybe when I don't smell?" Emilia hoped her face and voice showed how much she genuinely meant it.

"Yes. Lil's a great cook. Have we mentioned that enough yet?"

"Don't think I haven't noticed how all your dinner invitations involve zero cooking on your part," said Lillian.

"I cook," Angie said. "Pasta, bread, pizza . . ."

"If it's a carbohydrate, she cooks it."

"Not all of us feel the need to slaughter entire villages of vegetables every time we eat."

"I'm keeping the population in check," said Lillian.

"Because Swiss chard is such a problem?"

"Have you been in the greenhouse recently? It's a Swiss chard jungle. Anyway, we're a bunch of workaholics, but you should definitely hang out with us," said Lillian.

"I'd like that."

"Oh, and Morgan told me to ask you if you need anything else for your house. We've got some painting supplies left over from the renovation."

"That would be perfect actually," said Emilia.

"Cool. I never want to see them again." Lillian shuddered.

"Storage room. Third floor," Angie said without prompting.

"There's a third floor?"

"Sort of. Here, I'll show you."

She followed Lillian up a staircase worn in the center tread by two centuries of feet, then down a long hallway to a second flight of stairs.

"Most of us keep our doors shut to keep James out," Lillian explained as they walked. "Morgan and I are on this end, and Stevie and Angie are on the other."

The stairs led to a large room filled with dust motes, boxes, and a few rolled carpets. Lillian rummaged through a corner until she pulled a crate out from a rusting collection of old bedframes. Paintbrush handles and trays poked out of it, along with a mound of what looked like drop cloths.

"This is a huge help."

"It's yours."

Emilia accepted the box and they descended the stairs, leaving the dusty room shut behind them.

"Lil, have you seen the first aid kit?"

Emilia stumbled when she heard Morgan's voice and barely caught herself against the wall. The support, it turned out, was more than necessary. Morgan waited at the base of the staircase, still damp from her shower and wearing only a sports bra and sweatpants. She didn't seem to have noticed Emilia yet, which gave her a moment to compose herself. Unfortunately, it also gave her more time to stare. The black sports bra accented Morgan's fair skin, and the dip of cleavage drew Emilia's eyes down to the line of muscle beneath. She bit her lip. Abs like that just weren't fair. Especially abs that ended at those hips, attached to that ass. What was it Anna Maria had said? *Fuckable?*

She raised her eyes slowly, alerted by the pause in the conversation. Morgan stared at her in shock.

"I'll grab the first aid kit," Lillian said with poorly concealed amusement.

"Um. Hi. I had no idea you were here." Morgan rubbed the back of her neck in a gesture Emilia was beginning to recognize as her go-to move when she was nervous. It also accentuated the attributes Emilia had just categorized as decidedly fuckable, along with her biceps.

"Your truck isn't in the driveway."

"Stevie dropped me off and went to get gas. I got stepped on by a cow." She pulled up the hem of her pants to reveal a bruised and swollen ankle.

"Shit. Should you be walking on that?"

"It looks worse than it is. Ace bandage, ice . . ." She trailed off. "I should put a shirt on."

"No." Emilia felt herself blush. "I mean, it's your house. I'm the intruder. I can take off."

"Fuck." Morgan swore under her breath and sagged against the wall. Nell chose that moment to bound up the stairs in search of her person and paused to give Morgan an exuberant greeting.

"She met James."

"And you're still alive?" Morgan asked Nell.

"It was a near thing."

"I bet it was." Morgan stroked Nell's narrow head.

"Where are you broken this time?" Lillian asked when she returned.

"Her ankle," said Emilia.

"And you're standing on it, why?"

"It's not that bad."

"This is why I went into small animal medicine." Lillian positioned herself next to Morgan. "Let's get you downstairs."

Morgan shot Emilia a rueful look and allowed Lillian to place her arm around her shoulders and lead her, limping, away. Emilia stared at Morgan's back and was glad no one could see her face as she pictured digging her nails into the smooth, freckled skin. Maybe Anna Maria was right.

"Oh yeah," Angie said when they showed up in the living room. "Forgot to tell you. Morgan's home." She stroked the still-bristling James with an expression of feigned innocence. It occurred to Emilia, as it should have sooner, that Morgan's friends must have opinions of their own about her sudden appearance in Morgan's life.

"I'm just going to head out." She turned, the box of painting supplies shifting awkwardly in her arms, and fled.

Morgan sank into the armchair with a groan. "Thanks for that, Ange."

"What? It's not my fault you didn't put a shirt on."

"I would have if I'd known Emilia was here."

"Why? You're decent."

"By your standards, maybe," said Lillian as she pulled up Morgan's pant leg to examine her ankle.

"The human body is nothing to be ashamed of," said Angie.

"I'm not ashamed of my body."

"Emilia's seen women in sports bras before. I assume she's gone to a gym at least once in her life."

"Ange . . . *ow.*" Morgan didn't finish her sentence. Lillian's gentle rotation of her ankle had ended, and she began poking around one of the more tender areas.

"You should stay off this for a few days."

"You know that isn't an option. I'm booked."

"Then let Stevie drive and use crutches as much as you can."

"I'll try."

"Let me get you some ice. Where's the dog?"

"With Stevie still. Traitor."

"You really didn't see Emilia's car when you pulled in?"

"No."

"Look." Lillian returned with an ice pack and placed it on Morgan's elevated ankle. "I know you're being very noble about the whole situation, but there's clearly something going on between you two."

"Can we focus on my ankle?"

"No," Angie said before Lillian could answer. "Because I don't understand the problem."

"The problem is that Morgan thinks Emilia is fragile," said Lillian.

"That's not her call," Angie said.

"Nope. It also isn't the reason she's scared."

"Right here, guys," said Morgan.

"Kate?" asked Angie.

"Kate."

Morgan tried to stand as she had zero interest in hanging around for the rest of this conversation, but Lillian shoved her back down. "Stay off the ankle."

"Then can we not talk about this?"

"Hell, if you're not into her, I could be," said Angie.

"She's not your type." Morgan couldn't help bristling.

"I could make an exception."

"What's going on with Lana, anyway? I thought you were done with her."

"I am."

"Then why was she over the other night?"

"Because I wanted to get laid on my birthday." Angie folded herself into the corner of the couch. "Is there a problem with that?"

"She's not good for you."

Angie's hazel eyes were unreadable. "Also not your call."

"Children," Lillian said warningly.

"I just don't get it. You're kind, beautiful, funny, and smart. You deserve someone who appreciates that, not someone who . . ." She gestured vaguely, unwilling to put into words what women like Lana did to Angie.

"If that's what I wanted, I'd date you, Donovan." Angie stood abruptly, clutching a spitting James to her chest, and stalked out of the room.

Lillian sighed.

"What? Everyone gets a say in my private life, but I can't say anything about hers?" said Morgan.

"You're . . ." Lillian paused. "You and Ange are different."

"Lana is a dick."

113

"Lana isn't the problem, Morgan."

Lillian's quiet words deflated her anger. "I should go apologize."

"Later. Stay off that foot. I'll talk to her and make sure she's okay."

Okay, and not hurting herself. Morgan leaned her head against the back of the chair. Today had been an unmitigated disaster. First the cow, which should have been avoidable, then Emilia, and now Angie. Tomorrow promised more trouble. One of the local riding stables had purchased a new group of school horses, pending veterinary examination, which meant long hours on her feet on concrete. Then there would be the inevitable emergency, followed by an appointment with a bad-tempered horse with laminitis whose hoof never seemed to bother her enough to prevent a kick. Danielle needed to hire someone soon, even if it was just on a temporary basis. Maybe they could snag a new grad who hadn't found work yet, not that she relished that idea. What Morgan really needed was a day on the water, no pager, no cell phone—just her, her dog, and the ocean.

Angie came back downstairs an ice pack change later.

"Ange," Morgan said, sitting up. Angie's large hazel eyes gave her a soulful look. "Come here."

Angie approached cautiously, reminding Morgan of a feral kitten. She patted the armrest, and Angie perched on the edge.

"I'm sorry I snapped at you."

"It's okay. I'm sorry I pushed the Emilia thing."

"Don't worry about it. You doing okay?"

Angie slid into Morgan's lap. The vulnerability in the gesture brought a lump to Morgan's throat, and she wrapped her arms around her friend. Angie curled her head under Morgan's chin.

"No," she said.

"Is there anything I can do?"

Angie shook her head and burrowed deeper—a five foot, seven inch-tall puppy looking for comfort. Morgan stroked her hair and met Lillian's questioning gaze with a mouthed, *I don't know.*

She'd met Angie through the clinic. Angie had been Stevie's friend first and had kept her distance until Morgan realized her reserve stemmed from fear. Once she'd started treating Angie like a skittish filly, things changed. There had never been anything besides platonic affection between the two of them. Morgan held no threat for Angie, which she suspected had more to do with this current embrace than anything else. She might not understand Angie's love life, but she understood wounded animals.

"We've got you," she said into Angie's hair.

"I know."

The sound of a truck door slamming roused Angie from her fetal position. She blinked up at Morgan, mascara smudged under one eye, then unfolded herself and stood. Her mask was back in place by the time Stevie and Kraken waltzed through the door.

Chapter Nine

Emilia's hand shook. Primer dripped onto the drop cloth at her feet.

"Am I doing this?" she asked the house. Silence answered her. She didn't know what her father would have wanted. No. That wasn't true. He would have wanted her to be happy. He didn't care about the color of the walls or what she did with the house. Still trembling, she set the paint roller against the dark wood and brought it down in a broad stroke. White shone back at her. White, bright, beautiful paint.

She burst into tears.

Nell, whom she had once again relegated to the porch, whined at the sound of her person's distress. Emilia recharged the brush, still sobbing, and made another pass. She'd decided to start in the living room. It was the room she most associated with her father, which made it the hardest, but it was also the room she wanted to see transformed first. The dark whorls of the knots in the wood showed through the first coat of primer. They watched her like the eyes she'd imagined them to be as a child.

Her sobs faded as the morning wore on. The primer brought sunlight into the room with it, ameliorating her doubts. No longer would shadows dominate the living area. She refused to consider the analogy between her desire to paint the house and her desire to rid her own life of its shadows. Her therapist could have fun with that. She'd content herself with the work.

She almost managed to go most of the morning without thinking about Morgan. Her mind periodically offered up images of perfectly sculpted abs, but she bit her lip until the pain drove them out of her head. Her body had enjoyed the challenge of her run with Lillian, and she listened to her father's music as she painted. Leonard Cohen's voice reminded her of his, and she remembered, too, his hands on the guitar.

Come lunchtime, however, the paint fumes drove her out of the house, far more successful than her attempts to banish her thoughts. She gathered Nell and walked the two miles into town for lunch. It wasn't as if she was in a hurry. Walking, unfortunately, freed up her mind for more thoughts of Morgan, as did her destination: Stormy's.

Running out on Morgan had been rude. After her conversation with Anna Maria and the palpable chemistry the night of Angie's birthday, however, her body's visceral reaction to seeing Morgan half-dressed had triggered her fight-or-flight response. And by fight, she meant fuck.

So do it, her body suggested. *You're only here for a few months. You like her friends. You clearly like her. It doesn't matter that you're barely managing to function, and isn't human contact—the desire for human contact—a sign of progress?*

She kicked at a dandelion, earning herself a quizzical look from Nell. *What if I get attached?* Her mind remained obstinately silent on this front, and so she answered for it. *I have too much to figure out without adding someone else's needs and wants into the equation. Especially a vet.* Hannah had been a vet, and far from making her more understanding of Emilia's situation, it had shortened her already short fuse. She'd never had much patience for Emilia's doubts.

"Tough it out." That had been her advice.

Then she'd left.

"Fine," she said out loud. She would not get involved with Morgan. Nor, however, would she attempt to deny the electric potential. *I'll talk to her like the adult I'm supposed to be.*

Her mood lifted when she entered the café. The first tourists of the season filled most of the tables, but the corner in the back where she'd shared a beer with Morgan remained empty.

"Hey, lady," Stormy said from behind the register. Emilia blinked at the polka-dotted dress and vibrant red headscarf over Stormy's thick curls, which somehow suited her but would have looked garish on anyone else.

"Do you have anything strong enough to wash the taste of paint out of my mouth?"

"Out of your mouth? Yes. Your hair . . ." She smiled and reached across the counter to tap the side of Emilia's head. The familiarity unsettled her, but not unpleasantly so.

"I don't see much point in trying to get rid of it until I'm done. You should see my legs."

"Are we talking coffee or something stronger?"

"Just coffee."

"Latte? Black? Americano?"

"Espresso?"

Stormy winked. "Very Italian. Whipped cream on top?"

"Normally I'd say no." Cafes rarely offered espresso con panna without prompting. Her nonna had made it like that when she went to visit her in Italy, and it seemed fitting to drink it here in memory of her grandmother and her father.

"But you've got that paint taste to get rid of."

"Exactly."

"Whip for the pup?"

"As a vet, I can't really condone that."

"You've never given her whipped cream?"

Emilia looked down at her dog, who gazed adoringly back up at her. *What the hell*, she thought. "A small cup. And don't tell anyone."

"My lips are sealed," said Stormy, and she shot whipped cream into a sample cup with a flourish.

Emilia laughed in delight as Nell's pupils dilated so widely they nearly swallowed her irises. The greyhound's narrow snout shoved its way into the cup with the kind of joy only experienced by dogs and small children.

"How's your boat?"

Emilia waited for the sound of the coffee grinder to fade before responding. "Haven't had a chance to find out. And there's a hole in my skiff." Morgan had promised to help her mend it, she remembered. Maybe she could use that as an excuse to talk to her about mending other things—or rather, avoiding breakage all together.

"Skiffs are the little rowboats, right?"

"Skiff, dinghy, rowboat . . . I've never been sure if there was a difference between them or not. My dad used the words interchangeably."

"Either way, they scare the hell out of me." Stormy slid the espresso across the counter. "Especially ones with holes."

Emilia retreated to her corner and drank the espresso while she contemplated her lunch options. Nell eyed the whipped cream on top hopefully. *Sandwich, panini, salad, muffin* . . . all she could think about was Morgan.

ER: *Can I take you up on that boat repair?*

She hit send. No point putting things off.

Her bagel was nearly gone by the time Morgan replied.

MD: *You free tonight?*

ER: *I could be.*

MD: *Good. Then I'll text you when I'm off.*

Emilia laid her hand over her phone and felt the bagel solidifying in her stomach. Maybe that hadn't been such a good idea after all.

It vibrated again.

MD: *Afternoon appointment just canceled. You free now?*

She checked her reflection in the café bathroom mirror, using the break as an excuse to put off responding for another minute. Paint spattered her hair. The T-shirt she wore had belonged to her father, and the pants had seen too much bleach in their lifetime to hold much claim on the color black.

Good. If she didn't feel sexy, maybe she'd manage to keep her cool.

ER: *Yeah. I'm in town.*

119

MD: *Meet me at the dock in 20.*

"No," she said to Nell, who was sniffing the toilet with curiosity. The word summed up most of her own feelings, too. *No to all of this.* No to Morgan, no to good sense, no to inhibition. She splashed water on her flushed face, gathered her dog, and made her way down to the dock.

Morgan arrived in the clinic truck without Stevie. The ensuing blend of relief and dread dried her mouth.

"Hey," said Morgan as she swung herself forward on a pair of crutches.

"Oh god, I shouldn't have asked for your help until your ankle healed."

"It's fine. I'm only using these to keep Lillian off my back. Plus, it's the left, so I can drive if I'm careful."

"Still, you shouldn't . . ." she trailed off. Morgan was fully clothed in a clinic polo instead of just a sports bra, but Emilia's imagination filled in the blanks for her.

"I'll just sit and tell you what to do if that makes you feel better."

"Why do I feel like I don't believe you're capable of that?"

Morgan grinned in response. "Let's take a look at it in the daylight, yeah?"

They moved toward the boat together, and Emilia caught a whiff of horse. She pictured Morgan calmly running her hands along a broad brown back, whispering soothing words into a cocked ear. It soothed her. Once, she'd had an interest in large animal medicine, but she'd been persuaded out of it. She knew too many vets who'd ended up switching to small animal after one injury too many, and the hours and pay were dismal. Not, of course, that shelter medicine had turned out to be any better. She shut down the thought and returned her focus to the Russo rowboat overturned on the grass outside the boathouse. The crack looked smaller in the full sunlight. Morgan tossed her crutches to the ground and knelt beside it. Her fingers traced the hairline fracture in the fiberglass.

"Technically, we should sand this down."

"If only I'd thought to bring the sander I'm renting at great expense," said Emilia.

"I think I have some sandpaper in the boathouse. For splinters on my oars," Morgan added when she saw Emilia's raised eyebrows.

"Are you prepared for everything?"

"If you can find it in a standard toolbox, yes."

"So we sand, then what?"

"Then we lay new fiberglass cloth and resin until it's patched, apply an activator, and let it cure."

"Well, since I'm basically an expert sander, where can I find that grit?" Emilia asked.

"I'll grab it. You get your patch kit."

Emilia held out a hand to help Morgan up. Her warm, firm grip reminded her of something. "How's your hand from the other night?"

"You must think I'm a mess. Burning myself, cow-kicked . . ."

"I assumed you were still trying to make me feel better about falling overboard."

"I should have led with that," said Morgan.

"Here." She slung Morgan's arm over her shoulder. "It's just a few feet. Forget the crutches."

"You sure?"

No, Emilia thought. *This is exactly what I promised I wouldn't do.*

"Friends help friends," she said instead. "Besides, it's your turn to be the damsel in distress."

Morgan's blush rewarded her as color peaked beneath Morgan's freckles. She settled her weight over Emilia. Emilia wrapped her arm around Morgan's waist, where the abs she'd seen the day before tensed beneath her fingers. The short stretch to the boathouse seemed to simultaneously take years and end too quickly. Morgan also seemed a little more out of breath than the exertion required, but the dim flicker of the overhead lights failed to illuminate the expression in her eyes when they stopped by the locker Morgan indicated.

She stepped away. Her body tingled where it had been in contact with Morgan's, and Morgan fumbled with the lock without looking up.

The locker contained a jumble of boating supplies: oars, extra seat cushions, life vests, salt-stained jackets, cans of oil, rags, towels, ragged ball caps, a radio, and faded cardboard boxes the size and shape Emilia associated with hardware stores. Morgan rummaged through these until she pulled out a few sheets of sandpaper.

"You really are prepared."

Morgan turned off the locker light, which was just a lightbulb and a chain. "Keep that in mind if zombies start popping up."

"I'll remember that."

"Although a lot of it depends on if zombies can swim. That would make the boat less effective."

Are we really talking about the zombie apocalypse right now? At least zombies lacked sex appeal. Even necrophiliacs would agree. "I better grab that patch kit just in case they can't. Besides," she added as she left Morgan to access her father's locker. "Sailboats don't require fuel."

"Then I want you on my team," said Morgan.

"Just because I have a boat? I have other skills, too, you know."

"Like what?"

"Like . . ." Her voice faded as she turned on her own cobwebbed bulb. Her father's green jacket waited for him on its hook, along with the canvas bags and odds and ends she'd grown up with. The patch kit sat on a shelf, but she didn't reach for it. If she moved too quickly, she might jostle his clothing and the familiar smell would summon tears.

A hand settled on her shoulder, but Morgan said nothing.

"How did you and my dad become friends?" Emilia asked eventually.

"He helped me out a few times with my boat. I got it from my uncle when he moved. It was a piece of shit and I was broke, but the engine ran. My parents aren't big on boats. They've got the farm, so I had to figure a lot of it out on my own."

"I didn't think my dad knew much about motorboats."

"He knew the water. That's most of it really. Especially around here."

"Did he ever talk about me?" The blunt question would have embarrassed her anywhere else, but here in the boathouse, confronted by the ghost of her father, she couldn't help asking.

"A little. I didn't realize you were around my age, though."

"Always daddy's little girl," Emilia said quietly. She grabbed the patch kit and shut the door.

"You ready to do this?" Morgan asked. "We can always come back later. You can borrow my skiff if you need one."

The inundation of grief receded, but she felt like something raw and exposed left on the sand by the tide. In the shadows of the dim aisle, out of the glare of the June sun, the loneliness that had followed her since his death assailed her. It clawed at her breath, and she closed her eyes in sudden pain.

Morgan squeezed her shoulder. Emilia knew the gesture was meant to reassure, but the human touch against the rawness of her grief severed what little control she'd managed to maintain. Need raced along her synapses and forced everything else out of its way. The scent of Morgan's shampoo flooded her senses, erasing the smell of the ocean and the slightly musty odor of the boathouse. Heat from her body cut through the chill of shaded concrete and damp wood.

Something that might have been a curse or a prayer beat its wings in her throat. She pushed Morgan against the row of lockers, taking her by surprise and knocking her off balance. Her blue eyes flew wide open, and she didn't move from where Emilia had pinned her. Beneath Emilia's hands, she felt like the only solid thing in the world. Barely four inches separated them. She searched Morgan's face. Shock faded, and the sound of Morgan's rapid breathing filled her ears. This close she could count the freckles peppering her cheekbones. There was still time to pull away, apologize, and blame her actions on grief and emotional instability. Her eyes fell on Morgan's lips. Need lanced through her again. She met Morgan's eyes and saw the same need reflected there.

Morgan's mouth met hers with hunger. Her lips brushed over Morgan's once, and then she deepened the kiss with her body, pressing her full weight into Morgan. Hands pulled her hips in closer. A moan escaped her throat. The hair tangled in her fingers was thick and soft, almost as soft as the mouth beneath hers. She drew her teeth over Morgan's bottom lip, brushing her tongue along it as she did.

This isn't a first kiss, she thought, breathless. *This is . . .* Her mind blanked as Morgan ran her fingers up her back, thumbs dragging up her sides and drawing a whimper of desire with them. Morgan's lips moved downward, but Emilia closed her hands more tightly around her hair and stopped her. Instead, she kissed the smooth line of jaw leading down to her throat, tasting sweat and something else, something purely Morgan.

Morgan gasped when Emilia nipped at the skin along her neck. The sound, so feminine and so at odds with her androgynous persona, drove any last shred of resolve out of Emilia's mind. She abandoned her hold on Morgan's hair and raked her nails down her arms.

"Fuck." Morgan flung her head back as Emilia's tongue passed over the hollow of her collarbone. She tried to push Emilia off and turn her against the wall, but Emilia stopped her, taking Morgan by the wrists as her mouth moved back up to brush her ear. Morgan gasped again. Emilia traced the curve of her ear and felt her shudder. Still gripping Morgan's wrists, she returned to her mouth, teasing her lips with long, slow strokes. She knew Morgan could have fought her off if she'd really wanted to top Emilia, but she also knew with growing certainty that Morgan wanted no such thing right now.

It felt good, intoxicatingly good, to set the pace herself. She released Morgan's wrists and skimmed her fingertips up the bare skin of Morgan's arms. Morgan clung to Emilia's belt, her muscles rock hard, and whimpered into Emilia's mouth as Emilia ran her fingertips just as lightly down along the sides of her breasts and down farther, lifting the hem of her shirt to trace the smooth skin of her stomach. She wanted to slide her hand past Morgan's belt. She wanted to be inside Morgan, needed to feel her, needed to taste her hot against her.

"Emilia." Morgan's voice, raw, stopped her hand. She leaned her forehead against Morgan's as their breath mingled in the space between them.

"Do you want me to stop?"

Morgan groaned in frustration, and her hips pushed into Emilia's. "No. Fuck no. I just—"

Emilia slipped her hand into the waistband of Morgan's jeans. "Just what?"

"Just . . ." Morgan's chest rose and fell, and she kept her eyes shut as she tried to speak past the shudders wracking her taut body. "Is this what you want?"

Emilia drew a line along the border of Morgan's briefs. "Is this what *you* want?"

"Not. What. I asked."

Footsteps sounded on the wood of the wharf. Emilia kissed her hard on the mouth, willing the intruder back into their boat so that she could fuck Morgan Donovan blind against this wall, right now, right here.

A child laughed in the distance.

"Fuck," she swore as she pulled away. Morgan's flushed cheeks glowed in the near darkness, and removing her hand felt like the hardest thing Emilia had ever done. She allowed herself to linger in the shelter of Morgan's arms until the footsteps drew even with the boathouse.

"We should patch that boat of yours," Morgan said in her ear. Each word vibrated through her.

"Or we could go out in your boat." *Or your truck, or a locker, or anywhere we won't be interrupted.*

"I have a four o'clock appointment." Morgan's voice dripped regret.

"That gives us an hour," Emilia said. She supported Morgan as she put weight back on her damaged foot and waved at the small boy and his father as they walked by.

"If you think I'll be done with you in an hour, then you've

severely underestimated me," Morgan said. She nipped Emilia's ear and drew her lips slowly along the outer curve. The sensation nearly killed her. Only her hold on Morgan kept her upright.

"Come on," Morgan continued and, limping, she led Emilia out into the sunlight.

Emilia sank onto the grass by her boat. Morgan slid down beside her and produced the crumpled sandpaper from her pocket, but made no move to use it as they both caught their breath.

Desire and rationality warred in Emilia's head. All the reasons to avoid an entanglement battled the aching, immediate need that swept her body in shock waves. This was the problem. This was why she couldn't do this. Her mind stopped working when Morgan was around, making informed choices impossible. She had nothing to offer this woman. Nothing besides her body and her confusion, and she'd come here to find answers. Losing herself in Morgan would cloud that. It was also all she wanted to do. *That kiss* . . . Mustering her thoughts was like herding cats. Her mind presented her with recent and vivid memories of Morgan, and anything else faded to white noise.

"Look." Morgan's tousled curls tumbled over her forehead, and Emilia dug her nails into her palms to prevent herself from brushing them back.

"What?"

"You're . . . This has to be your call."

"What do you mean?"

"I can't . . ." Morgan trailed off again as she looked at Emilia with those dark, blue-gray eyes. "I can't fucking resist you so if this isn't what you want, it has to be your call."

The words settled in her mind, heavy and sobering even as they thrilled her. The naked vulnerability in Morgan's face mirrored the ache in Emilia's chest. She wasn't the only one this could hurt. That realization cooled some of the heat in her blood.

"I don't really know what I want."

"That's kind of what I guessed."

"I actually came here planning to tell you that. I didn't mean to . . . for that . . . it's your fault."

126

"How?" asked Morgan.

"You're too goddamn perfect."

"Sorry?"

"I'm a mess, Morgan."

"A hot mess."

"I don't even know what this is." She gestured between herself and Morgan. "Besides the fact that I would have fucked you in a heartbeat back there if you hadn't stopped me."

Morgan's sharp intake of breath reawakened Emilia's need to touch her. She put her hand on Morgan's good ankle.

"Trust me. I would have let you," said Morgan.

"So what do we do?"

"I told you." Blue eyes fixed on hers. "That's your call. If you need a friend, I'm here. If you decide you want something more, I think I just proved I'll be here for that, too."

"That's not really fair."

"No," said Morgan. "It isn't."

"But what do *you* want?"

Morgan's wistful smile tore at Emilia. "Right now, I want to help you fix this boat so that you don't drown before you make up your mind."

Nell, who had observed her person's behavior with canine indifference, chose this moment to flop down next to Morgan. *Traitor.*

"Okay then. Let's do that."

Stevie took one look at Morgan's face when she hopped into the truck and frowned. "What did you have for lunch? Bad fish?"

"I didn't eat." Instead, she'd helped Emilia spread epoxy over the crack in the rowboat's hull and had done her best not to scream in frustration.

"That was stupid. Here, eat this healthy bar thing that I stole from Lil." Stevie handed her a protein bar, and she chewed without tasting it. Her body ached with unreleased tension.

"Then what did you do?" Stevie asked when Morgan didn't volunteer any information.

"I helped Emilia with her boat."

"And how is the good doctor?" Stevie's banter carried a concerned edge.

"Fine."

"So fine that you look like you want to hit something."

"I don't."

"You most definitely do."

"Drop it, Stevie."

Stevie settled back in her seat with a hurt expression. Morgan hadn't meant to snap at her. White showed in her knuckles where they gripped the wheel.

"She's a top," she said, not looking at Stevie.

"Oh no." Stevie's voice softened. "Morgan, you're totally fucked."

"I know."

"How, exactly, did you discover this, Sherlock?"

"I don't want to talk about it."

"Can I play devil's advocate?"

"Do you ever play anything else?"

"*Touché.* Seriously, though. I think I get why you're fighting this, but let's be real for a second."

Morgan glanced at her friend. Stevie's face was uncharacteristically sober.

"You're going to get hurt either way. You might as well get laid in the process."

"Thanks for that bit of wisdom."

"You're welcome."

They drove the rest of the way in silence, listening to the radio. Morgan tried to calm the urge to beat her fist against the steering wheel. *Why.* Why did she have to be so responsible? Why hadn't she pulled Emilia into the back seat of this truck . . . or maybe someplace with less dog hair, like the bathroom of the boathouse, not that that option was much more appealing. She hadn't been with anyone since Kate, and her body screamed at her in thwarted fury. The memory of Emilia's hand brushing near her clit as she withdrew from her pants nearly made her swerve into the shoulder. *Fuck.*

Women expected Morgan to take the lead. Even Kate, who had known her better than anyone, hadn't managed to unhinge her quite so totally and had left things mostly up to Morgan in bed. Morgan had, once, drunkenly confessed to Stevie how much this disappointed her.

Emilia hadn't initially struck her as assertive. That haunted look in her eyes engaged Morgan's natural protective instincts and lowered her defenses. Today, she'd paid the price, and if she had any sense she'd run.

Instead, all she could think about was how Emilia would look riding her, head flung back, hair cascading down her shoulders as she came. The image distracted her so much she missed her turn. Stevie didn't offer any snarky commentary as Morgan corrected their course and pulled into their next appointment.

She'd been honest with Emilia. Probably too honest. She didn't have the willpower necessary to resist her, and it felt too damn good to feel wanted.

Stevie cleared her throat. Morgan realized she'd been staring at her hands on the wheel with the truck in idle. Killing the engine, she let her head fall back against the headrest with a groan.

"I hate ponies, too, but they won't vaccinate themselves."

"Stevie."

"What?"

"What do I do?"

"How did you leave it? Besides blue-balled."

"I put the ball in her court."

"Why are you such a masochist?"

"I don't want to push her."

"No. You want her to push you," Stevie muttered. Morgan glared at her. Louder, Stevie said, "Then I guess all you can do is see what happens and try not to fall too hard. You're still the only doctor on ambulatory, and Danielle will kill you if you break yourself any more than you already have."

"Good talk."

"Morgan."

She paused with her hand on the door. "What?"

"Be careful. If you can."

"I'll try. Ready to wrangle some minis?"

"Never."

Watching Stevie wrestle miniature horses significantly brightened her mood. Her friend kept a tight smile on her face to soothe the anxious owner of the small herd, who hovered nearby but made no move to help. Morgan was never sure whether to be frustrated when owners stayed out of the way or relieved. She settled on amused as Stevie held a particularly badly behaved yearling for her to examine.

"Easy," Morgan murmured to the little horse. It cocked one curved ear at her and snorted, unconvinced.

You're right, little dude. Nothing is ever easy. Better to know, better to accept Emilia's imminent departure instead of daring to hope that this time things might be different.

They swung by the grocery store on the way home. Morgan limped along behind Stevie, who wielded the cart like a weapon as she pulled food off the shelves.

"What brand of pasta does Lil like? I can never remember," Stevie asked.

"The kind I can't afford. Go with the store brand."

"She'll kill you."

"She'll get over it."

"Sometimes I think, 'Stevie, is being a vet tech really what you want to do with your life?' Then I go shopping with you and I feel better."

"Very funny."

"Your student loans are terrifying. Do you see me laughing? Ooh, check out this sauce." Stevie held a jar of livid red sauce in front of Morgan's face.

"Why would you ruin pasta sauce for me like that?"

"Because I know how much you love chili peppers."

"Moderation," said Morgan. "That's all I ask."

"That motherfucker." Stevie froze with her hand clenched around the jar. Morgan followed Stevie's gaze to where Lana stood with a slender brunette who was definitely not Angie. Lana waved lazily at them with the hand not buried in the other woman's back pocket. Morgan's hackles rose.

"She's not Angie's girlfriend," she reminded Stevie, even as she inventoried the bruises on the brunette's neck.

"She was with Angie last night," said Stevie, before raising her voice to Lana. "Who's your friend?"

"Stevie—" Morgan took her arm.

"You got a problem?" Lana's eyes glittered. Morgan recognized the look. Dogs got it when they wanted to pick a fight.

Lana's friend looked nervously between Lana and Stevie. She had a sweet, open face, and Morgan pitied her. Lana would eat her alive. *Lana Piranha.*

"I do."

Morgan snapped her attention back to Stevie. Several other shoppers had paused to watch, some of them with looks more dangerous than Lana's. Maine might be a blue state in theory, but this was Trump's America, and dyke drama drew deadlier things than heartbreak.

"Let's get out of here." She positioned herself between Stevie and Lana. Maneuvering with crutches slowed her down.

"Fuck off," said Lana.

Morgan dropped her crutches and caught a lunging Stevie across the chest. "She's not worth it."

Lana laughed as she walked away.

"She's a piece of shit," Stevie spat.

"I know."

"We could slash her tires."

"You have probable cause written all over your face. And the store cameras," Morgan warned.

"I don't care—"

"I do. I need my tech, and as we established, I can't afford to bail you out." She released Stevie cautiously. "You good?"

"Yeah."

131

"You sure?"

"We're not on call tonight, right?"

"Nope."

"Then I'll be fine if you promise to get drunk with me."

"Deal." Whiskey did sound like a more pleasant alternative than lying alone in her bed. They finished the shopping and headed for home without another encounter with the piranha.

"Piranha. I love it," Stevie said later when Morgan shared her lexical revelation over a bottle of whiskey. Light still glowed in the evening sky, and Kraken and Marvin lay in the grass at their feet by the fire pit. The small blaze kept the chill off—as did the whiskey.

"I don't get it. She deserves so much better. Why that little fuck?" asked Stevie.

"Maybe she doesn't believe she deserves anything better." Morgan remembered how Angie had curled up in her lap the day before.

"I hate caring about people," said Stevie. "Dogs are so much easier."

"To dogs." Morgan raised the bottle in a toast.

"Maybe Marvin will bite her next time she comes over."

"Have you met your dog? He's the poster child for pittie love."

"Tell Kraken to do it then."

"Maybe James is just biding his time."

"A terrifying thought. I never thought I'd agree with that cat." Stevie stared into the fire. "Do you remember senior year?"

"High school?"

"Yeah. Who was that girl you were obsessed with?"

"Nora?"

"God, she was hot."

"She has three kids now," said Morgan.

"Are we getting old?"

"Thirty-one isn't old."

"Look at us, though. Single. Childless. Still living with house-mates," said Stevie.

"The American dream."

"And I still can't believe Kate left."

Morgan groaned. "Don't."

"I thought you two had it made."

"So did I." The whiskey was inadequate to burn away that pain. Months later, she still didn't understand how she could have been so blind to Kate's unhappiness.

"Have you heard from her at all?"

"No. But I see her face every time I drive by one of her listings." She'd learned to avoid looking at any realtor signs she saw on her work routes.

"You should sleep with Emilia."

"You're drunk, Stevie."

"Yes. Which makes me smarter than you. Sleep with Emilia and forget about Kate."

"Maybe you should take your own advice."

"I can't sleep with Emilia. She's too tall. I'd never be able to reach anything."

"Asshole."

Chapter Ten

Emilia turned in a slow circle, balancing her weight on Nell's collar. The house looked almost unrecognizable. Cream-colored walls. Blue trim in the living room, raw beams in the kitchen, and all the shadows chased back beneath the suddenly faded chairs and end tables. She'd taken up the rugs, too, and mopped and polished the hardwood floors until they gleamed in the morning sun. Her father wouldn't have recognized his own living room.

The paint job also highlighted the out-of-date kitchen and older appliances. Problems for the new owner, she decided. Her father hadn't left her enough money to fully update the house, but at least the potential was now visible, and she could turn her attention to the outside.

She reached for her phone to text Morgan, as she had a hundred times since that day at the boathouse a week and a half ago. As she had each time, however, her fingers faltered. What the hell was she supposed to say? Leaving the decision to her had been a dick move on Morgan's part, and she'd spent several days stewing over Morgan's words. Claiming a lack of agency was a cop-out, and an unfair one at that.

Then there were her dreams. Try as she might to block her imagination from dwelling on Morgan Donovan during the day, at night her mind betrayed her. The result of her frustration and confusion was this: a freshly painted house. Crossing the task off her mental checklist left the following list of things to resolve before she could get out of Seal Cove: put the house on the market, scatter her father's ashes, and figure out the rest of her life. It didn't bring her the sense of closure she'd hoped. Paint met her nostrils instead of the lingering whiff of tobacco. The walls looked significantly less terrifying without their taxidermy occupants, but she almost missed their glassy stares.

"What did we do, Nell?"

The dog leaned against her leg in response.

Had this whole thing been a mistake? Not that she'd had much choice as executor of her father's estate, as well as the inheritor of said estate. The house had needed work. She could have paid someone, but that would have come with its own anxieties.

"Mom?" she said when her mother answered her call.

"Hi, sweetie. Is everything okay?"

"No. I don't know what I'm doing here."

"Oh honey. It's hard. It's so, so hard. Do you need me to come up?"

"I don't know." She sniffled and wiped at her eyes. "I finished painting, and now I don't know what to do."

"Take it easy for a few days. Take Nell to the beach and read a book, or see your new friends. Then think about contacting a real estate agent to help you."

A real estate agent. Someone who would set a price on what was left of her father's life.

"Do I have to?" She sounded like a child.

"You don't have to do anything, love. Your stepdad and I can take care of everything if you want us to."

"I just . . ." She took a deep breath. "I just can't believe he's really gone."

"I know."

"I thought it was supposed to get easier."

"It does, and it will, but easier doesn't mean easy."

"Do you ever miss him?"

A long pause echoed on the line.

"Parts of him. I miss the way he used to make me laugh. I miss listening to him play guitar. I miss how much he adored you."

Emilia heard the unspoken litany of the things she didn't miss. The drinking. The infidelity. The unpredictability of his moods and his refusal to change. Ben, her stepfather, was a much better husband, and he'd been a more reliable father.

"Tell Ben I say hi."

"He misses you. You should give him a call."

"Sure." She couldn't call Ben, though. Not about this. It seemed unfaithful somehow.

"I still don't like you being all alone up there."

"Anna Maria said she'd come up some time."

"Good." Another pause. "Anna mentioned you met someone."

Emilia sighed. "Of course she did. She spends too much time with toddlers."

"Are you sure you're ready to date again?"

"Mom. I'm not dating anyone."

"Okay, okay. Would you tell me if you were?"

"Mom."

"Ben offered to egg Hannah's car for you."

"Ben?" Gentle Ben, threatening violence on her behalf? She smiled into the phone. "Tell him he needs to work on his aim first."

"Have you thought at all about going back to work? I'm not pushing, just curious. You're so talented, Emmy. There's so much you can still do if you don't want to go back into practice."

"I've been trying not to think about it."

"Ben suggested business school. You could go into veterinary management. You'd still get to be a doctor, but you could own your own business."

"I'll think about it when I've decided to stop *not* thinking about it."

"Or horses. You used to love horses. Couldn't you switch to large animal? You'd be like James Herriot!"

Her mother's idea of large animal medicine remained firmly rooted in the James Herriot books she'd read to Emilia as a child, despite Emilia's best attempts to persuade her that times—and medicine—had changed.

136

"It's a whole different field. I haven't thought about equine medicine in years, mom. I can't just switch."

"Why not?"

"Because . . ." Morgan's face rose in her mind. "Because that's not who I am."

"You can be whoever you want to be."

Emilia laughed without humor. "I can't. Not with my loan. And thinking about going back to work makes me . . ." she couldn't finish the sentence.

"You promised to call me if you felt yourself going downhill again." She heard the panic in her mother's voice.

"I'm not. The meds are working, and it's nice to be out of the city. I talk with Shanti twice a week. I'm okay. Just overwhelmed."

"Of course you're overwhelmed, love. Remember what your father used to say?"

"Day by day," they said in unison.

"So go and enjoy this day. Get out of that house. Eat something. You are eating, right?"

"Yes, Mom. I'm eating."

"I love you."

"I love you too." She slid the tear-dampened phone into her pocket.

"What do you want to do today, Nell?" Big brown eyes widened hopefully at her tone. "Should we go for a sail? A real sail?"

The dog tilted her head.

"Don't worry. I bought you a life jacket."

The skiff didn't leak as she rowed them out to the sailboat with a bag packed with water, snacks, and a nautical radio. Nell sat in the prow with her ears perked forward, apparently accepting the fate that her human insisted on repeating this strange activity. The creak of the oars settled the feeling in the pit of her stomach. *This, at least, I can do.* She secured the skiff to the mooring without incident, hoisted Nell into the boat, and stood on the deck of the *Emilia Rosa* with the wind in her hair and salt on her lips.

"Okay," she said to herself as she untied the ropes that bound the mainsail. Hoisting the boom had been her father's job, often accompanied by a few choice curses when the sail jammed, while she'd been in charge of raising the jib. She eyed the sail with trepidation. The lines had been coiled and stowed neatly. She gave an experimental tug on the sheet, hoping the sail would thread through the groove without catching. It rose slowly. Wind snatched at it, and Nell slunk into the storage space beneath the bow as the boom swung back and forth. Emilia's arms strained, but at last the sail made it to the top, and she secured the line on its cleat and stepped onto the prow to raise the jib.

The line flew through her fingers in its eagerness to unfurl the smaller sail. Balanced on the prow, she felt thirteen again, almost too old to pretend to be a pirate, but still thrilling to feel the deck rocking beneath her and the canvas billowing all around her.

Both sails snapped loudly in the wind. Emilia reached down to loose the boat from the mooring, then paused. She'd promised Morgan she would tell someone before she went out for her first real sail.

I don't owe her anything, and I have an engine.

She also had a boom. If she got knocked out cold and fell into the Atlantic, she'd want someone to rescue Nell and retrieve her body. She sat with her legs over the side, the mooring framed beneath her bare feet, and pulled out her phone.

ER: *Hi. Taking the boat out.*

She deleted the text and tried again.

ER: *The skiff is seaworthy. I'm taking the boat for a sail.*

What else could she say? *I've been thinking about kissing you every minute of every day since I last saw you?* That would complicate everything. *I want you and it scares the hell out of me* would be honest, as would, *I really shouldn't get involved with anyone right now, but maybe you should come over tonight.*

She deleted her text again.

ER: Remember how I promised you I'd let someone know the first time I went for a real sail?

She hit send. Morgan was probably busy. Waiting for a response could take an hour at the least. She was about to add more when Morgan began typing.

MD: *I do.*

ER: *If you don't hear from me by 5:00, will you come looking?*

MD: *Of course.*

ER: *And if I survive, would you want to grab dinner with me tonight?*

The three little dots danced for a full minute before Morgan replied.

MD: *I'd love that.*

ER: *Great. See you later.*

She shoved her phone deep in her pocket, untied the sailboat, and leapt back in time to grab the lines and settle them more tightly around the winch as she turned the tiller to catch the wind.

Nell raised her head from her bed of cushions in alarm as the boat took off. Emilia let some of the tension out of the sail to reduce how much they keeled. The rush that came with skimming over the water filled her chest with an almost painful lightness. The harbor, with its lobster pots and lobster boats, opened its arms to them as she tacked down the Damariscotta River, doing her best to avoid the ledges and snags, past East Boothbay and Rutherford Island until the waters of Johns Bay met the Atlantic. Her hand knew which way to tack. She'd worried the instinct might have faded over the years, but instead it roared to life as if her father's hand still lay over hers on the tiller.

Wind whipped around the point past Christmas Cove. She braced her feet against the opposite deck as the boat keeled sharply. Blue-green water hurled itself past them. She'd run her hand through this same water as a child, enjoying the insistent pull of it against her fingers. Small swells rolled beneath the hull. Nell glared at her, then crept closer, her long nose burrowing beneath Emilia's leg for reassurance.

"You've got your life jacket on," she told the dog. This did not seem to comfort her. Sighing in regret, she released more of the sheet and slowed their progress. The deck leveled. "Better?"

Nell sat up and looked around.

"See? Not so bad. Look, Nell, a water puppy!"

The seal's head bobbed a few yards away. Nell, however, didn't notice. She'd lifted her nose to sniff the salt breeze, and Emilia kissed the faint roundness of her muzzle.

I missed this, she realized as they sailed on. Her father's drinking had worsened in the years following the divorce. After she'd made the mistake of telling her mother about how he'd left the house, drunk, to pick up more beer with her in the car, she'd been forbidden from staying with him for more than a few nights. Even that had been negotiated with tears and solemn oaths from her father. Her Maine summers had ended, replaced with more mundane, if equally fraught, summers at home in the Boston suburbs with her friends.

What if she'd contrived some way to keep coming? Would Morgan have eventually noticed her? Would the pressure of guilt for those lost years with her father weigh any less?

Probably not. Even if she had caught Morgan's eye, she still would have gone to Tufts for vet school, and she still would have met Hannah. She tried to feel something about her ex's potential infidelity or about the breakup. The wall that had cut her off from her life still separated her from those emotions. Or, maybe the greater grief had simply eclipsed them. Hannah still lived. Her father did not. Tears, snatched by the wind, added more salt to her cheeks as windblown sea spray—spindrift, her father had called it—flung itself against the hull.

Lillian glanced up at Morgan from the kitchen counter. "You look nice."

"I showered."

"No, I mean the outfit."

Morgan examined herself. Dark jeans. The black work boots she tried to keep cleaner than her other pair. A white button-up rolled at the sleeves. "It's not fancy."

"Hang on." Lillian wiped her hands clean of whatever leafy

green vegetable she'd been murdering and rounded the island. "Your collar," she said as she straightened it.

"Thanks."

"Where are you off to?"

"Dinner with a friend."

Lillian gave her a flat look. "Does this friend happen to be named Emilia?"

"I'll see you later."

Moving in with her friends had kept her afloat after Kate left. It also saved money, which she needed to do if she ever wanted to pay off her student loans. Sometimes, however, it didn't seem worth it.

Her small pickup growled to life without offering any complaints about her neglect. She'd started it up a few times over the past months, but since she was always working, it usually made more sense to drive the clinic truck. Peeling out of the driveway without a ton of equipment in the bed made her feel like the vehicle had wings.

She'd told Emilia to meet her at the dock. She hadn't told her where they were going. Warm, mid-June air blew in through the truck's open window as she veered around potholes. Hopefully, few tourists would be out. Tuesday nights weren't exactly like the weekend rush hour.

Emilia's car sat in the lot, but she didn't see Emilia. Maybe meeting here was a bad idea, she thought, remembering the last time they'd been in the boathouse together. She parked, still looking around, and passed through the danger zone and out onto the wharf.

A woman leaned against the rail. Her dark hair blew around her shoulders, and the simple navy blue dress hugged her body as the wind caught it like a sail. Morgan froze. The dress was casual. It was the sort of summer dress women wore all the time, she reasoned with herself. It wasn't Emilia's fault that she looked a thousand times better in it than any woman Morgan had ever seen. Granted, Emilia looked good in everything.

Emilia looked up and waved as Morgan ordered her feet to

continue their approach. She leaned against the rail beside Emilia, feeling impossibly gawky and out of her league, and stared at the ocean below. "See anything down there?"

"Yeah. Remind me never to fall in again. I just saw a crab big enough to eat my foot."

"Alternatively, we could eat him. Do you like seafood?"

"I like all food."

"My kind of woman." Belatedly, she realized how that might sound.

"I haven't eaten here in ages. Half the restaurants I know are gone."

"Ever been to Sally's?"

Emilia frowned. "I don't think so."

"Then that's where we're going." She set off down the ramp that led to the dock but paused when she realized Emilia had not followed.

"We're not driving?"

"Technically, yes, we are. We're just driving a boat."

Morgan gave up trying not to watch Emilia as she walked down the ramp. Emilia navigated the slight incline in a pair of sensible flats, her feet sure and her hand lightly brushing the railing as she looked out over the water. *She's letting me look,* Morgan realized with a jolt. She had no idea what that meant. Surely Emilia wouldn't invite her to dinner only to push her away? Then again, what did Morgan know about what Emilia would or wouldn't do? *Stevie was right. I'm going to get hurt either way.*

"Do you want to row out with me or should I come back for you?" she asked to clear her head.

Emilia scrutinized Morgan's skiff. "Is there a hole in yours?"

"Not last I checked."

"Then I'll come with you. Unless, of course, you want me to row?" She arched a dark brow.

"Would you like to?"

"Would you let me? Last I checked, you had zero faith in my boating skills."

"You made a strong first impression."

"*Annnnd* I'm rowing." Emilia stepped into Morgan's skiff and snapped the oarlocks into place before Morgan could protest. *You deserve that*, she told herself.

Sitting in the back of her own rowboat unsettled her. More unsettling was the proximity it brought her to Emilia, who maneuvered them away from the dock with none of the awkwardness Morgan had noted that first day.

"You've been practicing," she said to distract herself. The neckline of Emilia's dress, while modest when Emilia stood upright, dipped each time she leaned into the oars. Morgan threaded her useless fingers together and did her best to pretend she hadn't noticed.

"That, or I set the bar very low. Tell me if I'm about to hit anything."

"You're clear. Head a little toward starboard."

"Why not just say right?"

"We're in a boat. The boat's right side doesn't change, but if I say right, you might not know if I meant my right or your right. That, and I can only think of left and right in terms of patient charts."

"Really?"

"Why do you sound like that is worse than midnight cheese theft?" What she didn't say was that Ray had taught Morgan port and starboard. Using the terms with his daughter felt right, but she didn't want his ghost rising between them. The muscles in Emilia's arms shifted smoothly beneath the sleeves of the dress, and her tanned skin burned a warm gold in the evening light.

"Where is this restaurant?"

"Near Pemaquid. It's faster to get there by boat, and I'm on call tonight."

"There are plenty of restaurants in town."

"But you've never been to Sally's. It's my duty to change that. And here we are." She held out her hand to catch the side of her boat as Emilia startled and looked over her shoulder. They clambered in, careful to account for the other's weight. "I can get the mooring."

"I got it," said Emilia, who still had the skiff's bowline in her hand. She knelt in the prow. Morgan abandoned trying to be polite and settled for keeping her hands firmly to herself. The dress hugged Emilia's ass, and again she got the sense that Emilia knew exactly what she was doing. Sweat pricked her palms.

"Thanks." She cleared her throat. Her voice appeared to have dropped an octave. "Uh, it might get chilly on the water. I've got a spare jacket on the boat if you need it."

"I'll just stand back here with you," said Emilia as she stepped behind the shelter of the windshield.

Morgan started the engine. A spectacular evening spilled over the harbor. They had maybe an hour before sunset, but the running lights on the boat would see them home safely, and she'd checked the forecast.

"How was your sail?"

"Incredible. I think Nell hated it, though. Or maybe she just hated her life jacket."

"It looked like a good wind."

"It was." Emilia's hair flew into her face as she turned to grin at Morgan. "I forgot."

"Forgot what?" She had to raise her voice over the roar of the engine as she picked up speed. The fastest way to get to Pemaquid Harbor was cutting underneath the South Bristol bridge, but she wanted to go the long way around.

"How fucking amazing this is." Emilia's gesture included the ocean, horizon, and sky.

"Isn't it?" She wanted to put her arm around Emilia so badly it made her jaw ache. *She could be about to tell you she just wants to be friends*, her mind warned. *You need to be prepared for that.* Emilia shivered as wind straight off the ocean sliced up the river.

"You sure you don't want a jacket?" Morgan asked.

"It feels good," Emilia shouted back, but she took a step closer to Morgan.

She could slow the boat and insist on grabbing a coat. That, however, might tempt Emilia to move away, and so she drove on, past summer cottages and darkening pines. It was nearly high tide, and the golden water lapped at the rocky shoreline, hiding the ledges and snags beneath the surface.

Emilia never came so close that she invited Morgan's arm, but her hair whipped the back of Morgan's neck and her hip rested against Morgan's in a way she didn't think someone about to ask for distance would permit. Morgan pointed out her favorite parts of the landscape, but mostly sailing along in companionable silence, as talking over the thrum of the engine was difficult. Porpoises surfaced ahead and chased each other into the pooling gold of the sun's reflection. Emilia leaned away to get a closer look, but she returned to Morgan's side, and the warmth of her thigh brought more color into the world than Morgan remembered ever noticing.

Sally's restaurant came into view too soon. Perched on a wharf hanging out over the water, the light from its windows always made Morgan think of the sort of kitschy seaside paintings she never bought but secretly enjoyed when she passed them in any one of the art galleries that had sprung up along the coast in recent years. Flower boxes lined the restaurant's railings, and the "Cleat and Eat" sign attracted people from the summer cottages later on in the season. Now, though, only a few boats occupied the dock, and Morgan slid her boat into an empty berth.

"This is Sally's?"

"Best clam chowder in Maine. Everything's good here, and fresh."

She watched Emilia take in the cozy restaurant and the quiet cove beyond, wishing she didn't care quite so much whether or not Emilia liked the place.

"How did I not know about this?"

"It's harder to get to by sailboat, and a real pain to get to by car."

"I love it." She turned to Morgan with the most open expression Morgan had seen on her face. "Thank you."

"No problem. You can't live here and not get the Sally's experience, even if you're just here for a little while." While she kept her words light, her heart felt heavy as an anchor.

Emilia walked at her side up the ramp. Her hand brushed Morgan's several times, and each time she managed not to twine her fingers through Emilia's, but it was a close thing.

"Do you want to eat outside or inside? It's getting a little chilly," said Morgan.

Emilia looked like the decision pained her.

"The restaurant isn't going anywhere. I can always bring you back later in the summer."

If there is a later.

"Inside, then," said Emilia, although she hesitated one more time as she looked at the wooden tables by the water.

The air inside Sally's hit them with a wall of warm steam from the kitchen. Morgan explained that they placed their order first, then chose a table, and brought Emilia to the counter. The menu listed the seasonal offerings. Lobster, oysters, clams, scallops, catch of the day, crab, chowder, and the usual assortment of fried American cuisine. If Emilia stuck around, Morgan thought perhaps she'd take her to the high-end Italian restaurant that served squid ink pasta and overpriced wines, just for the pleasure of staring at her across a candlelit table, but Sally's had its own charm.

Emilia ordered a bowl of chowder after some deliberation. Morgan, grinning at the older woman behind the counter, ordered the same, along with a side of steamed clams and two beers.

"Glad to see you, Dr. Donovan," said the woman as she took Morgan's card.

"You don't—" Emilia began.

"You got drinks last time. How's your flock doing, Sue?"

"Oh, the usual. Lambs all good this year. I'll have you out soon to take a look at them, along with Bruce."

Bruce was Sue's livestock guardian dog, although the dog was so old that the only real deterrent from predators he provided was his bark.

"Client?" Emilia asked as they sat at a small table.

"Yeah. She has a flock of Jacob sheep."

"Are those the ones with the double horns?"

"Someone paid attention in class," said Morgan.

"I wanted to go into mixed practice when I was in vet school."

"What changed?" She tread carefully, remembering the pain on Emilia's face the last time she'd spoken about her career. Emilia took a drink before answering.

"Do you really want to know?"

"When you put it like that, yes."

"I fell in love with one of my professors."

Morgan tensed. "Was it mutual?"

"I thought so at the time. She got me into shelter medicine before she called things off. Then I met my ex, Hannah, but—I don't know. I think I went into shelter medicine partly to spite Thao."

"Your professor?"

"Yeah. Toward the end she told me I wasn't cut out for it. Turns out she was right."

"You couldn't have known that, though."

"Couldn't I? Come on, didn't you have at least one professor who warned you shelter medicine wasn't for everyone?"

Morgan rocked back in her chair to evade the question.

"Anyway," Emilia continued, "I don't even know if I want to practice anymore."

"Did something happen? If you don't mind me asking." Just because she thought she could guess didn't mean she didn't want to hear the truth from Emilia herself.

"No, it's okay. And probably better that you know." Emilia's mouth twisted bitterly. "I'd been having a hard time for a while. Everything I did was either euthanasia or duct tape doctoring. None of the shelters ever had enough money to actually treat their patients. I just wanted to practice actual medicine once in a while, you know? Then Dad died, and I just . . ." she trailed off.

"I'm so sorry, Emilia."

"Hannah left me while I was in a treatment facility."

"That's shitty." It was more than shitty. Morgan wondered how hard it would be to find out where this Hannah lived.

"Yeah. She's not a bad person, just incapable of understanding human weakness."

"You sure that doesn't make her a bad person?" She wanted to reach out to comfort Emilia, but that half-feral edge had returned to Emilia's eyes, and Morgan worried she might bolt if she touched her.

"It's how she does what she does, I think. She's in shelter medicine, too. Nothing gets to her. I thought I was like that, too."

"I'm glad you're not." Morgan hated losing patients. That was part of what kept her on call night after night, and part of the reason, ultimately, that Kate had left her.

"Basically, what I'm saying is that your first impression of me was pretty accurate."

"Angry and wet?"

"Drowning."

"Hey." Morgan couldn't stop herself from cupping Emilia's face in her hand. "You're not drowning. You patched your boat, remember? And you're alive."

Emilia leaned her cheek against Morgan's hand. "Alive."

"Sometimes staying alive is the bravest thing you can do," said Morgan, thinking of the colleagues who had lost that fight.

"You're a good friend, Morgan."

Friend. She smiled past the pain that word caused and gently withdrew her hand.

Sue called their order number from the counter, and she rose to retrieve it. It should not have come as a blow. Hadn't she been the one who kept saying that Emilia needed a friend, not complications? *I can be that.* She picked up the tray, but her appetite had abandoned her, and the freshly baked bread and creamy, steaming chowder no longer held any appeal.

"Morgan," Emilia said as Morgan sat back down and served their food. Her voice sounded tight and worried.

"Eat first."

"I don't think I can. And it's probably too hot anyway."

Morgan braced herself. "Okay. Then we should probably talk."

"Yeah."

Morgan drank some of her beer, wondering if Emilia expected her to begin.

"First off," said Emilia, "what you did was totally unfair."

"Huh?" Morgan blinked in surprise.

"This isn't just my call, and you can't put this all on me."

"I didn't want you to feel any pressure. I didn't—"

"Really? Because to me it just looks like you don't want to take responsibility."

"That's not it at all."

"Are you sure?" The challenge blazed in Emilia's eyes.

"Yes," She wondered if there was any truth to the accusation despite her disavowal.

"So you know what you want out of this." Emilia turned the question into a statement.

"I want to do whatever is right for you."

Emilia shook her head. "That is not what I asked."

Morgan held her stare and felt her face flushing with embarrassment and annoyance. She didn't deserve this attack. Did she?

"Emilia," she said quietly into those flashing eyes. "Please don't make me say it."

Emilia tore her small loaf of bread in half and broke eye contact. "I think this is probably a mistake."

Morgan composed her face and prepared herself to say whatever she needed to get through the rest of the evening. Perhaps she'd receive a call from the clinic, giving her a graceful exit. Coming to Sally's had been stupid. Now she had to face a boat ride home with Emilia.

"But I can't stop thinking about you," Emilia finished.

Morgan froze.

"I can't be friends with you, Morgan. I'm an emotional train wreck, and my therapist would probably kill me if she could see inside my head."

"I'm confused," Morgan admitted.

Emilia toyed with the hunk of bread in her hand. "Are you going to make *me* say it?"

"Yes."

"Fine." Emilia dropped the bread into her chowder and lowered her voice. "I can't be friends with you, because when I look at you, all I can think about is how much I wanted to fuck you against the boathouse wall. Happy?"

Morgan's smile threatened to split her face in two. "Yes."

"Good. Now I want to try this chowder."

Morgan watched in amazement as Emilia's blush spread across her cheeks. Emilia's words repeated themselves in her mind. *I wanted to fuck you against the boathouse wall.* That was suddenly all she could think about, too.

"Oh my god, this is good," Emilia said as she took her first bite.

Morgan watched Emilia close her eyes as she tasted the chowder. Her head spun. Too many thoughts flashed across her brain, but none found purchase save for one: Emilia wanted her.

She took a bite of her own chowder to prevent her mouth from hanging open in shock. The creamy base exploded on her tongue, warm and spiced and redolent of potatoes and fresh pepper, and yet she tasted these things like afterthoughts. Her heart seemed to be having trouble remembering its job, and a slow heat unfurled in her core—the kind of heat not even a plunge in Arctic waters could dispel. Emilia wanted her, and nothing in Morgan's experience had prepared her for the strength of her reaction to that confession. Emilia continued to praise Sally's kitchen and staff while she met Morgan's gaze shyly across the table.

You, Morgan thought. *You are going to wreck me.*

It was dark when she led Emilia back down the ramp to the boat. High tide had receded, and the steepened slope of the ramp gave her a convenient excuse to put her hand on Emilia's waist, though this made it challenging to concentrate on her own footing.

Once onboard, she pulled two flannel jackets from the boat's small storage cubby and handed one to Emilia. It hung loosely around her shoulders. She would have kissed her right then if another group of diners had not chosen that moment to join them on the dock. At least her pager hadn't gone off yet.

Moonlight illuminated their way across the bay toward South Bristol. Emilia stood behind her without speaking and wrapped her arms around Morgan's waist, resting her chin on her shoulder. The rightness of it reverberated with the humming of the engine. She kept the boat at a lower throttle on the way back. Starlight spotted the surf, and the smooth water unfurled the moon's path before them.

Emilia's lips brushed her neck. Morgan's hands tightened on the wheel, and her breath hitched. She felt Emilia smile, and then her lips closed over the sensitive skin above Morgan's shoulder and it took all her concentration to keep them on course. She swore under her breath.

"This is cruel, you know that, right?" she said when Emilia untucked her shirt.

Emilia's nails trailed over her stomach in response. Her muscles tensed beneath them, and she willed Emilia not to stop as her hands traced the hem of her jeans. Then Emilia's nails dragged up over the planes of her abs and across the fabric of her bra.

"Fuck, Emilia," she said into the wind. She eased the throttle forward, and the boat picked up speed. Emilia laughed in her ear.

She groaned when Emilia's hands paused again at her belt. Half of her wanted to stop her, wanted to turn regardless of the speeding boat and pull Emilia to the deck. The more assertive half stood rigid, her breath coming in gasps as Emilia eased her belt buckle open, followed by the top button of her jeans, and then slid her hands back up Morgan's stomach and under the wire of her bra.

If we crash before she touches me, I'll never rest in peace.

Emilia's lips closed over her ear as her palms cupped Morgan's breasts. Her thumbs brushed over her nipples with excruciating slowness. Morgan saw the distant lights of the bridge and prayed no other boats were around.

Keeping one hand on Morgan's left breast, Emilia's other hand drew a line down Morgan's stomach to the open front of her pants and toyed with the waistband of her briefs. Morgan took one hand off the wheel and reached behind her to grab hold of any part of

Emilia she could reach. The hem of Emilia's dress met her fingers, and she slid her hand underneath just as Emilia eased one finger beneath the waistband of her briefs and over the sensitive skin below. She gripped Emilia's thigh to keep herself from falling.

"Please," she begged.

Emilia's fingers tightened on Morgan's nipple as she trailed her other hand over Morgan's aching clit. The shudder of pleasure made the water briefly vanish behind her closed eyes, but she forced herself to pay attention to the ocean and not to the insistent, mirroring circles Emilia traced over her nipple and center.

Sheer willpower kept her climax at bay. Emilia seemed to sense this as they passed beneath the bridge and up the river, until at last they entered the no wake zone of Seal Cove and she stroked lower, teasing Morgan's opening with every dip of her fingers.

"Wait," Morgan said. "I can't moor us if—oh fuck, Emilia." Her hips bucked as Emilia's first two fingers curled inside her, urging her closer, each stroke temporarily blinding her. Emilia bit the skin below Morgan's jaw and increased her tempo. Still half-blind, Morgan held on to the steering wheel as her knees gave out, and the only other thing keeping her upright was Emilia's hand. She managed to avoid collision with other watercraft by instinct alone until, finally, they drew even with the mooring. Emilia removed her hand to catch the line, leaving Morgan shaking against the wheel.

The harbor lights barely reached them out here. As she switched off the ignition, she wondered if she would have even cared if they did. Emilia straightened from securing the bowline. Her lips parted as Morgan caught her around the waist, and her hands fumbled at Morgan's pants again.

"Nope." She grabbed Emilia's wrists. Emilia struggled against her grip and bit Morgan's lower lip in frustration. Then, abruptly, she stopped fighting. Morgan loosed her hold and buried her fingers in Emilia's wind-snarled hair.

She didn't realize she'd been outmaneuvered until the back of her knees hit the captain's chair. Emilia's tongue danced across hers, distracting her again, and she sank onto the cushion.

Moonlight lit Emilia's face as she gazed down at Morgan with a triumphant smirk. She straddled Morgan in a slow, fluid motion that hitched the fabric of her dress up her thighs.

"Do you have any idea how fucking gorgeous you are?" Morgan asked as her hands explored the exposed skin. Emilia arched her back as Morgan cupped her ass, and she leaned in to kiss Emilia's taut nipples through the fabric.

"God, Morgan." Emilia tugged the collar of her dress down over one shoulder to bare the black bra beneath. Morgan didn't need further instructions. She teased Emilia's nipple free with her tongue, sucking in time to the jerk of Emilia's hips against her. The swell of breast filled her mouth as Emilia pulled her head closer, and she kissed down the valley between them. Emilia gasped in frustration until Morgan took her other nipple in her mouth. She cried out then, not loud enough to carry over the water, but enough to bring Morgan close to climax once more. She needed to be inside Emilia. She wanted to tease Emilia the way Emilia had teased her, though she was loath to leave off running her hands down Emilia's legs. However, when she pushed past the slick fabric of Emilia's underwear and felt her swollen clit, she changed her mind. *No teasing.* She needed her now.

Emilia grabbed her hand. For a moment, Morgan thought she'd made a mistake. Then Emilia plunged Morgan's fore and middle fingers inside herself, crying out again. Morgan wrapped her other arm around Emilia's waist to support her, still teasing her nipple, and eased deeper into her.

"Harder," Emilia panted in her ear.

Morgan came.

The shock waves rippled through her as Emilia rode her hand. When she added a third finger Emilia muffled a scream in her neck, her hips pushing Morgan in deeper still. She felt the first beginning of orgasm quivering through Emilia.

Not yet, she thought, and slowed her pace.

"God, Morgan, please don't stop."

"Come here."

Emilia's lips met hers with an openness that begged Morgan to take everything. She swirled her thumb over Emilia's clit as she eased her back up. Emilia whimpered into Morgan's mouth.

"Another," Emilia gasped.

"Are you sure?"

"I'm fucking sure."

Morgan entered her with her fourth finger, awed as Emilia expanded and then contracted tightly around her hand. Emilia broke off the kiss and tilted her head back, her nails digging into Morgan's shoulders, hips rocking faster and faster as she took charge of her own climax.

Sweet fucking Jesus. Morgan watched in awe as Emilia came.

They breathed heavily together for a few minutes. Morgan periodically moved her hand, eliciting further spasms and gasps, until Emilia put a quelling hand on her arm with an almost pained expression of bliss.

Leaving her almost physically hurt Morgan. She wanted to spend days inside this woman, and the sudden eviction felt brutally unfair.

"You. Are. Incredible." Emilia punctuated each word with an open-mouthed kiss that made Morgan remember other things she could do to Emilia Russo. She didn't say anything in response. *Couldn't* say anything. Instead, she slipped both hands back over Emilia's ass, trailing some of her wetness along the cleft between her cheeks. Emilia squirmed and moaned Morgan's name.

"I need to taste you," Morgan said.

Emilia bit her ear, not hard enough to hurt, but with enough assertiveness to get her full attention.

"Get on the deck of the boat." Emilia commanded. "Now."

Morgan obeyed, half carrying Emilia down with her. The rough texture of the deck against her back only heightened her arousal. Every nerve ending hummed, sensitive to changes in the wind, the salt in the air, and Emilia still straddling her hips. She began unbuttoning Morgan's shirt while Morgan watched, transfixed by the way her tousled hair softened her face.

"You nearly killed me the other day." Emilia parted the shirt and ran her gaze appreciatively over Morgan's stomach.

"Sorry about that."

"Mhmm." Emilia lowered herself to lie across Morgan's legs, kissing the waistline of her pants with languid strokes of her tongue. "You should come with a warning label."

"Speak for yourself." She gasped as Emilia's tongue dipped lower. "And didn't I say *I* wanted to taste *you*?"

Emilia tugged Morgan's pants down in response and kissed Morgan through her briefs. Further protest died in her throat. Expertly, Emilia slid the last barrier between them over Morgan's hips. The sound of her own ragged breathing drowned out the waves. Warm air drifted across her clit, and she shuddered. Emilia's weight pinned her legs, and she feared she might burst if Emilia didn't take her in her mouth. Another breath, and then Emilia's tongue ran everywhere but where she wanted. She tried tangling her hands in Emilia's hair to direct her, but Emilia simply stopped teasing her entirely until Morgan loosened her grip. Each thwarted attempt to seize control only turned her on more, and she was just about to point out that the ocean was supposed to be on the outside of the damn boat when Emilia's tongue pushed deep inside her.

The temperature of the cool night air rocketed several thousand degrees. Morgan uttered something she wasn't sure was English as Emilia plunged her tongue in again, then slid out, and it was replaced by Emilia's hand as her tongue at last caressed Morgan's clit.

Stars shone inside her eyelids as Emilia sucked in long, hot strokes, the tip of her tongue fluttering over her at the end of each one. Her fingers moved equally slowly, pushing up against Morgan and holding her there, every molecule centered on Emilia's touch. She had to know she could make Morgan come in a second, but she kept her movements torturously slow, changing rhythms each time Morgan's hips bucked too quickly, until the horrifying sound of her pager's buzz cut through her shredded breathing.

"You've got to be fucking kidding me." She groaned as she opened her eyes.

Emilia chose that moment to take Morgan fully in her mouth, running her tongue along her clit faster and faster while her fingers drove Morgan up and over the edge, then up again. She came once and then a second time when Emilia refused to stop.

It took several minutes for the sound of her pager to register again. Emilia lay against her chest, gazing down at her with soft eyes. "Hey there."

"You," Morgan began, but she had no words to describe the way her body felt, except that Emilia had pinned Morgan's soul beneath her and called to it by name.

"I felt rushed," said Emilia.

"I'll let you try again anytime you want."

"Let me know when you're not on call," said Emilia as she sat up. "I promise you, it won't be over quickly. Now go save a life."

Chapter Eleven

Emilia's body ached pleasantly as she stretched the next morning, disturbing Nell out of a dream of running. Closing her eyes against the sunlight, she lay back on her pillow.

Morgan.

She pressed her bruised lips and savored the ache. When was the last time she'd had sex like that?

Have you ever had sex like that? her mind countered.

It didn't matter. Last night was all she wanted to think about. She conjured up the memory of Morgan lying on the deck of her boat with moonlight painting her fair skin. And her hands. Emilia turned her face against the pillow and let out a wistful sigh.

No. She'd never had sex like that before, especially not the first time. The way her body opened up for Morgan would have alarmed her if it hadn't felt so good. *Too good.* She grimaced as she realized how wet she'd gotten at the thought.

I'm hungry, she told her body, *and I want coffee.*

Ten minutes and two orgasms later, neither of which were even remotely as satisfying as last night's, she roused Nell and padded to the kitchen. She managed to get a cup of coffee and a slice of toast down before her phone rang.

Anna Maria. She put it on speaker and poured herself a second cup of coffee as her sister's voice filled the kitchen.

"Guess what?" her stepsister asked.

"Good morning to you, too."

"Is it still morning? Kids got me up at four. Whatever. The good news is that I'm coming to see you."

"Awesome." Emilia tried to remember when—or if—she'd invited her.

"Mom said you were having a hard time."

"I was."

"Was?"

Trust Anna Maria to pick up on semantics. "Yeah."

"Spill."

"Jesus, Anna Maria, I just woke up."

"It's almost ten o'clock."

Emilia glanced at the clock on the stove and blinked. "Oops."

"Are you okay?"

"Yeah. How many cups of coffee have you had this morning? You sound like a parrot on speed."

"Very funny. I should be at your place in three hours."

"Wait, what? Today?"

"Blame Mom. She got worried and ordered me to check on you."

"Some warning might be nice, next time."

"Why? You got a house guest?"

"No. But I need to clean, and buy food—"

"Emmy. It's me. I don't give a shit about any of that."

"Hang on." She slurped down half her coffee and leaned against the counter. "Okay. Start over. You're driving up today, you don't have the twins, and Mark is . . .?"

"Taking a few days off. And I didn't want to overload you. I was planning on staying two nights if you're up for it, but you can kick me out sooner. I just need a photo of us together to send to Mom as proof."

"The worst part about all of this is feeling like I'm sixteen again. Remind Mom I turned thirty last year, will you?"

"Funny how suicidal depression makes people protective," Anna Maria said a little too sharply.

The glow of last night faded. She couldn't really blame her mother or Anna Maria for their worry. "I'm sorry. Do I need to call Mom?"

158

"Please don't. I wasn't supposed to call you until I was ten minutes away."

"Thank you for not doing that."

"Anytime. Okay, go do whatever you need to do to roll out the red-carpet treatment for my imminent arrival. See you soon."

"Why, Nell?" she asked when Anna Maria had hung up. Nell wagged her tail from her spot in a pool of sunshine on the floor. She paused before putting her phone away.

ER: *Hope you got some sleep last night.*

Texting Morgan brought some of her good mood back. Humming, she hopped in the shower, and was rewarded with a response when she hopped back out.

MD: *A little. Want to keep me up again tonight?*

Dammit, Anna Maria. Her stomach tightened.

ER: *More than anything. Unfortunately, my sister is paying me a surprise visit. Can I see you when she leaves?*

MD: *Yes.*

ER: *You don't have to buy me dinner this time.*

MD: *Can I cook it for you?*

She pressed the phone to her forehead and took a steadying breath, wondering if she could manage to ditch Anna Maria tonight after all.

ER: *Only if you come to my place. I want you shirtless.*

MD: *You sure you're not free tonight?*

ER: *You're not ready to meet my sister.*

Briefly, she toyed with the idea of introducing Morgan to Anna Maria. "Hi, you're the fuckable one," Anna Maria would say. And then she would start asking questions, and Emilia didn't have any answers. *One day at a time.* She smiled at the emoji Morgan fired back and went to do battle with the guest bedroom.

Anna Maria's Subaru Forester pulled into the driveway a few hours later, playing the sort of music Emilia was positive she didn't listen to with kids in the car. Nell raced off the porch to greet her with leaping bounds that never quite managed to land on any physical part of the new arrival.

"At least someone's excited to see me," her sister said. Anna Maria and Emilia looked like they shared blood relatives, thanks to her stepfather's equally Italian heritage. The main difference between them lay in Anna Maria's larger chest, which she crushed Emilia into mercilessly.

"I can't breathe."

"You're too skinny. You're not eating enough."

"I am eating—"

"Don't worry, Mom sent lasagna, gnocchi, and some vegetable thing that looks like barf but tastes amazing. Oh, and half a thing of chocolate chip cookies."

"Half?"

"There may have been more a few hours ago."

"I see."

"So, this is it?" Anna Maria looked around, sweeping her dark hair into a sloppy bun.

"I forget you've never really been here. Yeah, I need to fix up the yard, but the inside is coming along."

"It's really nice. Mom always made it out to be so . . ."

"I know. Oh, and I hid the animal heads."

"Hid? You mean you didn't get rid of them? I'm not going to find one in my closet, am I, because I swear to god, Emmy, that isn't funny."

"But I saved some squirrels for you."

"You're kidding, right?"

"Yes, I'm kidding. Let me help you with your stuff."

Anna Maria opened the trunk, and Emilia balked.

"Please tell me all those coolers aren't for me."

"Yep. You have a freezer, right? Otherwise you're gonna have to throw a party."

"I have a freezer, but it's the normal kind, not a restaurant walk-in."

Emilia seized one end of a cooler and hauled it out of the car, irritation and affection vying for supremacy. Leave it to her mother to forestall any impending disaster with a wall of food.

Once the bulk of the edible matter had been stowed away and

Anna Maria's small suitcase huddled against the banister, Anna Maria collapsed into an armchair and leaned her head back.

"I love my children," she said, "but I cannot wait until they turn five."

"What's so special about five?"

"They'll use words besides 'no' and 'why.'"

"You'll miss this in a few years."

"Probably. Mark has so much more patience with them than I do. They're good kids. Monsters, but sweet when they want to be. I'll be crying because I miss them by the time I leave, but god it feels good to get away."

Emilia's phone vibrated. She glanced at it, hoping it was Morgan, but it was just a text from her mother.

"So," Anna Maria said, coming back to life. "What can I help you with while I'm here?"

Several dusty, tear-filled hours later, the remainder of the attic's population had found its way into the trash or the back of their cars to be donated, and Emilia stood in the doorway of her father's room with Anna Maria at her side. She'd left this room for last. Some of the boxes of things she'd decided to keep cluttered one corner, but the bed remained made in the same sheets, and the dresser and closet were still filled with her father's clothes.

"I can't do it," she said.

"You don't have to. You've got me. Have you thought about what you want to keep?"

Quite a few shirts and sweaters already mingled with her own clothes, but she'd grown accustomed to pulling out a piece of his clothing whenever her grief grew too hard to contain.

"All of it?"

"You can if you want to. But that's a lot of mismatched socks. Come sit." Anna Maria steered her to the bed, where she sat with her knees tucked under her chin while her sister opened drawers and rifled through the closet, taking inventory of the contents under her breath. She turned to Emilia when she finished. "I have a plan."

Emilia nodded to indicate her willingness to listen.

"If this were my dad, I'd want to keep things I could wear, right? Like this." She held up a faded flannel shirt. "So we leave anything like that for later and start with things you're less attached to, like boxers, socks, undershirts, pants, and shoes."

Emilia nodded again.

"And when we're done, I'll pour you a big glass of wine, feed you, and we'll call it a day, okay?"

"Okay." She wiped a rivulet of tears from her cheeks.

"Now. Let's start with these. Ooh, trout-patterned boxers? He was a man of taste."

"Do you ever think about what it would be like to end a day not smelling like an abscess?" Stevie asked as they pulled out of the Stevenson's barnyard, the mingling odors of pus and manure joining them in the cab of the truck. Kraken sat up and sniffed the air with interest.

"Honestly? No," said Morgan. "I've got to swing by my parents' house and check on a horse for my mom. Want to come?"

Stevie brightened. "Yes. I haven't seen your mom in ages."

Morgan's mother was in the barn feeding hay to her motley assortment of animals. She waved to them and dusted her hands off on her coveralls.

"Hey, Ma, how's the gang?"

Several sheep, a blind llama, and a spotted donkey raised their heads at her voice before they resumed nibbling on their forage. Her mother's horse, an old gelding named Bill, scratched his rear on the paddock gate at the end of the small barn. Horse hair flew into the air in clouds.

"Alive and well." She kissed Morgan's cheek. Shannon Donovan's short, curly hair was lighter than her daughter's, but they shared the same slate-blue eyes and straight nose. She also stood nearly as tall as her daughter, which left Stevie craning her neck more often than not in their company. Shannon extended her arms to Stevie. "And how's my favorite?"

"I'm right here, Mom," said Morgan.

"You're her daughter," said Stevie. "She has to love you. I'm special."

"Say hi to your father before you go. He's got some new lures he wants to show you."

"Hey, Ma, do you remember Ray Russo's daughter?"

"I remember seeing Francesca with a baby girl. Cute little thing. Looked just like Ray."

"She's in town for a bit to deal with his estate."

"Poor girl. Have you seen her?"

Stevie pulled a suggestive face behind Shannon's back.

"We're friends. She's got Ray's boat back in the water."

"You tell her she's welcome here anytime. I remember losing your grandfather when I was your age. No one's ever prepared for that. Be nice to the girl."

"Don't worry, Mrs. D.," said Stevie. "Morgan's taking good care of her."

Morgan quailed under the piercing stare her mother turned on her and vowed to throw a fresh pile of horse shit at Stevie the moment Shannon left the barn.

"Really? Then you should have her over here for dinner."

"She's busy dealing with Ray's house."

"That wasn't a request, Morgan."

"Ma," Morgan protested, "you can't force me to invite people I barely know over to your house. I'm not five."

"Morgan knows her pretty well," Stevie supplied helpfully. "We've had her over to our house a few times. I like her dog."

"I'll make that lamb pie you like."

"Seriously?" Morgan looked between her mother and Stevie.

"Morgan took her to Sally's the other night."

"I'm going to go check on the horse," she said, glaring at her friend.

The problem with knowing someone her entire life, she decided as she turned her back on the conspirators, was that Stevie felt more like a sister than a friend, right down to her inexplicable habit of throwing Morgan in front of the bus that was her mother.

Stevie was the second youngest of five, whereas Morgan was an only child, and she didn't have the survival skills to counter Stevie's attacks.

The thought of Emilia and Shannon in the same room made Morgan's skin prickle with unease. Shannon's lips thinned dangerously each time Kate came up in conversation, and Emilia didn't need to deal with the fallout of Morgan's previous relationship. Especially since Emilia wouldn't be sticking around for long. She tried to bury that thought.

"I'm going to kill you," she said in a conversational tone when Stevie came to join her.

"I'm sorry." Stevie's large blue eyes looked up at Morgan beseechingly.

"That was a dick move."

"Your mom's cool."

"My mother is the Irish goddess of vengeance."

"Well, it's not like you're dating Emilia."

"But now my mother thinks I am. Thanks for that, by the way."

"Why would she think that?"

"Morgan's taking good care of her," Morgan said in a high-pitched imitation of Stevie.

"Well you are. You take good care of everyone. Besides, it's not like you've slept with her."

Morgan lifted one of the gelding's hooves and prodded the frog, checking for tenderness.

"Wait," Stevie said, zeroing in on Morgan's silence. "You told me nothing happened at Sally's."

"He seems sound on this one." Morgan lowered the front hoof and moved to the back. "I'll have you run him for me in a minute just to check."

"Morgan."

She straightened, resting a hand on the horse's warm rump. Without looking at Stevie, she said, "I don't push you about Angie. Don't push me on this, Stevie."

Stevie circled around to face her with her arms folded. "You like her, don't you?"

"You know I do."

"No, I mean you really *like* her."

"Fuck off."

Stevie recoiled, but Morgan didn't care. She was tired of her friends' repeated attempts to push her toward Emilia. She didn't need pushing. She needed restraints, because falling for Emilia Russo had one possible outcome, and she'd only just recovered—barely—from the last time she'd had her heart broken.

Stevie didn't speak to her as she finished up her exam. Morgan left her with the horse and strode up to the house to say hello to her father—and to put out the dumpster fire her idiotic best friend had started.

"Over here," her father said when she entered the sunroom of her childhood home. He sat at the table surrounded by fly fishing lures, wires, and bits of feathers, string, and shiny beads. "Look at this."

A life-size dragonfly perched on wire legs on the table, spreading gossamer wings.

"That's beautiful," she told her beaming father.

"When's your boss going to hire a relief vet so we can go fishing?"

"Not soon enough." She collapsed into a chair.

"Want some tea?" her mother called from the kitchen.

"Sure, Ma."

"Stevie there?"

"No."

"Your mother says Ray's daughter is in town. Is she selling that house?"

"Probably." She explained Emilia's situation as best she could.

"I'm glad you've found time to make a new friend," her mother said as she set a mug of tea in front of Morgan and another by her husband. Morgan took note of the emphasis her mother put on the word *friend*.

"Stevie's full of shit, Ma. She's just a friend."

"What did Stevie say?" asked her father.

"Nothing, Dad."

"No one ever tells me anything," he said to his dragonfly.

"Hush your whining. I tell you everything you need to know," said Shannon.

"According to you." He winked at Morgan.

"I told Morgan to invite Ray's daughter here for dinner, and she got defensive."

"Embarrassed of your folks?"

"No, Dad. I just don't think overwhelming people is the best way to support them when they're already dealing with a lot."

"We're not overwhelming; we're hospitable," said Shannon.

"Fine. I'll ask her."

"Bring the rest of your crew if you want."

"And tell Lillian I need some new tomato starts," her father said. "Damn groundhogs."

"Sure." She felt her mother's worried eyes on her. "What, Ma?"

"You look tired, honey."

"I've been on call."

"Morgan." Shannon put her hand on her shoulder. "Burning yourself out doesn't prove anything to anyone."

"I don't have anything to prove."

Kate's name hovered unspoken between them.

"Just take care of yourself. That's all we're asking."

Stevie shut the truck door harder than necessary when they left and made it all the way back to the house before she turned in her seat. "Still want a beer?"

"Oh, you're speaking to me, now?"

"You were a jerk."

"Stevie—"

"Also I'm sorry I ratted you out to your mom."

Morgan laughed. This was one of the things she loved about Stevie: she didn't hold grudges. "And I'm sorry I snapped at you."

They stopped by the house. Angie wasn't home, so they settled for cajoling Lillian out of her sweatpants and into jeans and made their way to Stormy's.

"I've seen more of you this last month than I have in ages," Stormy said with a gratified smile when they walked in.

"Forced time off," said Morgan.

"Also Morgan was mean to me," Stevie said.

"Boifriend."

"She deserved it."

"Look at those baby blues." Stormy leaned over the counter and squeezed Stevie's cheeks. "She's the picture of innocence."

"Or the picture of Dorian Gray," said Lillian.

"Who's Dorian Gray?" Morgan looked between the three of them.

"It's a literary reference," Stevie said airily. "I wouldn't expect you to understand."

"Here's a reference for you," Morgan began, but Stormy scooted their usual drinks across the bar and Morgan had to concentrate on not letting the head of foam spill over. She had a suspicion Stormy had poured the beer badly on purpose.

"Go grab a table and I'll join you in a minute," Stormy said. "I've got customers."

Barely five minutes had passed when Stevie perked up, looking like a golden retriever with a squirrel in its sights. Morgan had a premonition this didn't bode well for her, and wished Angie had been able to join them to keep Stevie in check.

"Hey." Stevie nudged Morgan with her elbow. "Your friend's here with another woman."

"What?" Confused, she followed Stevie's meaningful gaze to the register, where Emilia and a woman with a curvier figure surveyed the menu. "Oh. That's her sister."

"We should say hello," said Lillian.

Stevie had already slid off her stool and sauntered over. Morgan experienced several temperature extremes as the blond ponytail bobbed away.

"You okay?" Lillian asked.

"Yeah," Morgan said in a croak. Even from here, she could see that Emilia's eyes were red as if she had been crying, and she wore an oversized man's sweater with leggings and a defeated set to her shoulders. Nell pressed herself close to her person and eyed the crowd dubiously. Morgan's heart leapt across the space between them as Emilia laughed at something Stevie said, then raised her eyes to look around the room until she found Morgan.

Fuck. Morgan smiled as best she could, remembering Emilia on the boat. At least, she thought, unable to look away, she wasn't a man. Hiding her desire was just a matter of keeping her hands to herself. Much harder to suppress was the surge of protectiveness that rose in her at the thought of Emilia crying.

Lillian stood and prodded Morgan's thigh. "Move it, lover boi."

"Look who I found," Stormy said with her irrepressible smile.

"Hi," said Emilia. She sent Morgan a look through her lashes that drowned the protectiveness in a much more basic emotion. "This is my sister, Anna Maria, and this is Morgan, Lillian, Stevie, and Stormy."

"So nice to meet you," Anna Maria said. Her gaze lingered on Morgan a moment longer than it did the others. "You should join us."

"Done," said Stevie.

"Only if we're not intruding," said Lillian.

Morgan raised her eyebrows at Emilia in a question. Emilia shrugged, as if to say, *too late now.*

Anna Maria placed her order and led their way to an open table. Her thick black hair swayed like Emilia's as she walked, but something about the assertive way in which she commandeered an extra chair from a nearby table reminded Morgan of a Jack Russell. She saw enough of the tiny terrors on her rounds to recognize the indomitable and slightly crazed air of a creature determined to bend the world to its will.

Stevie, Lillian, and Anna Maria sat, leaving two chairs side by side for Emilia and Morgan. She didn't think this was an accident.

"What do you think of Seal Cove? Is this your first time here?" Lillian asked Anna Maria.

Morgan tried to listen to her answer, but her body focused exclusively on Emilia's proximity. Their legs brushed beneath the small table, and she wanted to run her hands along Emilia's thighs again or, better yet, have them wrapped around her waist while she . . . *stop*, she scolded herself.

". . . change of pace," Anna Maria was saying.

"She's hiding from her children," Emilia explained.

"You have kids?" If Lillian were a dog, her ears would have perked toward heaven.

"Twins," said Anna Maria with grim satisfaction.

"How old?"

"Three. They say twos are terrible, but it's the threes you have to watch out for."

"I need to see pictures," said Lillian.

"And we've lost her," Emilia said to Morgan.

"Lil, too."

"What did you think of Sally's?" Stevie asked Emilia. Her face radiated innocence, and even Morgan doubted for a second that she had any ulterior motives.

"The food was amazing. Beautiful view, too."

Stevie's eyes flickered over at Morgan while her lips twitched in a suppressed smile.

"You went to Sally's?" Lillian looked up from Anna Maria's phone.

"What's Sally's?" asked Anna Maria.

Emilia placed her hand on Morgan's leg beneath the table and dug her nails in.

"Local restaurant," said Morgan. "Really good seafood."

"Yum." Anna Maria fixed Morgan with a charming, but predatory, smile. "What do you do, Morgan?"

The talk turned to Seal Cove Veterinary. Anna Maria asked thoughtful questions, and Stevie regaled her with several embarrassing stories about Morgan, which she tolerated when she saw the amused curve of Emilia's lips.

"Morgan knew my dad." Emilia's words steered the talk away from a deteriorating conversation about calving, which involved a detailed account of the time Morgan had her shoulder dislocated by a cow she'd been elbow-deep inside.

"What was he like?" Anna Maria's attention sharpened.

"You probably know better than I do," Morgan said. Emilia's hand now rested on her inner thigh, which made concentration increasingly difficult.

169

"I never got to know him." At their blank stares, she continued. "I'm Emmy's stepsister. My mom died when my brother and I were really little, so Emilia's mom basically raised me. Emilia went to see her dad without us."

At their puzzled looks, Emilia swirled the last few sips of beer in her glass and, without making eye contact, said, "My mom didn't trust my dad. He . . . sometimes made irresponsible choices."

"What did you think of him?" Anna Maria asked Morgan.

"Ray was a good guy." She removed her hand from her beer to reach for Emilia but stopped herself. It didn't feel right, in front of Anna Maria, to advertise their contact. "We share a dock, and he helped me with my boat."

"Is that how you met Emilia?"

"I fell in the ocean. Morgan pulled me out," Emilia admitted.

Anna Maria leaned forward to look at Morgan more closely. "You mean the perfect Emilia fell into the ocean?"

"Perfect Emilia?" Morgan said.

"This one," Anna Maria explained, "was a nightmare to grow up with. Perfect grades, perfect behavior, perfect daughter. I think you got into trouble what, maybe three times?"

Emilia flushed. "I wasn't perfect."

"True. Mom never found you playing Barbies." She winked at the group. "I knew Emmy was a lesbian the first time I caught her doing unspeakable things with our dolls."

"Anna Maria!"

"What?"

"I did the same thing." Lillian came to Emilia's rescue.

"Tell us more embarrassing things about Emilia," said Stevie.

"Please don't," said Emilia.

"Her first crush was Sporty Spice."

"Remember how I didn't actually invite you to visit?"

"Which means you can't uninvite me."

"Watch me." Emilia glowered as she drained her beer.

"Can I get you another?" Morgan asked her.

"Yes," Anna Maria answered for Emilia. "I'm driving, and she's had a long day."

170

Morgan stood, already missing the pressure of Emilia's hand, and headed to the bar.

"How's it going over there?" asked Stormy.

"Besides being interrogated, good."

"You can handle it. What do you need?"

"Another of whatever Emilia is drinking."

"Fetching her drinks now? Such a gentleman."

"I fetch you drinks."

"Are you still trying to play the whole 'we're just friends' card?" Stormy filled a mug from a tap and held it hostage while she waited for Morgan's answer.

"Shut up."

"Just promise me you're not lying to yourself, at least."

"Give me the beer, Stormy."

"She could be good for you."

"Do I give you shit about your love life?"

"I don't have one."

"Please?"

Stormy sighed dramatically and released the drink, accepting the cash Morgan handed her in return. "Oh, and Morgan?"

Morgan turned back to the bar. "What?"

"I closed up a little early the other night and took a walk by the water."

"That sounds nice."

"Emilia sounded pretty nice, too."

Morgan opened her mouth to say something, anything, but the blood overtaking her cheeks and throat made it impossible to speak.

"I won't tell anyone." Stormy shooed her away and turned to her next customer.

"You okay?" Lillian asked when she sat back down.

"Yeah." She cleared her throat. "Swallowed wrong."

She set the beer in front of Emilia and willed her face to regain its normal complexion. Stevie patted her on the back.

Stormy's words stuck in her head as she rejoined the conversation. Embarrassment warred with vivid memories of the sounds

171

Stormy referred to, and when Emilia shifted closer in her chair, Morgan laid her hand on her thigh, unable to stop herself.

Emilia uncrossed her legs and laughed at whatever Lillian had just said. Morgan slipped her hand between Emilia's thighs and stroked the fabric slowly, grateful their seats were against the wall. The only way someone could have seen was if they ducked underneath a table. Emilia tightened her thighs around Morgan's hand as she moved farther up, trapping her against her heated center. Morgan gulped more of her own beer and hoped the cold liquid would cool her off. It didn't. Emilia arched her hips so subtly none of the others could possibly have noticed, but it sent a shockwave through Morgan.

"Anyway, my mom sent Emilia enough food to feed an army, so feel free to invite yourselves over anytime."

"That reminds me," Morgan said to Emilia while Stevie inquired about the exact nature of the feast. "I mentioned to my parents that Ray's daughter was in town, and my mother ordered me to invite you over for dinner. You don't have to come," she added, "all things considered."

She moved her hand with the last word, and Emilia covered her sharp intake of breath with a fake cough.

"I'd love that." The eyes she turned on Morgan were half-lidded with desire, and the color in her cheeks could have been from the beer. Morgan suspected it had a lot more to do with the gentle, insistent pressure she was currently exerting on Emilia's clit through her jeans.

"Stevie was invited too," she said. "It wouldn't just be you."

"Either way is fine by me."

"What are you whispering about? I heard my name."

"I was insulting you," Morgan said to Stevie. "Obviously."

She managed to get through the evening without hauling Emilia to the pub bathroom. When Lillian yawned for the fifth time, however, she remembered she had promised to get them home at a reasonable hour.

"It was great to meet you," she said to Anna Maria as she pressed against Emilia's slick jeans. "But we should probably head out."

Emilia's expression was glazed as Morgan withdrew her hand.

"It was so nice meeting you." Anna Maria rose and hugged them all, pausing as she embraced Morgan. "Take care of my sister," she said in her ear.

Morgan nodded, aware that Emilia was watching, and certain that she would object to the idea that she needed looking after.

"We should probably head out, too," said Emilia. "Nell's put up with enough." The dog raised her head from her spot beneath Emilia's chair.

"My dog would have chewed her way out of the door by now," said Anna Maria. "But you're perfect, aren't you, Nell?"

The sweeping tail and flattened ears of the happy greyhound brought an adoring smile to Emilia's face. Morgan's heart constricted.

They walked out together after saying farewell to Stormy, who gave Morgan a suggestive wink. *Friends are overrated*, she thought, blushing again and hoping the darkness outside would hide it. She waved good bye to Emilia and bit back a groan of frustration as the other woman walked away. She had opened her mouth to call her back, damning the rest of them, when Lillian took her arm and pulled her to the car with a look of mingled amusement and pity.

The short car ride back to the house took a geological era. Anna Maria kept glancing over at Emilia in silence with a speculative gleam in her eyes.

"What?" she asked finally.

"Nothing."

"Then stop looking at me like that."

"I'm not doing anything."

"You just did it again."

Anna Maria pulled into the driveway and parked before turning in her seat to face her. "You didn't tell me you went on a date with Dr. Fuck Me."

"I hadn't gotten around to it."

Anna Maria patted Emilia's cheek with a tenderness that made her want to weep. "She's not Hannah."

"No," said Emilia. "She's not."

"She's also even hotter in person. Makes me wish I was a horse."

"That's revolting."

"Like you haven't thought it."

She opened the car door and escaped before Anna Maria could see her face. The memory of Morgan's hand inside her shuddered through her, spurred on by Morgan's teasing at the pub.

"Emmy," said her sister, following. She hurried to catch up with Emilia, who stood watching Nell race around the yard. "Are you seeing her?"

"You seem to want me to."

"I'm just an asshole. You know I worry about you, though, right?"

"Isn't that why you're here?"

"Morgan seems . . ." Anna Maria hesitated, as if searching for the right word.

"Fuckable?"

"Besides that. What's the word?"

"I have no idea."

"Real."

Emilia stared at her sister and tried to make sense of the lines creasing her forehead. "Real how?"

"Real in a way I'm not sure you're ready for."

"Doesn't matter." She pasted a smile across her lips. "We're just friends."

Anna Maria searched her face, then shrugged. "I'm glad you found good people. Come on. Let's put you to bed."

Real, she thought as she lay in the darkness of her father's house. Real was a good word for Morgan. Real. Solid. Grounded. Everything that was missing from her own existence. Was that why she was so drawn to her? Hannah had been real in a different way—never stopping, always moving, creating the universe she wanted around her. Emilia had been sucked in like a satellite. What, she wondered now, would life be like in Morgan's orbit? It

174

occurred to her suddenly that she knew very little about Morgan's past. Far less, in fact, than Morgan knew about hers. The disparity was disquieting.

But do I want to know? She'd had to tell Morgan about her recent past because it informed so much of her present—including the unspoken matter of her imminent departure. Falling for Morgan would complicate that and make it even harder to decide what to do about her father's house. And falling was a very real danger.

Anna Maria was right. She wasn't ready for someone like Morgan, nor was she capable of pushing her away.

"I'm so fucked," she said into her pillow.

Anna Maria stayed another day, helping Emilia minimize the rest of her father's possessions. For now, she'd settled for stripping the furnishings down to what she'd need if she decided to rent the house out for a few years.

"I know Mom's pushing you to sell, but I say keep it and run an Airbnb. Or pay someone else to manage it. You don't need to make any big decisions right now, and probably shouldn't, anyway."

What she really needed to do was deal with the yard. She'd mown it, but the flower beds looked, as Anna Maria put it while getting into her car to leave, "like moldy dog shit," and the vegetable garden had been overrun with weeds and weedier tomato plants and squash vines left over from last year's fallen fruits. She figured it was probably too late to do much with it besides make the best of the volunteer crops, but she decided to take Lillian up on her offer of spare seedlings. Gardening would also dispel some of the tension that shivered beneath her skin in all the places Morgan had touched her. A short text exchange confirmed the availability of all things green and growing, and Lillian invited her to stop over that evening. She stared at the rioting mess of a garden at her feet, then texted Morgan.

ER: *I'll be at your place to get plants from Lillian later. Will I see you?*

The reply was instant.

MD: *Wouldn't miss it.*

She dug a shovel, rake, and garden hoe out of the disorganized shed—a project for another day—and proceeded to do her best to remove the worst of the weeds. Her muscles burned with the unfamiliar abuse. Nell lay in the shade and chewed on a stick. She looked up each time Emilia swore at a particularly entrenched weed tree but made no move to help.

By five o'clock she was sweaty, sunburned, and exhausted.

"I am not a farmer," she told her dog as she slumped on the porch. She'd tended houseplants in the apartment she no longer shared with Hannah. Most had probably perished by now. She doubted Skylar would care for them, and Hannah had no time for things that didn't serve a purpose. Air purification and décor didn't count.

Still, it would be nice to have fresh vegetables and herbs, assuming the effort involved to get them didn't kill her. She glanced at the flower beds, where more weeds staked territorial claims over the faded mulch. *One day at a time.* Starting with the beds visible from the driveway probably would have been smarter than focusing on the vegetable garden, but she'd always hated the way mulch managed to wedge itself underneath her fingernails even with gloves.

The house felt empty without Anna Maria. Peaceful, but bereft, as if another departed human presence amplified her father's absence. Floorboards creaked under her feet more loudly than usual when she got out of the shower, and she wiped the steam from the mirror to remind herself that she wasn't a ghost.

"What are you doing here?" she asked her towel-clad self.

A message blinked at her from her phone.

MD: *Running late today. Stay for dinner?*

The crush of doubts dissipated, replaced by what was, without a doubt, pure and unadulterated lust.

ER: *I'd love that.*

MD: *Bring Nell.*

Nell currently sprawled across the bed with all four legs in the air. She snapped a photo and sent it to Morgan.

MD: *Your dog expired. Did you buy the warranty?*

ER: *I was hoping you could fix her.*

MD: *Wait, she's not spayed?*

Emilia snorted at the lame joke and wriggled into a pair of jeans.

ER: *That was a Stevie-level joke.*

MD: *Ouch. I'll tell her you said that.*

ER: *You wouldn't.*

The next message contained a picture of Stevie's devastated face behind the wheel of the truck. Kraken loomed in the background with his head out the truck window. Emilia kissed Nell on the snout and tapped one of the limp paws.

"Come on, slug-a-bed. We're going to see your new friends."

Chapter Twelve

Lillian ushered her into the greenhouse, still dressed in slacks and a blouse that wore its own coat of pet hair.

"I've got a few flats left over. You can see if the kale lasts in the heat, and it's a bit late for peppers, but I've got chard, beets, and actually these tomatoes and peppers might do it. I forgot I potted them up. And cucumbers. Ooh, and this summer butterhead lettuce is pretty heat tolerant."

"How do you have time for all this?" Emilia asked.

"Not sure I really do, but I make it work." Lillian pressed her finger into the soil at the base of a small tree with fat, glossy leaves. "I bring some of it in for my patients. And, of course, Circe." The tortoise poked her head up from behind a row of carefully stacked planters.

"Is she the only exotic you have?"

"At the moment. I almost took in an African Grey parrot last year, but a better option came along for him. I'm glad, honestly. Circe does okay when I travel, and the dogs come with me, but birds are tricky."

"How often do you travel?" Emilia sneaked a glance out the greenhouse window to the driveway. Still no sign of Morgan.

"Hah." Lillian put a few seedlings in an empty tray. "Usually whenever I can to see Brian, but since he's in South America and couldn't be bothered to come see me before he left. . . ." She took a steadying breath and smiled. "Sorry. You don't need to hear that."

"I don't mind at all. Long distance is hard."

"You can say that again." Lillian brushed her hand over an herb planter with an expression of muted frustration. "Want any herbs?"

Emilia breathed in the fragrances that stirred in the wake of Lillian's hand: thyme, rosemary, sage, and lavender. "Just annuals for now, I think."

"Right." Lillian's dark eyes focused on her face. "I keep forgetting you're here for only a little while."

"Me too." Doubt crept into her voice. *I can't afford any more doubt*, she thought as she met Lillian's gaze.

"Well, this should get you started, though you might not see any tomatoes until September. Until then, help yourself to some of mine."

"Thank you so much." She looked at her tray of plants. "You've all been way nicer to me than I deserve."

"Bullshit. We're all just sick of each other, and you fell into our clutches. This house is a Venus flytrap, by the way. Watch out."

And Morgan is the nectar.

"Has your boss found a new large animal vet yet?"

"No." Lillian unbuttoned her blouse in the heat, revealing a sensible undershirt. "No one wants to come out here. The pay isn't as good as it is farther south, and Danielle doesn't want to hire anyone out of desperation. Any chance you want the job?"

"I haven't touched a large animal since vet school."

"The position could be half and half."

"I . . . I don't think that would be a good idea."

"Oh yeah." Lillian grimaced. "I'm sorry. I'm still in doctor mode. Are you worried about Morgan?"

"It's complicated." The desire to confide in Lillian nearly overpowered her, and she knelt down to greet the tortoise to buy time to collect herself. Anything she said to Lillian might make its way back to Morgan. Then again, it wasn't like she had any good friends left, and her family was likely to overreact. "I don't want to put you in a difficult position."

"I'm not going to tell Morgan what you say here, unless you're planning on hurting her intentionally."

"I'm not. At least, I hope I'm not."

"Fair enough."

"I don't even know if I want to stay in the field. If I took a job at your hospital, assuming I was even offered one, I'd always wonder if I did it for the right reasons. I got into shelter medicine because of my ex."

"And you want to make sure you're choosing for you, not someone else."

"Not to mention what would happen if things didn't work out."

"Also fair. Morgan and I had a policy in vet school when it came to dating: career first." Lillian pulled a dead leaf off a hanging vine and crushed it. "Not that it worked out particularly well for either of us."

"Well, I can't recommend following your heart."

"To no good options." Lillian raised an imaginary toast. "Speaking of Morgan, are you sticking around till she gets home?"

"I don't want to intrude."

"You won't. Here, leave your plants for now and help me harvest something for dinner."

Angie joined them in the kitchen later on, dressed in a tank top, sweatpants, and a noticeable lack of bra. "I still smell like diarrhea, no matter how many times I've showered," she said, wrinkling her nose.

"Will all great Neptune's ocean wash this poop clean from my hands?" Lillian asked. Emilia thought she might be quoting Shakespeare but wasn't positive.

"What can my royal poopiness assist you with?"

"Want to grate some carrots?"

"Give 'em here." Angie held out her hands, and beneath the scratches Emilia recognized as signs of overenthusiastic dog play she noticed bruising around her wrists. Lillian had to have seen it, too, but she didn't comment, so Emilia didn't either.

"I'm sorry I missed meeting your sister," Angie said.

"Count yourself lucky. Do you have siblings?"

"Yeah. Morgan is the only only child under this roof. Did you find the banana bread I left for you in the fridge, by the way?" Angie asked around a mouthful of tomato.

Lillian set down her knife and opened the refrigerator, pulling out a large container labeled "bean sprouts." "You're the best. Want a slice, Emilia?"

"But you have to keep it a secret," said Angie.

"Morgan and Stevie don't respect labels," Lillian explained, "so we've resorted to subterfuge. Neither would ever look in this."

"Sometimes we put a layer of sprouts on top just to keep up appearances."

"Morgan did mention she has a cheese problem," said Emilia.

"It's not a problem. It's a pattern of criminal behavior." Angie scowled. "I still haven't forgiven her for eating an entire wedge of my good brie."

"And let's not forget the case of the missing mozzarella," said Lillian.

"Or the ghost of Gorgonzola."

"The stilted Stilton."

"Lillian's Limburger," said Angie.

"Monster of muenster."

"Ravisher of ricotta."

"I can't think of anything for Havarti," Lillian said.

"Ooh, pilfered provolone and the Havarti holdup."

Tires sounded on gravel outside.

"Quick, hide the banana bread." Lillian shoved the loaf back in its hiding spot and resumed slicing a cabbage as the front door opened and Kraken bounded in. Nell, who had taken up residence on the couch, slid down to greet him. Lillian's Italian greyhound merely opened one eye from her spot on the back of an armchair, and the other dogs remained in the backyard.

Emilia wished she could bound up to Morgan like her dog, who had moved past Kraken to lean against Morgan. She scratched Nell's ears as she looked around the room. Her eyes softened when they found Emilia's, and the late afternoon sunlight suddenly seemed to shine more brightly.

"Guess who got baby donkey cuddles," said Stevie.

"And guess who got to show the owner how to induce ejaculation in a jackass," said Morgan, somewhat dampening Emilia's current fantasy about bending her over the table. "Stevie had the better deal."

"Can't have one without the other," Lillian pointed out. "If you're doing artificial insemination."

"I love the dinner table topics in this house." Angie shook her head. "Especially when there's company."

"She's one of us," said Stevie. "Any chance you're feeding us, Lil?" Morgan asked with a hopeful expression as she surveyed the island counter. She ambled closer to examine the contents of a large blue bowl, and her leg brushed against Emilia's.

"I'm feeding Angie and Emilia."

"We've landed in enemy territory," Stevie said to Morgan. "If we abort the mission now, we may still have time to get burgers."

"I'm glad you stuck around," Morgan said, ignoring Stevie and fixing those flawless eyes on Emilia again.

"We've decided you can't have her all to yourself," said Angie.

Morgan placed an arm around Emilia in a show of playful possession.

"Careful, Donovan," said Lillian. "Angie's holding a knife."

The banter—and Morgan's proximity—left Emilia feeling dizzy.

Morgan dropped her arm, but let her hand linger on Emilia's lower back. The touch drove all thoughts of dinner from her mind, and while a moment before she'd been basking in the overwhelming warmth of this kitchen, now she desperately wanted to be alone with Morgan. Her body reminded her unequivocally that it had not forgotten the pressure of Morgan's fingers through her jeans, nor forgiven her for the ruthless teasing. Smiling at her sister and her friends while she wanted nothing more than to straddle Morgan right there in the coffee shop had been agony.

Agony she would happily relive again and again.

Lillian's salad, she reflected a few moments later, was worth the temporary deprivation.

"What did you do to these vegetables?" she asked.

"She's the vegetable whisperer," said Angie.

"It's unbelievable."

"That reminds me." Stevie launched into an elaborate story involving one of the clients they'd seen that day. Emilia followed along as best she could, but she kept glancing over at Morgan. Her clinic polo showed off her muscular arms, and a bit of sunburn colored her fair cheeks. Her eyes drifted to meet Emilia's, and she raised an eyebrow almost imperceptibly in a question that sent a shiver of anticipation through Emilia.

"Oh," she said as casually as she could after adding her dish to the dishwasher. "I brought back the shop vac."

"I can grab it for you." Morgan walked to the front door. Emilia and Nell followed.

She caught Morgan's hand as soon as they were hidden from view by the clinic truck and pushed Morgan up against the warm metal. Morgan grabbed her by the hips and held on as Emilia kissed her, all of the frustration she'd felt since Sally's boiling over into the embrace. Her hands were underneath Morgan's shirt and feeling the line of muscle down her abs before she remembered they were still visible from the road.

"Stay the night?" Morgan asked when Emilia let her up for air.

"What about your friends?"

"I don't fucking care." Morgan leaned in to kiss her again, but Emilia kept herself just out of reach.

"I like your friends."

"I like them too, but they're not what I am interested in right now."

"It won't bother them?"

"They'll be thrilled." Annoyance flickered across Morgan's expression. "And then they'll find a way to take credit for it."

"Oh yeah?"

Morgan attempted to kiss her once more and growled when Emilia held her at bay by bare centimeters. *I could invite you to my place*, she wanted to say, but the words refused to form. It wasn't her place, not really, regardless of what the deed now read. It was her father's, and she wasn't ready to claim it or to bring someone else into it as completely as she knew Morgan's presence would fill it.

"Please," Morgan said. Her sea-dark eyes stole Emilia's breath.

"Yes." She let Morgan pull her in, and the sweet smells of clean barn, horse, hay, and sunshine surrounded her.

The others had dispersed when they returned. Lillian sat on the couch with a mug of tea and a copy of *Clinician's Brief*, Hermione curled up on her lap and Muffin sprawled beside her. Angie and Stevie laughed from down the hall, and she heard what sounded like a video game in the background.

"Come upstairs." Morgan linked her hand with Emilia's and gently tugged. She followed, caught up in a riptide of inevitable longing.

Morgan's room overlooked the orchard. A window seat framed the sunset view, and Emilia sat there while Morgan hopped in the shower. She still hadn't set foot in the orchard. Old, gnarled apple trees spread across the sloping hill. *No wonder Angie bought this place.*

The rest of Morgan's room was plain. Her queen-sized bed took up one wall, a dresser another, and a large, comfortable-looking dog bed occupied the floor by the window. A painting of a field of cows hung over the bed, and a few smaller photographs lined her dresser. She left Nell on the window seat—Kraken had been quick to claim the human bed—and approached for a closer look.

The first photo showed a small child with a profusion of dark curls holding a sheep by a blue ribbon-festooned halter. The second featured the same child, younger, held in the arms of a woman who was clearly Morgan's mother. The family resemblance was almost uncanny. A taller man with Morgan's broad shoulders stood behind them with his arms around his wife's waist. *Happy families are all alike,* she thought, a line from a college English class floating into her head. The other two photos were of an older Morgan. Lillian and Morgan smiled out of one, dressed in graduation robes with the Cornell sign behind them, and the last could have been taken yesterday. Stevie, Lillian, Angie, and Morgan stood in front of 16 Bay Road surrounded by their dogs. James hissed in Angie's arms.

She wondered again what it would be like to have friends like that. She set it back down on the dresser. Kraken sighed deeply and stretched out further on the bed.

Morgan's bedside table caught her eye.

A lamp with a sheep-patterned shade adorned the top. She checked to make sure the shower was still running, then opened the top drawer, curiosity overriding guilt. A pair of reading glasses. A dog-eared reference book. Notepad. And at the bottom a small velvet box and another photo frame. This one was turned face down. She eased it out, careful not to disturb the drawer's contents, and held it up to the light.

Morgan stood with one of the most beautiful women Emilia had ever seen. Her smile lit the frame, and her face radiated warmth and kindness. Morgan gazed at her with total adoration.

She put the photo down as if it had scalded her. *You shouldn't have snooped*, she told herself, but that look on Morgan's face cut through her. Nausea boiled in her gut. Morgan was *hers*. She opened the velvet box with shaking hands. Two rings nestled in their grooves. One had a small diamond set with sapphires, and the other was comparatively plain, just a simple golden band with a tiny stone set in the center. Both looked like they'd been worn.

The sound of running water stopped. She shut the box and the drawer hastily, but couldn't resist opening the bottom drawer, wondering what other shattering things she might find.

Three dildos stared up at her. Jealousy still reigned supreme among her emotions, but her body reacted to this new find regardless, with a deep pulse of desire. All were a deep blue. She stroked the middle one, passing over the smallest, and then turned to the third and largest. Ridged silicone met her fingers and she felt herself give at the thought of it entering her.

Her perch on the window seat was less comfortable after that. She throbbed with need while her mind fixated on the rings and the overturned photograph. The story seemed obvious. Morgan had an ex-fiancée, one who was recent enough that she hadn't gotten rid of the picture and rings, serious enough that she hadn't gotten over the breakup, or both.

Good, she tried to tell herself. If Morgan had baggage, it would make it easier for both of them to keep an emotional distance. *I'll be gone in a month or two anyway. I have no right to be jealous about anything in Morgan's past.* The woman's face flashed before her again, sun-kissed and smiling.

Emilia hated her.

"Sorry about that." Morgan reentered the room in sweatpants and a men's V-neck T-shirt loose enough to almost cover up the fact that, like Angie, she had forsworn bras. The sight distracted Emilia from her confusion.

"I had hay in places I didn't think possible." Morgan stopped talking, as if considering the implications of her words.

"Well, I hope you got it all out."

Morgan flushed. "Did I mention I was smooth?"

"No, but I have heard you referred to as the Monster of Muenster."

Morgan leaned against the wall by the window. Emilia suspected she would have sat with her on the window seat had Nell not occupied all available space, but Emilia didn't nudge her dog out of the way. The air between her and Morgan had a new tightness. Last time had been unplanned, excusable as accident or momentary lapse in judgment. This felt different. Intentional. Awkward, almost, although she still pulsed with unreleased tension, and flavored with consequence. The image of Morgan with the beautiful stranger besieged her every time she blinked.

"Can I get you a drink?" Morgan asked.

"Yes please."

"Whiskey okay?" Morgan still leaned against the wall. Freckles scattered across her chest like constellations Emilia longed to connect with fingers and tongue.

"Perfect."

Morgan opened the top drawer of her dresser and pulled out a bottle.

"Secret stash?" said Emilia.

"It's an old habit."

"Who did you hide it from?"

Morgan took a drink straight from the bottle and passed it to Emilia. "A cat I used to live with. And before that, my parents. I grew up in Maine, remember? Drinking is what we do to stay warm in the winter."

"This is good." The whiskey had a smoky finish, and she rolled it around her mouth.

"I know." Morgan watched her. "What are you thinking right now?"

Emilia motioned for Nell to scoot over, and Morgan sat, one knee up to accommodate the dog, the other leg stretched out.

"I'm thinking I don't know anything about you."

"What do you want to know?"

Emilia touched the arch of Morgan's bare foot lightly. "You seem so stable. Are you?"

"That's a question." Morgan drank. "I'm employed, but drowning in student loans. I have a place to live, but I'm a thirty-one-year-old with three housemates. I love what I do so much that I'm single, and you're the first person I've slept with in half a year."

"Who was it before me?"

Morgan held the bottle up to the window. Amber light flowed over her face. "My fiancée. Ex-fiancée."

She'd suspected as much, but that didn't make the words sting any less. She ignored the pain in Morgan's eyes and pressed on, the sick, coiling jealousy in her stomach refusing to let her stop. "What was her name?"

"Kate."

"What happened?"

"This is really what you want to know?"

"You know about Hannah. You know I was committed to a psych ward. You know my father is dead."

"Fair enough." Morgan patted Nell. "Kate wanted a partner who was available. I wasn't."

"Available how?"

"Not on call all the time. Reasonable hours. That sort of thing."

"But she knew you were a vet."

"She did. She told me . . ." Morgan began. Nell lifted her head as the hand petting her paused. "She told me she had expected things to get better. Easier. Obviously, they didn't."

"I'm sorry."

"I had no fucking clue. I was happy. I thought she was, too. Here." She passed the bottle back and rolled her shoulders as if to shrug off the memory. It lingered in the tight line of her jaw and the tremor that passed through her lower lip. Emilia recognized the effort of pretense it took her to keep her voice level and her fists unclenched—it was the same pretense she carried with her every day. *I'm fine, I'm fine, I'm fine,* that posture said. *Please believe me so that I can believe myself.*

"So, that's my story."

"Thank you."

Morgan raised a brow.

"You were too perfect." She slid her palm up Morgan's calf, then dragged her nails back down. The tightness in Morgan's body retreated, replaced by a new kind of tension.

"And now I'm not?"

"Now you're . . ." She set the bottle on the floor and dislodged Nell with a loving tap. Morgan waited, her dark blue eyes catching more of the sunset as Emilia straddled her. "Human."

"I've always been human, to my knowledge."

"Do you have any idea what you looked like to me that day on the dock?" she asked, running her fingertips over Morgan's lips.

"*You* looked like you wanted to kill me."

She sank into Morgan's lap. "It didn't seem fair. I was a wreck, and you were this cocky, unfairly attractive witness to my total incompetence."

"You weren't that incompetent."

Emilia moved her hips and Morgan sucked in her breath.

"You're a bad liar," she said.

Morgan smirked. "Fine. Then I admit I enjoyed rescuing you."

"I knew you got off playing hero."

"I save lives every day."

Unlike me, Emilia thought. She let it go, relishing the feel of Morgan's hands on her waist.

"You have no idea what you looked like to me either," Morgan added.

"Angry?" Emilia guessed.

"Angry and gorgeous."

"You didn't always think so." At Morgan's frown, Emilia laughed to hide her embarrassment. "You clearly don't remember me, but I had the hugest crush on you growing up."

It was easier to admit than she'd thought it would be—eased in part, no doubt, by the blatant longing in Morgan's face as she squeezed her waist.

Morgan's eyes widened in what was unmistakably delight, followed by a grin that made Emilia simultaneously want to deny her confession and push Morgan inside her the way she had on the boat. "You didn't."

"Yep. I remember your ponytail and how you would dive into the water like a seal."

"I can't believe I would have missed you."

"It's not like we ever talked. And you would have had to stand still long enough to notice me," said Emilia.

"I see you now." Morgan's hands slid over Emilia's ass and pulled her closer.

Emilia's mind strayed to the bedside table drawer and the strap-on. Admitting that she'd seen it, however, would reveal to Morgan that she'd gone through her things. She settled for rocking her hips, reveling in the way the movement made Morgan's eyelids flutter. It had been a long time since she'd felt like she had control over anything, and the tight lead she held on Morgan's desire thrilled her.

"I promised you I'd take my time." She laced her fingers through Morgan's and held them away from their bodies.

"That you did."

"Are you on call?"

"Not tonight."

"Good." She ground her hips against Morgan, whose pupils dilated as she groaned. Morgan tried to break her hands free from Emilia's grip. She shook her head. "No."

Morgan's eyes closed as she exhaled sharply.

You like this, Emilia thought in wonder. Hannah had never let her take the lead, and she felt as if she'd been cut loose, freed to act as she'd always longed to. She pinned Morgan's hands beside her and leaned in, still rocking her hips, to hover over Morgan's lips. She could smell the whiskey on her breath as she took Morgan's lower lip gently between her teeth and tasted the malt with the tip of her tongue. Morgan struggled against Emilia's grip on her hands. Emilia bit down, not hard enough to hurt, but hard enough to make her point. Morgan stilled.

She released her lip and pulled far enough away to take in Morgan's blown pupils and flushed cheeks. "Don't move."

Morgan gave her a small nod.

She let go of Morgan's hands and leaned back. Slowly, holding Morgan's eyes with hers, she pulled the hem of her shirt up toward her breasts. Morgan reached out to touch her.

"I said don't move."

"Emilia—"

She let her shirt fall back down. Morgan stopped fighting. She repeated the slow motion, letting the sunlight warm the bare skin of her stomach, then her breasts, which ached for Morgan's hands beneath the sheer fabric of her bra, until finally she pulled it over her head.

Morgan struck while her view was obscured by the shirt. Her hands stroked Emilia's ribs and the curve of her waist before cupping her breasts, and Emilia gasped as she ripped the shirt off.

"I said—" she began, but Morgan had her mouth on Emilia's nipple, and the lace of her bra did little to shield her from the heat. Her hips pressed as deep into Morgan as jeans allowed. Morgan's tongue flicked her through the fabric, driving thoughts of control out of her mind, and she felt each touch in her clit.

She regained conscious thought when Morgan undid the catch of her bra. Tangling her fingers in Morgan's hair, she pulled her away from her breast and kissed her hard. Morgan tried to push her down on the window seat, but she resisted, fighting with her body as she surrendered with her mouth. Morgan growled low in her throat and tried to break the kiss. Emilia stroked her tongue with hers, and the growl turned into a moan. One of her hands tugged Morgan's curls. The other, she noticed absently, was curled around Morgan's biceps. *God, I love strong women.*

Morgan turned them on the window seat and sat up, bracing her feet on the floor. This freed Emilia to wrap her legs completely around her. Thighs gripped hips as they kissed, and she remembered how Morgan had tasted on the boat.

Morgan's sudden movement took her by surprise. She was lifted into the air, and the muscles beneath her hand flexed with the effort in a way that tightened muscles deep inside her in response. She thought they were headed for the bed. Instead, the smooth, hard surface of the wall met her back as Morgan pushed her up against it.

Oh, fuck. Only a whimper of longing escaped her mouth. Morgan drove her hips into Emilia this time, and she abandoned her grip on Morgan's arm to bury both hands in her hair. Morgan moved her hips in a practiced way that made her heart race with promise. Breathless, she let Morgan kiss the side of her jaw and down her neck. She'd intended to stay in control, she remembered faintly, but this felt too good to stop. She pictured Morgan with the strap-on. How *good* it would feel to have her inside her, just like this, with the cool wall at her back and Morgan's lips on her neck.

"Fuck, Morgan, do you have—"

"Yes." Morgan bit the muscle of her shoulder as she answered. Emilia did not need to clarify the question as Morgan adjusted her hold on Emilia and tumbled her into the bed, dislodging Kraken in the process.

Morgan opened her dresser drawer, her hands clumsy with desire. Emilia lay on her bed, still wearing jeans but gloriously topless, and Morgan held up the smallest of her toys. Emilia shook her head. She presented the second. Emilia hesitated, leaning forward in a way that sent her hair rippling over her shoulder.

"Do you have any more?" she asked.

Morgan swallowed hard, biting back a moan as she held her favorite up for Emilia to see.

Emilia's brown eyes darkened as she gazed at it in Morgan's hand, and then she nodded. Morgan reached for the harness.

Emilia plucked it from her hands.

"Strip," Emilia said.

She set the toy on the bedside table and did as she was told. Her sweatpants fell to the floor and she tossed her shirt off after it, grateful she hadn't bothered with bra or underwear. She held out her hand for the harness, but Emilia shook her head.

"Emilia—"

Emilia stood, leaving the harness on the bed. She ran her palms down Morgan's arms and up her waist until she stood close enough that the cold metal of her belt pressed against Morgan's clit.

Emilia cupped Morgan's breast in her hand. "You're like a sculpture. It's ridiculous."

Morgan didn't much care if she was a work of art or a pile of trash. Right now, she could only focus on Emilia. She wrapped her arms around her and tried to kiss her, but Emilia pulled away with that damned teasing smile and somehow must have managed to grab the harness, because she felt the cool leather circle her waist. The first buckle snapped as Emilia tightened it, and the sound might as well have been fingers stroking her. Emilia knelt, holding Morgan's eyes in that way she had, as if she knew Morgan couldn't look away even if her life depended on it, and slipped the dildo in place. The silicone nestled against her. Emilia fastened the second strap, brushing against Morgan's slick inner thigh, and lingering long enough to let her thumb tease Morgan's opening before fastening the second buckle. Morgan's hips jerked. By the time Emilia finished with the third and final strap, she knew she'd come hard and fast the minute she entered the woman on the floor before her.

Emilia rested her hand on the dildo. Desire rippled through

Morgan. She started to tell Emilia where to find the lube, but it was already in Emilia's hand. She slid it over the toy in long, even strokes that pushed the silicone into Morgan and made her gasp. Emilia kissed her thigh where the leather sat. She almost died as she watched Emilia run her tongue along the strap.

"Fuck." She pulled Emilia to her feet, loving and hating the way the woman laughed, as Morgan allowed herself to be pushed down onto the bed.

Emilia removed her own jeans with the same torturous slowness with which she'd taken off her shirt. Morgan marveled at the length of her legs and the long muscles of her thighs, mesmerized by the way Emilia moved. Her full breasts with their dark nipples swayed with her body, and Morgan longed to take them into her mouth one at a time, or to just hold them, letting them fill her hands. Then there were the soft curves of Emilia's waist, her lean, runner's body forgetting itself and spreading into hips and an ass that Morgan couldn't keep her eyes off even in polite company. How had this woman ended up in her bedroom?

She didn't pursue that line of thought. Emilia crawled onto the bed and over her, her hair curtaining Morgan's face and her breasts—*fuck me*—at last within reach. She held them, the nipples hard against her palms, and watched Emilia's eyes close in pleasure as she kneaded them. She could have stayed there forever, but Emilia's ass pulled her hands down, and she stroked the curves of each cheek while Emilia's breath came hot and fast. When she grabbed her ass, Emilia whimpered, and the tip of the dildo touched her. Morgan felt the pressure and bit her lip to keep from crying out. She'd never been this sensitive. Not to her own body, and not to her lover's.

Emilia sat up and scratched Morgan's sides with her nails, blinding Morgan with bright lust, which cleared to reveal Emilia with her hand on the dildo, teasing herself with the tip. *Jesus fucking Christ*, Morgan swore to herself as her body threatened to come at the sight. Emilia's hair almost covered her chest, wild and tangled from Morgan's hands, and her breasts caught the light again as Emilia arched her back.

Morgan's gasp mingled with Emilia's as she guided the shaft into herself. The length of blue vanished inch by inch as Emilia took it in, and Morgan felt her shudder through the silicone as it entered her. She waited for it to settle, not wanting to hurt Emilia, but desperate to take her in her arms. She wanted to please this woman. God help her, she wanted to give Emilia everything, and the danger in the thought was nothing compared to the strength of the longing.

Emilia's hips rocked slowly as she experimented with the length and width of the strap-on. Morgan felt the beginnings of her own orgasm start low inside her and clamped down, holding it at bay with sheer willpower as Emilia moaned and her hips surged, taking the dildo in deeper. Emilia, Morgan already knew, wasn't afraid to take control of her own pleasure. She studied the way desire changed Emilia's face, softening it, color flushing her cheeks and throat. She tried to tell herself she wasn't memorizing it.

As Emilia's breathing grew ragged, her brown eyes met Morgan's, and Morgan read the message there: *take me, now.*

She rolled Emilia over onto her back, and Emilia's legs wrapped around her waist, bringing her in closer as Emilia bucked, her hips desperate. Morgan's thrust answered her.

"Oh my god." Emilia breathed, almost laughing as she threw her head back. "Oh my fucking god."

Fire scored her back as Emilia's nails dug in. Her own desire peaked and shook her, but she didn't break her rhythm. *Not yet,* she told herself, fighting through dizzying shockwaves of pleasure. Not with Emilia so close. Emilia was soft beneath her, and she whimpered into Morgan's ear as Morgan picked up her pace, then slowed, loving the widening of Emilia's eyes as she begged Morgan with them not to stop.

"Fuck you, Morgan Donovan," Emilia said when Morgan slowed again.

Morgan did not bother pointing out that technically speaking she was, and came to a halt with her hips pressed hard against Emilia. Emilia's entire body quivered.

194

"What are you doing?" Her voice broke with frustration and Morgan kissed her gently, aware that gentleness was the last thing Emilia wanted right now, but unable to resist her flushed and parted lips.

"Roll over," she said.

Emilia's answering smile was slow and heavy. Morgan pulled out with her pulse hammering in her throat. She wasn't sure why she'd given the command, only that it had felt right in that moment, right in a way that would have startled her if she had been capable of self-analysis. Emilia turned and looked at Morgan over her shoulder as she obeyed. The trust and certainty in that look, paired with the smolder, twisted around Morgan's heart. She stroked Emilia with her hand and felt the heat of her. Briefly, she contemplated ditching the strap-on so she could feel Emilia come around her hand again, but there was a need in the way Emilia's body tilted toward her that she could no more deny than she could cease to breathe of her own free will. She paused long enough to taste her before sliding the shaft back inside her.

"God, yes," Emilia said. Morgan took hold of her hips and felt the curve of her ass against her as she thrust. She watched the muscles in Emilia's back shift as she clutched the sheets and marveled at the strength of her body. The darkness on the boat and the necessity of cover had concealed the steel beneath her curves. Here, in the fading evening light, she saw the raw power of Emilia Russo laid bare against the pale blue of her sheets.

"Harder," Emilia begged.

Morgan obeyed.

Emilia slammed her own hips into Morgan, forcing her to pick up her pace. Emilia's hair cascaded over her shoulders as she flung her head back. Had she ever seen anything this beautiful? She leaned forward to hold her closer, taking her breast in her hand and rocking with her.

"Morgan." Emilia's voice went high. "Morgan, please don't stop."

"I won't," Morgan said into her ear.

"Oh my god. Morgan. Morgan—" Her last word broke as she came, shuddering, in Morgan's arms.

Morgan held her until she stopped shaking, then gently withdrew the dildo and undid the harness. Emilia turned beneath her and rested her head under Morgan's chin, kissing Morgan's neck as her breathing settled. Morgan touched her hair, then her back, fingertips skimming the smooth skin and feeling the dip of her waist and the curve of her spine. Their legs tangled together. Morgan could feel Emilia's heartbeat pounding against her own, but something else beat in her chest: a fluttering thing with wings too small for its body, struggling to stay aloft. Morgan closed her eyes as she recognized it for what it was. When Emilia slid her hand between Morgan's legs, she nearly wept, and her second orgasm shook her down to her marrow. She cried Emilia's name as she kissed her and filled them both with the sound.

Emilia held her close after the last aftershocks passed, and she lay with her head on Emilia's breast and breathed in the scent of her skin and their sex. The fluttering thing grew stronger. As Emilia toyed with her hair and the distant sounds of her housemates filtered into the room, she wondered if she'd ever had a choice, or if she had fallen for Emilia Russo the minute she'd met her eyes on the dock.

Then Emilia rolled her over, those same eyes sated, and those full lips curved in a wicked smile.

"You didn't think we were done, did you, Morgan Donovan?"

Emilia woke in the darkness hours later as the unfamiliar sounds of the house broke into her dreams. Had a dog barked? She stirred, tangled in the sheets, and felt the warmth of Morgan's body beside her. The pattering of kitty paws in the hallway caught her ears—James, hunting some small rodent or engaged in the kind of midnight romp that made sense only to cats.

She'd ended up on the side of the bed against the wall. Morgan's sleeping outline was framed by the faint light from the window, and starlight painted her cheek. The sheet had slipped down over her shoulder. Emilia drank in the strength of her, the solidity, the grace of her body and the soft, feminine curl of her lashes.

In the darkness, with the heavy breathing of sleeping dogs rising from the floor and the pale whisper of light from the window, Emilia curled her body around Morgan's and wrapped her arm around her waist. Morgan moved in her sleep to press closer, and her hand found Emilia's and tucked it underneath her chin. They exhaled together. She could feel the steady beating of Morgan's heart through the meeting of their ribs, and she rested her forehead against the smooth blade of her shoulder.

Something in Emilia's chest split open. It hurt. For a moment she couldn't breathe. Morgan's breath brushed her fingers, warm, trusting, completely vulnerable in sleep. The ache in her chest spread through her body. Pain, mixed with a longing so intense she had to bite her lip to keep from gasping. It would have terrified her in the daylight. Here, though, with the stars as witness, she let herself feel, and she told herself she did not think about the names for these emotions as the steady beat of Morgan's heart lulled her back to sleep.

Morgan woke to the sound of two dogs whining. Kraken shoved his nose under her head and snuffled in her ear, and another dog lay on the bed beside her, beating her with its tail. It took her a moment to work out the details, and then she turned to find Emilia watching her.

"Good morning," Emilia said, her words shy.

Morgan twisted a strand of Emilia's hair in her fingers and ignored the dogs. Her body felt drugged, sluggish, and heavy with satiety, and she remembered Emilia pushing her up against the headboard the third—or was it the fourth?—time, riding her hard, and then finally, after copious pleading on Morgan's part, letting her take Emilia in her mouth. She'd tasted sweet and heady, and, remembering, Morgan elbowed Nell out of the way and rolled on top of Emilia.

"Good morning," she replied as she looked down at the woman pinned between her arms. Emilia writhed a little beneath her as the shyness in her eyes gave way to something more familiar.

Morgan moved her hips and Emilia's legs parted, and they were both wet where they met.

"I should offer you breakfast," Morgan said as she kissed Emilia's neck.

"Oddly, I'm suddenly not hungry," said Emilia as her body arched.

"Cup of coffee?" She worked her way up to Emilia's ear and whispered the words.

"Morgan—"

"We get really good coffee from Stormy." She drove her hips slowly into Emilia with a steady purpose that had them both breathing hard. Teasing Emilia was new. She liked it, she decided, finding the spot on Emilia's neck that made her gasp. Then Emilia raised her leg, hooking it over Morgan's shoulder, and the feel of her clit against Emilia's severed her ability to think.

Stevie's knock broke them apart some time later.

"Rise and shine," she said through the door. "We've got an eight o'clock."

"Shit," said Morgan, who was wrapped between Emilia's thighs.

"Coming," she said louder, ignoring Stevie's, "I bet you are."

She pushed hard into Emilia, who pressed a pillow over her face to muffle her scream as Morgan took her in her mouth and sucked, hard.

Two very disgruntled dogs awaited them. Kraken was used to being the center of her attention in the morning, and his face said both his bladder and his stomach were considering mutiny. Nell had scrunched herself onto the window seat in a tight ball that radiated betrayal.

"I need to take a quick shower." Morgan stood reluctantly. "Care to join me?"

"Are you sure that's a good idea?" Emilia lay prostrate on the bed, her body still flushed, and her half-lidded eyes ran up and down Morgan's body.

"Not at all." She grinned as an aftershock visibly shook Emilia and offered her a hand. "But I don't want to make our dogs wait much longer."

Keeping her hands to herself in the shower was impossible, but she managed to get them out in under ten minutes, aided by the brutally abrupt end of the hot water supply.

The other residents of 16 Bay Road were congregated in the kitchen with an air of forced innocence that didn't fool Morgan for a second. The chorus of "good mornings" that greeted them reeked of suppressed amusement, and Emilia's cheeks glowed pink with embarrassment. Morgan poured her a cup of coffee. Her own face felt hot, but she didn't care. Let her friends smirk with satisfaction at their correct predictions. Emilia was all that mattered.

They pounced on her the moment Emilia's car pulled out of the driveway.

"You're such a good friend." Stevie batted her eyelashes and sashayed toward Morgan. "Thanks for being there for me, Morgan. I just love our platonic fuck fests."

"Fuck you," Morgan said without heat. Her abs ached and her entire body felt like she'd gone to one of Angie's CrossFit sessions. She grinned despite herself.

"I'm happy for you," said Lillian.

"I'm genuinely impressed." Angie grabbed a banana from the fruit bowl and peeled it suggestively. "You two went late. I didn't think you had it in you."

"This is a conversation I am not having," said Morgan.

"And yet," Stevie leapt onto her back like a monkey and rested her cheek against Morgan's, "here we all are. Having it."

"Can you get off me?"

"I can if you say the magic word."

"Please get off me."

"Incorrect. '*Please*,'" Stevie said in an unnervingly accurate portrayal of a woman about to orgasm.

"I will kill you and feed your body to the nearest pigs."

Stevie slid off her, slammed her ball cap on her head, and smirked. "Ready to hit the road?"

Chapter Thirteen

The next week passed in agonizing slowness. Emilia didn't see Morgan, though they texted constantly, as a string of emergencies kept Morgan on the road, forcing her to cancel their plans. Emilia tried not to feel like this was the end of all things and distracted herself with a visit home for an in-person session with Shanti.

"How are you feeling?" Shanti asked.

Emilia did not mention Morgan. Instead, she told Shanti about the doubts that still shadowed her every step and the ache in her chest where her father's love had lived, and Shanti nodded, sympathetic, no doubt assessing her for risk.

"I don't want to die anymore," she said at the end of their session.

"Good. What changed?"

Everything. Nothing.

"Honestly? I think it was the meds."

It wasn't a lie. It also wasn't the entire truth. It was Seal Cove and her new friends and the water and Morgan, too much Morgan, and people were fragile things to pin a life on.

Shanti studied her but did not interrogate her answer.

I'm here, she wanted to say. *I'm here, seeing you, instead of throwing myself at Morgan's feet. Doesn't that count for something?*

Why then could she not bring herself to tell Shanti about Morgan? She met her therapist's gentle brown eyes and wondered when the shadow of the irrevocable mistake she'd nearly made would dissipate. Would it ever? Or would the people who cared about her always carry worry with them behind their smiles?

"You seem brighter," said Shanti as Emilia stood up to leave. "I am proud of you."

"For what?"

Shanti held the door open, her dark curls catching the soft light of her office. A few strands of gray gleamed.

"Every day is a choice. I am glad you keep making it."

She nodded, mute, and ducked out before tears overwhelmed her.

Every day is a choice.

One day at a time.

And at the end of each day, she wanted Morgan. She'd have to reckon with that eventually, but for now, at least, she could weep without unraveling.

It was a start.

The buzz of her phone kept her company as she began to sort through the remaining bureaucratic matters of her father's estate. She'd had no idea death was so complicated. Bank accounts needed to be closed, as did all the varying insurances, debts, and contracts she hadn't known her father was involved with. To make things even worse, they all wanted proof of death. Repeating the words began to strip them of their meaning.

"I am Emilia Russo, executor of Ray Russo's estate, calling to inform you of his death."

Perhaps none of this was real. Perhaps the urn in her bedroom contained someone else's ashes, and her father was merely far away, instead of gone—impossibly—forever.

She stopped by Stormy's every day just to get out of the house. The temptation to invite Morgan over when she texted late after an emergency at three in the morning beat in her throat so fiercely at times that she could barely swallow, but that in itself was enough to stay her hand. She could not afford to need Morgan. Not right now when so much was unsettled.

So she gardened. She cleaned. She argued with insurance agents and hospital billing departments and poured herself more glasses of wine than was healthy, but she liked watching the sun set through the red glow of merlot while she listened to her father's music.

He'd never gotten into digital music. His CD and vinyl collections took up most of the shelf space in the living room, and she played the music he'd loved and held her dog as Leonard Cohen and Bruce Springsteen filled the house. She'd keep his music and his guitars because that was who he'd been to her in the end. A voice on the end of a phone line. A remembered lyric. Rough hands on guitar strings, playing softly.

Then Morgan called her on a hot summer afternoon.

"Hey."

Her phone moved as her cheeks curved in a smile at Morgan's voice. It poured into her, and she felt full and thirsty all at once.

"Hey yourself."

"We're having a small barbecue for the Fourth if you're free. I was just informed a moment ago."

She hadn't realized it was already the Fourth of July. Time moved too quickly. She covered her sudden panic with words. "That depends. Will you be grilling?"

A distorted voice shouted something in the background.

"Was that Stevie?" she asked.

"Yes."

"What did she say?"

"Nothing repeatable."

The sounds of a scuffle ensued, and then Stevie's voice, breathless with victory, spoke into her ear. "Hey stranger."

"Hi, Stevie."

"You coming over?"

"Your friend grilling again?"

"Who, Morgan? You know she keeps things hot."

Emilia was glad the phone hid her blush. Morgan swore and Stevie yelped, and then Morgan regained control of her cell.

"Yes. There will be a grill. And food. On it. Cooked by me."

"Then I'll be there. What time?"

"Four? And bring Nell. I'll let Stevie explain about Dogpocalypse." There was another flurry of static. "Explain when she gets here, you dumbass. I am not letting you anywhere near my phone again."

"You got things under control?" Emilia asked.

"Totally."

"Sounds like it. Anything I can bring?"

"Yourself."

The way Morgan said the word left Emilia momentarily speechless. She swallowed, tried to respond, paused, and tried again. "I can do that."

"Great." She heard the grin in Morgan's voice. "See you soon."

She changed out of her ragged, paint-stained cutoffs and into a tank top and jeans, glancing at the mirror. The tank top dipped low over her breasts. *Too low.* She tore it off and wriggled into a T-shirt. *Too casual.* Her favorite blouse, however, was too dressy, and the short-sleeved, breezy button-up didn't look right, despite the fact that it was another one of her favorites. Getting desperate, she seized another tank top and stared at her rumpled hair and wide eyes. *I'm hideous*, she decided, turning to examine the way the shirt clung to her waist. Nell turned a circle on the bed on top of her discarded clothes and settled with a huff.

"Okay, fine, you're right, I am being ridiculous," she said to her dog. The current shirt was the least offensive of the brood. Simple, with a casual elegance in the drape of the fabric and a neckline that was flirtatious without drawing attention to itself.

Her damp hair hung in a curling mess around her shoulders. She twisted it into a knot and pinned it up, then let it down again, remembering the way Morgan had buried her hands in it. *Damn her*, she swore internally as she blew it dry. It made no sense to feel this nervous. This wasn't a first date. It was a barbeque. And after the night she'd already spent at Morgan's, nerves seemed preposterous. They'd done things that left no room for misgivings. She shivered and sat on the bed. Thinking about that night had robbed her of sleep every night since. Morgan shouldn't have been able to get under her skin the way she had. Nobody should. But whenever she blinked she saw Morgan beneath her, face filled with awe as Emilia rode her, or prone before her as she lifted Morgan to climax with her tongue. It made simple household tasks difficult.

Nell investigated the baggie of extra dog food she packed with interest. Not wanting to seem presumptuous, she settled for shoving a travel-sized bottle of mouthwash into her purse instead of a toothbrush, and then she killed time while she waited for four o'clock to roll around.

"Hi I brought strawberries," she said in a rush when Morgan opened the door.

Morgan glanced at the quart of fresh strawberries she'd picked up from a farm stand, then back at Emilia's face. The air between them hummed with unresolved tension.

Do I kiss her? Emilia chewed on her lip. They needed to talk, soon, about whatever this was, but until then—

"Come in." Morgan interrupted her panicking thoughts and took the fruit from Emilia's hands, then tugged her lightly into the doorway. Emilia let the berries go without protest, hypnotized by the way Morgan's plain T-shirt clung to her body. Morgan's smile widened.

"I probably should have picked up some whipped cream or shortcake—"

Morgan kissed her. Hunger blazed between them. She didn't realize she had pressed Morgan up against the doorframe, Morgan's strawberry-free hand on her ass, until Stevie cleared her throat.

They broke apart. Stevie took a bite out of the strawberry she'd stolen from the unattended container.

"Uh . . . hi, Stevie."

"Don't let me interrupt."

Morgan blushed a deep scarlet and pushed past a grinning Stevie into the house. Emilia and Nell followed.

"Beer?" Stevie offered her a cold bottle, which she accepted. Morgan, she noted, had not tasted like alcohol.

"I'm on call," Morgan said, correctly interpreting Emilia's look. "Come help us choose a movie for later? We need a tiebreaker."

Stevie explained Dogpocalypse as they scrolled through Stevie's extensive movie collection. The tradition had started a few years ago, before they all lived together, and had carried over. All of their dogs except Marvin—who Stevie said was too dumb to understand the threat—were petrified of fireworks. This made it impossible to enjoy the Fourth or to go out, and so they'd decided to spend the holiday watching apocalyptic movies and comforting their freaked-out animals.

"And the movie has to be apocalyptic?" she asked.

"Naturally."

"Too bad there are so few of them," she said as Stevie continued to scroll through a seemingly endless collection of the genre.

"I know. Hollywood really hates the subject."

"Is that actually a movie about zombie sheep?"

"Don't ask," Morgan warned.

They settled on a B horror flick about colossal tidal waves destined to take out coastal cities, complete with monsters in the water.

"We'll watch it later when the fireworks start and we have to go inside with the dogs. Have you seen the orchard yet?"

The three of them strolled through the twisted trunks and settled in the shade of a particularly gnarly apple tree to wait for Lillian and Angie. Emilia nursed her beer while Stevie and Morgan drank soda, listening to the drone of the bees in the apple blossoms. Morgan's arm lightly encircled her waist, but they took it no further. Their dogs lay in panting heaps in the hot sunshine.

"It's beautiful out here," she said.

"Wait till the fall—"

Emilia couldn't tell if she'd imagined the ripple of stillness that passed through Morgan as she cut herself off.

"How are the apples?" She hoped the words would rescue them both from the unspoken question of what the changing season would bring.

"Amazing if you don't mind a few worms," said Stevie.

"Lil makes an amazing apple pie. And Stormy will do small batches of cider for us."

"Not that we'll ever get to enjoy it," said Stevie.

"Danielle will find someone eventually." Morgan rested her head against the trunk of the tree.

Emilia felt Stevie's measuring look and did not meet her eyes. She could not work at Seal Cove. Even if she was looking for a job, which she wasn't, throwing herself completely into Morgan's world would be a disaster on so many levels. To begin with, she still hardly knew the woman, for all that her body begged to differ, and if things didn't work out between them—which was highly likely—she'd be stuck working with her. Secondly, once again she would have made a career decision based on her heart instead of her mind, and that hadn't exactly worked out splendidly last time.

That didn't mean she found the idea repulsive. She allowed herself to sink into the fantasy. Large animal medicine *had* interested her at one point. Perhaps she could embrace that latent passion and do what Morgan did now, driving around the countryside, or leave ambulatory for Morgan and take over the large animal duties at the hospital. The pay raise alone was tempting. Large animal vets didn't always make as much as their small animal counterparts, but compared to a shelter vet, she'd be rich—in more ways than one. The Seal Cove practice felt like a family. They cared about each other. They loved what they did. She desperately wanted to be a part of something like that.

Angie's shout of greeting floated over the orchard. With matching sighs, the three of them stood, stretched off the somnolent atmosphere, and walked back to the house. Emilia felt the absence of Morgan's hand in hers but did not reach out to take it. She was an adult, not a sixteen-year-old. She didn't need that kind of constant reassurance, and she had never been one for PDA. Walking beside Morgan was enough. The backs of their knuckles brushed every few steps, and the warmth of the summer afternoon encircled her like Morgan's arms. She shot her a lazy smile over her shoulder. Morgan's answering grin poured down her spine like sunlight.

Angie stripped out of her stained work polo as they entered the fenced yard.

"It's hot." She slumped into a lawn chair in her sports bra. "Why is it hot?"

"It's July. Need a hose?" Stevie made a move toward the spigot on the side of the house.

"Don't you dare, Stephanie Ward."

Stevie lunged.

Angie was up and shrieking before the water hit her. Stevie, Emilia conceded, was almost freakishly fast, and a spray of water slapped Angie across the back as she tried to flee to the shelter of the house. Dripping, she turned, and Emilia covered her own burst of laughter with her hand as Stevie got Angie across the chest.

"You are so dead."

Morgan pulled Emilia out of harm's way and toward the grill as Angie forged through another blast of water to wrestle the hose out of Stevie's hands. They went down in a heap of arms, legs, and enthusiastic dogs, who had decided this was the best game in the entire world.

"Not in the mood for a wet T-shirt contest?" Emilia asked as Morgan knelt to check the gas.

"Why, are you offering?"

"To spray you?"

"No. To get wet."

Emilia wished the line, which was borderline Stevie-bad, hadn't worked on her, but her body energetically disagreed. She tangled her fingers in Morgan's hair, glad the grill blocked them from view, and shook her head in disapproval. Her expression held for the two seconds it took for Morgan to close the distance and nip the fabric of her jeans, and then she had to fight not to gasp. Stevie and Angie were still entangled in a ball of curses and laughter. At the moment, Angie appeared to have Stevie pinned and was dousing her entire front with the hose while the dogs took turns diving in to bite at the water. They vanished from her sight as her eyes closed. Morgan's hands found her ass, pressing the zipper of her jeans against Morgan's mouth in a kiss that left Emilia clutching the grill for support.

"Plenty of gas."

Morgan stood and opened the top of the grill with a self-satisfied set to her lips that Emilia found simultaneously frustrating and incredibly hot.

"Morgan! Save me!" Stevie's cry for help was interrupted by Marvin, who had chosen that moment to lick her face enthusiastically.

"You started it," said Morgan.

Stevie, however, didn't look like she wanted rescuing. Emilia couldn't help noticing the way she was grinning, or the way Angie, whose bare skin glistened, leaned over her to shove the hose down the front of Stevie's shirt with a victorious expression that had one too many layers for a simple water fight.

"Children," said Lillian from the doorway of the house. Hermione glared regally down at them all from her stronghold in Lillian's arms.

Angie got one last spray in, then let the hose fall to the ground. Lillian turned it off and skirted the soaked grass on her way over to Morgan.

"Good day?" Morgan asked.

"If I have to hear one more person complain that I should treat their animal for free because, and I quote, *I would do it if I really loved animals*, I'm going to scream."

"Ask them if they would do their job for free," said Morgan.

"I think I would prefer to just have you help me bury the bodies."

"That's what friends are for, Lil."

Emilia was all too familiar with the problem. Owners, who rarely saw the real cost of human medicine, failed to appreciate how much their medical insurance covered, and then there was the fact that vets paid just as much for vet school as human doctors did for medical school, only to make a third, if not less, of their salary. To say vets were in it for the money was to confess complete and total ignorance of the American medical system.

They had just finished eating when Morgan's pager went off.

"Noooo." Stevie slumped in her chair.

"At least you got dinner. And hey, maybe it will be an easy one," said Angie.

The rest of them stared at Angie in horror.

"She's been out of the field too long," Stevie said with a wide-eyed expression. "She's forgotten the curse."

"The curse is bull—"

"It is not bullshit and you know it. The veterinary gods are cruel and unforgiving. We'll probably be stuck out all night now."

"Then at least you got dinner."

"Don't make me get the hose again."

"It's Abby Killmore."

The name meant nothing to Emilia, but Stevie broke off arguing with Angie and blinked at Morgan.

"One of her sheep?"

"No. It's Olive."

"Olive?" Emilia asked.

"The horse Stevie's in love with," said Angie.

Morgan whipped out her cell and called Abby while Stevie explained that Olive had been a teenage girl's barrel racing prospect, only to develop stringhalt and get dumped at her mom's cousin's. Emilia's heart twinged. Shelter dogs and cats had it rough; horses, perhaps, had it even worse. Long-lived and expensive to keep, they got passed around from owner to owner, and so many ended up as pasture ornaments before their time, out of shape and bored, or at slaughter.

"All right," Morgan said as she hung up. "Emilia, I'm sorry."

"It's fine. I knew you were on call. How's the horse?"

"Colic." Morgan turned to Stevie. "Is the truck gassed up?"

Stevie nodded, and Emilia felt words bubbling up in her chest. She tasted them, but she wasn't sure of their meaning until they left her mouth.

"Need a hand?"

Morgan's eyes widened in surprise, and Emilia felt her own face stiffen like a mask. She didn't know what her expression revealed about just how much those words had taken her unawares. This was a disaster in waiting, wasn't it? Hadn't she sworn to take a few months off from the field to think about things? She knew what a bad case of colic might mean: euthanasia. Could she handle that?

"We'd love a hand," said Morgan, and Emilia didn't know whether she was grateful Morgan hadn't questioned her decision or terrified. "Need a pair of coveralls?"

Emilia considered her shirt and sandals. "Maybe a pair of boots if you have them?"

It turned out that she and Lillian wore the same shoe size, and Morgan lent her a Seal Cove Veterinary polo that she shoved into her jeans in a French tuck. Morgan's shoulders were significantly broader than hers, and the shirt hung off her. Not that it mattered how she looked, she reminded herself, but focusing on her clothing felt safer than thinking about what lay ahead.

She refused to let Morgan kick Stevie out of the front passenger seat. Instead, she rode in the back with a confused Nell. Kraken remained behind with Lillian and Angie. The shirt smelled like Morgan's detergent, and she stopped herself with difficulty from burying her face in the sleeve while Stevie fiddled with the radio as they drove down country roads lined with forests and fields. She caught Morgan watching her in the mirror more than once and took comfort in those steady blue-gray eyes.

I'm a doctor, she told herself as they drove. *This is my job. Nothing to panic about.*

Panic, however, was determined to have its say. Her last work memory pounced. Pushing the bright pink Euthansol. The phone call. Her father's death, and the sense, illogical but irrepressible, that she had somehow caused it, as if all the death in her wake had added up to that moment. *What a waste of life. What a waste of a fucking life.*

It had never mattered that if it hadn't been her pushing the drug it would have been someone else, or that the people working at the shelters did their best to find homes for all their animals, even if it meant filling their own homes with more animals than they could afford. It had never mattered because everyone who had warned her against the field had been right, she hadn't been cut out for shelter medicine. She couldn't detach, and so her brain had done it for her, but it had taken things several steps too far—severing instead of shielding. Would things have been different if she had gone into general practice? Would she have still burnt out only a few years out of school?

Think of this as a ride-along, she tried to tell herself. She'd done plenty as a student. This could be a litmus test for how she was feeling toward work. It had nothing to do with the job opening at Seal Cove.

That last thought froze her. She sat, her hand tight around Nell's collar, as she weighed the implications of even considering what that could mean.

"I haven't had a ride-along in a while," Morgan said from the front seat. "Last one was a vet student on summer vacation."

Emilia had a sudden and vivid picture of how she would have reacted as a student to a ride-along with Morgan. Buckets of drool would undoubtedly have been involved. And swooning. She met Morgan's eyes, and Morgan seemed to guess her thoughts because she grinned. The flash of white teeth calmed her. This did not, after all, need to be as big a deal as she was making it. Downed horses were tricky, and they might very well need a hand to get the mare back on her feet. She was simply fulfilling the oath she'd taken when she became a vet.

They pulled into a small but neatly maintained farmstead fifteen minutes later. Sheep dotted the hillside pasture, and a woman stood waiting outside the red barn doors. Morgan opened Emilia's door for her, and before Emilia had time to register whether or not the gesture irritated her, Morgan touched her arm.

"Are you up for this?"

"I'll find out," she said. Morgan squeezed her forearm and looked as if she wanted to say more, but didn't.

"Dr. Donovan," said the stocky woman Emilia assumed was Abby. "Thank you for coming."

"Of course. Where is she?"

"The back paddock."

Stevie had her hands shoved deeply into her pockets and a worried expression on her face as she fell into step behind Morgan with Emilia.

The back paddock was small, and it was clear that Olive had done her best to eliminate every single blade of grass.

"I took her off pasture because she was getting fat, and this afternoon I came out and found her like this."

A Belgian mare sat in the dirt, more like a dog than a horse. Emilia recognized the symptom. The horse raised her head at their approach but made no move to stand.

"How long do you estimate she's been like this?" asked Morgan.

"She was up this morning, but didn't eat all her breakfast. I thought that was unusual, and I ran some errands, then came home to keep an eye on her. She's gotten up a few times, but she keeps biting at her sides and rolling. She's been sitting like this for about an hour."

Morgan walked around the horse while Stevie knelt at her head, whispering something to her. Emilia cast her mind around for what she remembered about colic. It could be caused by any number of things, ranging from a buildup of gas to an infarction. With luck, this would just be an impaction—perhaps the result of ingesting too much sand from the paddock.

"Let's get some blood; then we'll try and get her up." Morgan joined Stevie at the head and accepted the vacutainer collection needle Stevie handed her. The mare didn't move as Morgan held the tubes up to the vacutainer to fill them, but her sides heaved, and sweat soaked her shoulders and flanks. *Classic signs of pain.*

Olive struggled to her feet as Stevie tugged on her halter and Morgan shoved at the horse's hips. Emilia and Abby urged Olive on with encouraging chirps and words of praise, and at last Olive staggered to her feet. She stood with her legs splayed and her eyes glazed.

Morgan motioned for Emilia to step forward. With her borrowed stethoscope, she joined Morgan in listening for intestinal sounds. Absolute silence met her ears.

That's not good.

"Okay," said Morgan as she checked Olive's heart rate and mucous membranes.

"Rectal exam?" Emilia offered.

Morgan worked through the exam methodically, her face taut with concentration, and Emilia marveled at the steadiness of her own hands against the horse's flank. Sheep *baa*ed in the distance. Hay and manure mingled in her nostrils, along with the warm smell of horse. If Olive was badly obstructed, there were steps that could be taken. She ran through them, trying to recall her large animal rotations. Olive stood patiently while Morgan probed, and Emilia appreciated the steadiness of the animal's temperament. *This isn't a shelter,* she repeated to herself. *We can help her. I can help her.*

"Let's get her some butorphanol and place a nasogastric tube," Morgan said when she withdrew. Emilia noted the grim set to her face and looked over at Olive again. The horse was clearly in severe pain; this was not a case of mild colic.

"Do you think it's an impaction?" Emilia asked.

"If it is, it's further up than I can feel. We'll see how she responds to fluids and the lubricant. The butorphanol should kick in soon, too."

Despite the confidence in Morgan's words, the pain medication had little impact on Olive. Her respiratory rate remained high, and after several hours with no increased signs of motility, Morgan turned to Abby.

"Dr. Donovan?" Abby asked with fading hope.

"I'm worried she's got a strangulating obstruction."

"What does that mean?" asked Abby.

Emilia knew the answer. It meant without surgical correction, the blood supply to the rest of the intestine could be cut off, killing the tissue—and the horse.

"It means we need to talk about next steps. I'm not comfortable waiting this out." Morgan explained the risks to a white-lipped

Abby Killmore. Emilia thought she saw the shine of tears in the older woman's eyes.

"Abby," said Morgan, "is the horse in your name?"

"No. My cousin has the papers."

"We have three options here." Morgan spoke calmly, but with authority. "My recommendation is that we get her to a specialist for surgery. The nearest one is Portland. Your second choice is to wait and hope it works itself out with lubricant, but I don't recommend it."

"What's the third choice?"

"A quality-of-life discussion."

Euthanasia. Emilia's stomach writhed at the thought. *Death follows me everywhere.* She shouldn't have come. Perhaps if she had remained behind, the prognosis would be better for Olive. She knew the thought was superstitious. It didn't change the clenched certainty inside her.

"I need to call my cousin," said Abby.

Abby stepped away and pulled out her phone. Emilia studied the slump of her shoulders and felt Morgan's hand on her back.

"You okay?" Morgan asked her.

No, she wanted to say. *I am not okay.* Instead, she nodded.

Stevie stroked Olive's nose and crooned something into her ears. Olive's flaxen mane mingled with Stevie's blond hair. The sight tightened Emilia's lungs.

When Abby returned, her face had turned from gray to a sort of pale mustard color, accented by two bright spots of anger in her cheeks.

"They don't want to pay for treatment. They'll turn her over to me, but Dr. Donovan, I can't afford to have her hospitalized."

"I understand." Morgan and Abby stepped to one side and spoke in the low tones of people making funeral arrangements. Morgan nodded sympathetically as Abby gesticulated, but Emilia saw the set of her shoulders and knew Morgan was angry.

"I'm sorry," she said to Stevie.

"It's okay. She's not mine. It's not my call, is it, sweet girl?" The last words were for the horse.

214

"I get it, though." She stroked Olive's strong neck. "Sometimes we just click with them, and it hurts."

Stevie looked up at her with overbright eyes. The jokester was gone. A woman in pain sat before her, and Emilia's heart broke. They both knew the outcome. She saw the conflict twist Stevie's face, and she knew what it was like to fall in love like this. It happened. Though she would never put it into words, she believed in soul mates. Not human soul mates, especially after Hannah, but animals sometimes reached out and touched a part of her that she could only identify as soul. That's how she'd ended up with Nell, but there had been others: dogs and cats in her care who had wormed their way past her professional barriers. Animals she'd fostered and found homes for who still haunted her dreams. Animals she hadn't saved. She rested her hand on Stevie's shoulder as Stevie wiped at her eyes.

"Allergies," Stevie said in an attempt at levity, but neither of them smiled.

"We don't deserve them."

"We really don't." Stevie shook her head and stared into Olive's large brown eyes. Olive looked up at her with trust and pain and confusion.

Morgan and Abby conferred for a while. Stevie talked to Olive, and Emilia braided her long mane for something to do with her hands. The coarse texture of mane brought up childhood memories of horseback riding lessons, and she remembered the farm her father would take her to in the summer, with its old lesson horses and the grizzled instructor. Her father had watched her ride around and around in circles with pride filling his eyes.

Forgiveness savaged her, ripping into her body with a pain that made her gasp. Stevie looked up in alarm, and Emilia shook her head, unable to speak as her hand tightened around Olive's mane.

Her father had loved her. His drinking had stolen him away from her, but he had loved her, and he had been proud of her, and that was what she had now: the memory of his love.

"Emilia?"

"I'm . . ." she started to say she was fine, but stopped herself.

"My dad. He liked horses." An idiotic statement, and yet, here in the mud with a dying mare, she could not find any other words. His love scorched her. Missed opportunities sparked, flared, and burned out, along with some of her anger and resentment, charred pieces landing on the exposed parts of her heart. Her father had loved her, and now he was gone.

"I'll pay for half her treatment," Emilia found herself saying to Stevie.

Stevie's mouth fell open.

"Get Abby to sign her over to you."

"Emilia—"

"You two belong together if you want it."

Furrows sprung up on Stevie's brow. "I could talk to Ange. We could fence off part of the orchard, and there's an old hoop house we could use as a run-in." She held Emilia's eyes. "I can't ask you to pay for her treatment, though."

"Can you pay for it yourself?"

"No, but—"

"Then let me help. Please."

"Why?"

Because I can't bear to lose anything else. It wasn't a professional thought. It wasn't even a rational thought, but she could not take the feeling that death followed her everywhere and it seemed crucial suddenly that this horse live. She felt the way she had when she was a child begging fate for favors: *If the next car that passes is blue, my parents will get back together. If this horse lives, everything will turn out okay.*

"Because I want to feel like I've done something good."

Light blue eyes, so different from Morgan's, held hers, and Emilia understood as she held them why that friendship had lasted over the years. Stevie might prank and clown, but beneath that veneer she sensed the same intensity and sensitivity that drove Morgan. Stevie nodded once as if she'd heard the words Emilia had not said aloud.

"If you change your mind, I can always open up a payment plan. You're not bound to this."

216

"Fair enough."

Stevie dug her phone out of her pocket and dialed Angie. Emilia listened to their conversation with half an ear. She felt light and heavy all at the same time, like she might drift away in slow motion if she wasn't careful.

Stevie hung up with a dazed expression.

"What did she say?" Emilia asked.

"She said yes."

She hadn't expected Angie to say no. Stevie, however, appeared stunned. Taking on an animal was always a big decision, and horses were a thousand pounds of responsibility with legs and bodies that seemed designed to fail. This could beggar Stevie, but Emilia did not point out what she was sure Stevie knew.

Morgan turned back to them as the resolve in Stevie's face hardened.

"Stevie, I need you to—"

"Morgan."

"What?"

"Ask Abby if she'll sign her over to me."

"To you?"

"Yes."

"Stevie—"

"I've decided to get into mounted archery."

Morgan looked at Emilia, who shrugged.

"Mounted archery?"

"Yep."

"With Olive?"

"Yep."

Morgan rubbed the back of her neck and looked over her shoulder at Abby, who stood with the air of someone going to their execution.

"She can't afford this, and she feels guilty," Stevie said in a rush before Abby could enter hearing distance. "I can stable her at the house."

"Or Olive could die, leaving you in debt."

"I don't care."

"Stevie—"

"Please, Morgan."

Morgan searched Stevie's face and then shifted her gaze to Emilia, who felt a shadow pass over her. She didn't want Morgan thinking she'd pressured her friend into a rash decision. More than that, however, she didn't want this animal to die for the same reasons that had shadowed her work in shelters: finances. It wasn't the animal's fault she'd been discarded by one owner and dumped on another who had never asked for a horse and could not afford to take her to surgery. Neither was it Abby's fault. Sometimes, though, the right person was in the right place at the right time, and if she could help Stevie save a life, she would.

Saving Olive would not bring back her father.

It *would* be a tribute to his memory.

"I'll talk to her," said Morgan.

By the time they got Olive on the trailer, the sun had long since set and the lights of distant fireworks lit their faces with reds, blues, whites, and greens. Stevie's laughter buoyed them, and Emilia couldn't help joining in.

Emilia lay awake long after Morgan fell asleep. Morgan's dark hair was damp with sweat, and the relaxed curve of her body warmed Emilia's, which hummed in contentment even as her mind roamed. She stared at the stars out the window. They'd arrived back sometime after 3 a.m. after situating Olive at the surgeon's where Stevie had remained, and then she'd tumbled Morgan into bed before Morgan could ask her the questions Emilia could see hovering around her lips. A breeze from the nearby ocean blew in through the open window and ruffled Morgan's hair. She trailed her fingers through it and twisted a curl around her middle finger as her heart beat in her too-tight chest.

She'd practiced today. Technically, of course, it had been Morgan's case, and all she had done was assist, but she'd offered up differentials and assisted in a treatment plan, and she hadn't panicked. She hadn't shut down. Instead, she'd witnessed good medicine in practice and played a role in it, and the complicated roil of emotions that had brought to the surface now assaulted her from every quadrant.

"You're awake," said Morgan.

She hadn't noticed Morgan's breathing shift into wakefulness. "You shouldn't be. You might get called in again."

"I'll be fine." Morgan stroked the bare skin along Emilia's hip. "Do you want to talk about anything?"

"No," Emilia said.

"I thought you were Italian."

"Only when I'm angry."

The soft snore of a dog punctuated the calm quiet of the night.

"Do you love what you do?" she asked Morgan eventually.

"Professionally?"

"Yeah."

"More than anything."

Emilia considered the statement. "What does that feel like?"

"Frustrating? Satisfying? I can't see myself doing anything else. I've never even wanted to do anything else."

"Not even when you were a kid?"

"I had a brief pirate phase, but besides that, no. I wanted to be a vet."

"I thought I knew what I wanted," said Emilia. Morgan waited for her to continue. "I was so sure of it, you know? And then everything fell apart, and now I'm not even sure who I am, let alone what I want to do."

Morgan remained silent.

"God, now I'm unloading on you and we hardly even know each other." The last statement rang false in her ears, but she didn't know how to correct it.

"Don't apologize. You've had a lot happen, and you're allowed to be confused."

"Confused." She repeated the word. "Yes."

"Was coming along tonight too much?"

"No," she said, needing the warmth of Morgan's hand on her hip too badly for comfort. "I mean, maybe? It felt good to be in the field again. Although now I have professional jealousy about you to deal with, too. You're a good doctor."

Morgan didn't laugh at her attempt at humor.

"I'm sorry. You really should go back to sleep."

"Who made you feel like your feelings weren't valid?"

Morgan's blunt question knocked the wind out of her. She fixated on a particularly bright star. Venus, perhaps. Not a star then. A world.

"I don't know."

She did know, though. Hannah. Thao. All the women who had mistaken her softness for weakness and exploited it or smothered her with misguided protections.

"Whoever it was, they were wrong." Morgan tucked Emilia's hair behind her ear. "This is your life, Emilia."

"Is it?"

"Yes. I have doubts about almost everything else besides my career if that makes you feel better."

She looked at Morgan. Her eyes were nearly black in the darkness, and her mouth was no more than a soft shadow. "What about this?"

Morgan resumed stroking Emilia's skin. "Are we talking about us now?"

"We don't have to," said Emilia.

Morgan lapsed into silence for a few moments. "I like you a lot."

Warmth trickled into every part of her body at Morgan's words.

"But you've got a lot going on," Morgan continued before Emilia could speak, "and I don't want to complicate that."

"You're not."

"Are you sure?"

She didn't answer. If she said yes, she'd not only be lying, but she'd be discrediting both of their feelings. If she said no, though, Morgan might feel obligated to call things off. She settled for a different truth.

"It's too late." She touched Morgan's lips with the tips of her fingers and traced the bow of the upper, then the full sweep of the lower.

"We could—"

"Morgan." She cut her off. "You don't need to protect me."

"But—"

"Shut up, Dr. Donovan." Morgan's lips parted beneath her fingers and Emilia pressed them closed. "I want this."

A small, nearly inaudible sound vibrated against her fingers. Emilia shifted beneath the sheets to lay flush against Morgan's body, half rolled on top of her, half tangled in her arms.

"I want this," she repeated in a voice that broke against itself as she framed the words, and Morgan's hands gripped her hips with a fierceness that mirrored her own.

Chapter Fourteen

The first few weeks of July passed in a blur of heat, appointments, and moments spent with Emilia. Morgan took her out on the boat and melted at the sight of her in a bikini, cursing the number of other boaters on the water who prevented Morgan from fucking her on the deck again. Stevie spent every spare minute with Olive, who had recovered from surgery without complication and who now lived at Morgan's parents while Morgan and Stevie built a paddock in the orchard. She saw Stormy in snatches behind her bar, usually while grabbing a cup of coffee on a midday break with Emilia, as she was now.

"This must be Ray's daughter."

Both Morgan and Emilia jumped. Morgan slopped her iced coffee down her front as she looked up into her mother's face. Shannon Donovan handed her a napkin and surveyed a startled Emilia over one of Stormy's outdoor café tables.

"Yes. I'm Emilia Russo. And you must be Morgan's mother?"

"Shannon," she said with a smile.

"I can see the family resemblance."

"I've been telling Morgan to bring you by the house. My husband, Aaron, knew your father. You're always welcome. In fact," she shot Morgan an inscrutable look that promised trouble, "why don't you come over tonight if you aren't busy?"

Morgan opened her mouth to stop this disaster, but only a squeak came out.

"I'd love to," said Emilia.

"Wonderful. Stop by whenever you get out of work."

"It's my day off," said Morgan, who had been looking forward to spending the day lying in bed with Emilia, not facing the Shannon Inquisition.

"Then we'll see you at five."

And with that, Shannon strode away.

Morgan stared after her mother, feeling like she'd been clubbed over the head.

"You okay?" Emilia asked.

She made what she'd intended to be a noise of assent, but what instead sounded like a strangled cat.

"Your mother seems nice."

"Hah." Morgan buried her face in her hands. "My mother is a force of nature. Nature is inherently cruel."

"Then we have that in common."

She peered out at Emilia through her fingers.

"My mother is one, too," Emilia finished.

"I don't want her steamrolling you. Don't feel like you have to come to dinner."

"Actually, I'd really like to." Emilia avoided her eyes and drew a line through the condensation on the table.

Morgan pictured the four of them sitting around her parents' kitchen table. Her mother would pick up on Morgan's feelings for Emilia faster than a bloodhound in a charnel house, especially given the tip-off Stevie had supplied her earlier that summer. Armed with that knowledge, she was bound to corner Morgan and interrogate her later. Not for the first time, she wished she had a sibling to distract her mother from her only daughter. As for her father, he'd be his usual affable self, but he reported to his wife. They'd be sure to compare notes. Morgan wasn't prepared to face that jury.

She took a steadying breath and said, "Okay then, but don't say I didn't warn you."

"You met my sister. I suppose it is only fair." Emilia still hadn't met her eye. "Do your parents . . ."

"I haven't told them that we're . . . whatever we're doing."

"If you don't want me to meet them, that's okay."

"No! That's not it." She floundered and cast around for words, feeling five years old again and caught making mischief in Miss Peters's classroom. "I just don't want you to feel uncomfortable."

"Really, don't worry about that. And if they knew my dad, I'd like to talk to them."

Of course, she thought, feeling even worse. This was about Ray, not her.

"Then wear something with an elastic waistband so my mom can shove you full of food."

"Does this mean you want to have a food baby with me?" said Emilia.

Morgan's laugh burst out of her, catching her by surprise and dispelling the black mood that had threatened to settle. "Yes. I totally do."

They spent the rest of the afternoon on the water instead of Morgan's bed. Emilia had invited her to come for a sail. It was the first time she'd offered, and it didn't take much guesswork on Morgan's part to surmise that it was hard for Emilia to sail with someone besides her father. She watched Emilia handle the lines of the sailboat with a confidence she'd seen in her only in the bedroom, and she was surprised to find she was more than content to make herself comfortable on a cushion as Emilia took them out of the harbor—though she eyed the currents and the hidden rocks with distrust. Sunlight teased red highlights out of Emilia's hair, and her skin glowed under the blue sky. The sight pierced Morgan with a fierce longing, and she tried to fix this moment in her memory forever.

Neither of them spoke much as they sailed. The creak of the boat and the snap of the wind in the sails each time they came about filled the air with enough conversation, and the distant shrieking of gulls harassing the lobster boats for discarded bait echoed Morgan's thoughts: *I want, I want, I want.* Emilia kept one hand on the tiller and the other on the lines, searching out the wind. Morgan let her own hand skim along the waves. Sailing wasn't like driving her boat. It was quieter. Slower. A different sort of exhilaration.

Emilia's shorts exposed her lean and muscled thighs. Not wanting to disrespect Ray's memory, Morgan did not run her fingers over the smooth skin, but her eyes strayed the longer they sailed. The buttons of Emilia's white shirt had come partially undone in the wind to reveal a curve of breast and the black cloth of her bikini top beneath. Reflections from the water played across the shadow of her cleavage, and Morgan's mouth went a little dry as she shifted. The heat between her own thighs was growing uncomfortable. Determined to behave, however, she stretched out on the bottom of the boat and propped her feet on the bow with her head resting on a life jacket near Emilia's calf. She studied the sway of the boom and the tight swell of the sail above her until Emilia leaned her leg against Morgan's head.

Unable to stop herself any longer, she stroked the arch of Emilia's bare foot and up her calf, thrilling at the feel of warm skin against her palm. Emilia didn't move away, and she continued the lazy caress, chewing on the inside of her lip to keep herself in check. Whenever the urge to slip her fingers under the hem of Emilia's shorts became too strong, she pictured Ray sitting across from her.

The image wavered, however, as Emilia opened her legs wider. Morgan chanced a glance up. Emilia's cheeks were flushed, and her lips were parted as she breathed more rapidly than normal. Still, Morgan hesitated. This boat clearly meant a great deal to Emilia, and she did not want to dishonor the memory of Ray Russo by going down on his daughter as she clutched the tiller, Morgan's name on her lips . . . *fuck*. She swallowed. *Be good*. But Emilia's thigh was pressed against her cheek, and she turned her face, dragging her palms down the underside of Emilia's calf as she kissed the salt-stained skin. Emilia gasped. The sound undid the last of Morgan's dwindling restraint, and she licked the sea spray from Emilia's thigh as her teeth and tongue worked their way up to the hem of Emilia's white shorts. Morgan could hardly be held accountable for the fact that those shorts covered so little.

She ran her tongue along the border of the cloth and paused whenever Emilia whimpered, savoring the way her body quivered as Morgan moved closer and closer to the place they both wanted her to be.

"Oh, god," Emilia said when Morgan nipped at the warm fabric over her clit. She pinned Morgan there with one leg while the other braced herself against the side of the boat. Morgan eased the hem up further, grateful for the scantiness of the material. Emilia shuddered as Morgan slid her hand along the line of her bikini bottoms, but Morgan didn't want to touch her with her fingers. She elicited a moan of protest as she withdrew and propped herself on her elbow to undo the top button of Emilia's shorts, then slowly eased the zipper down. It didn't give her enough access, but she kissed the skin of Emilia's stomach as Emilia lifted her hips to allow Morgan to slip off her shorts. She knew she should be on the lookout for other boats, but she was beyond caution. She teased Emilia through the fabric of her suit. Emilia's clit hardened as Morgan took it in her mouth through the cloth.

Emilia kept the boat on course—or if not on course, she at least prevented them from turning into the wind. Morgan gently pulled the fabric aside. Emilia bucked her hips, begging Morgan with her body, but Morgan had been teased too many times by Emilia. She wasn't ready to give in just yet. She cupped one hand beneath Emilia's ass and ran her tongue along the crease of her thigh, the heat from Emilia's center burning against her cheek.

"Fuck you, Morgan."

Morgan dipped lower and tasted her. Her tongue traced Emilia's opening in slow circles, now and then entering her in long strokes. Emilia's heel dug into her back. She intensified the thrusts of her tongue as she felt Emilia's body begin to shake. When she at last dragged her tongue out and up along the length of Emilia and over her clit, Emilia cried out. Morgan was gratified to see her knuckles whiten on the tiller. She repeated the measured strokes, beginning inside and moving up to take Emilia in her mouth before returning to the beginning. Emilia was almost sobbing as she repeated Morgan's name. Morgan gave her ass a hard squeeze as she entered her again. Emilia jerked the tiller to the left and swore as she corrected. The curse broke into another moan when Morgan drew a lazy circle around her clit, closing in and just brushing it before working her way back out, reveling in the way Emilia tasted.

"I'll come right now if you don't fuck me."

"Don't come." Morgan let her words vibrate against Emilia. As much as she loved it when Emilia was in control, right now she wanted to be the one calling the shots—while Emilia captained the boat. She'd unpack that one later. Emilia's head flew back. Her hair caught the wind and Morgan's breath. God, she was beautiful. Despite her command, Morgan could feel the beginnings of orgasm in the way Emilia's body shuddered. She closed her lips and tongue over her clit and drew Emilia into her mouth.

"Holy fuck," moaned Emilia. Morgan slid two fingers inside her to press against her, feeling her g-spot harden beneath her touch. She licked her clit with the tip of her tongue, moving her fingers in and out, then intensified the motion as Emilia's trembling turned into whole body shudders. She felt her open, accepting more and more, and her own body shook as she came with her.

"Oh my god," Emilia said as she softened around Morgan's hand. "Oh my god, Morgan."

Withdrawing reluctantly, Morgan looked up at Emilia's closed eyes and blissful smile.

I love you, she thought, and the knowledge hit her with so much force she thought they'd run aground.

She picked Emilia up at four forty-five after showering salt water and sex off her body. The shower, however, had done nothing to erase her revelation, and the thought of sitting in front of her parents and Emilia with it burning a hole in her chest made her feel sick.

"What's up with you?" Stevie had asked from the couch where she'd sprawled with Marvin and a dog-eared paperback of *The Hitchhiker's Guide to the Galaxy*.

"Nothing."

Stevie sat up and put the book down. "You're dressed up."

"Dinner with my parents."

"Since when do you look nice for that?"

Morgan smoothed her dark blue button-down and inwardly cursed herself. Should she change into something more casual? But this *was* casual by most people's standards. Just a dress shirt, jeans, and her nice boots . . . *Shit.*

"Since my mother cornered Emilia and invited her, too."

"Oh." Stevie's face softened with sympathy. "That could be . . . awkward."

"Yeah."

"Do you want me to gate-crash?"

Morgan considered the offer. Stevie would balance things out, but what would Emilia think if Morgan invited Stevie along?

"Can I leave you on standby?"

"Sure. I'll dig out my phone in case you text." Stevie eyed the couch cushions dubiously.

"Thanks."

"Morgan," Stevie called out as Morgan turned to leave. "It will be okay."

Now, as Emilia emerged from Ray's house wearing a simple, dark green sheath dress that emphasized her figure, Morgan wondered if she should have brought Stevie along after all. How was she supposed to carry on a conversation when Emilia looked like that?

"Hi," she said as Emilia got into the car. Her throat felt unnaturally tight. Emilia shot her a quizzical look, and Morgan tried to smile. It felt like a grimace.

"You okay?"

First Stevie, now Emilia. If she couldn't fool them, then there was no way she was going to fool her mother.

She nodded.

"You don't look okay."

Morgan put the truck in drive, but Emilia's hand arrested hers on the shift. "Look at me."

She obeyed and tried to crack a joke. "Just wondering how I am supposed to act like a gentleman when you look like that."

"Is it too nice?" Emilia's face fell, and Morgan tried to banish her own doubts.

"God no. You'd look good in anything anyway. But . . ." she swallowed. "You do look gorgeous."

Emilia blushed. "So, your mom is Shannon and your dad is Aaron?"

"Good memory."

"What do they do?"

"My mom was a vet, too. She just retired two years ago, and now she works on the farm. My dad still works for the fishery department and spends his free time fishing. Guy's obsessed."

"He knows what he likes."

"Absolutely," said Morgan, aware she had taken after her father in that regard. She knew what she liked, and it was sitting right next to her, heartbreak dressed in green.

"Sometimes I wish one of my parents had been a vet. Or my stepdad. They don't really get it, you know?"

"Even my mom doesn't get how things have changed, honestly."

"But I bet her eyes don't glaze over when you talk about work."

"Fair point."

Emilia stared out the window with obvious curiosity as they approached Morgan's childhood home. She tried to see it from Emilia's perspective: the older house, in need of a new coat of paint, not quite yet shabby but derelict by Boston suburb standards. The wide lawn, mostly blueberry scrub at this point, and the red barn with its aging cupola and lopsided weather vane. Kraken raised his head in the back seat and thumped his tail in anticipation.

"You grew up here?" Emilia asked as she took it in.

"Yep." She pulled in beside her mother's Jeep. "Ready?"

Emilia smiled. Morgan forcibly reminded herself Emilia was

here to talk about her father, not to meet her girlfriend's parents. They were not a couple. She had no right to the vivid fantasies now rolling through her head like some jackass's idea of a movie montage, about showing Emilia her childhood haunts or sitting on the porch with her father and her arm around Emilia's shoulders with a scratchy wool blanket over their laps to keep off the evening chill.

I love you.

Had the thought merely been the by-product of sex and loneliness? She wanted to believe that was the case. She didn't want to give a name to the tightness in her chest and the sickening ache that filled her whenever Emilia left her side.

Shannon greeted them at the door with an enthusiastic ear scratch for Kraken, a kiss for Morgan, and a handshake and warm smile for Emilia.

"You look so much like your father," she said to Emilia as she ushered them inside. "Did Morgan warn you about the dogs?"

"No, but I love dogs."

A streak of black, gray, brown, and white shot past them as her mother's two border collies circled the newcomers. Kraken raised his lips disapprovingly, then ignored them.

"Your father is out back trellising his tomatoes. Can I get you girls a drink?"

Morgan followed her mother into the kitchen, noting the smells coming from the oven. Her mouth, ever a traitor, watered in anticipation. "Lamb pie?"

"Yes. Unless you're a vegetarian, Emilia? I should have asked."

"I'm not."

"Good. Not that I mind, of course, but Morgan loves her meat."

"*Ma.*"

"Well, it's true."

Kate had been a vegetarian. Was probably *still* a vegetarian, she corrected herself. When had she started thinking about Kate in the past tense? She suspected this was behind her mother's comment and groaned inwardly.

Emilia admired the kitchen as Shannon poured glasses of wine, praising the hanging copper pots, trailing houseplants, and granite countertops. Morgan observed her mother warming to the praise with satisfaction, though she knew that Shannon would reserve judgment for now.

"Here you are," her father said as he came through the kitchen door bearing a handful of freshly cut herbs. Their fragrance filled her nostrils, and she breathed in the sharp, piney scent of rosemary. "And you must be Emilia."

Emilia smiled and stuck out her hand. Aaron Donovan shook it as he apologized for the soil still clinging to his fingers.

"I don't mind a little dirt," said Emilia.

"Careful, or he'll put you to work in the garden," said Shannon.

Aaron winked at Morgan and Emilia. "Come sit with me on the porch before your mother puts us to work in here."

"Do you want any help?" Emilia asked Shannon.

Shannon waved them away, and they followed Aaron out to the back porch, which overlooked the pasture and the woods beyond.

"It's nice to meet you again, Emilia."

Emilia gave him a puzzled look.

"Last time I saw you, you were maybe four years old. You wouldn't remember, of course."

"I remember seeing Morgan, growing up," said Emilia.

Morgan fixed her eyes on her wine to avoid blushing, remembering Emilia's confession of unrequited adolescent love. *How the tables have turned.*

"My little hellion." He smiled at Morgan. "She's slowed down some, although you still drive too fast in that boat of yours."

"Be nice," Shannon said as she joined them.

"My wife drives too fast, too," he said in a stage whisper.

"Your father and my husband were friends in high school, and from what he's told me, they were responsible for their fair share of trouble."

"Ray was the ringleader. Very charismatic. Charmed us out of a few detentions. Did he ever tell you about the time we filled the football team's lockers with shaving cream?"

231

"You're *that* Aaron?" said Emilia.

Morgan studied Emilia as her father regaled them with stories of Ray's youth. Emilia hung on his every word, laughing as he exaggerated their exploits, and biting her lip periodically in a way that made Morgan think she was biting back tears. Her hand twitched in her lap, desperate to hold Emilia.

A prickling sensation at the back of her neck alerted her to danger. She tore her eyes away from Emilia and found her mother watching her with a calculating expression on her face. Morgan stared back defiantly.

"We lost touch after school. He moved away and met your mother, and when he moved back after the divorce we saw each other occasionally, but it was Morgan who knew him best." His face softened. "Perhaps this isn't my place to say, but your father was a good man. I know . . . I know it must have been hard. If you can, try to remember the good parts."

"Aaron," Shannon said in warning.

"My father was an alcoholic, too," said Aaron. "It's not an easy thing to live with."

Emilia nodded and spoke softly. "No, it's not."

"Morgan tells me you're a vet, too," Shannon said.

"I am."

"Small? Large?"

"Small, but I like large animal medicine."

"How long do we have you in town for?"

Emilia glanced at Morgan before replying. "I'm not sure. I'm still figuring out what I want to do with my dad's house. At least another month."

"Your practice is generous with leave," Shannon said as Morgan counted off the days in her head.

"I—"

"Ma," she said, coming to her senses. "You're prying."

"I'm sorry. You're right. Emilia, don't mind me."

"It's okay." Emilia took a deep breath. "I've actually left my practice. I'm taking a few months off to reevaluate things."

232

Shannon shot Morgan another look.

"Good for you," said Aaron. "It takes guts to take time for yourself."

"I should check on the pie. Morgan, come help me set the table?"

"Don't frighten her with any of your dad jokes," Morgan warned as she slunk off into her mother's lair.

Shannon beckoned her over to the oven. "Well, she's certainly good-looking."

"Jesus, Ma."

"Does she know you're in love with her?"

Morgan pressed her knuckles into the counter to keep from punching something. "Do we have to do this?"

"I worry about you."

"Well, don't. And no, she doesn't know, and she's not going to. You heard her. She's leaving in a month." No point in trying to hide the bitterness in her voice, she reflected as she listened to herself speak. Her mother wasn't dumb.

"Have you asked her to stay?"

"I've only known her since May."

"Take these plates," said Shannon. "And Morgan—"

"Just stay out of it, okay?" A wave of rosemary wafted into the kitchen as Shannon opened the oven. Not even that smell could clear the sourness from her tongue. "She's not Kate."

"I can see that."

"So you'll leave it alone?"

Shannon stuck a thermometer in the pie and considered her answer. "You're an independent woman. I raised you to make up your own mind."

Morgan waited for the "but."

"But I do hate seeing you hurt."

"I don't enjoy it either, for the record." She turned her back on her mother, fuming. This had been a mistake. Of course her mother couldn't leave well enough alone. That had always been the case. *Have you asked her to stay?* The idea was preposterous.

233

Asking Emilia to stick around for her would be unfair and self-ish. She'd do her best to enjoy the time they had and deal with the rest later.

Her foul mood ebbed as she set the table. She could see out the door to the porch, where Emilia was laughing, probably at one of her dad's terrible jokes. She looked so right, sitting there. More so even than Kate, who her father had adored. Emilia said something Morgan couldn't hear, and her father threw back his head with mirth while Shannon emerged from the kitchen to place a hand on Morgan's shoulder in sympathetic silence.

Chapter Fifteen

Emilia paused her assault on the weeds in the front garden to wipe a stream of sweat out of her eyes. Late July, she'd assumed incorrectly, would be cooler here than in Boston, but the degree or two of discrepancy didn't make much of a difference once the temperature surpassed eighty-five degrees. At this rate, temps would hit ninety by noon. Maybe she'd head to the dock for a swim after she finished prepping the yard for the real estate agent.

Her hand tightened violently around the next weed. Calling the agent had been a good idea, she reminded herself. The real estate market was a total mystery to her, and she'd need an agent whether she decided to sell or rent. The woman had seemed nice enough on the phone. Professional, knowledgeable, and objective. Her insight would help Emilia make the decision she'd been putting off for months. Why, then, did the thought make her queasy?

It could be the heat, she reminded herself. Haze shimmered over the gravel drive. Nell had opted to remain on the shaded porch, sleeping. Emilia plucked a thistle from behind a wilting shrub and tossed it into the wheelbarrow before slumping. The yard looked fine. She'd mowed the meadow, and the garden was respectably weed free, provided no one looked close enough. The agent—Katherine something—had mentioned photographs. Maybe she could Photoshop the last of the weeds out. Would she have to pay a landscaper if she decided to rent, or would the tenant take care of that? A property management company? But what if the house fell into disrepair and no one told her? Once again, she considered the relative ease of selling. It made more sense, once her emotions were out of the picture.

The queasiness intensified. She wheeled the weeds to the ends of the yard and tipped them into the woods. If only her parents had been a better fit for each other, like Morgan's. Then this would be somebody else's problem: namely, her mother's.

Thinking about Morgan brought the now familiar rush of warmth. Dinner with the Donovans had been more enjoyable than she'd allowed herself to hope for. Shannon, she'd noticed, had held herself back a little, eying her daughter, but Aaron was one of the most genuinely wonderful men she'd ever met. He was so like Morgan that she smiled at the memory.

It hadn't just been talking about her father that made the evening feel special, either. The love in that house reached out and invited her in, so much so that she hadn't wanted to leave. Her own family looked at her with too much concern these days for her to appreciate the comfort of her mother's home. It didn't hurt that Morgan had been visibly flustered each time she reached for Emilia, catching herself at the last minute—although not, she suspected, before Shannon had seen. Morgan always seemed so cool and put together. Seeing her off balance made Emilia itch to push her down on the nearest surface and blow her cool even further open.

The forced platonic nature of the evening had ended in a spectacularly unplatonic night. She leaned against the handles of the wheelbarrow while her body tingled in recollection. Morgan had been even more intense than usual, and Emilia recalled the marks her teeth had left in Morgan's shoulder with a new wave of hunger. She'd wanted to take her again and again, until Morgan's breathing was so ragged it sounded like sobs, and afterward she'd fallen into a dreamless sleep sprawled across Morgan's chest with Morgan's hands still buried in her hair.

A buzz from her pocket broke her out of her reverie: the alarm she'd set as a reminder. Her campaign against the weeds had taken her longer than she realized. She hurried to get cleaned up, reflecting on all the things the agent would no doubt say needed updating: the upstairs bathroom, for starters. She trailed water out of the bathroom and past the open door of her father's room to her own bedroom with its twin bed. The bed was the main reason she hadn't invited Morgan to spend the night here.

The thought renewed the sense of unease that had briefly faded while she thought of Morgan. That was the reason, wasn't it? Moving into her father's room wasn't an emotionally viable option, even though the queen-sized bed was far more suitable. She couldn't bring Morgan into that room. That was all. It had nothing to do with the fact that having Morgan here, in this house, would bridge her two worlds too completely—and there was a guest room with a queen mattress that was perfectly serviceable, even if it squeaked.

These thoughts were still on her mind when the real estate agent knocked. She'd had the foresight to check the woman's name beforehand and was prepared to greet Katherine Kovaleski with a firm handshake and a smile.

The smile, however, froze on her face as the door swung open. It occurred to her, belatedly, that she should have checked the woman's photo for safety reasons if nothing else. If she had, it might also have occurred to her that *Kate* was short for *Katherine*.

Morgan's ex-fiancé greeted her with a polite smile.

"Katherine," she said as she offered her hand. Emilia shook it because she didn't see an alternative.

Smile, she told herself. *Act like an adult.*

"So nice to meet you. Please come in." Her voice sounded falsely chipper to her own ears, but maybe Kate—Katherine—wouldn't notice. *Fuck, fuck, fuckity fucking fuck.* This could not be happening.

"And who's this?"

"Oh my god, I'm sorry. This is Nell. I meant to put her away. I can—"

"Don't worry about it. I'm a dog person."

She'd have to be to have been with Morgan, Emilia reflected as Katherine greeted Nell. The pause gave her a chance to scrutinize the other woman.

Morgan clearly had a type. Katherine stood as tall as Emilia, and while her dark brown hair was currently pinned up in the sort of sophisticated twist Emilia had never been able to manage, she could tell that Katherine had the same thick waves as she did. Sure, Katherine's skin tone was lighter, and her eyes were more hazel than brown, but "leggy brunette" might as well have been stamped on their passports. Katherine wore a smart pair of black slacks and casually elegant pumps, giving her a slight height advantage, and her sleeveless blouse accentuated her curves. She was even prettier in person than in her photograph. Emilia felt an immediate need to hate this woman, which she stifled. She could get through this. Then she'd just tell Katherine she had decided to go with another agent. Nothing personal.

Katherine finished petting Nell and looked around appraisingly.

"You mentioned this house belonged to your father?"

"Yes." Grief, at least, cleared her mind of other thoughts.

Katherine gave her an understanding smile. "I've worked with quite a few clients in your situation. It isn't easy. One of my other listings is for a man whose father recently passed, too."

"I am sorry to hear that."

"Maine's aging population makes it inevitable, and I enjoy helping where I can. This isn't the kind of thing anyone should have to deal with on their own."

Emilia did not point out that it also wasn't the sort of thing she wanted to face with the help of her lover's ex-fiancé.

"This looks like a new coat of paint."

"Yes."

"You've done a nice job. It's hard, especially when you have so many decisions to make regarding what to keep."

"My father had a thing for taxidermy," Emilia said.

"Did he hunt?"

"Yeah."

"That's normal for Maine. I had a listing last year for a man who collected watches. The house was full of them. I could barely show the house, there were so many. Anyway, I appreciate the legwork you've done here. Shall we look around?"

Emilia followed Katherine from room to room, answering questions and trying to do her best to stay calm. Talking about showing the house was terrifying enough without having to stare at Katherine's perfect ass and picture Morgan—*nope, don't go there.* Katherine made notes as they covered the downstairs, then ascended the staircase. Emilia dug her nails into her thighs and pinched herself.

Katherine inspected her father's room, first. Cold sweat broke out on Emilia's forehead. She wanted to push the woman out of the way and slam the door before she could say anything. This had been a mistake. She wasn't ready. She would never be ready.

"Sometimes it is good to leave the master suite untouched," Katherine said, and Emilia realized she was being watched. "It gives prospective buyers a place for a personal touch, and you've done a wonderful job with the rest of the house. Have you had an appraisal yet?"

"Not yet." She could barely breathe.

"That would be the next step if you decide to list. An inspection, too—that way there are no surprises."

"Surprises?" She'd had enough of those already.

"Like a failing septic."

Things are already shitty enough.

"I—"

"This is a lot of information, I know. Why don't I meet you back downstairs?"

Emilia fled.

Back in the kitchen, alone with her dog, she rested her forehead against the fridge and held on to the sides of the appliance. Nausea wracked her body. She wanted to call Morgan, craving her stability, but that wasn't possible with Katherine in the house. The idea of other people poking around her father's life was intolerable.

A warm hand touched her arm. She blinked into Katherine's hazel eyes and flinched.

"Can I pour you a glass of wine? A cup of tea?"

Tears sprang to her eyes and overflowed in a hot torrent at the simple kindness. She gestured wordlessly at the fridge she'd been clinging to and accepted the small glass of white wine Katherine poured her. The cool liquid trickled down her throat, and she mopped at her eyes with the back of her hand, smearing her mascara.

"This is incredibly difficult," said Katherine. "Would you like me to come back at another time?"

Emilia shook her head. She did not want Katherine coming back. Only after she'd finished the gesture did she realize she had inadvertently let an opportunity for escape slip past her.

"Why don't I lay out the steps for you? That way you have all the information in front of you." She guided Emilia to a seat at the kitchen table and took the chair opposite as she laid out a folder.

She listened as Katherine explained about inspections and appraisals and the various rental opportunities available in the current market, as well as the likelihood of a quick sale. She had a low, melodic voice that gradually pushed back the sparkling darkness at the edges of Emilia's vision. Her desire to hate Katherine abated. It didn't matter anymore that she was Morgan's ex. The reality of dealing with her father's house was so much larger than that. When Katherine at last stood to leave, Emilia thanked her with sincerity, shut the door, and sank to the foyer floor to weep until her head ached and her throat was raw.

Another glass of wine and an icepack to her forehead later, she FaceTimed Anna Maria.

"What's up, chicken butt?"

"Seriously?"

"Toddlers, Emmy, toddlers. It's all butts all the time."

"Can you spare a minute for my butt?"

Anna Maria squinted at her through the phone and frowned as she no doubt registered the bloodshot eyes and puffy face of someone who had very recently been sobbing.

"Of course. Do not bite your sister. Babe, kids are yours."

Anna Maria walked briskly to a different room and settled into a chair. "What's wrong?"

"Everything."

"Can we start a little smaller than that and work our way up?"

Emilia sniffled. "Maybe."

"Did something happen today?"

"The real estate agent came over."

"Oh honey."

"I can't do it." Emilia squeezed her eyes shut and willed herself not to start crying again. Considering her empty tear ducts, her victory was perhaps not much cause for pride.

"Was she nice at least?"

Laughter bubbled up and out of her mouth. Abruptly, the situation seemed hilarious.

"She's Morgan's ex," she said when she regained control of herself.

"Holy shit. You need a new agent."

"Trust me, I know. Oh, and I burst into tears in front of her."

Anna Maria shook her head. "Of course you did."

"Should I tell Morgan?"

"That you cried in front of her ex? Maybe not. That her ex is your agent? Definitely."

"Here's the thing, though." She explained about how she'd discovered the photograph.

"Just say you saw her picture online. Hang on." Anna Maria's eyes scanned the screen, and Emilia realized she must be stalking Morgan on social media, something that she probably should have done herself a long time ago, too.

Anna Maria let out a whistle. "Damn. She's hot."

"Not helpful."

"Sorry."

"She keeps her engagement rings next to her photo." She hadn't wanted to mention that part of the story, but she couldn't hold it in. Anna Maria's eyes snapped back to hers, and she knew her sister had closed out of her social media apps.

"She still has the rings?"

"Yes. That's weird, right?"

"Not necessarily. What would you do if you still had rings from your ex?"

"Toss them into Mount Doom."

"Let me clarify. If you weren't Frodo Baggins."

"Pawn them? I don't know, actually."

"She might just not want to deal with them."

"If she isn't over Kate, I don't want to bring her up. Especially since I'm not staying here." Another lump filled her throat. "It will just make things awkward, and there's no point. Can't I just get a new real estate agent and not tell her?"

"I mean, you could." Anna Maria sounded hesitant. "Not mentioning it won't be weird for you?"

"Of course it will be weird. I just . . . I just don't want to ruin things."

"How far *have* things progressed since I was there?"

"Um."

"How many nights a week do you see her?"

"A few."

"How often do you talk to her?"

"I don't know, often?"

"Every day, often?"

"Yes."

"Hypothetically," said Anna Maria, her expression carefully neutral, "how would you feel about all of this if you were staying?"

"It doesn't matter."

"Humor me."

"I'd probably ask you to stalk Kate for me and then spend the next month comparing myself to her in every way."

"But would you tell Morgan?"

Emilia didn't answer. She didn't *have* an answer. If she and Morgan were a couple, perhaps, she'd feel obligated, but they weren't, and hypotheticals were extremely unhelpful in a situation that already had too many variables.

Anna Maria gave up waiting. "Fine, don't tell her, but if it backfires don't say I didn't warn you."

"I just can't deal with anything else right now." Her tear ducts made a renewed attempt at flooding.

"Emmy." Anna Maria brought the phone closer to her face. "I don't even want to say this because I know how overwhelmed you are, but have you thought about staying?"

"Staying?"

"Nothing says you have to move back to Boston. There are jobs up there, aren't there? You could get a fresh start, and you have a house. Obviously I'd miss my free babysitter, but you weren't available much anyway, and you're only three hours away."

Her ears rang. She wanted to chuck her phone across the room and watch it shatter against the stone fireplace, and she wanted Anna Maria to continue putting into words the idea she'd been tiptoeing around for weeks.

"You still there?"

"I'm here."

"Looked like you froze."

"I—" She broke off. "I have to go."

She hung up and stared at the living room walls. Half of her felt even more confused than she had in months, while the other half felt closer to clarity than she had in years.

The clarity scared her a hell of a lot more.

Could she actually stay here? Was that crazy? Or was she so out of touch with normality that she couldn't tell the difference? She tried to picture it: living in her father's house—her house— year-round. Mulled wine by the fire in the winter. Sailing in the summer. Her new friends.

Morgan.

And if things don't work out with Morgan? she asked herself. *Then you lose those new friends and you're back to square one.*

Except that wasn't entirely true. She could always sell the house later, and what did she have waiting for her back in Boston—besides family—anyway? The wildflowers she'd picked earlier that day stood in a vase on the coffee table, glinting as they caught the sunlight.

Could this still be a place where she could be happy even if things fell through with Morgan?

Does she know you're in love with her?

Shannon Donovan could have dropped a live grenade in her daughter's bedroom and had less impact than that sentence.

Once upon a time, falling in love had felt like discovering magic. Now it felt like a boulder sealing the mouth of her tomb. It had happened again: she'd fallen for someone who wouldn't stick around. Yes, she told herself, she had known that was a risk. That didn't diminish the urge to point her boat straight out to sea and stop only when she ran out of gas or reached a distant shore. She couldn't go through another heartbreak. Not so soon.

"Have you heard anything I just said?" Stevie asked on their drive home from their last appointment.

"No." She didn't bother lying.

"Love you too, buddy."

"Were you talking about *Game of Thrones* again?"

"It ended, dipshit. Doesn't matter. I thought you said dinner with your folks went fine?"

"It did."

"Why are you pissed off, then?"

"I'm not pissed off."

"Sure."

"Fine. You're pissing me off as of right now," said Morgan.

Stevie's temper flared to match. "I'm not the one ignoring her technician."

"Were you talking about work?"

"No, but—"

"Then I wasn't ignoring my tech."

"Just your friend?"

She opened her mouth to snap back, aware that her anger was misplaced and that Stevie was one of the few people who loved her unconditionally. *Get it together. Hold your tongue. Be reasonable.* A grunt emerged instead of an insult.

244

"Well, let me know when you're done. Your brooding bullshit doesn't turn me on, Donovan. It's annoying, and you're too old for that shit."

"Really? You're calling *me* immature?"

So much for reasonable.

"Adults talk about their problems."

"Because you do that all the time?" She knew she needed to stop herself before she said something unforgivable. If her world was determined to implode, she would need Stevie. The balled fist in the center of her chest, however, screamed for a target, and Stevie was the only person in range.

"At least I don't take it out on my friends."

Morgan tightened her hands on the wheel and did not yell, which took all her concentration. She did not need this right now. She didn't need any of this. Not Stevie's hurt expression, not her mother's catastrophic meddling, and not Emilia. Pain ripped through her.

I love her. I love her and she's leaving, and if I tell Stevie it will make it real.

"What, nothing to say to that?" Stevie folded her arms over her chest. Kraken whined in the back seat, made uneasy by the tension and the raised voices.

"Just—just leave me alone."

They pulled into the drive of 16 Bay Road in silence. Stevie jumped out the minute the tires stopped rolling and slammed the door. Morgan leaned her head on the wheel and closed her eyes. Everything was going wrong.

A knock on the window startled her upright. Lillian stood outside with a concerned—and slightly menacing—expression. She thought about telling her to fuck off too, then opened the door. Kraken bolted over her lap and out of the truck.

"Stevie says you're being a bitch."

Morgan shrugged.

"Want to tell me why?"

"Not particularly."

"You're not coming in the house then," said Lillian. Her dark brows lowered, threatening to skim her cheekbones.

"Think you can stop me?"

"Don't fuck with me, Donovan. You know I could kick your ass."

Despite herself, Morgan smiled. "You sure about that?"

"Please." Lillian shook her head dismissively. A crease from an abandoned hair tie crinkled her smooth sweep of black hair. "Shove that butch ego. You know I hate it."

Morgan released her death grip on the steering wheel and groaned. "I'm just tired, Lil."

"Then go apologize to Stevie and take a nap."

"I'm not a child."

"Then stop acting like one."

Morgan scrunched her nose at Lillian, whose glare softened. She grabbed Morgan's chin and shook it back and forth a few times. "Why are you so frustrating?"

"Genetics," said Morgan, thinking of her mother.

"How's Emilia?"

"She's fine."

"You're not in a fight?"

"No. Why would you think that?"

Lillian raised a skeptical brow. "Fine. I'm not going to force you to talk to me. If you want to pout and brood, that's on you."

"Christ, I don't brood!"

"Your call. But other people live here, so try to contain your negativity to your room."

She turned on her heel and marched back toward the house.

"Wait." Morgan hated herself for the neediness in her voice. "Take a walk with me?"

The corners of Lillian's eyes crinkled in a smile.

They strolled along the fencing Stevie was erecting around the orchard. T-posts stuck out of the ground at uneven intervals, and Morgan, despite her gloom, made a mental note to remind Stevie how a measuring tape worked. Evening had dispelled some of the heat of the day. The setting sun cast the gnarled shadows of the

246

apple trees over the grass ahead of them, and Morgan smelled the slowly ripening apples hanging in the leaves.

"I can't go through this again," she said without preamble.

"Sure you can."

Morgan opened her mouth in outrage, but Lillian continued. "I assume you're talking about Emilia. Is she leaving soon?"

"She said a month."

"You knew this was going to happen."

"I know."

"When are you going to break it off?"

"What?" Morgan stared at Lillian.

"If you're determined it's going to end badly, why not just rip off the Band-Aid?"

"I don't want to end it. That's the whole point."

"Then put on your big girl pants, tell Stevie you're sorry, and deal with your emotions."

"Don't feel like you need to go easy on me or anything."

"I would if you'd just act like an adult."

"I don't process. You know this about me. I leave that to you and Ange, and Stevie apparently."

Lillian stopped her forward momentum by grabbing both of Morgan's hands and holding them in hers. "Here's what you need to do. Find out when she's leaving and talk to her about how that makes you feel."

"Or I could not."

"Suit yourself." Lillian dropped Morgan's hands and tilted her face up to the sunlight, closing her eyes. Morgan saw the dark circles of exhaustion beneath them.

"How's Brian?" she asked.

"I don't know," Lillian said in a quiet voice. "We're not speaking at the moment."

"I'm sorry."

"Thanks."

Morgan really did feel like an ass, now. She'd been so wrapped up in her own problems she hadn't noticed her friend was suffering. "Do you . . . want to talk about it?"

247

Lillian let out a harsh laugh. "God that sounded like it was actually painful for you to say." Her eyes opened, and she seemed more like her usual self as she teased Morgan.

"How much of a dick was I to Stevie?"

"Super dick. The kind of dick that's too big to do anything with."

"Gross, Lil."

"Stevie will forgive you. She always does. Just, try not to explode at the people who care about you, okay?"

Morgan swung an arm around Lillian and pulled her close, both chastised and grateful.

"I love you," she said to the top of Lillian's head. "You know that, right?"

Lillian wrapped her arms around Morgan and squeezed. "I know. I love you too."

"Thank you."

"Talk to her, Morgan. You're stronger than you think you are."

She was glad Lillian couldn't see her face. Lillian was wrong. She was not strong enough for any of this.

She did, however, try to follow Lillian's advice over the next few days. Stevie accepted her apology and shrugged off the exchange. Morgan knew the length of their friendship played a part in her quick forgiveness. Stevie understood her, and she didn't hold grudges—which, Morgan reflected in a less than charitable moment, was good, considering how much Stevie enjoyed pushing other people's buttons.

The next time she saw Emilia was at the dock. She'd just returned from a short and fruitless fishing trip, hoping the water would clear her head, only to discover Emilia scrubbing the deck of her sailboat in a bikini and denim cut-offs.

Fuck me, she thought as she overshot the mooring and doubled back. Maybe her mother and her own heart were wrong, and this was just lust, because the way Emilia filled out that suit top should have been illegal.

Rowing in any direction besides Emilia's wasn't optional.

"Need a hand?"

"I could use some company."

Thoughts of distancing herself from Emilia floundered in her wake. She let them drown. Emilia's skin shimmered in the bright sunlight like a beacon.

"Swabbing the deck?" she asked as she hauled herself onboard and tied off her skiff.

"Figured it was time. It's growing things."

"Things?"

"Things." Emilia held up a strand of seaweed she had pulled from the waterline. "I don't like things."

"You need a scrub brush with a longer handle," she observed as Emilia bent over again to scrub at the scum on the side of the hull. Then again, the view the short handle afforded Morgan was totally worth a little extra effort on Emilia's part. "Don't fall in."

"Spot me if you're worried."

Morgan was more than happy to oblige. She placed a hand on Emilia's waist and wished the harbor contained far fewer people so she could put this angle to better use.

Stop it, she scolded herself. *Act less like a teenage boy and more like an adult. A respectful adult.* She couldn't help herself, though. Emilia's hair fell over her shoulder in a heavy ponytail, nearly trailing in the water, and a bead of sweat ran along her spine. Morgan's hands braced her hips, and she felt the muscles in Emilia's core work as she fought against the briny scum.

I need to keep a clear head, she thought. *I need to stop falling.*

Emilia gave one last scrub and straightened, turning in Morgan's arms.

"Hey." Emilia's lips were chapped from the salt air, and they caught and held Morgan's attention.

Morgan kissed her. She couldn't help it. Her mouth needed this woman, and her body—her body was falling, dropping out from underneath her feet as she understood for the first time in her life the definition of the word *swoon*. Her feet didn't waver on the deck, and the hands that held Emilia were steady, but inside she plummeted.

"Come to my place later," Emilia said, breaking off the kiss and bringing Morgan back to earth.

"I'm on call."

"I don't care."

"Okay."

Emilia had never invited her into her father's house. She hadn't wanted to ask why, guessing it had something to do with Emilia's grieving process, but her heart leapt at the suggestion even as her mind urged caution. This was a step in the wrong direction—the one that led toward Morgan sobbing in her truck and binge eating cheese when she couldn't sleep. She should keep things on her own turf, where she had control.

Her mouth had other ideas. "I'll cook you dinner," it said, because her mouth, like the rest of her body, was an idiot.

Emilia bit Morgan's lower lip and released it slowly. "You've cooked for me several times now. It's my turn."

"Can we go now?" Morgan asked. Her hand had wandered dangerously close to Emilia's bikini tie.

"Does this boat look clean to you?"

"Yes."

"Liar." Emilia pulled away. "Lucky for you, I have an extra brush."

"Any reason in particular you're spit shining this?" She tried to keep her tone casual, but if Emilia was planning on selling the boat, Morgan needed to know.

"Stress cleaning."

"That's a thing?"

Emilia brandished her brush like a weapon. "Stress cleaning is very much a thing."

"I can think of better ways to blow off steam," said her idiotic mouth.

"I bet you can. And you missed a spot over there."

"Why are you stressed?" Morgan asked as she doubled back.

"What am I not stressed about is the better question." Emilia spoke to the deck and kept her face downcast as she answered.

Morgan waited for her to say more. When she didn't, the

feeling of dread grew. *She's leaving.* The sunlight seemed to dim over the water, and Morgan resumed scrubbing.

"Did you catch anything?"

"What?" Morgan asked.

"You have a fishing pole in your skiff."

"Oh. No, I didn't, or else I really would insist on cooking."

"We could pick up some fresh mussels on our way back to my place," said Emilia.

Kate hadn't liked shellfish. She tried to block out the comparison, but her mind seemed determined to ruin this evening one way or another. Kate also hadn't liked fish, though she never objected when Morgan cooked it for herself.

"Will you sell the boat?" she asked to shut her mind up.

"What? No. I mean . . ." Emilia trailed off. "I hadn't even thought of that."

"You could always lease it."

Her brow wrinkled, and Morgan longed to smooth it away. "God, all of this is so complicated."

It doesn't have to be, Morgan wanted to tell her. Instead, she said, "Or you could sail away into the sunset. Live off your boat."

"Nell wouldn't like that."

"She could play with the seals."

"True." Emilia's smile brought light back into the evening. "And I also wanted to be a pirate when I was little."

"Oh yeah?"

"If you make a joke about my booty, Morgan Donovan, I'll throw you overboard."

"Harsh."

"I run a tight ship."

The brush fell from Morgan's fingers. She stepped toward Emilia, who backed away with a coy smile until her back hit the mast. Morgan took the scrub brush from her and sent it to join its mate on the deck.

Emilia placed her hands on Morgan's shoulders. She moved to kiss her, but Emilia used the momentum of a passing wake to turn the tables on Morgan. She ended up with a cleat jabbing into her back and her head flush against the mast, half sitting, half leaning on the bow with the boom to her left and Emilia Russo between her legs.

Slowly, deliberately, Emilia took Morgan's hands and pinned them over her head.

"Should I call you 'captain'?" she managed to say.

"I'd like that."

"Then I'm all yours, Captain."

Morgan broke against her as Emilia put her full weight into her kiss. All of her hunger and confusion distilled into desire beneath that weight, and she tried to communicate what she couldn't say in words: *please stay with me, I love you, please stay.*

Emilia fidgeted with the hem of the crop top she'd thrown on after a quick shower. The shirt had a tendency to slip off one shoulder, and she rather hoped Morgan would take advantage of the opportunity. Morgan, who was coming here, for dinner, in her father's house.

The large pot on the stove stood waiting for the mussels, and a smaller pot and saucepan occupied two of the remaining three gas burners. A simple dish. Pasta with mussels in a white wine sauce. She could manage that even with her head full of ghosts.

Morgan's knock broke into her reverie. She wiped her palms on her shorts and was surprised to find them sweating. This wasn't a big deal. She'd eaten with Morgan numerous times at the farmhouse. All that had changed was the location.

Her thoughts flew to the urn on her dresser. Was he watching? What would he think about the dream she'd been keeping close to her chest since she'd met with the real estate agent?

"Come in," she said. Nell sniffed the paper bag in Morgan's hands enthusiastically. Morgan, Emilia saw, hadn't gone home to change. She still wore her work Carhartts, but she'd swapped her clinic polo for a soft blue T-shirt. Part of Emilia wished Morgan would wear less blue; it made her eyes impossible to ignore.

"Not for you," Morgan told Nell as she stepped into the house and shut the door.

Nell's continued attempts to investigate the bag of mussels helped muffle the impact of the door clicking shut.

"Wow. This is Ray's place?"

"Give or take a coat of paint and a few dozen animal heads."

"That makes more sense. You painted all this?"

Emilia followed Morgan's gaze. The front door opened into the living room, with only a small foyer area for boots and coats and dog toys. They could see into the kitchen from here, and the only other room on the first floor, besides the bathroom, was a small, multipurpose room that had served as an office, toolshed, and storage room when her father was alive. The house looked so different now, and yet most of the furniture was the same. It still amazed her what paint and a few light fixtures could do to a room.

"I did," she said in answer to Morgan's question. "I think I like it."

"You think?"

"The walls were so dark, before, and my dad's tobacco stained them pretty badly." She didn't say the rest of her thoughts out loud, but Morgan seemed to understand.

"Change is hard."

"Yeah."

"Where should I put these?"

Grateful for the shift in conversation, Emilia led Morgan into the kitchen. "I hope you like pasta," she said as she put the mussels in the sink.

"How very Italian of you."

"I will throw a potato at you," she warned Morgan.

"Luck of the Irish is on my side. You'd miss."

"Try me."

Morgan leaned against the counter a few feet away. Emilia started steaming the mussels; then, once the pots were all lidded and on their way to boiling, she stepped into Morgan's embrace. They stood like that in the kitchen. Morgan had a curiously seri-

253

ous look in her eyes, and while Emilia's body still ached from the kiss they'd shared earlier in the boat, she refrained from acting on any wayward impulses.

"This is the first time you've had me over," Morgan said.

"Yeah."

"Are you okay?"

She tucked her hands into Morgan's belt and toyed with the loops. "It's . . . weird."

"We can go to my place, if you want."

"It's not weird in a bad way. I . . . I don't know how to describe it."

"Do you believe in heaven?"

Startled, Emilia bit her lip before answering. "I don't know. I didn't, before Dad. I'm not religious. But now . . ." She trailed off, then forced herself to continue. "I just can't believe I'll never see him again, or talk to him, or . . ." Her throat closed up.

"One of my best friends died a few years ago." Morgan wiped a tear from Emilia's cheek as she spoke. "It's the hardest thing in the world to lose someone you love. Nothing about it makes sense."

Emilia nodded, unable to speak.

"The only thing that ever helped me was thermodynamics."

She stared at Morgan, here in her father's kitchen, brushing her strong hands through her hair. "Thermodynamics?"

"Yes." Morgan's thumb rested on the curve of her jaw. "Conservation of energy. Science can prove they are still with us."

"I can't talk to protons and atoms."

"Have you tried?"

"What do I do, call his cell?"

"Out loud. Talking out loud."

"No."

Morgan pulled Emilia's loose hair toward her and let it drape over her shoulder, running her hands through the strands. The gentle tug soothed something deep and animal inside her, and the door she'd slammed shut on her feelings opened.

"I'm so angry at him for leaving."

Tears followed the confession. Morgan pulled her in, and she sobbed convulsively into her shoulder until the sounds of rattling pot lids punctured the bubble of her grief. She surfaced, aware she must look like a wreck, and aware also that Morgan was looking at her with a compassion born not of pity, but of understanding, and in this moment she was friend and lover and could not have cared less about puffy eyes and tear-stained shirts.

"Pasta," Emilia said.

"Hey." Morgan tilted her chin to look her squarely in the eye. "I'm here for you. Whatever happens. Whatever you need. Okay?"

"Okay." She let the warmth of those words flow through her. *Thermodynamics.* If that was true, then her father's energy filled this house. Perhaps the heat created by her body bumped against the lingering heat of his, and the molecular evidence of his footsteps echoed hers. It still wasn't enough.

Morgan, though, was real, and for the first time since her father's death she allowed herself to come apart with the knowledge that one day she would, and could, put herself back together.

Morgan studied Emilia as she chopped garlic for the sauce and sautéed it in a fragrant olive oil. Her shoulder was still damp with Emilia's tears.

Emilia held the wooden spoon in a practiced grip as the sound and smell of cooking garlic filled the kitchen. Her shirt had slid off one shoulder, and her hair, now piled on top of her head in a messy bun, curled in the steam. The sight of that smooth skin distracted Morgan from her thoughts. It didn't matter that she'd already memorized the way that skin felt beneath her lips. Each memory just fueled the longing. Only the damp reminder of fresh grief restrained Morgan from standing behind her as Emilia had stood behind Morgan on her boat, kissing her neck while her hands lifted the loose cotton of her shirt and felt the warm skin of her stomach. She tightened her grip on the counter.

Emilia chose that moment to glance over her shoulder. The side of her mouth quirked in a lopsided smile. "What?"

"You're beautiful."

It was the truth. No one could deny Emilia Russo was hot, but the roughness of her own voice, thick with the words she couldn't say, invoked far more than physical beauty.

Emilia glanced down at the stove and then up again. "So are you, Morgan."

She wanted to brush off the compliment. A joke rose to her lips, but she bit it back and instead closed the distance between them. Emilia couldn't turn her back on the stove without burning the garlic, so Morgan wrapped her arms around her waist and rested her cheek against Emilia's. The fragrance of her shampoo mingled with the smells of cooking. Morgan decided she could happily smell ginseng and garlic for the rest of her life.

She didn't speak. She watched Emilia stir the garlic and accepted a strand of pasta to test, all the while aware of the sense of rightness, of belonging, that suffused her.

Had it felt this right with Kate?

Comparing Emilia to Kate was a mistake, and yet the last time she'd been in the kitchen with a woman like this had been in the apartment she'd shared with her fiancé. Comparison was inevitable.

Emilia shifted her weight as she cooked. The motion should have disrupted the way they fit together, but all it did was bring her closer. Perhaps it had felt like this with Kate in the beginning, back when they were younger and dumber and unaware of the consequences of a shared life. She hadn't felt Kate pulling away. She hadn't seen her tears or her anger, her frustration about one lonely meal after the next as Morgan worked and worked and worked, pushing herself to build them a better life and completely unaware that with each late night she pushed Kate further and further away. How could she trust in this if she had failed so totally before?

Emilia added some of the freshly chopped herbs to the garlic and put her back to the gas burners. Morgan instinctively pulled them a step back and out of the way of the open flame.

"Hey, are you okay?"

"Yeah," said Morgan.

"You got quiet."

"I was enjoying the garlic."

"That's not what I meant." Emilia laced her fingers around Morgan's bicep.

"I'm just thinking."

"About what?"

"Stuff."

"Stuff," Emilia repeated. "Any of it interesting?"

"Maybe."

"What do I have to do to get you to tell me?"

A few possibilities flashed through Morgan's mind. Desire struck, spreading like electricity from the places where Emilia touched her. "Depends."

"Depends on what?"

"On how much you care about burning the garlic."

"Oh, shit." Emilia spun around and snatched the saucepan from the stove. "Fetch me the bottle of white wine on the counter."

Morgan obeyed, enjoying the command more than was probably healthy.

Emilia wrapped up the meal preparation with a surge of steam from the pasta and mussels and a generous swig from the bottle of wine, which she passed to Morgan. The pinot grigio wasn't bad, she noted as she took a sip.

"Okay." Emilia surveyed the bowls before her. "Now we just need a drink."

"Can I get you one?"

"I'm the hostess. Pick your poison. Wine? Beer? I don't have anything harder, but—" She stopped talking when Morgan slid her hands beneath the sheer fabric of her crop top.

Drinking could wait.

∽ ∽ ∽

257

Emilia swirled the wine in her glass as she breathed out a contented sigh. Dinner had turned out even better than she could have hoped. The mussels dripped flavors, and the memory of Morgan's eyes closing as she took her first bite, moaning, caused a physical reaction in Emilia that made sitting deeply uncomfortable.

"You," Morgan said as she twirled one last strand of pasta onto her fork, "are a goddess."

Emilia used her next sip of wine as a cover to stare at the flush in Morgan's cheeks and neck, planning to deepen it very soon. They would not need to be quiet here.

"Seriously, why have I been cooking?"

"Because I like seeing you behind a grill."

"Yeah?"

"Yeah. It's a reminder I'm playing with fire." She held Morgan's eyes and was rewarded by her dilating pupils. She could get used to this. The small dining nook in the kitchen held the table she'd polished to a sheen a few days before, and the house felt less haunted with Morgan in it. Still holding Morgan's gaze, she allowed herself to imagine sharing this house with her, waking next to her—she'd figure out the bedroom situation—and spending evenings just like this. She couldn't, however, tell Morgan about her tentative plans. Not yet. Not until she was absolutely certain.

"Are you going to tell me what you were thinking about earlier? There's nothing to burn now."

Morgan leaned back in her chair. "I could light something."

"No fire pit, here." *Although I could build one.*

"That's a pity."

"Truly." She put down her glass and stood. Morgan made to follow suit, but Emilia pushed her back down in her chair and straddled her.

"Fuck, girl," she whispered as Emilia ran her hands over her chest, not quite touching her breasts.

"Please tell me?"

"I was thinking about you."

"How?"

Morgan's hands slid beneath her shorts and pulled her closer. "Do you really have to ask?"

She tangled her hands in Morgan's hair as she struggled to come up with a meaning for Morgan's words. She knew what she wanted them to be; she also knew she couldn't afford to misread this.

"Yes."

"I was thinking . . ." Morgan paused and Emilia held her breath. "Boston doesn't deserve you."

The air between them stilled. Emilia discarded half a hundred responses in the space of a heartbeat. Morgan hadn't asked her to stay. She knew Morgan well enough to know she would find that disrespectful, but it was so close to a request the air in her lungs turned solid. *I'll stay if you ask*, she thought. Morgan's dark curls were locked around her fingers, and with that thought came the realization that by not asking, by keeping the question sealed behind those slate-blue eyes, Morgan had broken down the last of the flimsy barriers Emilia had managed to keep in place.

How long had she been in love with Morgan? She searched Morgan's face, counting the freckles across her cheeks and loving the dark curve of her eyebrows, such a contrast to the pale skin beneath.

I love you, she thought, testing the words she'd forbidden herself to think.

She kissed Morgan fiercely. Morgan matched her in intensity and lifted her, growling as she backed Emilia into the kitchen wall. She kept her legs wrapped tightly around Morgan's waist. The solid wood of the wall provided leverage for her hips, and she pressed into Morgan as Morgan broke the kiss to bite the place where her neck met her shoulder. Love and lust blurred. She needed Morgan. Needed her with a ferocity that filled her with a heady, feral joy. She wanted to break herself against this woman. She'd been broken so many times already this year, never by choice, but in Morgan's arms she knew she could come undone without losing herself.

"The couch," she said as best she could with her breath ratch-

259

eting into new gears. It would take too long to get upstairs, and upstairs—she shut the thought down. She would not think about her father's room. Morgan's hips surged with hers, and she let the thought and its suppression go.

"Please," she begged Morgan. "I need you."

Morgan's hands tightened on her waist and Emilia felt the certainty of her heart beating against her palms. She felt, too, the effect her words had on Morgan, and slid to the ground so she could tug Morgan into the living room. Then she pulled Morgan down on top of her on the couch. Her legs rewrapped themselves around Morgan's waist, and she dug her nails into the hard muscles of Morgan's back. Morgan whimpered, half with pain, half with desire, and when Emilia paused for fear of hurting her Morgan said, "Don't you dare stop."

She ripped Morgan's shirt over her head and fumbled with her bra until it gave. Her nails marked Morgan's back, and while a distant part of her wondered at this new intensity, she was too lost in it to care.

Her own shirt went next, though she complicated this by refusing to relinquish her grip on Morgan.

"Girl," Morgan said, and for the first time since they'd started sleeping together, she used her superior strength to take control without Emilia's permission. Pinning her with one arm, she eased Emilia's shirt over her head while Emilia's chest heaved with a new thrill of longing. She was dimly aware that she had never been this turned on in her life.

"Every time," Morgan said as she touched the curve of Emilia's breasts. "I forget how fucking perfect you are."

The skin around her nipples screamed as Morgan stroked it, and she writhed with unaccustomed sensitivity as her mind went white. Morgan bent her head and closed her lips over her right nipple. The hand not still pinning Emilia kneaded the other, rolling it between her thumb and forefinger, and lightning traveled through Emilia. Morgan's tongue lashed her with fire as her climax took her by surprise. Up and up she sailed, Morgan's teeth raking over her between exquisitely, almost painfully tender kisses, and she screamed into her father's house as every filament of her being aligned.

"Did you . . .?" Morgan asked her when she regained consciousness.

"Holy. Fuck." Each word was a struggle. Language was a struggle. Why were there so many words? Her body was a mess of nerve endings, each alive and desperate, and she shivered as Morgan's breath passed over her skin.

"Holy fuck," Morgan agreed, and another shudder passed through Emilia at the look of reverence on Morgan's face. She let her head fall back as it claimed her.

Morgan's hands tugged at her shorts, and she raised her hips to let her remove them. She seemed to know Emilia was in no condition to return the favor, because she kicked off the rest of her clothes before settling against Emilia again. The contact of skin on skin, softness and curves and muscles and bone and Morgan, Morgan—Emilia slid her hand between them.

"Emilia," Morgan said as she parted her. "Oh god, Emilia."

"Look at me."

Morgan's eyes flew open. Emilia entered her, and the full strength of Morgan's body closed around her hand as Morgan propped herself on one elbow to hold her gaze. Emilia moved her hips in time with her hand, and Morgan's body answered. The tight line of her stomach was just visible, but Emilia forced herself not to look away from those slate-blue eyes as she gathered Morgan to her, bringing her slowly and inexorably to the brink. She watched Morgan's pupils expand as she came, but Morgan did not break their eye contact even as her body trembled and she breathed out Emilia's name.

"You," Emilia said in wonder as Morgan fought to hold herself upright.

"No. You," said Morgan, and though she should not, in Emilia's opinion, have been capable of such immediate reaction, she slipped three fingers inside Emilia, then four, rocking with her while her thumb teased her clit and the room spun again.

Her body no longer belonged to her. It belonged to Morgan,

and Morgan eased more deeply into her with sure, strong, inexorable strokes. She opened. The complete and total surrender as Morgan filled her unlocked something. She arched against her, wanting her deeper, more totally, more completely than she'd ever wanted anything.

This orgasm did not take her by surprise. It built from the tips of her fingers and toes and erased every other touch her skin had ever felt. Her throat was raw, though she was unaware of making a sound, and the blue of Morgan's eyes eclipsed everything. She fell through that blue, weightless, and Morgan caught her as the last of the evening light bled out of the sky and painted the room a gold that lit her face and framed it forever, eyes sea-gray and sea-blue, black lashes and warm lips, and love, so much love, pouring out of her and into Emilia as her soul splintered and re-formed around the waves of ecstasy that drowned her. She came, sobbing, as the pieces that had for so long drifted, sharp-edged and brittle, fit back together with a pain so exquisite she could not tell if it was agony or bliss, and then it passed, leaving her more fully herself than she had been in years.

After, she lay with Morgan's arms wrapped around her and Morgan's heartbeat thundering beneath her ear. Her body ached in its wholeness. She'd come here to grieve and to find a new direction. Instead she'd found Morgan. While her scientific mind balked at the idea of spiritual guidance, she couldn't help but feel her father's hand in this. Of course she'd fall in love with this place and with the one person besides her father who had always embodied it. She'd be a fool to throw that all away for a life she no longer wanted.

It's time, she decided, and sat up.

"You okay?" asked Morgan.

"I need to talk to you about something."

Morgan's face clouded. She dropped her eyes and then frowned. Emilia followed the direction of the furrow and froze.

No. This can't be happening.

Wedged between the couch cushions was a business card. One corner had been crumpled by their bodies, but the couch had preserved the rest. Kate's photo looked up at them, the embossed real estate logo reflecting the last of the half-light.

Chapter Sixteen

Morgan's blood cemented in her veins. She stared at the innocuous bit of card stock. Slowly, as wary of the card as if it were a fractious animal, she picked it up. The face that had shattered her world smiled up at her.

A brittle laugh erupted from her lips. Sometimes the universe sent clear signs after all.

"Morgan?"

She continued gazing at the card as her last fight with Kate echoed in her skull. *I thought things would get better.*

Things never did, though. Now here she was again, blind to the truth before her. Emilia would sell her house and leave. Alone, she would stare at the mooring where the *Emilia Rosa* had lain at anchor while the boat's owner moved on with her life. Morgan had been a distraction, maybe even a friend, but she was not the sort of person women stayed with. It fit, didn't it, that Kate would be the one to remind her of this. Maybe it was even a kindness.

Emilia needed to figure out her life.

What Morgan needed didn't matter.

"Morgan," Emilia said again, this time more urgently.

She met those brown eyes. Emilia looked frightened. Her face had lost its flush, and Morgan wondered what her own face looked like. "I think I should go."

"What? No!" Emilia grabbed her hand.

She stood. "Yeah. I'm sorry."

"It's not what you think."

"What am I thinking then?" She couldn't keep the hurt out of her voice any more than she could prevent it from rising in anger. Emilia's throat worked as she swallowed, but she didn't answer. "You're leaving."

"No, I—"

"It's not your fault. I knew this was coming. I'm happy for you, really."

"Morgan, I'm not—"

She cut off Emilia's protest. "Do you know who this is?"

Emilia paled further.

"You know what, it doesn't matter. She's a good agent." It was bad enough she saw Kate's name and face on signs in yards on her rounds. But here? She couldn't take it in the room where she'd just exposed her heart so thoroughly. She began pulling on her clothes.

"Wait. Please."

The pleading in Emilia's voice halted her.

"I'm staying," Emilia said. "I'm staying in Seal Cove."

Disbelief coated Morgan's tongue. "Then why are you listing the house?"

Emilia tucked her knees to her chest. "I'm not."

Morgan held up the card in a counter.

"I wasn't sure. I called her a few weeks ago to set up an appointment. I thought I should consider all my options. That's what I wanted to talk to you about. Me staying. Us."

She wanted to believe Emilia. She wanted to let those words soothe the agony shredding her insides. Emilia, though, had made it clear from the start that she had come here searching for clarity. Morgan had been a wrench in that machinery from the beginning.

"Why?" she asked.

"Because I love you." Emilia's voice broke on the words.

Morgan stood with her shirt in her hands and her jeans half zipped, a cold ringing in her ears. Emilia's vulnerability was a scalpel in her gut. This was everything she wanted, but hearing

265

it, hearing Emilia echo the words that had been knocking around inside of her, bruising her, changing her, she felt fear close around her like the winter ocean.

"I can't," she heard herself say. She'd told herself she needed to keep her distance from Emilia to protect Emilia. Now, the shell of that lie had cracked, and she stared at the shriveled, cowardly thing inside and knew she didn't have the strength to watch it get crushed again.

"You can't what?" Emilia said, stricken.

"I can't do this."

I love you, Emilia'd said, a harpoon to her chest, hooking her sternum and full of deadly promise. Kate had loved her once too, and Kate had left. She could not survive a second time. Not when what she felt for Emilia so fully transcended what she had felt for Kate, whom she'd been ready to commit the rest of her life to.

What would she lose to this woman?

"Morgan—"

"Good luck with everything, Emilia." She turned, pulling her shirt on backward and abandoning her bra entirely, and grabbed her keys. She heard Emilia stand behind her. Not waiting to hear what else she had to say, Morgan fumbled with the latch on the door and ran into the night air. The truck started up with a growl that covered her scream. As she backed out of the drive, she saw Emilia silhouetted in the doorway. The image seared itself into her retinas, and she knew she'd see it every time she blinked. That didn't change anything.

Some things couldn't be changed.

Morgan didn't answer her phone. Not that night, nor the next, and by the third day Emilia stopped trying. Everything had gone wrong. She forced herself out of bed each morning, but without Morgan to look forward to her days lacked structure. The house was finished. The gardens were in check. There was only so far or so fast she could run on her morning jogs, and going to the dock felt too much like seeking Morgan out. She avoided her boat for

266

that first week, and instead of sailing drifted around the empty house while her dog watched her out of worried eyes. Sometimes she went back to bed, lying in a half-sleep for hours at a time. This wasn't anything new. Sleeping was what her brain did when it snapped. Some people drank. Others raged. She slept.

Her phone buzzed periodically. Anna Maria, or her mother, or an email. Never Morgan. She gave brief answers when needed, unwilling to let on that, once again, she'd made a crippling mistake.

Morgan hadn't given an explanation for her sudden departure, but Emilia wasn't stupid. She'd seen the flash of betrayal in Morgan's eyes when she picked up Kate's card.

She wondered, in the moments where she felt capable of thought, how she would feel if Morgan showed up and announced that she'd gone into business with Hannah. Shitty, probably. But shitty enough to call things off? No, she decided. She would not have done that. Not without an explanation. Or perhaps Morgan was still in love with Kate. She couldn't even blame her after meeting the woman, but then what had this summer meant to Morgan? A fling? Something to be tossed aside the moment the season changed? The anger warmed her, and she clung to it until it dissipated and left her once again empty and floating in the void.

The knock on her door roused her out of one of her naps. Nell perked her ears and slid off the bed. Emilia contemplated getting up and then thought better of it. Whoever it was would go away.

The person knocked again. She rolled over and buried her face in her pillow.

Beside her, her phone buzzed. She peered at the screen.

LL: *I know you're home. Open up?*

Lillian? She sat up. Why was Lillian here? Nell trotted downstairs while Emilia weighed her options. She could lie here like a broken toy, proving to herself and everyone around her that she was still too fragile to function, or she could answer the goddamn door.

Lillian and Stormy waited on the doorstep. Stormy hefted a growler of a pale beer, and Lillian scratched the backside Nell presented her.

"Um, hi," she said, belatedly realizing her hair was a tangled mess and she'd been wearing the same pair of sweats and one of her father's old T-shirts for three days straight.

"Morgan's an idiot," Lillian said by way of greeting, "but you're not getting rid of us unless you want to."

"And even then we'll put up a fight," said Stormy. "You got some glasses for this?"

Emilia stared at the two of them with her mouth open in shock. None of her old friends—Hannah's friends—had come forward like this after their breakup. Sure, one or two of them texted her to say they were sorry about her dad before they drifted out of her life, but not one had physically shown up for her. Their eyes met hers, full of compassion, and she burst into tears. She'd been doing that a lot lately.

Five minutes later, sniffling on her front step with two pairs of arms around her, she managed a smile.

"Thank you."

"Did you really think we'd let you disappear on us?" said Stormy.

"I would have come by sooner, but it took me six days to dig the truth out of Dickhead." Lillian rubbed soothing circles on Emilia's back. "I love her, but sometimes she's impossible."

"I'll be right back." Stormy disappeared into the house and emerged with three glasses, which she filled with the contents of the growler. "Blueberry ale."

Emilia took a long drink and let the subtle notes of blueberry linger in her mouth.

"Good, right?" Stormy grinned.

"So, now that you're properly hydrated, we need to talk," said Lillian.

Emilia nodded.

"First of all," said Stormy, "we love you. Whatever you decide to do, we support."

"Yes." Lillian, still in scrubs, undid the knot of hair on top of Emilia's head and began detangling it with deft fingers. "And you're good for Morgan."

"That's not what she thinks."

"I thought we established that she's an idiot."

"What do *you* want?" asked Stormy. Her curls framed her face as she leaned toward Emilia.

The answer came to her at once. "I want to be with her, and I want to stay here. I want to stay here even if she doesn't want to be with me."

Lillian nodded. "And you're sure of that?"

"As sure as I can be."

"What about Kate?"

"My sister found her for me. I had no idea she was Morgan's ex. Listening to her talk about listing is part of what made me decide to stay. I tried to tell Morgan that, but she . . ."

"Yeah." Lillian's tone softened. "I think finding Kate's card short-circuited her brain."

"How . . ." Emilia trailed off, then tried again. "How is she?"

Lillian and Stormy exchanged dark looks. "She's a nightmare. Stevie's going to kill her soon, and I don't blame her."

"Really? *Morgan?*" Emilia couldn't reconcile the easygoing, gentle, caring person she knew Morgan to be with the person they seemed to be describing.

"Snapping at anyone who comes near, brooding, vanishing for hours . . ."

"She hasn't even come by the bar."

"That's because she's living off cheese and whiskey," said Lillian. "You have to understand something about Morgan. She's one of the best people I know, but when she's hurting badly she acts like a wounded animal."

The idea of Morgan in pain squeezed her heart, even as a part of her was glad to know that Morgan, too, was upset.

"She won't answer my calls."

"That's because she's told herself how this story ends," said Stormy. "I see it all the time at work. People are dumb."

"Morgan is scared," said Lillian. "Give her time."

"Time?"

"You each have things to figure out. You do you right now. I promise you Morgan Donovan isn't going anywhere," said Stormy.

She wanted to believe them both, but too much could go wrong.

"And if she doesn't come around," said Lillian, arranging Emilia's hair around her shoulders, "you'll still have us. You can make this place home if you want to, Emilia, with or without Morgan."

"I'll have to move my boat."

"No." Lillian shook her head. "You have just as much right to be here as she does."

The anger in Lillian's voice surprised Emilia.

"What about work?" asked Stormy. "I know you were figuring that out, too. I could always use help at the bar although I know you are obscenely overqualified."

"Actually," said Emilia, meeting Lillian's eyes, "I think I might look for a vet job. As a general practitioner."

"Please apply to Seal Cove," Lillian said at once. "I'll be a reference."

"I don't know if working with Morgan is a good idea. I've been there before. Besides, I don't have the large animal experience."

"We can train you," said Lillian. Then she hesitated. "But, and I can't believe I'm saying this, I do know of a smaller practice a few miles up the coast that needs a new doctor."

"Really?"

"It's very small. Two doctors. One's retiring, and I know the other, Dominique. I feel like you'd do well there. I can call if you'd like."

The prospect of a real opportunity, one where she made a decent salary for work that didn't drain her, flooded her with a mix of hope and terror. She pushed aside the terror and nodded. "I'd appreciate that."

"Besides. With climate change, you want to get out of Boston. Floods too easily," said Lillian.

"Thanks for the warning."

"And you'd miss out on my coffee and beer." Stormy refilled their glasses as she spoke. "And let's face it. That's an even bigger crisis."

Emilia raised her glass and toasted Stormy. At her feet, Nell sighed in contentment, and despite the ache in her chest a little of the same feeling crept in.

Morgan rubbed her face in her hands and remembered too late that they were covered in Kraken's slobber from the leftovers she'd fed him. Normally, she abstained from giving him any people food, but it seemed a shame to let food go to waste just because her appetite had vanished along with Emilia.

No. She wouldn't go there. She'd done what she'd needed to do for them both. Emilia deserved the chance to make a clean start, and Morgan had gotten out while she still had the willpower to do so. Emilia couldn't stay for her sake. She'd only grow to resent Morgan, and it would be Kate all over again. Emilia might think she wanted Morgan—might genuinely want to be with her, but soon enough Morgan's schedule would wear her down. And she couldn't help wondering, as she had ever since Kate left, if there was something else wrong with her that it had taken Kate years to see, but had, at the last, made her impossible to love. Why else would Kate have left her? Pushing Emilia away had been the only option.

Shoving the thoughts aside, she got out of her truck. Danielle had some more applications she wanted her to take a look at, and for some reason—despite Morgan's rational explanation of how email worked—she wanted to do this in person. Stevie had chosen to eat her lunch inside where she was no doubt complaining to Lillian about Morgan's behavior.

August heat baked the parking lot. She killed the truck and jogged across it with Kraken to spare his paws. Inside, even the front desk staff greeted her warily. Guilt flickered into irritation. It wasn't like she'd snapped at any of *them*, but they'd probably heard Stevie ranting. Another apology loomed over her future.

Danielle motioned for her to shut the office door behind her when she skulked inside, having managed to avoid everyone she might have felt obligated to interact with on the way.

"Good news," said Danielle before Morgan could open her mouth. "I've found a replacement for Sellers."

"What?" Morgan stared at the folder in Danielle's hand. Her words took longer than they should have to make sense, and then she blinked. "Really?"

"Excellent references, good track record, and she has family in the area so she knows what she's getting into."

"May I?"

Danielle handed the folder over as she continued to speak. "She's been working at an equine practice out in Colorado, but she's been looking to move back East. Cornell grad, too."

Morgan opened the folder and stared down at a familiar name. *You've got to be kidding me*, she addressed the universe at large. She recognized the name on the CV in her hands. "Can you pull up her picture?" she asked Danielle. "I think I may have gone to school with her."

"You did," said Danielle. "She speaks highly of you and Lillian."

Lillian. Her mind worked quickly. Lillian would lose her shit if she knew that Danielle was considering hiring the girl who had tormented her all through vet school although, to be fair, the hatred had been mutual. Lillian hadn't ever pulled her punches when it came to Ivy Holden.

"Something wrong?"

She couldn't bring herself to lie to her boss. "She and Lillian didn't . . . get along."

"Is it something Lillian can get over? I don't think I need to tell you that this is the only decent application we've had all summer, and unless you want to downsize we need to strongly consider it."

"I need to talk to Lil."

"No you don't." Danielle leaned forward. "I'm hiring this woman for your service, not Dr. Lee's. I'll schedule them on different days if I have to. Do you, based on what you remember of Ivy Holden, think she would be a good addition to our large animal team?"

"Yes," she said, mentally apologizing to her friend. "I think we'd be lucky to have her."

"Excellent. I'll enter negotiations. She can't start until the end of September, but relief is in sight." Danielle clasped her hand. "I'm just sorry that it took us this long."

Emilia wiped her eyes as she finished talking and blinked at her open laptop where Shanti's compassionate face studied her from her Boston office.

"I just don't know what to do," she finished with a sniff.

"It sounds like you *do* know what to do," said Shanti. "Although I would like to explore why you did not feel comfortable telling me about Morgan."

"I—" Emilia swallowed. "It seemed too . . ."

"Tenuous?"

"Yes. And . . . I wanted something for myself. I needed something that was mine."

"Something that hadn't been touched by the recent past," said Shanti.

"Yes."

"We can talk about how to move into a healthy relationship—"

"There is no relationship." Morgan's last words cut her open again.

"But you were ready for one, which is just as important. Before we get there, however, can you talk about why you want to stay in Seal Cove?"

Emilia nodded, and the words poured out of her. Her new friends. The quiet. Her sailboat. The meadow and the distant surf and the connection she still felt here, to her father and Morgan. Morgan, despite what had happened in this room. Despite—or because of—the pain she'd seen on Morgan's face.

"You are not running away," Shanti observed. "Good."

"I can't run. Not from here." She looked up from her computer as she spoke, her eyes glancing over the living room walls before focusing on her sleeping dog. Speaking the words made them somehow true. There was no place on earth she could go to escape the depths of darkness she'd discovered within herself, but she might learn to live with it if she gave herself a chance. She might relearn how to live.

Shanti smiled at her. Her own lips responded, and despite the gulf in her world where Morgan had been, she felt ready. She could do this. The road would be arduous and long, and she knew she would encounter things that would make her want to turn back, but that no longer seemed like a reason not to set out.

"Well then," said Shanti. "Let's get started."

Morgan ran the last of the mesh electric fencing along the line of fence posts. Olive's pasture was nearly complete. She'd checked it thoroughly for problematic forage and helped Stevie resurrect the old hoop house, which would act as hay storage and shelter for Olive during the winter. Stevie waved at her from the electric panel they'd installed. "Ready?"

"No," Morgan shouted. Electric shock therapy would not solve her problems. She secured the mesh and stepped back before giving Stevie the signal.

"Okay, it's live."

Morgan plucked the tester from her pocket and stuck the ground line into the earth before checking the strands. All lit up. She paced the remainder of the pasture just in case, but by the time she returned to Stevie she'd established a solid perimeter.

"We good?" Stevie asked.

"We're good."

Stevie beamed. Morgan still didn't know how she felt about Stevie's impromptu decision to adopt Olive. Sure, the horse was sweet, and yes she had survived her bout of colic, but horses were expensive. She had no idea how Stevie was planning to pay off Olive's bills, let alone the cost of upkeep on her technician's salary. Not that it was her business.

"Want to go get her?"

"Hell fucking yeah. Let me get Ange."

Stevie sprinted across the field while Morgan followed at a walk. Lillian was still at work or else she would no doubt have wanted to come too, but Morgan was relieved she could put off talking to Lillian for one more day. Broaching the subject of Ivy Holden was the last thing she wanted to do. It was hard enough keeping her foul mood under wraps so as not to ruin Stevie's happiness.

Angie and Stevie chattered the whole drive to Morgan's parents'. Morgan even managed to crack a real smile as Stevie expressed her concern that Olive wouldn't like her new home.

"She's going to love it," she said.

"What if she's lonely?"

"Ooh, we can get a goat," said Angie.

Morgan groaned. "This is how it begins; you know that, right?"

They pulled into her parents' drive, and she backed up to the trailer. Stevie jumped out and began the process of hitching, calling out directions to Morgan.

"Love the way you back it up," said Angie with a wink at Morgan.

Morgan snorted.

They loaded Olive without incident. She boarded willingly and with her usual tranquil curiosity, coaxed along by a few treats. Shannon hopped into the passenger seat when they'd finished shutting Olive in.

"Coming along for the ride?" Morgan asked.

"I've gotten attached to her."

Morgan was willing to bet that was only half of what was driving her mother. The other half, she suspected, would become clear soon enough.

"Oh no," said Angie when they were almost home.

"What?" Morgan asked, afraid something had fallen off the trailer.

Angie, however, was staring at her phone. "It's Lil."

"Is she okay?" Or had she found out about Ivy?

"Brian just dumped her."

"No." Stevie and Morgan broke into simultaneous outrage.

While this wasn't exactly a surprise, Morgan had been harboring a secret hope that Lillian would break things off before Brian could hurt her further. She hadn't believed Brian capable of decisive action.

"Poor Lil," said Angie.

"Although now you won't be alone," Stevie said to Morgan. "You two can be grumpy together."

"Why are you grumpy?" asked Shannon.

Stevie at least had the courtesy to look sheepish as she realized what she'd done.

"I'm not grumpy, Ma."

Shannon turned around in her seat and directed the same question at Stevie.

Stevie quailed. "Um . . ."

"Morgan broke it off with Emilia," said Angie.

Morgan threw her hands in the air.

"Hands on the wheel," Shannon said, but she didn't press.

Fucking great. Morgan felt like she had a very good idea about how the ride back to her mother's house was going to go.

"Tell Lil I got her a pony," said Stevie.

"Yes, I'm sure that's exactly what she wants," said Angie, but she began typing anyway. "I wonder if Brian was sleeping with someone else."

"I hope not," said Morgan. Lillian didn't deserve that, and while she'd never found Brian particularly interesting, he was sweet, and she didn't think he'd do that to Lillian. Then again, what did she know? And how was she going to tell her about Ivy now?

She'd deal with that another day. Today she would focus on getting Olive to her new home and comforting Lillian, not to mention dealing with her mother.

Olive pranced around her new pasture, stringhalt and all, with her ears pricked and her neck arched. She even threw a playful buck as she broke into a canter. Morgan was pleased to discover that her canter, at least, was unaffected by her damaged gait.

"She looks so happy," said Angie.

"Yeah." Morgan wasn't looking at Olive, however; she watched her best friend's face alight with joy.

"I'll be back soon," she told them as she hopped back into the truck to return the trailer and her mother to their rightful places—miles away.

Shannon wasted no time broaching the last subject on earth Morgan wanted to discuss with her.

"What happened with Emilia?"

"I'm not talking about this with you."

"Is she leaving?"

"Probably. I don't know, Ma."

"What do you mean, you don't know?"

"I mean I don't know. That's usually what people mean when they say that."

"Did you ask her to stay?"

"Ma!"

Shannon ignored Morgan's shout and waited for her to answer her question.

"No, I didn't, and it isn't any of your business."

To her horror, tears obscured her vision.

"Pull over."

"I can drive."

"It's my trailer. Pull over."

Morgan pulled to the side of the road, shaking from fury now, along with grief. She slammed her door as she crossed in front of the truck, only to get swept into her mother's embrace.

"Just promise me you're not running away from something good," Shannon murmured as she held her through her sobs.

Chapter Seventeen

No sign of Morgan. Emilia swallowed her disappointment as she climbed into her skiff and rowed out to the sailboat. *It's okay*, she reminded herself. She was staying here. Morgan would turn up eventually, and today she had something else she needed to do.

A brisk wind pushed her out of the cove and into the harbor. Sailboats dotted the horizon. She couldn't have asked for better weather, and she grinned as the boat keeled. Spindrift drenched her as she made her way into deeper water. Pulling more tightly on the jib sheet, she increased the angle of the keel until the boat flew over the swells. Leaving Nell behind had definitely been the right choice; the dog would have hated this. Emilia, however, laughed as spray slapped her in the face. Off to port, a pod of porpoises swam parallel, racing with her across the sunlit sea.

She sailed until her body ached and her hands were raw from the wet lines. Evening brought a lull to the wind. In the calm, she reached into her bag and took out the small metal canister that held some of her father's ashes. This is what she'd brought for this moment.

"Dad," she said to the horizon. The next words wouldn't come. He knew she missed him. He, better than anyone, knew about regret and missed opportunities and poor choices. She opened the urn just as the wind ruffled the surface of the water.

Ash flew out over the Atlantic to mingle with the waves.

"One day at a time," she said.

Nothing about his death had changed. He was still gone, and the hole he'd left behind remained as large as ever, but she might be able to grow around it with enough time, until the balance tipped in the other direction.

"Morgan?"

Three weeks and two days after she'd left Emilia standing in a doorway—not that she was counting—Morgan heard a familiar voice call her name from farther down the grocery store aisle. She groaned. Of fucking course.

"Hi," she said to Kate. She'd clearly come from a showing, judging by the skirt and blouse she wore although Morgan noted she'd changed into the pair of sandals she always kept in her car so that she could ditch her heels. Remembering that detail would have sent her reeling two months ago. Now it just made her tired.

"Jesus, you look awful. Are you okay?" Kate set her shopping basket down and took a few steps closer, pausing at a respectful distance as she peered into Morgan's face.

Morgan knew what she saw. Deep circles under bloodshot eyes. The clenched set of her jaw. Sleep, like Emilia, no longer shared Morgan's bed.

"And you look great. I thought you didn't shop here anymore." Too blunt. Too rude. She didn't care.

"I had a showing up the road, and I was too hungry to wait." Kate flashed her an apologetic smile.

"The Russo place?"

"Russo?" Kate wrinkled her forehead.

"On Pleasant Street."

"Oh." Her face cleared. "No, she decided she didn't want to sell. I'm not surprised, honestly. It's a great property. Do you know her?"

"I knew her dad." Talking about Emilia with her ex was not how she wanted this—or any other day—to end. "What do you mean she's not selling?"

"I guess she could have gone with a different agent, but I haven't seen the house on any listing sites. Are you sure you're okay?"

"I'm . . ." The world went in and out of focus as she struggled to comprehend Kate's words. Emilia wasn't selling. "Is she renting?"

"I don't think so." Concern laced Kate's voice. "I've been keeping an eye on it. I have a few clients who I think would love it. So far, nothing."

Emilia hadn't changed her mind about staying then, even with Morgan out of the picture. She was still here. The lights of the grocery store seemed overly bright suddenly, and the shelves swayed in the corners of her vision. She had been so sure Emilia would leave.

It still didn't change anything.

"Morgan?"

"Tell me something," Morgan said, gripping her cart to keep herself upright. "Why did you break things off?"

"Morgan—"

"I need to know."

"We've been over this." Kate's expression of sympathy was hardening into a defensive mask.

"This isn't about us. Just please tell me, okay?" Her breath caught oddly in her throat, like someone had let air out of her lungs and she couldn't replenish it quickly enough.

Kate crossed her arms over her chest and spoke in a strained, raw tone. "It wasn't easy. You know that. I just needed someone who was around more, and you deserve someone who understands your work and what it means to you."

"That's it?"

"That's it."

"Why didn't you tell me sooner you weren't happy?"

Kate bit her lip. "What was I going to do? Ask you to leave your job?"

"I could have tried—" Morgan broke off the rest of her sentence as a man pushing a toddler in a cart paused at a nearby shelf.

"I didn't want to be the person who made you miserable. I care about you too much."

"There isn't something wrong with me?" The question leaked out of her, poisonous, pathetic.

Kate's mouth opened in shock. "Of course not. Is that—that's not what you've been thinking, is it?"

"What the hell else was I supposed to think?" The man glowered at her and strode off, his toddler still reaching for a box of crackers. Fighting with Kate felt familiar and good. "You never told me you were lonely. How was I supposed to believe you? I never knew. I missed every sign. How am I supposed to trust myself now?"

"Trust yourself—oh, Morgan." Kate's face cleared, and she put her hands over Morgan's white-knuckled one. "*I'm* the one you shouldn't trust, not yourself. *I'm* the one who didn't say anything, who kept hoping I would find a way to make it work instead of telling you I was struggling. None of that was your fault. Do you really not know that?"

Morgan couldn't speak.

"There is nothing wrong with you, Morgan."

Her ex searched her eyes, and it occurred to her that Kate had no reason to lie now. They were no longer partners. They were no longer even friends, and while Kate's face was full of compassion, her own heart did not ache at the tenderness in those eyes. She'd moved on. So had Kate. And if there really was nothing wrong with her, if the only thing keeping her away from Emilia was her own fear, then—

"I'm a fucking idiot," she said to a very confused Kate. "Sorry. It was good to see you."

"Morgan?"

"I have to go." Abandoning her cart, she cut through the lines of people jostling around the cash registers and out into the parking lot. Early September sunshine blinded her as she jogged to her truck.

Emilia was still here, and she could either be a coward for the rest of her life or beg the woman she loved to forgive her for running.

281

She punched the accelerator as she hit the main road, cursing the slow drivers in front of her. Emilia probably wouldn't vanish between now and when Morgan got to her house, but the depth of her own idiocy spurred her on. She couldn't bear to let another minute pass.

Emilia's car wasn't in her driveway. Panic closed around her throat as she stared at the log house.

"Breathe," she told herself. She could wait here. Emilia would be back eventually.

The seconds ticked by. A dog's face appeared in the window, then vanished. Nell, at least, was home. She drummed her fingers on the steering wheel.

The dock. Putting the truck in reverse, she sped toward the harbor, spraying gravel, and slowed down to some semblance of the speed limit only when she left the back roads and hit traffic.

Emilia's car sat by an empty spot. Morgan pulled in, hardly daring to breathe, and stared at the water. No sailboat. She was out there then, enjoying the perfect—why hadn't she appreciated how perfect it was?—evening. Waiting in the truck felt stifling. She walked down to the dock and debated whether or not to take her own boat out to look for her. Only the chances of missing her entirely stopped her from rowing to her mooring. Instead, she paced the dock until she felt stupid, and then sat with her feet in the cold water until a familiar sail turned into the cove. Abruptly, she realized she had no idea what to say to Emilia. Panic tightened its grip. As the sailboat grew larger, however, and the setting sun glinted off a pair of sunglasses she recognized, the panic vanished. It didn't matter. Emilia was here.

Emilia raised a hand to her eyes as she tacked across the cove. Morgan wondered if she'd recognized her yet, or if she'd turn back out to sea once she did. The boat kept coming. Emilia turned it into the wind and caught the mooring in a practiced maneuver she'd clearly perfected over the summer. Morgan thought about diving in and swimming straight out to the boat, but that felt too much like cornering her. She'd walked out, and now she had to let Emilia come to her.

Not, of course, that she was going to do anything so chivalrous as leave the dock. If Emilia wanted to escape her that badly she would have to find a different port.

She watched Emilia coil the lines and furl the sails with excruciating slowness. Was she avoiding her, or did it always take this long and Morgan had just never noticed? She chafed at the distance. After a geological era, Emilia at last got into her skiff and began to row. Morgan counted the strokes. *One, two, seven, thirty-seven.* Emilia's back was to her, concealing her expression completely.

Morgan caught the bow as Emilia pulled hard on the right oar and slid into the dock. Her tongue had glued itself to the roof of her mouth, making it difficult to swallow and impossible to talk. Emilia stowed her oars without meeting Morgan's eye, and the moment stretched, time turning to taffy as Morgan's hopes—and organs—twisted. When Emilia at last looked up, her sunglasses shielded her eyes and the rest of her face gave nothing away.

I've lost her, Morgan thought, but she held out her hand anyway, and forced her tongue to remember its duty.

"I'm an idiot."

"Yes," said Emilia as she took her hand and allowed Morgan to pull her onto the dock. "You are."

Standing this close to Emilia without reaching for her physically pained her. "I thought I was doing the right thing. I didn't want . . . I didn't want to complicate your life."

"And I already told you that wasn't your decision to make."

"I know."

Emilia pulled her hand out of Morgan's. "Do you? Because I can't be with someone who doesn't trust me."

"That's not—"

"It is, Morgan. If you don't trust me to make my own choices, how can I trust you to respect them, or me?"

"I respect you."

"Then prove it." Emilia's mouth, normally soft and full, hardened into a thin line.

"I trust you." Morgan could see her own reflection in the sunglasses: desperate; lost. It was time to tell Emilia the truth. She met her own eyes in the glass and said, "I didn't trust myself."

Emilia's mouth softened as she waited for Morgan to continue.

"With you, I feel—" She broke off as she searched for the right words, failed to find them, and stumbled on. "I feel right. I didn't think I would ever feel that way again after Kate. But you were going to leave. I knew that. I reminded myself every day."

A seagull swooped low over their heads and shrieked, throwing her off. Emilia's lips quirked in a faint smile. That smile gave her the courage to continue.

"I got so good at telling myself I was going to lose you that it scared the shit out of me when you decided to stay."

"Morgan—"

"I ran into Kate today."

Emilia's face froze.

"She said you hadn't sold the house. I was so sure you would leave after I was a dick."

"My world doesn't revolve around you, you know."

"I fucked up so badly with her, Emilia. I didn't see her hurting. I didn't see anything." She was talking too quickly now, her words rushing together. "What if I was doing the same thing with you? And if you stayed—"

She couldn't say the rest.

"If I stayed?"

"What if you changed your mind? About me."

There it was: the fear that had been eating at her for months. The worry that Emilia would leave her either way, no matter what she did, and the bleak comfort in the certainty of heartbreak.

"I might," said Emilia. She took off her sunglasses and held them loosely in her hand. "And you might, too."

"No."

"I spread my father's ashes today."

Morgan's heart stuttered. She should have been there for her. She should never have left her to grieve alone.

"People leave, Morgan. People leave, and sometimes we never get them back."

"God, Emilia—" She took the hand that held the sunglasses and brushed her thumb across Emilia's wrist. Emilia's expression hardened.

"I'm willing to take that risk. But if you're not, then that's on you, not me."

Morgan felt each word like shrapnel. She wanted to hold them inside her forever, the pain proof that she'd been wonderfully, beautifully wrong. Suddenly, words weren't enough. She'd used up all the ones she had anyway, and so she did the only thing she could think of. Morgan Donovan fell to her knees and stared up at a stunned Emilia.

"Please stay with me," she said. "I need you."

Emilia's eyes searched her face, and the wind tousled her hair as it blew off the September ocean. Her hands found Morgan's chin, holding her steady, and then she knelt to face her. The wood of the dock bit into Morgan's knees as Emilia rested her forehead against hers with a sob of breath that was more answer than anything she could have said, until she spoke, and then Morgan broke around her like surf.

"I'll stay with you forever."

Epilogue

Emilia dropped her bag on the table and stared around her kitchen. Morgan's sweater hung over the back of one of the kitchen table chairs, and she touched it lightly with two fingers. Her house. Her kitchen. Her girlfriend.

Morgan wouldn't be home for another hour or two, and Emilia unbuttoned her shirt as she stretched. Late September light flooded the kitchen, and the golds and reds of the trees beyond the windows stained the glass. Nell nudged her with her long snout.

"Yes, yes, I will feed you, monster."

She scooped food into Nell's bowl and put the kettle on to make herself a cup of tea. August's heat had departed with the month, and the house retained the morning's chill even late into the evening. She shed her button-up and tugged Morgan's sweater over her head. The scent of horse, shampoo, and the underlying intoxicating scent of Morgan's skin wrapped around her.

Friday. The end of her first week at Briar Hill Veterinary Clinic. She warmed her hands over the kettle and let herself feel the stream of joy pour out of her like steam. This work was so different from her old job. Yes, she had euthanized two patients, but they'd been older, and it had been a matter of quality of life rather than overcrowding. There would always be difficult decisions and difficult clients—she was not that naïve—but there would also be continuity of care, joy, and satisfaction.

The kettle's whistle shrieked, and she poured the hot water into her cup, breathing in the fragrant mint. Tea, Nell, and a detective novel she'd borrowed from Lillian moved with her to the porch to watch from her favorite Adirondack chair the birds flit over the meadow.

Tires on gravel broke her out of her reading trance some time later. Nell leapt off the porch in a streak of greyhound muscle and speed to greet Kraken. She set her empty tea mug down and stood to watch Morgan walk up the drive. Morgan knelt to pick up a stick and tossed it for the dogs. Nell got to it first, but overshot and kept running, bounding over the grass that Emilia had let grow tall again because she liked the wildflowers. Kraken seized the opportunity and loped back to his person with the stick clamped firmly in his jaws. Morgan ruffled his ears and then looked up to smile at Emilia.

Would she ever get used to that? she wondered as electricity pulsed through her. Morgan walked toward her with her sure gait, her strong body moving smoothly as she mounted the steps to the porch and pulled Emilia into her arms.

"Nice sweater," Morgan said.

"Kiss me, you idiot."

Morgan obliged her. Emilia put her arms around her neck and allowed Morgan to remind her, quite thoroughly, how much she'd missed Emilia over the course of the day. She broke away only when they were both breathless.

"I've been thinking," she said.

Morgan kissed her neck, distracting her.

"About what?" Morgan asked between gentle nips.

"About getting you a key."

"Really."

Morgan's hands broke Emilia's train of thought. She let Morgan pull her toward the chair and was more than happy to curl up on her lap as Morgan banished the evening's chill with her lips.

"Really. If you'd like one."

Morgan looked up at her. As always, she fell into those eyes.

"I'd love one."

287

"Well then." Emilia dug into her pocket and pulled out the key she'd had cut on her way home. *Home.* She savored the word. Home was here, in this house, in this town, with this woman.

Morgan accepted the key like it was something precious. Emilia watched her face, loving the freckles across her cheeks and nose and the way her eyelashes brushed them when she blinked, and loving, too, the tenderness in the way Morgan held her—and beneath that tenderness, beneath the warm certainty of her smile, the sense of permanence that this, at least, was hers to hold onto.

Acknowledgments

Being married to a veterinarian opened my eyes to the realities faced by veterinary practitioners. The people who care for our animals do so despite pressures the rest of us can't fathom, and Emilia's struggles are not unique. They are, in fact, the norm. The next time you visit your vet, take a moment to thank them. Your words make a difference, and in some cases could even save a life. To learn more, check out Not One More Vet at www.nomv.org.

Tiffany, you inspire me every day with your dedication to your profession and our family, and you're the best first reader a writer could ask for. The scenes in the rowboat are for you. (I will always be the better oarswoman, but you can be the captain.)

I would also like to thank Mx. Rey Spangler, editor, Jedi master, and all-around writing support guru. This book would have much more brooding without your intervention. Ann McMan continues to create exceptional covers that manage to capture the essence of a thing. Frankly, she is too talented to be allowed. I also owe a huge thank you to the team at Bywater Books, who are devoted to bringing queer literature to our community and the world. We need all the stories we can get.

I have managed to write three books without thanking my dogs in the acknowledgments. However, my pups really did help with this one—and not just as inspiration for Nell and Kraken. Their cuddles and reminders that fresh air is good for writers helped me stay sane during what turned out to be a turbulent year. Between illness, loss, and a pandemic, their unconditional love kept me going. Animals give me hope that we can do better.

Most of all, I want to thank my readers. Sharing my stories with you is a blessing. Thanks for sticking with me; you make this possible. If you want more stories and behind the scenes glimpses into these and other worlds, consider joining me on Patreon at www.patreon.com/annaburkeauthor or following me on Twitter @annaburkeauthor.

On a side note, my Seal Cove is not a real place. There are several Seal Coves in Maine, but this is not one of them. Any coincidences are coincidences. The rest of the geography *is* based in reality, and Tiffany, those waters will always be ours.

About the Author

Anna Burke enjoys all things nautical and generally prefers animals to people. When she isn't writing, she can usually be found walking in the woods with her dogs or drinking too much tea, which she prefers hot and strong—just like her protagonists. She is the award-winning author of *Compass Rose*, *Thorn*, and *Nottingham*.

Bywater BOOKS

At Bywater Books we love good books about lesbians just like you do, and we're committed to bringing the best of contemporary lesbian writing to our avid readers. Our editorial team is dedicated to finding and developing outstanding writers who create books you won't want to put down.

We sponsor the Bywater Prize for Fiction to help with this quest. Each prizewinner receives $1,000 and publication of their novel. We have already discovered amazing writers like Jill Malone, Sally Bellerose, and Hilary Sloin through the Bywater Prize. Which exciting new writer will we find next?

For more information about Bywater Books and the annual Bywater Prize for Fiction, please visit our website.

www.bywaterbooks.com